GOOD
FOR
YOU

Lucy Vine is the bestselling author of novels *Hot Mess*, *What Fresh Hell*, *Are We Nearly There Yet?*, *Bad Choices*, *Seven Exes*, *Date with Destiny* and *Book Boyfriend*. Her eighth novel is *Good For You*. Her books have been published in seventeen territories, with *Hot Mess* optioned for a TV series in America. In a previous life, Lucy was a journalist, writing for publications including *Grazia*, *Stylist*, *Heat*, *Fabulous*, *Marie Claire*, *Sugar* and *Cosmopolitan*. You can find her on Instagram and TikTok @lucyvineauthor. Her website is www.lucyvine.co.uk.

Also by Lucy Vine

Hot Mess
What Fresh Hell
Are We Nearly There Yet?
Bad Choices
Seven Exes
Date with Destiny
Book Boyfriend

As Elly Vine

The Lottery Winner Widows Club

Praise for Good For You

'My new favourite Lucy Vine novel. Her writing is always a delight – fresh, smart, hilarious – but this book was extra special. Full of empowerment, friendship and the best kind of rage, with a gorgeous romance too, it truly brightened my week'
Beth O'Leary

'I ADORED it. Lucy has such a gift for writing books that are utterly hilarious and hugely emotionally intelligent too. I'd recommend it to anyone who needs some serious cheering up, or cheering on'
Daisy Buchanan

'A smart, modern romance, *Good For You* is funny, sharp and sexy'
Louise O'Neill

'A vibrant, funny, big-hearted romcom with a relatable heroine and a swoonworthy hero. It's as empowering as it is emotional, and left me with a huge grin on my face and a reminder not to settle for less than I deserve'
Cressida McLaughlin

'This was pure joy from start to finish. Hilarious, warm and delicious, but also a really satisfied and nuanced exploration of female rage'
Lauren Bravo

GOOD FOR YOU

Lucy Vine

**SIMON &
SCHUSTER**

London · New York · Amsterdam/Antwerp · Sydney/Melbourne · Toronto · New Delhi

First published in Great Britain by Simon & Schuster UK Ltd, 2026

1 3 5 7 9 10 8 6 4 2

Simon & Schuster UK Ltd, 1st Floor
222 Gray's Inn Road, London WC1X 8HB

Simon & Schuster Australia, Sydney
Simon & Schuster India, New Delhi

www.simonandschuster.co.uk
www.simonandschuster.com.au
www.simonandschuster.co.in

The authorised representative in the EEA is Simon & Schuster Netherlands BV,
Herculesplein 96, 3584 AA Utrecht, Netherlands. info@simonandschuster.nl

Simon & Schuster strongly believes in freedom of expression and stands against
censorship in all its forms. For more information, visit BooksBelong.com

A CIP catalogue record for this book
is available from the British Library

Paperback ISBN: 978-1-3985-3205-2
eBook ISBN: 978-1-3985-3206-9
Audio ISBN: 978-1-3985-3207-6

Typeset in the UK by M Rules
Printed and Bound in the UK using 100% Renewable Electricity
at CPI Group (UK) Ltd

FSC
www.fsc.org

MIX
Paper | Supporting
responsible forestry
FSC® C013604

For Mum

ViralVideosTranscribed

one hour ago

THE TRANSCRIPT OF **THAT MELTDOWN** IN FULL!

Sound of chair scraping across floor

LC: You can't be serious, Justin, tell me you're not being serious?

cutlery clattering

Justin: [inaudible]

LC: No, you were ... this wasn't ... this was ... look at my NAILS. These are Instagram ready nails, Justin! This is SHELLAC.

Unidentified female: [hissing] Are you filming this?

Unidentified male: Yeah, shush! This is so fucking funny.

Unidentified female: Oh, it's mean, don't!

Unidentified male: Shhhhhh!!

LC: [raised voice] I thought you were *proposing*, Justin. What the fuck is this? Is this real – are you being real?

Justin: [quietly] Can you sit back down?

LC: No, I'm not sitting back down, I want you to tell me you're not serious.

Justin: [barely audible] I am serious. Look, it's just not working out. I think you're, y'know, great but—

more cutlery clattering

Justin: Babe, can you put the dessert spoon down?

LC: No, because I ordered a tiramisu and I'm going to eat it. You can dump me but you can't stop me eating my pudding.

Justin: Sit back down and we can both finish our food . . .

LC: [shouting] WHERE'S MY TIRAMISU? I ORDERED IT AGES AGO! I
WANT TO EAT MY TIRAMISU!

Waiter 1: We have your dessert, madam, if you'd like to take a seat?

LC: [sob-shouting] THIS ISN'T A TIRAMISU, WHAT IS THIS?

Waiter 1: It's the cheesecake, madam.

LC: [still sob-shouting] I DIDN'T ORDER THE CHEESECAKE, I
ORDERED A TIRAMISU! WHERE'S MY SODDING TIRAMISU?

sound of chair falling over

LC: ASK THAT MAN OVER THERE! HE'S THE WAITER I ORDERED
MY TIRAMISU FROM. EXCUSE ME, SIR? I'VE JUST BEEN
DUMPED WHICH IS REALLY, REALLY HILARIOUS BECAUSE I
THOUGHT I WAS GETTING ENGAGED! *maniacal laughter* SO I
REALLY NEED TO EAT MY TIRAMISU.

Waiter 2: You ordered the cheesecake, madam.

LC: NO I DIDN'T! I ORDERED THE TIRAMISU, I WANT TIRAMISU!
PLEASE BRING ME TIRAMISU!

Justin: Can you stop saying the word tiramisu?

Unidentified male: [whispering] What even *is* tiramisu?

LC: *weird long wail that sounds a bit like the word tiramisu*

Waiter 2: I'm afraid you didn't order the tiramisu, madam. I know that for
a fact because we don't have it on the menu.

LC: [silence]

Justin: [silence]

Waiter 1: Would you like this cheesecake, madam?

LC: [quietly] Yes.

clattering of spoon

Justin: Look, I am really sorry, it's just not [incoherent]

LC: [through mouthfuls of cheesecake] I do your WASHING, JUSTIN.

Justin: [incoherent mumble]

LC: [sob] I have to wash all your boxers on a 90-degree cycle you know? Because they're so disgusting. You're going to do that on your own now, are you? You don't even know how to operate a washing machine. Do you actually know what a hot cycle is?

Justin: [quietly] No.

LC: You're really doing this? You're really breaking up with me?

Justin: [silence]

sound of drink being glugged and empty bowl being dumped back on table

LC: [to Waiters 1 and 2] THANK YOU FOR THE CHEESECAKE. IT WAS DELICIOUS.

Waiter 1: You're welcome. It's a special recipe, people come from miles away for—

LC: [to Justin] BY THE WAY, I HATE YOUR MOTHER.

sound of high heels clacking furiously across room to exit

sound of high heels returning, even more furiously

LC: HER SUNDAY ROAST IS THE WORST I'VE EVER HAD AND HER NEW SOFA IS THE COLOUR OF VOMIT. I WAS BEING POLITE WHEN I SAID IT WAS NICE.

more heel clacking

LC: [from across the room] AND I ALSO HATE HER LIVING ROOM CURTAINS.

[watch again?]

"by the way, I hate your mother"

#Hilarious #LivCarpenter #BBCMorningTea #RelationshipTherapist
#PublicMeltdown #PublicFreakout #FunnyVids #funnyvideo #funny
#funnyvideos #lol #memes #meme #comedy #funnymemes #fun #memesdaily
#funnymeme #lmao #dankmemes #funnyshit #video #viral #funnyposts

273 comments

Dan
This is so fcken funny

Glo
Did you see her nearly drop the cake? Lol

Josie
I thought she was going to throw it in his face!

Sam
This is brutal

Kom
You can hear everything so clearly. MORTIFYING!

LovesIt
I've seen that woman on Morning Tea?!!?!

> **Sarah**
> Me too! She's their relationship therapist!!!

> **TomFG**
> I bet she's not actually a qualified therapist

> **HiiiitThat**
> I used to really like her but she's clearly maaaaaad

DogLover
I feel bad for her!!! Men are the worst!!!!!

> **Sop99**
> I agree. Who the hell dumps someone in a TGI Friday's like that
> anyway?

Gary

Someone gave this dude some shit breakup advice

IAmWhoIAm

Lol, showing this to my boyf next time he tells me I have a temper

Fredi

She's famous isn't she???

> **Vee**
> Barely

Al

She is actual wel fittt I would bang her

> **Haz**
> Too high maintenance for me
>
> **Haz**
> Fuk em and ditch em
>
> **Al**
> That guy tried to!!!! She wouldn't let him!!

DailyExpress

Hi! @DailyExpress here! We love your video. Can we use it for an article? We'll credit you

> **ViralVideosTranscribed**
> No

Andrew

Can't wait for someone to do a dance remix of this vid

JZ

100th comment!!!

> **JellyTots**
> 200th!!!!!!!

Kel

She's seriously going to regret this

> **ELP**
> You can say that again

CHAPTER ONE

'OH GOD, HELP! HELP ME, PLEASE!'

I make a panicked run from my bedroom and down the hall, my heart hammering in my chest. I throw myself into the bathroom, slamming the door shut and locking it quickly behind me. I'm panting hard.

'Help!' I call out again, leaning for support against the towel rail. I try to make an action plan. What are my options here? Go through the window? There's a flat roof just outside the bathroom window that could take my weight, but then it's three floors to the ground. I'm fairly sure the drainpipes are sturdy though and I could— oh wait, that won't work. The window's painted shut, of course it is. There's no way. If my flatmate Samira doesn't hear my shouts, I've got no chance now.

'HELLLLLLLLLLP!' I scream one last time, any hope draining away as my voice reverberates back at me across bathroom tiles.

'Liv?'

It's Samira. I almost sob at the sound of her lovely, familiar voice on the other side of the door. I sag against the loo roll holder, feeling my heart rate slowing. Thank god. Thank god she's here. My best friend speaks again, sounding half-asleep. 'It's 4am, babe, what's going on?'

'He's back, Sam,' I half whisper. 'In my room. I only just got out in time.'

There is a judgemental pause on the other side of the door. 'Okay,' she says at last, not sounding nearly as sympathetic as I would've liked. 'I'll go get the thingymajig.'

I hear her creak her way down the hall as I wait in front of the mirror, staring at myself, my heart still pounding.

I look horrendous.

I haven't slept a wink, I have to go to work in a few minutes, and now the fucking daddy long-legs is back for the fiftieth time, trying to ruin my life. I'm deathly afraid of the bastards and this one particular arsehole daddy long-legs keeps creeping into my room at night through the open window, chasing me out, and scaring me to death. He's got a vendetta against me, I know he has. He comes in, flapping his weird fucking wings and his weird fucking legs, knowing I'll have to run for the panic room. AKA the bathroom. I swear to god, he knows I'm terrified and he thinks it's funny. He's *laughing* at me.

I visualise the creature coming for me again now, throwing himself at the bathroom door, flapping furiously as he tries to break the door down to reach me.

If Sam can't get him out this time, what then? Set the whole flat on fire, smash my way out of that sodding painted window, and begin a whole new life in another country? We definitely wouldn't get our deposit back from the estate agent, but what with everything that happened last night with Justin – not to mention this daddy long-legs vendetta – losing a battle with cunty estate agents doesn't feel like it would be the worst thing in the world.

I study my reflection in the mirror, taking in the cavernous eyebags and pallid skin. The fear recedes for a moment and the rage rushes back in.

I still can't believe Justin dumped me. Out of nowhere. In a *restaurant*. A restaurant that doesn't even serve tiramisu! What kind of decent restaurant doesn't have tiramisu? I hate him so so *so* much. I'm overflowing with fury; my chest burns with it. I'm not even sad – I'm too mad. I wasted a whole *year* and two months on that man. On that waste of space idiot. And he's not even good enough for me! I was doing him a *favour* going out with him and he had the AUDACITY to end it with *me*? The bitterness makes me breathe hard. I can taste the fury on my tongue.

I'm aware anger is not the healthiest way to process a break-up, but I have to admit, it's a lot easier than acceptance or misery. Being this cross feels like downing six cans of that mad looking Monster drink and washing it all down with a few tabs of speed. Which I only did that one time and do not recommend. The anger courses through my veins. I've had no sleep but I feel caffeinated to fuck. I am fired up with lividness. With *Liv*-idness. I'm ready to burn the whole world down with my rage. I feel ferocious and powerful.

And *angry*.

It's just so unfair.

I honestly, honestly, honestly thought Justin was going to propose last night. Things have been so amazing between us since we met at my thirtieth birthday party last year – it's been like a dream. And yes, okay, he's been a bit cagey for the last few weeks, but I thought that was him making secret plans. Y'know, picking out a ring, booking the restaurant, making *arrangements*.

And then I overheard him *in this very* bathroom last week, practising a proposal speech in the mirror. He was going on about how wonderful I am and how special our time together has been. It was so obviously a proposal speech – I was so sure. Even Sam agreed! Although she did keep harping on about how I have to stop saying I *overheard it,* when the truth is that I had an ear pressed up against the door. But overhearing or eavesdropping – either way – the very next day Justin invited me out to dinner at his favourite restaurant . . . what the hell was I meant to think? I even got my nails done in preparation – I was *so sure*.

But it turns out a proposal speech can sound an awful lot like a dumping speech.

'Liv?' Samira is back. 'He's gone, babe, the daddy long-legs has been taken care of. You okay now? Can I have a wee, please? I had too many Kefir yoghurt drinks last night.'

Sam is obsessed with her gut health.

I pull back the bolt slowly and open the door an inch. 'Are you sure?' I hiss, eyes frantically scanning the ceiling. 'He could be tricking you. He's wily. He could be waiting for you to turn your back and then he'll dart straight back in. He might be hiding in my wardrobe right now, ready to pounce and torment me. That's how he gets his kicks. Did you check my chocolate drawer?'

She sighs, still not as sympathetic as one might expect. 'No daddy long-legs can outsmart me,' she says firmly, pushing past me and into the bathroom.

She opens the loo lid, pulls down her pyjama trousers and takes a seat, totally uninhibited. She does it all the time, but her total lack of shame still takes me by surprise. Imagine being so chill with urinating in front of others! I guess that's what comes from having such a secure and loving childhood. Yuck, I'm quite glad mine was so dysfunctional.

'You know, you could close your window at night,' she offers, yawning and tucking curly dark hair behind her ear, as she helps herself to too much toilet roll.

'I need the cool air.' I shake my head. 'June starts tomorrow and I haven't yet swapped my 13.5 tog winter duvet for the 7.5. I get so sweaty, it's like bathing in the bedsheets.'

'Okay, well, then you need to just get over your fear.' Her face brightens. 'You should read up about the daddy long-legs. Get rid of the unknown element. Get to know them. Make them your friends. Immerse yourself in the most long legged of the daddies.'

Ever since Sam started having therapy a month ago, she's

become a bit of a know-it-all when it comes to trauma. But *I'm* the therapist here. I know plenty about exposure therapy, thank you.

She pauses, then looks excited. 'Ooh, or we could both take a month off and travel to the daddy long-legs' country of origin – probably the Amazon or something, right? – where we could camp out and become as one with the insect life there. That would cure you.'

'I'm not sure getting into debt to upend my life just so I can bond with mosquitoes and beetles would be a sensible choice,' I point out, before adding fiercely, 'And I *have* read about the daddy long-legseses. They're evil little bastards. They tear their prey apart with just their mouths.'

'Their prey being?' She raises an eyebrow as she pulls up her pants. I look away.

'Mainly grasshoppers and slugs.'

Sam snorts as she flushes and moves to the sink. 'They don't bite, they're not poisonous, they don't even spin a web or do anything annoying like that. They're mostly just . . . sort of . . . *silly*?'

Silly?

For a moment I consider telling Sam what happened with Justin last night. I could tell her how I got brutally dumped in a public place. That would make her feel bad for calling my very legitimate daddy long-legs terror *silly*.

'I'm going back to sleep,' she yawns again, drying her hands.

I open my mouth to say the words, to tell her about Justin, and then I shut it again.

I'm not ready to say out loud that I got dumped. I don't want to see the pity that I know will be there in her eyes. Yet another relationship Liv couldn't close, how sad. Sam's pity might dim my anger and I need to hold onto it right now. It's all that's keeping me standing upright.

Plus, it would seem that my best friend is not all that sympathetic at this hour of the day.

'Night night,' I call out, as she trudges back to bed. 'And thank you for saving me, I love you loads.'

'Whatever, loser,' she responds, as per our friendship protocol, slamming her bedroom door and laughing.

I glance out of the bathroom window. It's pitch black out there. My taxi will be here to take me to the studio in a few minutes. I have to be at work for 5am and I haven't even showered yet.

I turn on the water and start to strip, feeling adrenaline zigzagging through my body. I can't be late.

Justin's taken my romantic hopes away from me, the evil flappy daddy long-legs has taken my home from me – my work is just about all I have left. I'm not going to mess that up on top of everything else.

I climb into the shower, trying not to think about Justin – about my *ex* – and my ever-so-slight overreaction to the break-up last night. It wasn't *that* bad, was it? Sure, I was a little bit upset, but who wouldn't be a little bothered by getting dumped like that? I'm sure the diners at the next table understood if I raised my voice a little. I mean, I could've gone *really* postal. I wanted to flip the table and punch everyone in the room. So what if I hid under the table for a while, eating cheesecake? Is that *so* bad?

I put my face under the warm water, letting any doubt drain away along with the overpriced bodywash I bought off TikTok. I just need to get through my segment this morning – I need to focus on other people's problems – then I'll have the whole weekend to process this break-up; to decide what I'm going to do next. Two solid days to let go of all this anger bubbling away inside me and have a big old cry. I have the training for this very thing, for god's sake. I'm a relationship therapist! I know exactly how to handle this break-up with appropriate poise and grace. Mindful and demure, that's what I'm all about. Cool, calm, collected Liv Carpenter, that's what they call me. It's one of my many mottos. It's who I am.

And it will aaaaaaaall be fine.

CHAPTER TWO

The weirdness starts before I've even arrived at the *Morning Tea* studio. The taxi driver – usually morose and silent at 4.30am like any sane human would be – is twitchy and watchful. I keep glancing up to see him looking at me in the rear-view mirror, looking faintly amused. I check my compact three times for errant bogies and decide he's probably just alarmed by how exhausted I look.

Blame Justin and spindly-legged arsehole insects, I silently instruct him.

When the driver at last pulls up outside the cast and crew entrance, he grins as I thank him.

'You're welcome, Ms Carpenter.' He pauses, as I inelegantly clamber across the backseat. As I go to shut the door, he adds, 'Your nails look lovely, by the way. Very *Instagram ready*.' I laugh nervously and thank him again.

Weird.

Especially since one of them is broken and scuffed.

A member of the production staff called Maz is waiting just inside the building entrance. She's holding a clipboard and is deep in conversation with a guy I vaguely recognise as being a breakout star – slash narcissistic villain – from a recent reality show. He's probably one of today's guests on the sofa. Maz glances up as I enter, surprise registering on her face. I give her a quick wave and she returns it after a moment's hesitation, her expression confused.

The reality star looks up, clocking me. 'It's you!' he says, looking excited.

'It's . . . me!' I confirm, because how else is a person supposed to respond to that? I hear it a lot and always have to resist the urge to reply, 'Yes, it is me because I am me. And it's also you, and aren't pronouns fun?' I'm not famous-famous, but I am on TV three mornings a week – Wednesday through Friday – handing out relationship advice to the country's broken-hearted women. People do get like this from time to time. Although, I note with interest, this twenty-something bronzed triangle isn't my usual type of fan. They tend to be shy young betas who've been shat on from a great height by everyone for most of their lives. Often by men like this one, actually.

I smile my best public-facing smile at him and give Maz a half-hearted little finger wave. Then – clinging for dear life onto my bag to keep me upright – I make a beeline for the green room.

A few people are dotted around on sofas, looking

5am-glazed and buried in newspapers or their phones. I dump my bag by the espresso machine, making myself an extra strong coffee. I feel hungover even though I didn't drink much last night. I head straight for the make-up room, my head spinning. I love the beauty team and today I urgently *need* the beauty team.

'Morning, Jools! Hiya, Andi!' I burst into the small, well-lit room, mirrors glinting off every wall. 'How are you gorgeous creatures today?' I take a long sip of my coffee, feeling the joyous placebo effect of caffeine coursing its way through my nervous system.

'Liv?' Juliette – Jools – blinks at me with horror. 'You're here?' Andi stares at me vacantly, a strange look on her face.

I tilt my head at them and for half a second I'm certain I must've got my days mixed up. Am I here on my day off?

No, it's definitely a Friday, I know it is. And the taxi picked me up; it wouldn't have been at my house at 4.30am if this wasn't one of my scheduled appearance days.

So why are Jools and Andi looking at me like that? Like they can't believe I'm here?

Oh shit, maybe someone called to cancel me this morning. My phone died last night at the restaurant, and in the aftermath-y, up-all-night hysteria, I didn't plug it in. I wanted to ask the driver to charge it for me on the way in, but he was being such an oddball. Too dazzled by my Shellac, it would seem.

'Er, I am here, yes!' I laugh awkwardly. 'And I haven't slept at all. Please save me from my own eyebags. They are like

17

wet bin liners under my skin.' The pair exchange a look of concern but then Jools gestures at her chair.

'Of course, sweetheart, have a seat.'

I do so, pulling out my phone and charger. 'Do you mind if I plug this in?'

Jools nods towards the socket on the wall and prepares her make-up station. I settle in, readying myself for the usual soothing routine.

Jools is probably my favourite person at the studio, though I'm dimly aware it's part of her job to make everyone feel good. With nervous guests passing through this room just minutes before they have to go on air in front of millions of judgemental viewers, the head of make-up is required to be everyone's calming best friend. She's got a natural maternal energy, with her short, grey hair and big, knitted cardigans – and I always feel a million times better when I sit in her chair.

Her breath is cool and minty on my face as she gets to work, slathering on pounds and pounds of primer. I take her in for a moment, wondering like I always do, how her glasses don't get steamed up when she has to be so up-close-and-personal with people's hot breath every day.

Jools is, like, *known* for her glasses. She has a wide variety but they're always huge, always brightly coloured, and always sparkly. She has 400,000 followers on Instagram because of them, with people declaring her to be a style icon on a near-daily basis, but she confided in me once that she just copied Elton John's look from the late 1970s.

I close my eyes, the familiarity of her movements making my breath slow.

I've been doing this gig on *Morning Tea* for two years now, and I love it. Even the early mornings! There's nothing like that burst of nerves and adrenaline that floods me when I sit on that sofa, ready to go live. Plus, Jools isn't the only lovely person who works here, everyone is great, really, really gr—

'Olivia?'

Ugh, apart from him.

I open my eyes to see the show producer eyeballing me in the mirror.

Spencer Tate. Textbook narcissist. A prime example of nepotism in action – his dad owns the studio – and just a really horrible little man on a power trip to end all power trips. *And* he's younger than me! Yuck.

He's framed now by the doorway, his massive pores enlarged by the intense lighting. He's wearing a *Peaky Blinders* cap, which is so sad because even the worst of *Peaky Blinders'* fans have at last realised what fashion victims they were being, and stopped wearing them.

'Spencer,' I reply evenly, as Jools works scrupulously on my bin liner eye circles, ignoring the boss in her work space.

Nobody likes him.

'Can I see you for a minute, Liv?' he says coolly, and I nod.

'Of course. Can it wait ten minutes? I'm just having my make-up done.' Jools lightly strokes some kind of magical powder across my cheeks and nose, pausing for a moment to push the Elton John glasses from her bridge to the top of her head.

The reality star is suddenly in the door frame behind Spencer. He shoves his way past and into the seat beside me. 'All right, birds!' he crows, ironically sounding quite a lot like a bird as he addresses the room. 'Time to make me even hotter, yeah, if it's even possible!' He laughs and even this noise sounds like it's straight out of a David Attenborough documentary.

I catch Andi's eyes across the room and she rolls them, then turns to the boy, smiling brightly. 'You're on *Morning Tea* today, are you love?' she asks, so nicely, because she has been well trained by Jools. She picks up some brushes and asks carefully rehearsed questions about the reality star's recent bookings. He seems to be immensely enjoying the 15-minutes of fame reality circuit, boasting about slightly sad club appearances and his massive new TikTok following.

Spencer steps properly into the room.

Hovering a few inches away from my face, Jools moves on to my eyelashes. She coats the left eye with thick black mascara, and I can feel my face coming back to life. I always feel more like myself with make-up on, which might not make sense, but is a fact nonetheless.

'No, it *can't* wait,' he says starkly. 'Jools, put the mascara thingy down.'

'I've only got one eye done!' I protest, feeling suddenly afraid. What is so urgent? Why can't I finish? Why does the head producer need to talk to me anyway? We mostly just ignore one another. Honestly, I don't really ever like to get too close to Spencer because he smells of too much cologne. It's inescapable, clinging to me all day long, making me gag whenever I catch another whiff.

'Two minutes, Spencer.' Jools does not do as instructed with the mascara thingy. She is an institution around here – she's been head make-up artist for twenty-five years. She doesn't back down to snivelling little grotbag gnomes with daddy issues. She begins coating my other eyelashes and I watch Spencer carefully through my one available eye.

'Liv, you know what this is about!' Spencer cries, his voice raising an octave. 'You don't want me doing this in front of everyone!'

His threat gets the attention of the room, and the reality star spins in his chair to face us, rudely knocking over Andi's face powder. She tuts but he doesn't notice – or care.

'Oooooooh, you're in trouble,' the boy says like a small child delighting in a sibling scolding. He leans closer. 'To be fair to you, babe, I thought you were *well* funny in that video. And I've had loads worse from my crazy bitch exes! One of them once threw a shoe at my head just cause I cheated on her with her sister.' He scowls. 'And, like, I've never actually had tiramisu – I don't know what it is actually – but it was well annoying that they wouldn't get you some. It really pisses me off when I ask for a protein shake in one of those restaurants and they're too up their own arses to get it.' He scowls. 'I mean, like *who* doesn't have protein powder? Uptight knobheads.'

I stare at him, some of his words penetrating my fog of confusion. Crazy exes? Tiramisu? Video? Somewhere at the back of my brain, something jangles. An alarm bell.

Tiramisu.

The taxi driver mentioning my *Instagram ready* nails.

Tiramisu.

The reality star is grinning at me.

It's *you*!

Oh god no. What – *no*. It couldn't be.

'Liv?' Spencer says impatiently, and it is at this moment that my phone springs back to life on the table before me, vibrating aggressively as notifications start coming in. Message after message – missed call after missed call.

Ding ding ding.

Oh god no.

The tiramisu.

CHAPTER THREE

Spencer sits across from me in his office, squatting there balefully like a pouty toad. Except his pond would be overflowing with horrible Dior Sauvage.

He waits for me to speak first – a move I know he's gleaned from some awful advice article on being an alpha male – and so I do.

'Is everything okay? What's, er, what's going on?' I feel a little trembly, squeezing my phone in my right hand, feeling it vibrate again and again.

I haven't looked yet. I'm still trying to convince myself this isn't anything serious. It can't be to do with my Justin break-up last night. It can't.

'The video,' he says at last, and we stare at each other some more. I still don't understand what he means but my heart is thumping like mad. It's pounding in my ears as I fight waves of nausea.

'What video?' I ask in a quiet voice, and he sighs abrasively.

'Liv, for fuck's sake, don't pretend you don't know. Don't make me say it. You know what I'm talking about. The meltdown video? It's all over TikTok. The internet is having a field day. They're calling you The Tiramisu Girl.' He tuts. 'Someone's made T-shirts! Even though half of them can't spell tiramisu and the other half don't know what it is. Everyone's sharing it. It's everywhere! The *Daily Mail* have fucking called us for comment! They want to know how *Morning Tea*'s relationship expert – known for being cool, calm and collected, for advising women to be rational and balanced in their relationships – how she could go all Will Smith at the Oscars.' He pauses, looking exasperated, then half shouts, 'For fuck's sake, Liv, your mantra is Keep Calm and Carry Condoms!'

My heart is pounding wildly now. He *is* talking about last night. My break-up with Justin. Someone was . . . filming us? The video's gone . . . viral? But it can't. Why would it . . . ? Why would *anyone* . . . ? Oh my god.

I feel my breathing pick up as I try to get a handle on myself.

Okay. So, someone in the restaurant filmed Justin dumping me – and my reaction. But it wasn't even that bad, was it? I held it together for the most part. I was just blindsided and desperately needed some sugar. It wasn't *that* bad . . .

Spencer watches my expression curiously. After another moment, he swivels his monitor to face me. He clicks on a tab and presses play on some bright but grainy footage from inside last night's restaurant.

Fuck, it's me. I recognise us both – Justin and me – sitting at the table at a distance, our finished dinner plates in front of us. I can just about make out the half-finished mushroom pie I'd pushed around for half an hour, waiting for the big moment I was so sure was coming. There were onions in there I didn't want to eat before our post-proposal snog.

It takes me a minute to place the conversation point. It is just post-break-up; after Justin had generously told me it's not me, it's him. I'm shouting about my nails. My proposal-ready Shellac.

An image of this morning's taxi driver hits me again. The words he said as I got out of the car. He complimented my nails. '*Very Instagram ready,*' he'd said.

Oh my god. He'd seen this. That's why he was being weird.

On the screen, they've zoomed in on me. I'm flouncing around the table holding a spoon, yelling at waiters. I tell Justin his boxer shorts are disgusting.

Honestly, I don't remember it being this bad. Did I blank it out? Sure, I was upset, but this isn't me. Is it? I don't recognise myself at all.

I'm storming out now, screaming about Justin's mother. The video cuts out and TikTok asks if we want to watch it again.

Oh god, no thank you, TikTok.

My eyes travel with horror across the numbers on the right-hand side. They look all wrong. Under the heart symbol, it reads 34,019. There are 2,550 comments.

No.

NO!

I realise I am crunching my phone in my palm and release it. Pain shoots through my hand and up my arm. Saliva fills my mouth. I'm going to be sick. My cheeks chipmunk and I cover my mouth as Spencer regards me with pure horror.

For a second, his repulsion grounds me and the nausea recedes. Okay, that worked. I try to find something else to focus on. To stop me from losing my mind. What would I tell a client to do in this moment?

Metacognition.

The act of thinking about my thinking. I must observe my thoughts with detachment to avoid this negative spiral of horror running away with me.

So, what am I thinking?

Basically?

Fuck fuck fuck fuck fuck fuck fuck fuck fuck fuck fuck fuck fuck fuck fuck fuck fuck fuck fuck fuck fuck fuck fuck fuck fuck fuck fuck fuck fuck fuck fuck fuck.

What else?

I'm thinking that I'm screwed. That my life is over. There is a video on the internet of me being a proper mad person and thousands of people have seen it. My boss has seen it. My taxi driver had seen it. That reality star saw it. Maz at the front entrance had seen it. Clearly Jools and Andi on the beauty team had, too. I've been publicly humiliated – publicly *shamed*. This is the end of everything. Everyone I've ever met or known has no doubt seen this, or will see it. Every friend, every ex-boyfriend, every single person I went to school with, every teacher, everyone I've worked with over the years; they've all seen me behave like this. They've all seen me being this awful, crazy, hysterical dumpee, scream-ing at a room full of people about an Italian dessert made of lady fingers. Me, a renowned relationship therapist.

I consider all the WhatsApp groups out there in the ether, all alight right now with acquaintances I've met across the years, all sharing this link and mocking me.

'This psycho used to come to my coffee shop every day!! LOL! Good job I never got her order wrong!!!'

'I snogged this girl at a balloon party when I was a uni student. Soooo glad I ghosted her!!!!'

'I'm pretty sure I sit across from this woman on the train home, what a crazy bitch!'

Never mind all the people I actually care about seeing it and judging me.

And, oh god. All the clients I've ever seen or worked with will watch this and doubt everything I've told them. Because who would trust this awful, shrieking woman?

My head spins with the horror.

This is it. No one will ever love me again, no one will ever speak to me again, I will be a pariah in society.

I look up, making eye contact at last with Spencer. He looks grim as fuck.

And I'm clearly about to lose my job. The best job I've ever had. The only job I've ever really loved.

My life is over.

I take a deep, wholesome breath, trying to steady the thump-thump-thump in my chest.

See how helpful metacognition is?

Spencer takes a deep breath of his own and I steel myself for his words. I know what's coming.

'I don't want to fire you,' he says at last, and it is so unexpected that I can't understand the words. It's a jumble of mess that sounds like he's . . . *not* sacking me? He sighs heavily and continues, 'Not yet anyway. The viewers really like you. So do people here.' He turns his computer away from me while I stare at the back of the monitor, still seeing my wild, furious expression as I scream at Justin for not proposing. Like a mad-woman version of the bright sun seared into the back of my eyelids.

I stare down at my lap. The humiliation doesn't just burn, it's molten lava in my chest, making its way into my lungs and on throughout my whole body. Red, hot, liquid shame.

But I'm not fired?

Spencer begins speaking again and I try so hard to listen; to take in his words. 'We're going to give it a few days – you're obviously not going on air today – and we'll issue a public apology on your behalf. And then, if this has all blown over by Wednesday, we'll get you back to your regular schedule.' I breathe out heavily and he hastily adds, 'If! *If*, Liv! If it hasn't blown over – if people don't move on to the next big humiliating thing,'—I wince at his words—'then we'll have to . . . *revisit* this.' He gives me a second to take all of this in, looking at me with an expression I've never seen from him before: pity. 'Get one of the assistants to book you a car back home, okay? Get some rest. You look terrible.'

So much for Jools' hard work. Although, to be fair, she didn't get to my eyebrows, and I feel like my eyebrows do a lot of heavy lifting for my face.

I wander out of Spencer's office in a daze, my mind racing. I pass a few familiar faces in the corridor, and they all look away awkwardly. I feel my way to one of the bathrooms and just make it into a cubicle before I sink to the tiled floor, my head in my hands.

I sit there for a few minutes, everything spinning around me.

And then I look at my phone.

I stare at the screen. It looks ten thousand miles away and I briefly wonder if I'm having a panic attack. My fingers look tiny and delicate holding the device, as I swipe it open. Part of me hopes Face ID won't work, but it clicks open. Just about every app is lit up with notifications. Multiple notifications. Multiple messages. I ignore them all and open TikTok instead.

Shakily, I search 'tiramisu girl' and there it is. The video. There are hundreds more likes and comments now, though it's only been a couple of minutes since I left Spencer's office. I scroll through people's opinions, my horror increasing with every LOL and every unimaginative millennial calling me a Karen. I let the video auto play over and over, until it doesn't feel like it's me anymore.

I put my phone face down in my lap for a second and try to rationalise.

Okay, so maybe this isn't that bad. I haven't lost my job, after all. Maybe this will end up being a funny story I tell my kids.

I think of Justin again – has he seen this? Sure, he saw it happen in real life, but has he seen *this*?

In my lap, my phone vibrates and I turn it over. The video disappears, replaced by caller ID. It's Samira. I want to sob at the sight of her name and quickly hit answer, bringing my phone to my ear. It's not even 6am, she must've just woken up – but she sounds alert and worried.

'Liv?'

The sound of my own name, said by a person I know loves me and cares, is enough to push me over the edge. I start crying, tears rolling down my cheeks as she shushes me nicely. 'Babe, it's okay, it's okay. Everything's going to be okay.'

'You've seen it?' I ask through sobs.

'Yeah. Like, fourteen people have already sent it to me this morning.'

'Fantastic,' I say sourly.

'Why didn't you say anything earlier?' she asks. 'In the bathroom this morning?'

I shrug helplessly. 'I hadn't seen it! I didn't see it until my twat-head boss pulled me into his office and showed it to me. Everyone was acting weird, and I didn't know why. I thought my taxi driver just really liked my nails.'

I can hear her shake her head. 'No, I mean the break-up, dude. You didn't tell me about Justin – that he'd … ended things.'

'That prick can sod off and die,' I bark, the anger rushing back in. 'He's stolen my thirties from me.'

'You're only thirty-one,' she points out, then something occurs to her. 'Wait, you said your boss called you in? You mean boy child Spencer himself? Are you in trouble? They're not . . . ?'

'I think it's going to be all right,' I breathe out. 'He says as long as the internet moves on and this all quickly blows over, my job is safe.'

'Well, shit, that's almost halfway decent of him.' Sam sounds relieved. 'I'm glad I don't have to kick you out of the flat for being an unemployed layabout.'

'Me too,' I laugh.

'It *will* blow over quickly,' she continues with strength in her voice. 'You know what TikTok is like, it'll be onto the next viral thing within twenty-four hours. You'll be forgotten so fast.'

'I hope so.' I swallow hard, then feel anger rising in my chest. 'Why would someone share this though?' I ask. 'What kind of person would do that? What kind of horrible sad excuse would film it in the first place and put it on the internet?'

'I think we both know who posted this,' she replies sombrely, 'I mean, it's obvious. Who would want to hurt you like this? Who's already been torturing you for weeks and whose whole purpose is solely driven by tormenting and destroying you?' She pauses dramatically. 'It was the daddy long-legs.'

Despite myself, I laugh at this.

Everything always feels so much better when I've spoken to Sam.

And maybe she's right and things will be okay. Sam still loves me, I've still got my job, and all this drama will die down really fast. I just have to hang on in there.

The bathroom door opens and someone at the sinks calls my name. I recognise Jools' voice and say a quick goodbye to Sam, slowly standing up. 'I'm here,' I call out.

'Oh, sweetheart!' she says, throwing her arms out as I exit the cubicle. She pulls me close and I breathe in her familiar shampoo smell. 'I'm really sorry I didn't say anything! I was so surprised to see you turn up this morning and didn't know whether to mention it. I assumed you knew and were trying to be as normal as possible. I'm so sorry, my darling.'

I shake my head into her shoulder. 'Don't be silly, Jools, it's not your fault. I just can't believe it's happened. I'm so embarrassed.'

'You must be a wreck.' She shakes her head, her glasses sliding down her nose as she regards me with concern. Then she frowns. 'I can't believe that little knob Spencer wouldn't let me finish your eyebrows. He hasn't sacked you, has he? Tell me he hasn't? We'll riot.'

I shake my head, then straighten up. 'No, and I'm okay, honestly. Thanks for being so lovely, Jools, you're the best. But you don't need to worry, I'm all right, I think. I'm just going to ignore all the comments and wait for this to blow over. It was just one silly video where I made a fool of myself. There will be another idiot on the internet tomorrow, stealing focus from my temporary insanity. I just need to keep my head down for a couple of days.'

She nods slowly, looking worried and avoiding my eyes. 'Um, well ... yeah, maybe.'

I narrow my eyes at her. 'What?' She says nothing and I move closer, forcing her to look straight at me. I give her my sternest expression, which is effective even without eyebrows. 'Jools, *what?*'

She swallows dryly and removes her glasses, cleaning the glass with the corner of her cardigan. 'Oh, love. I'm so sorry. There's another video of you from last night. Someone just shared another one.'

From out in the hallway, I hear Spencer roaring. He's yelling my name.

ViralVideosTranscribed

one hour ago

LIV CARPENTER'S HILAR MELTDOWN PART
TWO – NEW FOOTAGE TRANSCRIBED!!!

Waiter 2: Oh god, she's coming back.

Waiter 1: Erm, madam—

LC: I would like another piece of cheesecake, please.

Justin: What are you doing, Liv? Come back to insult more of my
mum's soft furnishings?

LC: [still speaking to the waiter] I REALLY LIKED THAT CHEESECAKE,
PLEASE BRING ME ANOTHER SLICE. I JUST GOT DUMPED
AND I WOULD LIKE SOME MORE PUDDING PLEASE.

Waiter 1: Coming right up, madam.

LC: PLEASE STOP CALLING ME MADAM, I'M ONLY JUST 31.

Waiter 1: Sorry . . . miss? I'll get you some cheesecake.

LC: Unless you found some tiramisu?

Waiter 2: No.

LC: I really like cream. It doesn't sit well with me, but I love it.

sound of chair scraping across floor

Justin: [sighing] What are you doing now?

cutlery clattering

Justin: Come out, Liv, you can't hide under the table.

LC: Why not? I'm going to enjoy my cheesecake under here – is that a crime? I happen to like eating under the table. This is where I eat most of my meals.

Justin: [inaudible]

Waiter 1: Here's your dessert, madam, er, miss. On the house.

Justin: Please come out.

LC: No! I'm not coming out. I've chipped my Shellac getting under here, I can't risk ruining another nail crawling out. Look at this one, it got broken! On a spoon!

Justin: Please, Liv.

LC: Are you cheating on me? Is that why you're dumping me?

Justin: No.

LC: So, you just don't fancy me anymore?

Justin: [inaudible]

LC: Well, you should know your penis isn't even that great. I know I said it was, but I say that to every guy I sleep with, and I was totally lying in your case. It's not even in the top three of penises I've seen. I wouldn't even say top fifty actually.

Justin: [inaudible]

LC: Don't slut shame me! I had a very prolific university era, thank you.

Justin: [inaudible]

LC: Do you remember when I got you that supercar driving experience for Christmas, Justin? You said I was the best girlfriend ever. Was that just a lie? *And* I came along to watch even though it was the most boring day imaginable.

Justin: You said it was fun.

LC: I was *lying,* Justin. I was trying to be the best girlfriend ever, because that's what you said I was. Well, I want that souvenir model car I bought you back.

Justin: You can't just take gifts back, Liv.

LC: [through mouthfuls of cheesecake] You've taken back your love, so I can take Percy the Porsche back.

Waiter 1: Can I get you anything else, mada— miss?

LC: No, I'm done with this cheesecake and I'm done with this man. Please bring me the bill, I'm paying. Like always.

Justin: [muttering] Not always . . .

LC: [table scraping on floor] Oh! And yes, for the record, I would like to insult more of your mum's soft furnishings. THEY'RE FUCKING HORRIBLE. WHY WOULD SHE HAVE SO MANY PURPLE SCATTER CUSHIONS? AND I DON'T NEED TO BE TOLD TO LIVE OR LOVE OR LAUGH WHEN I'M IN THE DOWNSTAIRS SHITTER. IT WOULD BE FUCKING WEIRD TO BE LAUGHING WHILE HAVING A POO ACTUALLY. *WEIRD*, JUSTIN. AND REMEMBER HOW SHE BOUGHT ME ONE OF THOSE SIGNS FOR CHRISTMAS AND I LAUGHED POLITELY WHEN SHE WOULDN'T SHUT UP ABOUT HOW FUNNY IT WAS THAT IT SAYS LIVE, LOVE, LAUGH WHEN I'M CALLED LIV? WELL, IT WASN'T ACTUALLY FUNNY AT ALL, JUSTIN. I WAS LIE-LAUGHING. I WAS LIV, LIE, LAUGH.

Justin: [stunned silence]

LC: LIV, LIE, FAKE LAUGH, JUSTIN. THAT WAS OUR WHOLE RELATIONSHIP.

[watch again?]

"your penis isn't even that great"

#TiramisuGirl #WhatIsTiramisu #Hilarious #LivCarpenter #BBCMorningTea
#RelationshipTherapist #PublicMeltdown #PublicFreakout
#FunnyVids #WhatAnEmbarrassment #PurpleScatterCushions
#DownstairsShitter #CrazyEx #CoolCalmAndCollectedYeahRight

42 comments

Alayah

Tiramisu Girl!!!!!! This is even better than the last one

Blondie

A friend of a friend vaguely knows her and says she is a right
headcase!!

> **Grant**
>
> No way! She always pretended to be so chill

Kyro

Such a Karen lol

> **TLWWC**
>
> I don't know how those waiters stay so patient

Dothraki

Have Morning Tea commented anything yet? Bet they're sacking
her right now. LOL

> **Haj**
>
> I've been clicking refresh on their socials all morning! Wonder if
> they'll say anything on the show today?!!!
>
> **Jem**
>
> She usually does her segment on a Friday doesn't she?
> Imagine if she turned up!!!!!
>
> **Gary**
>
> No way, she is so fired. Too many women on that show anyway.
> Give men a chance! Down with DEI. I'd have a job if not for
> other people.

Andrew

New dance remix just dropped

Faddy

Lol, maybe we should rename her Cheesecake Girl

> **Indi**
>
> Or Cheesecake Woman because she's not a child

> **Jim**
>
> She is a low value woman. Did you clock that mention of her body count? Yuck. Wouldn't touch her. Did you know semen stays up there and goes into the woman's brain? That's why alpha men should only be with virgins.

Kel

TBF to Tiramisu Girl, I've wanted to hide under a table so many times. I feel her pain.

> **Fran**
>
> Me too. But I don't think anything's going to save her job now ...

CHAPTER FOUR

'SAM!' I yell out into my apartment as I open the front door, desperately needing the immediate comfort and reassurance of my favourite person.

'In here, babe,' she shouts from the living room. I enter to find her standing still on the arm of the sofa in the corner of the room. She has her arms raised in the air, hands like claws, and a goofy expression on her face. Her tongue lolls out of her mouth and her eyes are crossed. On her back, she is wearing giant plastic wings.

'What are you doing?' I ask after a moment of stunned silence.

She puts her tongue back in her mouth. 'Duh! I'm a daddy long-legs!' She sounds exasperated. 'I've come to take more videos of you and share them online.' She pauses. 'I thought it might distract you from your unbelievably shitty day.'

She resumes the pose, tongue hanging out of the side of

her mouth like an inbred Yorkshire Terrier. When I still don't react, she jumps down from her chair and starts chasing me around the room. I shriek and run away – and despite everything, I am laughing.

'It's not funny to mock my terror,' I scream through mirthful tears. 'You knobhead.' She collapses on the sofa, crushing her wings, and I sit beside her, still laughing. 'You're the best.'

'I know.' She closes her eyes.

'I love you.' I close my eyes, too.

'Fuck off,' she says mildly, and I reopen one eye.

'Where did you get the wings?' I take them in. They look familiar.

'You wore them last Halloween,' she confirms, thick, dark eyebrows raised. 'When you were dressed as a slutty fairy.'

'I was just dressed as a fairy, actually,' I point out. 'Any sluttiness was all me.'

'Fair enough,' she acknowledges. She leaves a beat, then turns to face me on the sofa. The left wing bends in half and I wonder if it will break. I consider asking her to take them off. If I'm going to be out of a job, I can't just re-buy fairy wings every Halloween, can I? She reaches over to poke me in the shoulder. This is Sam's idea of spontaneous affection. 'Are you okay?'

I wonder how to answer this. I want to tell her the truth, but I don't know how I feel right now. Not after that second conversation with Spencer.

'Did you see a second video went up?' I ask after a moment.

She nods gravely. 'I did.' She raises her eyebrows. 'I actually think you came off better in that one. Very relatable.' She pauses, waving open palms. 'I mean, who *hasn't* wanted to eat cheesecake under a table? Plus, Cheesecake Woman is a much cooler nickname than Tiramisu Girl.' She shrugs. 'At least everyone knows what cheesecake is.'

'Do people *really* not know what tiramisu is?' I ask, baffled. 'Are some people not obsessed with boozy, creamy desserts like me?'

'I guess not.' She shrugs, sinking into the sofa. It squishes the wings even more and I frown. Now I've remembered I own them, I want to be able to wear them again. Next Halloween I could dress up as Cheesecake Tiramisu Daddy Long-legs Girl.

'Did you read the comments?' I ask quietly, and she nods.

'Do you not want to cry or whatever?' she asks nicely. 'I know you love crying.'

'I do love crying,' I confirm, nodding. 'But no, not this time. I don't know, I feel . . . sort of hollow. Empty. A meat sack.'

'Like a Scotch egg without the egg because eggs are disgusting,' Sam comments in a wise voice.

'Erm, sure, yes, like that.' I nearly laugh again. Sam's very anti eggs. 'All hollowed out apart from my sausage meat.' I sigh. 'But at the same time, my stomach feels all spiky. I feel really sick, but also numb.'

'I expect you're in shock.' She continues quietly, 'I watched the show – *Morning Tea* – earlier I noticed you weren't on at your usual time ...' She pauses. 'They haven't ... you're not ... they didn't ...?'

'No, not fired.' I fill in the blank, then add quickly, 'Not quite.' She breathes a sigh of relief, before I add, 'Except I probably am.' I shake my head. 'Spencer, the cunty little frog, says I have to go to *therapy*. Can you imagine? He says the only way I'm going to keep my job on the show is to spend the next six weeks in therapy. It's rubbish. It's a bunch of pandering nonsense that people would see straight through! I *am* a therapist for god's sake! And they're saying I have to go speak to some parachuted-in counsellor. It's pure nonsense. Complete bullshit!'

Sam nods slowly. 'I can see you're upset,' she says carefully, and I want to knock away the therapy words pouring out of her therapised mouth. Doesn't she know I can hear them? That I know them inside out?

'You don't think I need therapy, do you?' I ask pointedly, frowning. 'Last night in the restaurant was just ... it was just a *moment*. I had a silly moment last night, that's all. It's not like that was the real me. I was just momentarily upset about the situation – like anyone would be – and some horrible dick leapt on the chance to film and humiliate me. I'm not the one in the wrong here. I'm not the one who should be punished. The guy who videoed and transcribed my break-up is the one who needs therapy!'

'I think everyone needs therapy,' Sam shrugs. 'And if it's the only way you get to keep your job, it would be worth it, wouldn't it?'

'But I've had a bunch of therapy! Every therapist has,' I cry. 'It's part of the training. I know it all! And it'll make me look ridiculous! A therapist in therapy, ugh. It'll undermine my credibility, and the viewers will see straight through it. They're saying I have to do this to save my reputation, but it'll ruin my reputation! Who's going to trust a therapist who's been ordered to go to therapy herself?'

'Yeah, but who's going to trust Tiramisu Girl?' she points out rather brutally.

'I thought I was Cheesecake Girl now,' I mutter, and she shrugs again.

'Tiramisu Girl, Cheesecake Girl, Cheesecake Woman – whatever. At least this could give you a clean slate.'

'I don't need a clean slate,' I tell her sulkily. 'I need none of this to have happened. I need Justin not to have dumped me when he was supposed to propose. I need arseholes not to have put it all on the internet. I need someone to go back in time and stop Spencer's parents from ever having sex or procreating. What I really *don't* need is therapy!'

'But what will you do if they sack you?' Sam looks worried and I shake my head defiantly.

'Fuck them!' I yell furiously, not meaning a word of it. 'I don't need therapy *or Morning Tea*.'

Sam looks suddenly excited. 'Hey, you know what you should do? Record a response video! We'll tell the entire internet that they're all stupid twats and that you did nothing wrong.'

Even in my fog of despair-cum-rage, I know this is a

terrible idea. Sam is the queen of terrible ideas. 'Er, thanks, dude,' I hedge. 'But I have been heavily *encouraged* to avoid the internet altogether for now.' Sam looks disappointed as I shake my head. 'No, I know what I'm going to do. I can go back to properly seeing clients at my office. I've barely been there for more than a few sessions a week in months.' Something occurs to me and I sit up straighter. 'And there's the book! I'm supposed to be writing my book and the publisher has been asking when I'll get the first draft in. This will give me a bit of time to really focus all my energies on writing it.' I pause, nodding. 'This will be good for me, actually. I'll hide away for a few months, write *Orange Flags: Your Ultimate Guide to a Healthy Relationship*, and when I'm finished, the internet will have forgotten all about any stupid viral videos of me. I'll be able to emerge from my cocoon like a beautiful therapist butterfly.'

'Or a beautiful therapist daddy long-legs.' Sam stands up, her wings flapping.

I nod enthusiastically. 'Sure, like a beautiful therapist daddy long-legs. And *Morning Tea* will be begging me to come back. I'll probably get an offer from one of the rival shows, and then there'll be a bidding war over me.'

I meet Sam's eyes and there is pity there, clear as day.

'Hey,' she says brightly, very obviously changing the subject. 'I know what'll distract you from all of this today!' She raises an eyebrow. 'Let's go trick or treating. I've already got my daddy long-legs costume on. You can go as that viral Tiramisu Girl. It's so *now*.'

'Oi!' I say, laughing despite myself. 'And what are you talking about, Sam, it's the 2nd of June, Halloween is nearly five months away.'

She grins. 'So what? Who says you can't celebrate early? You know some people start celebrating Christmas in June. Halloween is far more reasonable.' She looks at me faux-sternly. 'And if anyone asks us what we're doing, we'll say it's our trick, and then we can demand treats.'

'I *do* want treats,' I admit begrudgingly.

'I think seeing some ghosts might make you feel better.'

'It would certainly make me feel *different*,' I confirm. 'I'm not sure better is quite the right word.'

Sam looks thoughtful. 'Why are all ghosts from the Victorian era? Like, if ghosts were real, you'd think you'd see them from all different times. Where are all the caveman and dinosaur ghosts?'

'Maybe they've had long enough on earth to torment the living, and have passed on?' I offer and Sam accepts this logic.

'Okay, that makes sense. So, then you'd think the biggest number of ghosts would be, like, from recent times. But you never hear about some embarrassing nineties ghost wearing a crop top and Spice Girl white wedge trainers, on the arm of some loser ghost in a bucket hat and a bomber jacket.'

'Good point.' I nod, then peer at her closer. 'We're not really going trick or treating, right? Aren't you meant to be working?'

Sam works from home on a Friday. In theory, at least. She doesn't actually get much of anything like work done.

Before she can answer, our Ring doorbell goes and we both jump.

'Who the hell could that be?' I ask in a whisper. No one *ever* comes here. Even the Amazon delivery driver just lobs our loo roll deliveries over the back fence. It usually bounces into the neighbour's bird bath but who can be bothered to complain? Once the loo paper dries out, it works just fine.

'God knows,' Sam whispers back, as we stare at one another, me with horror, her with exhilaration. She loves the drama. 'Do you think we should check the video?'

'What if they see us checking?' I ask with a tremble.

'We've been through this,' she sighs. 'It's not a two-way video, Liv. They can't see through the camera.'

'I swear to GOD the postman could see me that time,' I say stridently, but she just rolls her eyes. We both jump as the bell goes again, and Sam picks up her phone and opens the app.

'Who is it?' I ask her, my eyes wild. She looks up at me – she's frowning. 'Who?' I ask again, suddenly feeling afraid.

She takes a deep breath. 'It's Justin.'

CHAPTER FIVE

It has only been – I check my watch, god, seriously? – about thirteen hours since we last saw one another. Thirteen hours since I finally stormed out of that restaurant still shouting about his mum. Thirteen hours since my life became pure turd. But I feel like I haven't seen Justin's face for aeons. I study it now on the phone screen, drinking him in as he waits patiently outside our building. His long, straight nose, his thick eyebrows. He pushes his hair away from his face now; a habit I once adored. Still do, actually.

'Let's ignore it,' Sam says firmly, and I gasp.

'We can't do that,' I tell her. 'He's come to see if I'm okay. This is *so* sweet.' I cling to a sudden hope. 'Maybe all of this can be undone, Sam! He'll take back his dumping and tell the world we were just messing about in that video. We'll show everyone how very in love we are – he might even propose for real now! – and Spencer frog-face will forget all about this silly therapy idea. Everything will be good again. We can undo this!'

Sam squints at me. 'You are majorly in denial, Tiramisu Girl. This arse-knob *dumped* you. The whole world has seen it. And just because he's here doing the halfway decent thing of checking you're all right after something awful happened, it doesn't make him a good guy. It makes him a human being at its most basic level.' She grins. 'Plus, it's funnier to ignore him. Look at his stupid face getting more and more irate.'

I tut at her, hitting the buzzer and telling Justin in my nicest voice that he should come on up.

A light tap on our front door comes a minute later and I quickly check my reflection in the hallway mirror. Jools' make-up is holding firm and everything looks good, apart from the missing eyebrows. Ah well. Justin has seen me without eyebrows before. Never without mascara, but a few times minus eyebrows. It was quite funny actually. He knew something was wrong with my face and I kept catching him examining me curiously, but it was obvious he couldn't figure out what. Men and eyebrows, LOL.

'Justin,' I say breathlessly as I yank open the door.

'Er, hi.' He nods nervously.

'Justin,' Sam acknowledges archly from over my shoulder. He gives her wings a quizzical look. She doesn't offer an explanation, and he doesn't ask.

'Come in,' I tell him warmly, and he steps awkwardly over the threshold.

'Umm, Samira.' I turn to her. 'Can you . . .' I gesture for her to go away, and she rolls her eyes.

'No fair!' she pouts. 'I want to listen.' We glare at one another for a long second, before she sighs. 'Fine, I get it. I'll give you guys some space.' She stays standing there for another moment, glaring at Justin, before finally turning in the direction of her room. She hops awkwardly along the hallway, then glances back at me.

'What? I don't know how a daddy long-legs would walk,' she explains as she continues to hobble-jump out of sight. I try not to laugh as I turn my attention back to Justin.

'Is she . . . ?' He peers after her, his eyebrows knitted together with confusion. 'What is . . .'

'She's a daddy long-legs,' I tell him simply.

He frowns. 'Daddy long . . . Aren't you scared of them?' he asks, and my heart gets all warm. He remembers. See, he *does* care about me.

Although, I suppose it probably helped that I talked about them *a lot*. One of our most in-depth chats ever was about what happens with a plural or singular daddy long-legs. Is it a daddy long-leg or are they daddy long-legses?

I smile and he clears his throat. 'I messaged but you didn't reply . . .' he begins.

'I haven't looked at my phone.' I shrug apologetically. 'I was avoiding it. For obvious reasons.'

'Right.' He swallows. 'Are you okay?'

'Not really,' I admit. 'It's been pretty awful. My boss is

going mad, my phone is radioactive.' I sigh. 'I can't believe those restaurant dickheads did this . . .'

He frowns. 'Wait, what? Why would your boss be angry? What's the restaurant got to do with it?' His eyes narrow. 'Are they charging you for getting cheesecake all over the tablecloth? And damaging that spoon with your nail?'

I stare at him. 'Er, Spencer's upset about the . . . y'know, the videos.'

Justin stares back. 'What videos?' He shakes his head. 'I thought you were upset about the break-up – avoiding your phone because of me. I thought this was about me du—' He swallows the words, but I know what he was going to say. *I thought this was about me dumping you.*

Jesus.

I take a deep breath. So, he doesn't know about Tiramisu Girl and the viral videos of me. Of *us*. How is that possible? I suppose it was mostly zoomed in on my face and I'm the one on TV, maybe no one's recognised him yet.

Which means . . . he's not here because he was worried about me.

But he could still be here to retract the break-up! To get back together?

'What are you doing here, Justin?' I ask and he looks away. 'Did you want to talk about us? About where we left things last night?'

'Erm, no,' he replies too quickly, looking at me all boggle-eyed. 'Christ no. I think we said all we needed to say. It's better off this way. Definitely.' He pauses. 'But I really need my washing back. I forgot you had all my underwear and these boxers I'm wearing are on day five.' He smiles bashfully like this is adorable.

I frown. He's not here because he's worried I'm upset about millions of people on the internet watching and mocking my tantrum. He's not here to plead forgiveness and ask me to be his girlfriend again. He's *definitely* not here to propose with a huge diamond ring like he was supposed to in the first place. He's here because he needs his underpants.

I feel the rage bubbling up in my belly again. It froths and sloshes there, fermenting in its own livid juices. And suddenly I want to hide under a table with sugary foods all over again.

I take a long, deep breath. Letting my anger win has already ruined my life enough for one week. I push it way back down, deep down inside myself and inhale slowly.

'It's in the tumble dryer,' I say after a moment. 'I'll go get it for you.' I turn for the kitchen and then turn back, fresh annoyance flooding me. 'Actually, no, I won't get it for you. *You* go get it for you.'

He nods silently, looking around himself helplessly. I sigh. 'The dryer is in the kitchen.' I pause, as he still looks baffled. 'Stacked on top of the washing machine?' He still has the same look. 'Fine!' I snap. 'Just follow me, I'll show you.'

I lead the way, muttering about how often he's stayed here over the last year. I point towards the machine and he approaches it cautiously. He pulls hard at the door handle. It doesn't open.

'There's a door release button,' I explain as nicely as I can. 'There is a clue in the form of the words *door release*?'

He nods, finding the clearly labelled button and gingerly pressing it. The door pops open and a waft of lovely floral softener fills the room. I bought those special dryer sheets just for his washing. Just so he could smell the extra effort and realise how much I care. Cared. No, *care*, present tense. I still want him to notice the smell.

But he doesn't. Of course he doesn't.

He peers inside the drum with some trepidation. 'So, I just . . . reach inside?'

He *cannot* be this incompetent.

When I first met Justin at my birthday party, I delighted in him being a whole ten years older than me. Of course, I thought, he must know sooo much about life. He must be so wise and experienced. Naturally, he'd be much more mature than men my own age, so much less shallow. He would understand women and know about the world.

But here he is; regarding the inside of my dryer like it contains a waiting Rolf Harris and Jimmy Savile.

I step forward, unable to cope with this level of uselessness. I pull out the pile of clean washing, dump it on the kitchen table and begin folding. He watches.

'Should I help?' he asks, sounding reluctant, and I shake my head.

From across the room, I hear Sam's horrified gasp.

'You're *not*!' she says, 'Please, Liv, tell me you're *not* folding Justin's washing for him? He's an adult man with an adult job. He *knows* how to do his own washing.'

Justin attempts a weak protest. 'It's a different kind of machine than the one I'm used to ...'

Sam ignores him. 'And you're helping him with his clothes twelve hours after he *dumped* you in the middle of a restaurant.'

'I offered to do it!' he cries. 'She wanted to fold them!' I tut at him.

'He doesn't know *how* to do it!' I tell her, and I can hear the defensiveness in my voice. Sam was never Justin's biggest fan. She'd constantly tell me off for doing his washing; for letting him manspread across our whole sofa; for letting him mansplain her own job to her; for – in Sam's words – letting him *man* all over the apartment.

'He's in his *forties*, Liv!' she almost shouts now, and he looks put out.

'Only just,' he says huffily. 'I'm only just forty-two. My birthday was only a few months ago.'

'I remember.' Sam eyes him coolly. 'Because you had Liv organise and host a party for you here. And then you turned up late, already drunk, and left us to talk to your boring old friends about how much they all hate their wives and kids.'

'My friends are not old!' he cries, missing so much of the point.

'Liv, this'—Sam waves at the pile of laundry I'm folding—'is weaponised incompetence and you *know* it is! He's pretending not to have any clue so you'll just get sick of watching him fail and do it for him.'

'That's not true either,' he says looking guilty. 'I can fold this washing just fine, thank you.' He steps forward, taking a shirt from my hands and shaking it out. He takes the sleeves in each hand and stares at them for a moment, then tries to make it into something resembling a shirt. It's laughable and cryable, but when I move to take over, Sam takes a step closer, glaring me down.

'So, um, Liv, what happened with the restaurant?' he asks as he crumples the shirt up into a pile, sleeves in all directions, and picks up some odd socks instead. 'You said something about them being dickheads with a video? Was there CCTV? Have they been in touch?'

Sam looks startled, turning to me. 'He doesn't know what's happened?'

He glances between us. 'What do you mean what's happened? What *has* happened?'

I swallow hard, eyeballing socks he's just paired incorrectly. He deserves to know. 'Our break-up has gone viral,' I sigh, then nod at Sam. 'You better show him.' Reluctantly, she retrieves her phone and pulls up TikTok. I can't watch, but I listen to the now-familiar dialogue as I wail from the screen about my nails and what pudding I did or didn't order. Justin's eyes get wider and wider as he watches, taking in the number of likes and the comments, no doubt still racking up and up with every passing minute.

'Nooooo!' he says at last, looking up and directly at me.

'I can't believe it, it's ... oh my god, it's *us*, and they're saying ... and there are hundreds of ... *thousands* of ... But ... but ...' He trails off, his eyes wide and full of fear. '... But they don't know who *I* am, right? They won't come for me, will they? I'll be okay? It's just you?'

'You are unbelievable,' Sam says, her face twitching with disdain. 'And it's time for you to go.'

She marches him out, the washing pile in his arms, un-folded and teetering. I resist a desperate urge to offer him a carrier bag. It would be the decent thing to do, especially since we have close to ten thousand under the sink. Sam slams the door behind him and returns to where I'm stand-ing. She eyeballs me with concern, waiting.

At last, she speaks first. 'Are you all right?' she says softly.

I shake my head sadly, then look up. 'Can you believe he doesn't want to get back together?' I lament and her eyes bug out. I take in her furious expression, adding quickly, 'I know, I know! I'm an idiot and you're wishing a plague of daddy long-legs would come eat me alive, aren't you?'

'Yep,' she confirms in a biting tone. But then she takes a deep breath and moves closer. 'What can I do? Tell me what to do. Do you want me to kill Justin? Do you want me to track down the person who posted those TikTok videos and eviscerate them? Do you want me to spend the day replying to every single comment calling them all cunts?'

I gasp. 'You kiss your mother with that mouth?'

She shrugs. 'I mean, no, not really. I hug her, but kissing my mother as an adult feels a bit creepy to me.'

'Okay,' I continue. 'You hug your mother with that mouth?'

She grimaces. 'Again, no. I'm not sure how that would be possible.' She nudges me gently with her elbow. 'But really, tell me what I can do to make this all right. Or, at least, to make this slightly less horrible. I mean it about the comments; I'll take on each and every one of them for you.'

I smile, my eyes watery. 'Thank you, but you're meant to be working. I'm about to be fired, so we need at least one of us to have a job. You'll have to support the two of us. I'm going to be your trad wife, cleaning the house, washing your clothes, making sure the meatloaf is on the table at 6pm for your arrival home from the office.'

'Ew,' she says. 'I don't know what meatloaf is and I never ever want another human being to touch my smelly pants.'

I raise my eyebrows. 'Are they that bad?'

She nods. 'Yes, they really are. They're, like, sell-them-on-OnlyFans-bad. I have a yeast infection something like eighty per cent of the time.'

I nod, knowing this. 'That's why you're trying to fix your gut health,' I say, and she parrots it back.

'That's why I'm trying to fix my gut health.' She grins.

When we met, Sam was a person who would steal other people's leftover chips in Wetherspoons. Now she's someone who recently pooed into a bag to send to one of those health companies for gut analysis. I guess this is what being in our thirties means. I sigh. 'But don't you want a partner one day who'll help you with your disgusting underwear? Who'll bring you home cranberry juice and Canesten Duo, and then take you to the GP to collect your antibiotics?'

She makes another face. 'God no. Why would I want someone stealing my energy and my "me" time?' She smiles at me. 'I've got you to share the rent and Canesten expenses with.'

'But what if I meet someone?' I hesitate. 'Or what if I . . . what if I get back with Justin?'

She looks disgusted. 'You'd actually want . . .' She waves at the door, in the direction he went. Then she throws up her hands. 'Ugh, Liv, you're impossible.' She crosses her arms, and I know she's really annoyed. 'But you're right, I better get back to my work.' She stalks away towards her bedroom, wings flapping.

'I LOVE YOU, SAM,' I shout.

'SHOVE IT, LIV,' she yells back as she slams the door.

I pull out my phone. Maybe I'll just message Justin quickly – just to check he got home safe with all that wash-ing. And to check he definitely doesn't want to get back together . . .

Sam appears like magic at her door. 'Don't you dare.'

I put it away.

MorningTeaVids

6 weeks ago

RELATIONSHIP EXPERT LIV CARPENTER ON MORNING TEA COUNSELS HEARTBROKEN WOMAN – WITH SUBTITLES!!

Liv: Morning – sorry, is it Suzanne we have on the line?

Caller: Yes, er, hi, I'm Suzanne.

Liv: Morning Suzanne, how can I help you today? What's on your mind?

Caller: Well, right, yeah, so, I was with my ex for nearly three years and he dumped me out of the blue, a few weeks ago, right.

Liv: Uh-huh, and what reason did he give?

Caller: So, he, yeah, he just said, like, that he didn't really love me anymore and he wanted something more.

Liv: How awful, Suzanne, I'm so sorry that happened to you.

Caller: Thanks, yeah, so that was three weeks ago, and I've been, like, a mess ever since.

Liv: Understandably!

Caller: Right? So, I'm staying at my mum and dad's and I get a message on Snapchat from him last night, saying that he, like, misses me—

Liv: On Snapchat?

Caller: Yeah. He likes Snapchat.

Liv: How old is he, can I ask?

Caller: Forty-eight.

Liv: [mutters something inaudible under her breath]

Caller: Anyway, right, he says he really misses me and wants to get back together. I still love him and I don't know what to do. I'm such a wreck, like, I'm all over the place. My mum keeps bringing me Pot Noodles, which usually snap me right out of anything, but, yeah, nothing's working, not even the Noods.

Liv: Oh Suzanne, this is so awful and I totally understand. But you need to take a breath and find some inner calm, if you can. We make rash decisions in moments like this and almost always regret them later. You need to keep a cool head and consider this objectively. Try and picture yourself six months from now. If you're back with him, can you see yourself being happy? Can you see yourself having let go of this betrayal? Can you see yourself trusting him when he says he loves you, after he did this to you so suddenly? [long pause] Suzanne, wouldn't you rather find a way to adjust to his absence, than adjust to a future full of uncertainty and fear?

Caller: [long pause] I think you're right.

Liv: Also the Snapchat thing is such an orange flag. Yuck. I bet he never went down on you either, did he?

Caller: He said his exes never liked it, so he doesn't do it.

Liv: I think we have our answer. You remember my motto, right, Suzanne? He should show up and go down.

[watch again?]

Liv Carpenter says never go back to an ex!

#LivCarpenter #BBCMorningTea #RelationshipTherapist #AgonyAunt #AdviceColumn #LifeCoach #Wisdom #LivCoolAndCollectedCarpenter #ShowUpAndGoDown

CHAPTER SIX

By Monday I have pretty much convinced myself that everything will be okay.

Ish.

I spent the entirety of Sunday repeating a series of mantras on a loop: I'm fine, I have my health, the world has not ended. The furore is going to die down online this week. By Friday, frog-face Spencer will have realised what a doofus he's being, and be begging me to return to *Morning Tea*. This therapy idea will get the thorough binning it deserves. I will graciously accept his offer to come back, and in the meantime, I will focus on my other work – my clients and my book, *Orange Flags*. Oh, and – just for good measure – Justin is also going to come to his senses, realise what a brilliant girlfriend I am, and propose. At which point I will of course tell him to get lost.

Probably.

Maybe.

'How do you think curiosity actually did kill the cat?' Walking along at my side, Sam starts thinking out loud. It's one of her amazing non-sequiturs – she does this a lot. 'I mean,' she continues, 'like, what was the cat *so* curious about that he got murdered for it?' She looks thoughtful. 'What could be so bad that someone would *off* a poor little pussycat?'

'She probably witnessed a murder,' I supply sombrely. 'That's the kind of curiosity that gets you killed, right?'

'Who would she tell?' Sam looks at me seriously. 'Liv, it's a *cat*.'

'Okay, fair point,' I acknowledge. 'So maybe it's more like, the cat was curious about the edge of a building and fell off?'

She gives me a withering look. 'Have you never met a cat? Firstly, they always land on their paws. And secondly, they're not fools. They wouldn't just fall off a building like some kind of clumsy dog. Most cats have a higher IQ than the average politician.'

'Another excellent point.' I nod, as we reach the office block. I tap in my code and the door beeps an acknowledgement. I hold it open for Sam, and she slips under my arm and into the foyer.

'The only thing I can think, is that maybe curiosity is a codename for the mob, or maybe some kind of serial killer?' She unbuttons her coat halfway, shaking hair off her shoulders. 'And don't they say most serial killers start by killing cats? I think curiosity is a euphemism for serial killer.'

'Or'—I check the wooden box by the door for any post

addressed to me—'maybe it's yet another one of those shitty sexist sayings designed to shut down little girls. I don't think we tell boys off for being curious, just girls. Like, *don't ask any questions, know your place, you little pussies!*' She frowns at this, then nods after a moment, accepting its truth.

We head for the lift as I rifle through a pile of pure junk mail. Ooh, fifteen per cent off at Optical Express!

Sam travelled into the office with me today as she's scheduled for a therapy session on the first floor. I work on the third floor, which we've decided is enough professional distance between us to be just fine.

I work here in this West London office as part of a sort of therapist collective, along with four other therapists: Edward, Fran, Jamal and Arshiya.

We all met when training at university – a many-year'd hell that would bond anyone for life. After we qualified, we initially all went our separate ways, spinning off into different areas of psychotherapy. We'd mostly lost touch until about four years ago, when we reunited as a group to set up an office together. We decided to call it a therapy collective, mostly because it sounds cool, though there was much back and forth about the possibility of the term 'therapy cooperative'. Edward argued for that one while I explained – as nicely as possible when someone is being a total arse – how that made us sound like a hippy-dippy many-sister-wived commune.

That particular conversation aside, the four of us mostly rub along very nicely, all offering something slightly different to clients in the convenient framework of one building. There's Arshiya on the first floor, who helps people with grief, anxiety and depression management. Jamal on the second floor specialises in family dysfunction and addiction. Fran works in the office next to Jamal, and their niche is psychosexual and identity issues. Then there's me, of course, the relationship expert on three. But these days, I only see a handful of patients, and just on a Monday and Tuesday.

Oh, and then there is the previously mentioned arse, Edward. He works in the office across from me, dealing mostly with trauma and anger issues.

We call the lift and Sam turns to me, pouting. 'Are you *sure* you don't want to blow off your day and come hang out with me?' she asks for the fiftieth time. 'Your patients won't care! They'll totally understand after what's happened with the videos and all that. Any normal person who's been publicly shamed would be getting day-drunk with me and maybe looking for some daytime hook-ups. Get the taste of Justin and his stinky laundry out of your mouth.'

I frown at her. 'I'm not sure any of that is a good idea . . .' I hesitate.

Usually I can ignore Sam's terrible life advice, but today it is a little too tempting. The prospect of spending today trying to work, knowing the entire internet – or, okay, what *feels* like the entire internet – is talking about me does not especially appeal. Maybe I *should* torpedo my professionalism for booze and my best friend?

I shake my head, trying to be my own shoulder-angel.

'No,' I say with finality as she pouts. 'It's a cardinal sin to cancel on clients. And if I'm going to be ousted from *Morning Tea*, I'm going to need them more than ever.' I sigh. 'Plus, I need to meet with Edward, he's—' Oh shit, speak of the uptight devil. Here he comes now.

'Can you hold the lift!' His deep voice echoes down the corridor. He's got one of those actor timbres that projects even when he's not trying. Sometimes I can hear it through the walls of our offices and it makes my brain reverberate in my skull. I don't know how his clients can stand it. Or him.

'Of course!' Sam yells back in a high voice as I repeatedly jab at the close doors button.

It's too late. His fingers close around the edges and the traitorous lift doors spring back open.

'Samira, Olivia.' He nods at us both, moving to a position as far into the corner away from us as possible, and turning his back.

'Hi Edward,' Sam says throatily. She fancies him, which is unusual for her. She doesn't usually much like men. Sam dates all genders, but mostly women, because men are *the worst*. She doesn't call herself bisexual though, because she doesn't like labels. Except slag. She likes the label *slag*. She says it's pure 90s nostalgia and the word is making a comeback.

Either way, apparently there's something unusual about Edward that she finds appealing. I can't see it, but then, I've known him forever. Maybe it's his hair? He does have undeniably good hair. It's all thick and dark and wavy – any woman I know would kill for Edward's lustrous hair. I asked him once if he uses heat protection spray and he looked at me like I'd shat on his desk. He's very uptight.

Whatever it is, Sam can't get enough of him. In fact, when she first started talking about having therapy, she said she wanted to start working with him. I told her it would be incredibly unhealthy to start seeing a counsellor you have a crush on. I mean *duh*. It would be sooo unprofessional, never mind the high chance of transference. That's when a person starts to redirect their feelings onto someone else – their therapist being a common recipient. It can be feelings of rage or distrust, but quite often it ends up being love or dependence. It's not real but it *feels* super real, and it's something we're all trained to watch out for.

'Ooh, weird energy in here today,' Sam says, always one to point out any elephants in the lift. I fight an urge to throw my handbag at her.

'Shut up,' I hiss, and she grins at me loopily, enjoying my discomfort. Of course, she's right. There is a weird energy, but it's not wholly my fault.

Edward is being extra clenched-jawed towards me today because I *maaaay* have missed our last few sessions of clinical supervision. But like I said, it's not my fault!

When you qualify as a therapist, as well as undergoing about a thousand hours of personal therapy, the UKCP – otherwise known as the UK Council for Psychotherapy – basically insists you regularly sit down with another counsellor, to talk through your client work and reflect on how everything's going. It's supposed to give you some perspective and keep you forever working towards best practice. Since Edward was such a goody-two-shoes at university and always got the best marks, we elected him as our clinic supervisor at the therapy collective. He's basically our therapy House Mother. Which makes me his least favourite child.

But hey, it's yet another reason it's totally absurd that *Morning Tea* wants to send me to therapy. I'm pretty much already *in* therapy with Edward, thanks to the supervision.

Except, yeah, I haven't been to many of our sessions lately because I've been very busy with my TV work and the book. And I don't even see that many clients these days to talk about with him. Oh, and – most importantly and as previously mentioned – Edward is an arse, so I do not need supervision from him.

Okay, so he's not actually *that* bad. He's just one of those horribly clever people who is impossible to relate to. He's infuriatingly calm all the time, and so sure of his opinions, even though they're usually super annoying. Sure, there are some basic tenets of psychology and therapy we can all agree on, but about literally everything else? We do not agree.

Example number one: He once mentioned that he's not scared of spiders, so I bet he *loves* a daddy long-legs.

'I'm out,' Sam says flamboyantly as the doors open on her floor. 'By the way, Liv, I've got a date tonight, so I'll be back late.' I nod, unsure if this is true, or if she's just trying to get Edward's attention. She winks at me, then adds, 'Late or maybe not at all, eh?' This is her embracing her preferred label: Slag.

She turns to Edward, smiling sweetly. He stares pointedly at the lift ceiling. 'Bye, Edward,' she calls as she bounces away.

'Goodbye, Samira,' he replies formally. He's very formal is our Edward. Always addressing people by their full names; always nodding at people by way of greeting; always wearing a full three-piece suit for no reason. He must have about a thousand of them. This one today is slim fit, cobalt blue. It looks expensive.

'Love you,' I call to Sam as the doors shut behind her. Through the gap, I just about catch her giving me the finger, and yell after her, 'I SEE YOUR AVOIDANT ATTACHMENT STYLE, SAMIRA.'

Sam is a patient of Arshiya's. She started having therapy quite recently – just a month or so ago – but it's been a long time coming after she lost her dad a couple of years ago. He was ill for ages – one of those hideously drawn-out things that brings as much emotional pain as it does physical. He wasn't super young or anything – Sam was one of those 'surprise' additions to the family, turning up when her mum and dad were both already in their mid-forties – but he was a brilliant dad. I've known Sam since nursery, so I got to see up close exactly how brilliant he was. With my dad buggering off with barely a word when I was three, Sam's dad was the only benevolent male figure in my life. And she truly adored him. So, of course, his death hit her really hard.

I get it in an abstract way, but if I'm being honest, it's quite hard for me to imagine being *so* close to family. I am extremely low contact with mine. My mum and dad are withholding, useless shitbags, so my grandparents essentially raised me. But they both died in my late teens, so now I struggle with relating to people who really love their parents.

We arrive at our floor and Edward gestures for me to exit first. I consider being stubborn about the outdated chivalry but quickly give in and stride away.

'Olivia?' he says sternly as I hurriedly stalk off in the direction of my office.

'Yes, Ed?' I turn back, pointedly using the shortened version of his name that I know he hates. I try to look innocent because I know what he's going to say.

'We need to have a conversation today if you're free.' He's talking about the supervision sessions. He's going to tell me off; give me a lecture about my duties and about sticking to my commitments. It's the last thing I need after the few days I've had.

At least it's unlikely Edward knows anything about my public dumping and ensuing meltdown. He definitely doesn't have TikTok. I'd be surprised if he even owns a TV. I'd bet large sums of money that he sits around at home of an evening, still wearing his three-piece suit even though it's after 6pm, with a crossword puzzle book in his lap, tutting about how frivolous and uncultured the rest of the population are. Then he no doubt changes into his three-piece pyjama suit at 9pm on the dot, does a quick Sudoku, has a perfunctory wank, and is asleep by 9.25pm. You know what, I bet he doesn't even have dreams. And definitely not confusing ones about ex-boyfriends having sex with each other.

'I'm actually really busy today, I'm afraid, *Ed*,' I tell him quickly. 'I have a full day of clients to see.' I pause, then add spitefully, 'Plus, my *publisher* is pushing me about my *book*, so I need to get some *writing* done.'

He nods, an odd expression on his face. I bet it's jealousy. Not that he'd ever debase himself by acknowledging such an untoward feeling.

I clear my throat, already reaching for my office door handle. 'I'll check my calendar and give you a shout about any availability I might have coming up, 'kay?' I don't wait for an answer, coolly turning to the door, twisting the handle and flinging myself at it.

It's locked and I bounce back off the wooden panelling.

Fuck, that was embarrassing.

I fumble for my keys, not looking up to see if Edward is still watching. At last I get it open, throwing myself into the familiar room and down onto the nearby sofa. I lie there, my face in the cushions, my cheeks burning.

At least no one was filming this time.

I turn myself over, face to the ceiling, breathing deeply. My first client will be here soon, I can't just lie here feeling sorry for myself all day. It's time to let go of everything that's happened – everything that is hurting me – and switch on the other Liv. Turn myself into cool, calm and collected, therapist Liv Carpenter.

CHAPTER SEVEN

'He said he barely knows who I am anymore.' My client, Wendy, says this in a whisper, head down, eyes on her lap. Her expression is one of devastation.

My heart hurts for her but I don't react. Even though I think her son is a selfish little shit. I wait, knowing she wants to explain and giving her the minute she needs first.

Wendy breathes deeply, then continues. 'Maybe I am being unfair, maybe I have changed too much. But I'm still his mum, you would think he'd want me to be happy! And this feels like the first time in my life I *am* happy! It's the first time I've put myself first.'

Wendy is a fairly new client. She says she came to me through a friend's recommendation, but I'm pretty sure she just saw me on the telly. I get most of my referrals that way these days, but a lot of them pretend they've never seen me on *Morning Tea*. I suppose it's a bit embarrassing to admit. Like maybe there's something sort of shallow about booking a session with a TV therapist who comes with catchphrases.

Wendy reaches for the glass of water sitting on the coffee table between us, her hands slightly shaking. I suppress the urge to grab the hand and squeeze it reassuringly. She seems like such a kind-hearted, sweet person and I so want to help her. She sips the water half-heartedly before looking up. 'Of course I want to be there for Mal and my grandchildren. I told Mal I could babysit next week instead, but he said that wasn't good enough. He wants me to cancel my plans and go back to the way things were before. I don't know, maybe he's right, maybe I'm being a horrible mother. Maybe I'm being unfair putting myself first like this.'

Wendy's in her early fifties, with a husband and two grown-up sons – the eldest of which, Malcolm, has recently procreated for a second time. The reason she's come to see me is, after thirty years of servitude – being a housemaid to her husband and children, with no hobbies or outside interests – Wendy has finally made some friends. For the first time in her adult life, she's been spending time with a group of women, all eager to finally have some fun in their lives. They've started a book club, they go for regular drinks, and even took a minibreak together last month, camping in the Lake District.

None of which has gone down well with the toddler-men in Wendy's life. Her son, Malcolm, has been throwing tantrums about her not being on 24/7 call for him and his children, like she used to be. He has repeatedly called his mother selfish and demanded she give up her new hobbies and the new pals. All so she can return to being a lifeless shadow person and support automaton for the men in her life, with nothing for herself. It *enrages* me.

'Do you really think you're being unfair, Wendy?' I ask her neutrally. She wrings her hands anxiously, looking at me beseechingly. I can tell she is deeply divided. Her instinct is to defend her freeloading idiot offspring, but there's also something righteously selfish and joyful growing inside that I can tell she so desperately wants to feed.

She starts quietly crying and I hand her a box of tissues. God, I *so* want to tell her what misogynistic arseholes her sons are being. Imagine feeling entitled to someone's whole existence! Especially when that someone has already given you so much of it! Imagine!

'Sorry I keep crying,' she sobs silently.

'Don't be!' I tell her, meaning it.

This is our third session together, and the first two meetings were 120 minutes of solid crying. Which – by the way – is totally normal. Some of my clients feel like it's a waste of their money coming along just to weep, which I do understand, but also . . . where else do you get to have an un-judged, full-on cry in front of a patient, sympathetic ear? Plus, crying is often a shortcut to intimacy with a newbie client. I'm hoping she's starting to feel like I'm a safe space.

Wendy hasn't cried as much today, but she is still vibrating with fragility. It makes me want to hug her – but that would not be professional. Although, my colleague Arshiya – Sam's therapist – told me the other week that she's looking into retraining as a professional cuddler. I thought she was joking, but apparently it's a real thing. People pay hundreds of pounds an hour just to be . . . *held*. There's even an official certification and membership body. It makes me feel a little sad, but I guess it's not that much weirder than spending money to cry in front of another person.

But you *know* loads of creepy old men would hire you just so they could grab a boob or stick you in the back with their boner after innocently asking for a spoon.

I lean forward as Wendy gulps down more water, trying to regain some composure. 'I think you have a little anxious attachment style, Wendy,' I tell her nicely. 'You're worried about losing your children and they're worried about losing you. But I think having an outside life – a life for yourself – is the best way for you to find yourself.'

Wendy blinks, eyes still leaking. 'I thought you said earlier that I have a disorganised attachment style?'

'Oh right, yes.' I nod quickly. 'Yes, that's right. You exhibit a . . . er, mixture of behaviours.' Dammit, usually I'm better at keeping track of which attachment style I've assigned to which client. I'm obviously a little distracted today.

'Sorry, would you mind if we talked about something else for a minute?' Wendy asks urgently, swiping furiously at her eyes as the tears keep coming.

I hesitate. Sometimes I am stern in these moments, forcing

my clients to confront the things that are painful and difficult. But we are early on in this process, and I don't think Wendy is ready. She still doesn't know me all that well and has all this confusing misplaced loyalty to the men she loves. I can see the guilt ravaging her insides as she tells me the awful things they've done.

We all have this cognitive dissonance about people in our lives that we love. It's easier to justify bad behaviour quietly, in our own heads, but saying it out loud – *hearing it* out loud – makes this so much harder. Sometimes you have to give clients more time to feel safe before they can be pushed to explore or change the things that need exploring and changing.

I nod. 'If that's what you'd prefer.'

She sighs. 'Oh dear. I don't really know what I want to say or what I'm doing here.' Her voice is wretched. 'I feel a bit silly, to be honest. I bet you have people coming to see you with real problems. I'm just an ordinary woman with an ordinary life. I've been so lucky, having a home and a family – what am I complaining about? I'm lucky! I don't know what I want you to say! I'm—'

'Hey,' I gently interrupt her self-flagellating trail. 'This isn't about anyone else. And you don't need to arrive here having already solved it all. That's what therapy is for. A lot of people don't know how they feel or what they're trying to untangle until they start to talk.'

Oh my god, that sounded wise. I should write it down. I'm always on the lookout for more Liv mottos and mantras.

Especially since I've already used up most of my attachment style stuff today.

Wendy nods slowly. 'You're right, thank you.' She swallows. 'My insides feel all mixed up and I don't know how to get anything straight.' She takes a long, deep breath. 'I feel like I don't know myself anymore.' She pauses. 'Or maybe I haven't known myself for a long time.'

'When did you last feel like yourself?' I ask her curiously, and she considers this.

'Probably before I got married,' she says. 'But I was only nineteen – just a child in hindsight really – so maybe I didn't know myself then either.' Her eyes widen. 'What if I've never known who I am?'

'How do you feel when you're around these new friends?' I ask, and a smile spontaneously breaks out across her face. She's really beautiful when she smiles and it is with effort that I keep myself from grinning back.

'Brilliant,' she beams. 'Really wonderful! I feel light – content and excited. We do things I enjoy and they ask me questions about myself. They seem like they genuinely care about the answers.'

Wendy is describing a normal friendship, and I hate that she is so blown away by it.

She continues, a faraway look in her eyes. 'We have such a good time together, you know? Sarah is so funny, and Gina never gets the jokes straight away. We giggle about the silliest things. For our last book club we read such a sad book – I wept my way through the whole thing – and yet, when we came together to discuss it, Trudy made a joke about trauma porn and then Sarah said the author was high on the smell of his own farts.' Wendy squeals with delight at the memory and I mentally log that farts expression because it's genius. 'Then nobody could stop laughing for the next half hour! It was so funny!' She pauses. 'Even though me and Gina had no idea what they were even talking about.' She hangs her head, speaking the next part in a whisper. 'I just don't understand how Malcolm can't see how happy they make me. I didn't stay in touch with my school friends after I got married, and I never worked, so I didn't ever have much of a chance to meet anyone new. Having my girls around makes me feel so special, but Mal says they've ruined my life by making me unhappy with who I was.' She shakes her head. 'But he doesn't see that I was already unhappy. I just didn't have any other options, so I got on with things.'

'You felt trapped,' I offer, and she nods a lot.

'All the time.' She breathes deeply. 'And – if I'm being honest – quite resentful a lot of the time.' She pouts. 'But I also don't want to make Malcolm unhappy. He's my son and I love him. I have a duty to him as his mother, and I feel so guilty that he's upset with me. I don't know how to make things better. Do I give up the friends that make me happy, or do I alienate my children and husband?'

Only dickheads would make a person choose between those things – but I don't say that out loud. Instead, I give her a second, then lean in, ready to paraphrase one of my favourite therapists, Philippa Perry. 'Wendy, if you have to choose between guilt and resentment, wouldn't you rather choose guilt?'

She stares at me, something dawning on her face. I internally high five myself. Yes! I'm getting through to her! I'll have her fully slagging off those knobhead sons of hers in no time!

Beside her, Wendy's handbag vibrates and she startles. 'Sorry.' She makes a face. 'I thought I'd turned my phone off outside.' She reaches in to retrieve the device, then smiles when she sees the message. 'It's the girls,' she tells me happily, and I can *see* how much this new circle of friends means to her. I cannot let her give them up. 'We have a WhatsApp group! We're called the Fifties Fillies! Isn't that silly?'

I grin warmly, gesturing at the phone. 'Please go ahead. We're nearly at the end of our time together anyway. Are they planning your next camping adventure?'

She flicks open the message, then frowns. 'They've sent a link,' she murmurs, tapping the screen. Noise immediately fills the room, and it takes approximately two seconds for me to recognise the sound of my own voice before she can close the video. I'm shrieking those now-familiar words.

'You can't be serious, Justin, tell me you're not being serious?'

She closes it quickly and we stare at one another, her face horrified and pale. I have a feeling mine is too.

I swallow hard, trying to find my voice. 'Um, well, er, Wendy, that's our time together for today, I'm afraid. I'll . . . see you next week?'

'Er . . . right,' she says half-heartedly, standing up and fumbling for her belongings. 'Of . . . course. See you . . . then, Liv. Definitely. Thank you for . . . today.' She practically sprints for the door as I stare after her.

CHAPTER EIGHT

I have half an hour before my next client arrives, and I use the first few minutes of it to stare at the wall.

I'm fine, I have my health, the world has not ended.

I repeat it five times, feeling my breath slowing. Nothing is ever really as bad as it seems in the moment.

Except maybe my life right now.

No, not even that.

I take a few more deep breaths. I need to stay being the 'other' me. The psychotherapist, Liv Carpenter; the calm, rational relationship expert who can face down any trauma with a cool head. The version of me who can totally handle the humiliation of what just happened. I am Liv, Laugh, Lose the Dysfunction. Not Liv, the ragey maniac – current laughing stock of the entire planet.

I take a seat behind my desk, wishing I wore glasses because I would feel so much more in character. I'd even take a pair of Jools' Elton John glasses in this moment. I turn on my computer, robotically checking my emails.

Ah.

Ah shit.

My next client has cancelled.

So has the one after that.

Everyone else scheduled for today – they all have.

Oh my god.

Everyone booked in for tomorrow, too.

And for the foreseeable.

No no no no! How can this be? This can't be real? Over some silly videos? Just because I had a very minor internet incident?

I'm not fine, I don't have my health, the world *has* ended. This is a disaster.

Fuck, there's also an email from my agent, Fabian, asking why I'm not answering his calls. I pull out my phone. I've been avoiding it all weekend, but I suppose I need to face real life at some point.

Sigh. I thought your phone was supposed to be where we all went to *avoid* real life, not confront it head-on.

I open the call log, noting Fabian's number in there on five separate occasions in the last forty-eight hours. Things must be bad. He usually takes the whole of June off to summer in France, never mind working on a *Sunday*, trying to get hold of me. I don't give myself time to think – or listen to his voicemails – and quickly tap his name.

'Liv?' he answers after half a ring. 'You absolute diva,

why have you been ignoring me?' Fabian always addresses me thusly, even when I'm not on the verge of career suicide.

'Sorry,' I tell him, meaning it. 'I've been hiding all weekend.'

'Darling,' he sighs, 'this kind of mess is exactly why you have an agent. It's what I'm here for. It's why I take so much of your money from you.'

'Sorry,' I say again pathetically. 'I was hoping it would all die down on its own.' I pause, feeling a tiny bit hopeful. 'Do you think it will?'

'Not without you doing something,' he replies sharply, and the hope fades. 'I spoke to that odious little man at *Morning Tea* – what's his name again, darling?'

'Ugh, Spencer,' I supply.

'Yes, Ugh-Spencer. He's told me the plan.'

'Plan?' My stomach sinks.

'We're sending you to anger management.'

'Oh, it's anger management now, is it?' I say hotly. 'On Friday it was just plain old straightforward therapy.'

'Tomato, potato,' he says. 'Who cares? It's about what plays better for the public.'

'But that's why I can't go, Fabian!' I cry. 'The public will never trust me again if they think I'm a therapist who needs therapy.'

'Nonsense darling,' he says, and I can picture him waving his hands about. 'It's relatable.'

'I don't need anger management, Fabian,' I say, my voice all reedy and thin. 'What happened in that restaurant was a one-off. An aberrance.' I leap on an example. 'Like, yesterday! My flatmate, Sam, said I had to stop reading internet comments and she dragged me to the cinema as a distraction. We were sandwiched right next to these horrible little teenagers, who were making out right next to us the whole way through – and I didn't say a thing. Then they started wanking each other off – *right next to us, Fabian* – and I still didn't lose my rag. I kept all my lovely, bubbly rage buried deep down inside me where it's meant to stay. I didn't even lose it when I realised Sam wasn't actually watching the film. She was trying to order stuff off Temu and they wouldn't let her check out without the ten thousand free gifts and prizes she'd 'won', so that had taken up the entire first half of the film. Apparently, she hadn't even noticed the teenagers being disgusting.' I pause but Fabian says nothing, so I continue, 'Oh! And as we were leaving, the teenagers spotted me in the foyer and one of them screamed *Tiramisu Girl* at me – and I *still* didn't say anything. I just smiled and gave them a thumbs up. Even when Sam told them not to call me that and I thought she was defending me, but then she said I go by *Cheesecake Woman*, which wasn't funny at all. So, you see, Fabes? What happened with Justin last week was just an anomaly; it wasn't really me. I don't need therapy. I have an excellent, *secure* attachment style.'

There is more silence down the phone.

'Fabian?'

He's suddenly back, his breath loud down the phone. 'Sorry sweet cheeks, I didn't catch any of that. Michael's trying to talk to me about the new coffee machine. This is life or death stuff – we've been waiting months for a new one in the office – let me put you on hold.' Fabian doesn't know how to put anyone on hold, and for the next two minutes, I listen to him berating his boss. 'I don't care if the coffee machines cost a thousand pounds or fifty thousand pounds, *Michael!* That piece of trash isn't even plumbed into the wall! You cannot expect me to keep refilling the water, it's *inhumane!* This is why I should've gone to France last week after all, this is unacceptable.'

I tap my foot impatiently, wondering whether to just hang up. I don't want to have this conversation anyway. Because I. Am. Not. Going. To. Therapy. They can't make me, and I don't need it.

Fabian is back. 'Darling, I'll call you back in five. Absolute emergency here. You wouldn't believe the coffee machine Michael bought for the office, it's a travesty. A war crime in pod form. I am on the verge of throwing it – and Michael – through the window.'

'Sure,' I sigh.

'You better answer when I call,' he threatens, not waiting for my reply before hanging up.

I breathe out for a second, staring at the wall, trying to gather my thoughts. I'm interrupted by a knock at the door. Edward's face appears in the frame.

'Have you got a minute, Olivia?' he says formally. 'I saw your last client leave and there doesn't seem to be anyone waiting to see you now.' I bite my lip and he continues blithely. 'I know you said you're busy today but I just need five minutes.'

I suppress a huge sigh. I might have five minutes – I might have five hours or five days – but not for Edward. I don't have the emotional or mental energy to sit across from someone this exhausting.

Even though Edward and I have known one another since university – and worked in adjoining offices for the past four years – we've never exactly been friends. He's just not my bag. He's too . . . frigid. Too cold and distant; a little sneery, like he thinks he's better than everyone else. He walks around this building, all broad shouldered and freshly washed, with this jaw that is aggressively square. Like, there's no need for anyone to be that square-jawed. It's just unnecessary. There's something grating about how together he is, too – how self-sufficient and organised, like he knows all the answers. It's why I call him Ed, even though I know he doesn't like it. It's just my small, petty way of bringing him down a peg or two. An Ed or two.

For the record, he doesn't have much time for me either. He's always made his dislike pretty clear. I can practically hear the disdain dripping from his voice when my TV work comes up in conversation during our supervision sessions. It's obviously not proper or *worthy* enough for the likes of Ed and his three-piece suits.

I hate that he's our clinical supervisor, tracking our work and expecting us to get his – I don't know – *approval* on our sessions. Maybe that's why I've been skipping out on them lately.

'Um, my next client . . .' I begin breezily but trail off. I can't say she's about to arrive – his office is across from mine, and there's a good chance he'd be able to see anyone coming or going. But I can't admit she's cancelled on me, he'd think I'm a terrible therapist. On the other hand, I don't want to lie and say I've cancelled on her, that makes me sound unprofessional. 'Erm . . . my client is . . . she's running late,' I tell him.

He nods and settles into the chair across from my desk. It's clear he's taken this as permission to stay. Must be nice being a man. They don't need to bother learning social cues like women do.

I try again. 'But I am waiting for an important phone call!' I glare down at my mobile, willing Fabian to ring me back.

I cannot handle being told off right now. I really can't. Not by Edward of all people! I'll lose my mind. And I'm definitely not up for a supervisory session. Imagine having to tell him what just happened with Wendy! No way.

'That's fine,' he says. 'I'll be quick. I just want to talk to you about—'

Like an Avenger swooping to the rescue, my phone starts ringing on my desk. I suppress a cheer. 'Sorry!' I yell at him cheerfully. 'I have to take this!'

He nods, but – surprisingly – still doesn't move. Can't this man take a hint? Or are his suit trousers so tight that he literally can't stand up? We'll need to have him craned out the window. Actually, I would pay good money to see that happen.

My phone continues to ring and Edward continues to sit, apparently unfazed.

Sighing, I answer at last, and Fabian immediately starts garbling in my ear.

'Sorry, cherry pie, you wouldn't believe the shit coffee machine Michael is trying to palm off on us. And after I delayed my summer vacation this year! I threatened to quit and he's given in, but then told me I'm only allowed to use the quitting thing a maximum of once a month.' He pauses to inhale. 'So, I threatened to quit again and he's upped that allowance to twice a month.'

Usually I find all of Fabian's chatter delightful but today I'm not in the mood. Especially not with Edward sat across my desk, eyeballing me, with his tight trousers and uptight expression. I wonder what he'd say if I told him he had a resting bitch face? I wonder if anyone's ever told him?

'Right, so, anyway,' Fabian breathes, 'this therapy thing, my darling . . .'

'No.'

'Yes, Liv,' he says calmly. 'This *has* to happen, my little scrumpy dumpy doodle.'

'It's ridiculous!' I say, feeling the heat of Edward's eyes on me. 'I don't need it. You don't understand, I had a whole story I tried to tell you earlier, about going to the cinema yesterday and teenagers wanking . . .' I make eye contact with Edward, who frowns. But his presence in my office gives me an idea. 'Oh, and I'm basically already *in* therapy, Fabian! I have regular therapy supervision sessions with Ed, here at the office.' I wave a hand in his direction, though Fabian can't see us. Edward raises an eyebrow. 'In fact, we're actually in a session right now. So, if you'll excuse us, Fabes . . .'

I pause hopefully, wondering if my agent will buy this.

'Right now?' Fabian sounds intrigued. 'This minute?'

'Yes.' I swallow, nodding at Edward who is watching me, eyebrows knitted together with interest.

'Perfect.' His reply down the phone is confident. 'Put me on speakerphone. I want to talk to him.'

'What?' Horror tap dances across my stomach. 'No! God no, why would you need to—'

'Now, Tinkerbell,' he instructs. I swallow hard, then I do as I'm told in slow motion. Fabian's distinctive voice fills the room. 'Hi, Ed?

'Edward,' he corrects crisply.

'Edward then,' Fabian calls out in a sing-song voice. 'I'm Liv's divine agent, Fabian, I'm sure you've heard all about me. I hear the two of you enjoy a spot of therapy here and there?'

Edward shifts uncomfortably. 'Well, I am the clinical supervisor here at the therapy collective, but—'

'Perf!' Fabian crows with delight and I want to scream as he continues, 'So, we'll just formalise that arrangement. Six weeks of sessions with Edward. That'll be easy peasy. You can do it at your own office, once a week.'

'No!' I stand up at my desk now, horror dawning. 'Absolutely *not*! Not Edward! He's . . . Edward is . . . *absolutely not*.' Edward raises his eyebrows at me. The animosity between us isn't exactly a secret but I've never been quite so brazen about it. I bring the hostility down a notch. 'What I mean is . . . erm, let's not agree to anything right now. I'll just have a tiny little think and come back to you both.'

'Liv.' Fabian says my name slowly down the phone and I try to listen. 'It's this or nothing, piglet. I'm serious, are you hearing me? *Morning Tea* are ready to let you go right now. And I'd bet all my bitcoin that you have patients cancelling on you—'

'We call them clients at the therapy collective,' I murmur, feeling the need to be right about at least one small thing.

Fabian ignores me. 'Edward, are you still there, honeybee? Are you happy to do six therapy sessions with Liv? The studio will pay you, just let us know your hourly rate.'

Edward shifts in his seat again, clearly blindsided. 'Well . . . look, I have quite a full roster of clients already and the next couple of weeks are fairly booked up—'

Fabian interrupts. 'Edward, sweetums, I'm going to call you directly to work out all of these lovely details. But just so you know – just so you *both* understand – this will save Liv's job. She doesn't have many other options right now.'

Edward and I lock eyes and it's the first time I've ever seen this man look uncertain. He's always had this innate confidence; this surety about him. It's infuriating, honestly. Who lives their life knowing all the right answers? Only sociopaths, surely.

He looks away at last and clears his throat. 'I understand. And if Olivia is happy for us to go ahead, then . . .' Edward's

Adam's apple bobs lightly. '... then yes, of course. I'm sure I can move some things around.'

I stare at him. This can't be happening. 'Both of you, just hold on a minute.' I jab at the phone's loudspeaker button, taking Fabian out into the hallway with me – away from Edward.

'Fabian, you cannot be serious,' I hiss into the receiver once we're alone.

'Okay, John McEnroe,' he snorts.

'I'm too young for that reference,' I murmur as he continues now, speaking over me.

'Look, Liv, I'm not kidding, darling. Your options are very limited. You have a few sessions with that hot-sounding therapist over there, who you say you're already working with anyway. Or you throw your toys out of the pram completely, lose your job and everything you've worked so hard for.' He sighs. 'And you know what's happening with the book, of course ...' he continues blithely.

'Wait, no, what?' I interrupt, suddenly very, very afraid. 'What's happening with the book? I'm working on it right now, it's all in hand. I have chapter headings and everything.'

'Oh, babe.' His voice is full of pity. 'You didn't listen to my voicemail? And you haven't read my email?'

I remove the phone from my ear and quickly pull up his email. I hadn't read any further than the first line; the one scolding me for ignoring his calls. I scroll down. There's another paragraph, and a forwarded message from my publisher. I hold my breath as I scan it.

They say – very nicely and with lots of enthusiastic energy – that they're 'pausing announcement' of *Orange Flags* for now. They're still 'hugely excited' about publication but there have been 'a few scheduling conflicts' that mean they need to 'hold fire' for now. Fabian has generously translated it for me:

'Babe, this means they're probably binning the whole project and you're unlikely to get the rest of your advance. They may even come after you to repay the money they've given you so far. That scheduling thing is bullshit, it's all about Tiramisu Girl going viral, soz.'

'No,' I whisper, reading and re-reading the email. 'No.'

'You see,' Fabian calls cheerfully from down the phone. 'There really isn't any option. Going to therapy is the only chance you have of saving everything you've worked for.'

'Can I think about it some more?' I whisper into the phone at last, my brain blinking on and off. 'I need to process this a bit.'

'Nope,' he says with even more apparent joy. 'I'm working up a press release right now. I'll have to get it okayed by odious little Spencer – do we know if he's gay by the way, because I would probably go there and yes, I know I also need therapy – then I'll send it out by lunchtime. Time is of the essence here, snookums.' He pauses. 'Anything else you want to add before I hang up on you?'

'Only that I hate you and I'm glad Mike bought you the shit coffee machine. I wish you'd gone to France and I wish I hadn't called you back.'

'Can't hide out forever, babe,' he sings and then the line goes dead.

I stare at the phone in my hand, then at my office door, where Edward sits just a few feet away.

Why *can't* I hide out forever?

MorningTeaVids

13 weeks ago

RELATIONSHIP EXPERT LIV CARPENTER ON MORNING TEA TELLS WOMAN TO STOP BEING A WUSS!!!

Liv: Hiya, Asha, can you tell us a little bit about your problem?

Caller: Okay, yes . . . [silence]

Liv: You still with us, Asha?

Caller: Yeah it's just . . . it's hard for me to . . .

Liv: Take your time.

Caller: [swallows] So . . . [long pause]

Liv: Would you like me to explain? My producer's given me your notes.

Caller: Please.

Liv: So, you found out your boyfriend is cheating on you . . .

Caller: Yes.

Liv: . . . with a friend . . .

Caller: Yes.

Liv: . . . and you found this out a month ago?

Caller: Yes.

Liv: . . . But you haven't confronted him yet? Or her?

Caller: That's right. I just . . . I've always . . . I can't face . . .

Liv: You're hiding.

Caller: [silence]

Liv: I'm guessing you have a history of avoiding confrontation, am I right?

Caller: [silence]

Liv: We can't hear you when you nod, Asha.

Caller: Yes, sorry, I don't like . . . having difficult conversations.

Liv: I think we can all understand that. This kind of issue sometimes comes from a childhood where you never had to face up to things. Was there always someone at home dealing with problems for you? Did you never learn to handle things for yourself as a child?

Caller: [mumbles] Maybe.

Liv: It sounds like you have an avoidant attachment style. It's something we all have to work on, because it can get worse as we get older. It's always easier to run away or hide from problems, but it's impossible to live a full life if you're always conflict-avoidant. If you stick your head in the sand and go la-la-la, then you're saying your own feelings aren't important. How can you have a real, honest relationship with others if you can't be yourself and when you never speak your truth? Never mind the cheating and your friend's betrayal, you'll only ever have half a relationship if you can't learn to stop hiding.

Caller: [sighs] I know you're right.

Liv: Asha, of course I'm right. Time to stop being a wuss, okay?

Caller: [laughs] Yeah, okay.

[watch again?]

*Liv Carpenter says hiding from your
problems means living only half a life*

#LivCarpenter #BBCMorningTea #RelationshipTherapist
#StopBeingAWuss #LivLoveAndLoseTheDysfunction

CHAPTER NINE

I'm really into this new game on my phone. You basically move bits of different coloured liquid around test tubes trying to find some order in the chaos.

I complete another level and smile, enjoying the tiny boost of dopamine.

'Olivia?'

I start a new level. This one looks a lot harder. Lots of test tubes, a rainbow of different colours to sort out.

'Olivia!' My head snaps up at the sound of Edward's sharp tone.

'What?'

'You can't just play games on your phone throughout the whole session. That's not what this is for.'

'Fine,' I sigh loudly, locking my phone and throwing it to one side with as much passive aggression as possible. I look up, and into Edward's dark eyes, channelling every last ounce of defiance.

It has been two weeks since that fucking press release went out to the world.

Following a recent incident in a TGI Friday's restaurant involving tiramisu, *Morning Tea*'s resident agony aunt, Liv Carpenter, has voluntarily taken some time away from the show. For the next two months, she'll be attending therapy sessions to work on her anger issues. She would really like to thank all the viewers for their well wishes and support while she gets the help she needs.

I'm still steaming over that last line in particular. Help I need? The absolute cheek.

But I got no say in it, no veto power over my own life. By the time I saw what had been written, the team at *Morning Tea* had already shared it across their socials. And then my agent, Fabian, posted it to my own Instagram, immediately changing the password and locking me out of my account. The utter bastard. Him and toad-producer Spencer deserve each other.

I'm raging.

Which, admittedly, isn't really helping my case when I try to explain to everyone that I don't have an anger problem.

And here's the worst part of it all: the man sitting across from me in an expensive dark green suit, legs crossed ever patiently, wearing that smug expression I can't stand.

Edward.

Ugh, I never should've mentioned his name to Fabian. He took the idea and ran with it, agreeing the whole thing with

Spencer and arranging it all before I had any more chances to object.

'Come on, Olivia, you know how this is supposed to work.' Edward takes his glasses off and leans forward. I swear Edward doesn't even need those glasses. I'd bet all of Fabian's bitcoin that they're just clear lenses he bought after googling 'How to look like a therapist'.

'This is the initial evaluation part,' he begins in a serious tone. 'I need to assess your situation, start looking at patterns and triggers. But I can't do that without your cooperation. You need to help me.'

'I don't need this,' I reply, injecting ice queen boredom into my tone.

How *dare* he tell me how this is supposed to work.

He leans back into his chair. It squeaks lightly around him and I try to imagine Edward ever farting. I honestly wouldn't be surprised if he'd had his butthole sewn up. No farting for me please, doctor, it's just not part of the Edward brand.

I wonder how he'd react to Sam weeing in front of him. Go mad? No, I don't think he'd lose his cool. He'd just watch with detached disinterest, no doubt pointing out that her lack of inhibitions is a sign of something deeper she should explore through CBT.

'Can we talk for a minute about that night at the restaurant?' he asks, his pen hovering over a pad in his lap. No one else in this building takes notes like that. Edward's not much older than me – mid-thirties – but it's like he's operating out of 1984.

'I'd rather not,' I say, matching his cool tone.

'Please,' he prods, and I sigh. I'm a sucker for someone saying please.

'Look, there really isn't much to say.' I swallow. 'I assume you've seen the video?' I don't wait for him to answer. 'I thought my boyfriend was going to propose. Instead, he dumped me in the middle of a restaurant. I felt like the right recourse in the moment was to ask for some dessert. It's *possible* I asked at a volume that wasn't completely appropriate, but who hasn't accidentally used their outside voice on occasion? I didn't deserve to be publicly shamed over it.'

I pick up my phone again, resuming the game and trying to focus all my rage and feelings of injustice into the silly little colourful test tubes. I can feel Edward's eyes on me, watching, waiting.

'Look,' I say, and I'm trying – I'm *really* trying – to keep the impatience out of my voice as I put the game down again. 'I know it wasn't my greatest moment. *Believe me*, I know it wasn't great.' I feel myself flush with shame yet again, before quickly pushing the feeling away. 'But I do feel like the reaction has been massively outsized.' I shift on the sofa, trying to find a more comfortable spot. 'And it's not like I get dumped every day, is it? So, it's not as if I'm going to be casually heading into random chain restaurants every day of the week, begging for creamy puddings'—I pause, aware this sounds somehow extremely dirty—'so I don't need to figure this thing out. I don't need a solution or an epiphany or some other self-realisation crap. I'm only here having this session as a PR stunt.' I wave a hand. 'It's just so the show can be seen by the viewers to be doing something. And that means that we – you and I, Ed – we can just sit this out. You can get on with your paperwork during these six sessions. And I'll just'—I shrug—'sit here and play Sudoku on my phone.' Edward doesn't need to know about the colourful test tubes. I lean forward, eager for him to understand. 'This can benefit both of us, y'know? I get my old job on *Morning Tea* back, and you get paid by the studio for doing nothing. It's win-win, especially because we don't need to talk.'

It's Edward's turn to move in his seat. 'I'm guessing you haven't been watching *Morning Tea* since all this happened?'

I shake my head, my stomach turning at the thought. 'Christ no. I don't need to see and hear a reminder of everything I'm on the verge of losing.'

For a moment he looks like he wants to say something. He puts his notepad to one side and clears his throat.

'Look, Olivia, we need to talk about *Morning Tea* . . .'

'No,' I say flatly.

'No?'

'No.' I am absolute. 'I don't want to talk about the show. I don't want to think about the show. I don't want to see the show.'

'You're not interested?'

I shake my head. 'Of *course* I'm interested. I'm dying to know what's going on over there, but I can't. Until I get my job back I can't hear about it or talk about it. And I definitely can't watch it. It would be too horrible.'

'But—' Edward shifts and I take a deep breath.

'I'm not talking about *Morning Tea*,' I say again. 'We can talk about that night in the restaurant with Justin, we can even talk about tiramisu if you really want to, but not the show.' When he doesn't say anything, I speak again, spelling out the most important thing. 'And just because I don't want to face one horrible thing, doesn't mean I have issues. I'm a *therapist*, Ed, I don't need therapy.'

He watches me now, heavy-lidded and thoughtful. Eventually he does speak and it's in his usual low, measured tone. 'We're nearly out of time today, Olivia. I think it's going to be really useful going forward if you work on some exercises at home – some therapy homework if you will.'

He's ignored everything I just said.

I sigh as he turns to find something on his desk. I zone out, casually picking up my phone again and opening Instagram. I don't have access to my public account – thanks Fabian, you arse – but I do still have my personal, private profile, where I post under a fake name. The one where I share all the goofy pictures of me and Sam that the *Daily Mail* would have a field day with.

I scroll through mindlessly, barely taking in the array of baby pictures and weddings from people I went to school with.

Then I stop. What did I just see?

I scroll back up a few posts.

No. No fucking way.

It can't be.

It's a post from Justin.

Justin. The man I was sure I was going to marry until three weeks ago. The guy I'm choosing to hold responsible for this whole mess I've recently made of my life. The person behind the ruination of my career and my reputation. The human-shaped reason I'll never be able to eat tiramisu again.

He's there, smiling his bloody head off, next to a woman I've never seen before. And there's the caption. Short and so goddamned sweet.

'Orla. #HardLaunch'.

I gape at it, horror creeping its way through my whole body.

No way. While my career burns down around me and I'm forced to make ash angels in what's left of my life . . . Justin's been busy finding himself a new girlfriend.

And she's *gorgeous*.

This can't be happening.

CHAPTER TEN

'Sam!' I scream as I enter the flat, slamming the front door behind me with such force, it makes the walls shake. 'SAM!'

'What?' She emerges from her room. 'Jesus, *what*? Are there more videos on TikTok of you being terrifying?'

I stare at her, my eyes filling with furious tears.

She gasps. 'No, it's something even worse . . . Is the daddy long-legs back?'

I shake my head. 'He's got a new girlfriend.'

She frowns at me. 'What? What are you talking about? Weren't you just with Edward for your first anger management sesh?' Her eyebrows shoot up. '*Edward?* Do you mean Edward's got a new girlfriend? Nooooooo!'

I shake my head. 'I don't think Edward even has a penis. He would've had it all surgically removed when they sewed up his butthole.'

She frowns again. 'Why would they sew up his—'

'Never mind that.' I shake my head again. 'I'm talking about Justin.' I wave the phone in my hand. 'Justin's got a new girlfriend. He's hard launched her on Instagram – he even used the hashtag. Her name is Orla. It's the coolest fucking name I've ever heard. And it probably means she's Irish as well, doesn't it?'

'Oh god, no way!' Sam moves towards me with sympathy. She knows Irish is my favourite nationality. All the best people are Irish. That's why all Americans pretend to be part Irish.

'He's shared a picture of her! Of the two of them together!' I cry, letting Sam lead me by the hand into the living room. She sits me down and fusses about, covering me with a blanket. 'He never, ever posts on Instagram! He always says it's a vacuous hole designed exclusively for thirsty woman and gym bros. He wouldn't post anything about me or us – not in the whole year and two months that we were together. He said it would go against his principles to post a picture of us. He wouldn't even "like" my post wishing him a happy birthday in March.' Sam takes the phone, examining the picture.

'Bloody hell,' she murmurs. 'It doesn't even look like him!' Sam brings the phone closer to her face, trying to zoom in on the image without touching it.

'Don't heart it,' I shriek, and she looks at me witheringly.

'This is not my first ex-stalking rodeo,' she says, returning her gaze to the picture. 'He looks so … good? What the fuck?'

'I've never seen him dressed so well,' I tell her with disgust.

'He had that shirt when we were together, but it was crumpled up in the back of his wardrobe. I offered to clean and iron it for him and he said what was the point in making the effort.'

'Classic Justin,' Sam says, and I shake my head again.

'But apparently it's not classic Justin,' I point out. 'Because for *Orla* he's willing to wear the nice shirt. He's willing to shave!' I lean over Sam to look again at the photo. 'He's willing to brush his hair! Look at it, Sam! I swear, I think he's actually washed it! He always said shampoo was for women and dogs.' She stares at me and I stare back. 'Was I not worth making all this effort for?' I ask her after a long silence.

'Of course you are!' she says defiantly. 'You're a total babe. He's just an absolute knobhead.'

I swallow hard. 'He looks really happy, doesn't he?' I say, and she doesn't answer. 'Do you think he was seeing her when we were together? This is awfully quick to have moved on. It's only been a few weeks.'

'He's just not capable of being alone,' she says with force. 'He's a small child who needs a mother. He has to jump straight into something else because he'll have run out of clean washing.'

'Why wasn't my mothering good enough then?' I wail, and she looks uncertain.

'Don't do that, Liv! You've had a lucky escape. He's the worst. You're too good for him!'

'I feel like we've been saying that stuff to each other about men our whole lives,' I tell her in a whisper.

'Maybe,' she acknowledges, looking a bit sad.

'I don't know why you still date men at all.' I shake my head. 'You should just stick exclusively to women.'

She grimaces. 'That date I had the other week – did I tell you? – he wore one of those minging vests that are actually *designed* to show off the nipples. You know what I mean? You can always spot the villain on a reality show because he's wearing one, exposing his horrible man nipples.' She shudders. 'There's just never a situation where we should have to see men's nipples. They don't look nice, they don't breastfeed, they contribute nothing to society—'

'Men?'

'Their nipples.'

'Their nipples contribute nothing to society?'

'Right!' She nods, like I am agreeing with her. And I suppose I'm not *not* agreeing with her. She stands up. 'I'll get us some tea.'

She returns from the kitchen after a few minutes with two steaming mugs, handing me one.

'Okay, I've got a plan,' she says with renewed determination. 'We take the eggs from the fridge to his house and we throw them at the windows.'

'Eggs are expensive,' I point out, and she shrugs.

'They're out of date anyway.'

'It's just a best before,' I protest, knowing this means nothing to Sam. We fall on different sides of the best before vs use-by debate.

'They're vile, rotten eggs and we need to throw them at

his house.' She grins. 'Ideally he'd have an open window and we can lob it straight in. Maybe we can also break in and hide some fish inside the curtain poles. They'll stink the whole place out in days.'

'All great ideas.' I nod, knowing they're not. 'But we shouldn't.'

She pouts. 'Why not? He deserves it and you'd feel better afterwards.'

I shake my head. 'I don't think I would.' I wrinkle my nose. 'Okay, maybe I'd feel better for five minutes, then I'd just feel ten times worse.'

As if I could feel worse.

Justin has a *girlfriend*. A new girlfriend. I'm in fake-therapy with anus-less Edward, while my ex is moving on, dating a dreamboat called Orla. It's so unfair.

Sam flops down beside me, deflated by my lack of enthusiasm. 'Are you okay, mate?'

'Not really,' I reply. 'Can I have a cuddle, Sam?' I add in a small voice.

'Ugh, fine, give me a sec.' She turns to offload the mug onto a side table, and I pout.

'You don't want to cuddle me,' I say forlornly.

'You know how I feel about cuddling,' she replies, arms now free and outstretched.

'Well, I don't even *want* a cuddle anymore,' I say, pouting even harder.

She tuts, then pulls me into her arms. 'Tough luck, the cuddle is happening. You don't have to cuddle back but you will be a cuddle recipient. The cuddle is happening to you. Enjoy the cuddle, Jane. I hope it makes you happy. Dear lord, what a sad little life.'

'Shut up, or I'll show you my nipples.'

I let myself be hugged. Sam doesn't volunteer for too much affection, but she is very good at it.

'How was the therapy session anyway?' she enquires after a moment.

'A waste of time,' I say stridently, head up. 'I kept telling Edward I don't need it and it's pointless, but he didn't listen.' I wave at the notebook on the coffee table. 'He's given me *homework* if you can believe it! He says there will be exercises every week for me to do at home.'

She sits up straighter. 'I bloody love therapy homework! I love it when Arshiya gives me stuff to work on at home.'

'You teacher's pet,' I sniff at her.

'What does he want you to do?' she asks curiously.

I shrug. 'I don't know. Something to do with anger journaling. I'm supposed to keep a diary of feelings for the week. Write down what triggers things, warning signs, how I deal with it. All that crap.'

'I'll make a diary of feelings I have for Edward.' She grins leerily. 'It would be weird and pervy.'

'Ugh, stop it.' I roll my eyes, and she laughs.

'No, but really.' She smiles. 'Anger journaling sounds like it'll be really useful and interesting.'

'Whose side are you on?'

'Yours, you idiot.' She leans out of the hug completely.

'But, look, you have to take some time off work, and you have to go to these sessions. You might as well try to get something out of it. Try and embrace this chill time, while also working on your mental health – kill two birds, etc.'

I regard her with horror. 'Why would I kill two birds?'

She looks amused. 'It's an expression.'

'An *expression*?' I gape at her.

'An idiom, a phrase,' she adds. 'Wait, you're telling me you've never heard someone say they're going to kill two birds with one stone?'

I gasp. 'Now I'm murdering these two birds with a *stone*? I'm taking a large pointy rock and I'm bludgeoning two innocent carefree little doves—'

'No one specified that it was doves,' she protests.

'Two little robins then,' I continue, 'a pair of cute, red-breasted robins who – after years of searching – finally found one another and fell in love. And just as they're building their happy little nest together, I come along with my bloodied rock to pummel the life from their limbs. I climb up the tree to find their tiny little sanctuary and one by one I—'

'It's a saying!' she cries.

'Serial killer's saying,' I mutter.

'Yes, fine, the Yorkshire Ripper came up with that and the one about curiosity killing the cat.'

'So you know all about bird murder sayings, but curious cats confuse you?' I query.

'We fill in each other's knowledge gaps.' She smiles mistily. 'And either way, dead birds work for this situation.'

'What's my situation?' I ask innocently. 'I've forgotten.'

'You're in therapy,' she reminds me. 'And I actually think you should take it seriously. It could be really useful.'

I throw myself onto the sofa cushions, feeling resentful. 'Since when do you give me good advice? Your whole thing is leading me astray! You've been getting me in trouble for decades, ever since you persuaded me to hide under the arts and craft table at nursery.' I sigh. 'And I don't need "useful" – I don't need therapy!' I whine, hearing and hating the tone of my voice.

I can't help it though. I know I lost my rag at the restaurant that night with Justin, but it was warranted, wasn't it? I didn't physically hurt any patrons; I wasn't even particularly rude to anyone but Justin. Apart from demanding pudding. Even then, I said thank you. And now I might lose my job and all my prospects because of a momentary loss of control. That is, unless I'm willing to go back to school and re-learn everything I already know; prostrating myself before a therapist work colleague I don't even like. A man who has a Ken doll groin bump. Not that I'm looking.

I don't understand why any of this is happening to me. And I hate how whiny I'm being about it all. Ugh, and my internal voice is even worse.

I sigh. 'Look, sorry, I know I'm being stubborn, it's just . . .' I wave a helpless hand. 'Can we talk about Justin and perfect, beautiful, amazing Orla instead of therapy and bird murder?'

'She's not perfect!' Sam scoffs loyally. 'I'm not saying she's not pretty.' She wrinkles her nose. 'We're not doing the depressing noughties thing where we hate on her because she's a rival, but c'mon, *no one* is perfect, Liv.' She picks up her phone, searching for Justin's post and re-examining the photo. 'You know, actually, she looks like you.'

I laugh. I spent the entire journey home from my session with Edward staring at this image. Orla does not look like me.

Okay, so on a very surface level, she looks a *tiny* bit like me. We both have dark hair and dark eyes. We look like we might be about the same height beside Justin. But everything else about this woman is just . . . better. Her hair is cut into a modern, sassy style. It's cute, cut short around her ears. She has thick, arched eyebrows and a light smattering of freckles across glossy, perfect skin. She has make-up on, sure, but it doesn't look like much; a little mascara here, a dab of clear lip-gloss there. She's smiling sweetly in the picture, but without fear. She doesn't look nervous or anxious – just happy. Everything about this woman is all just . . . perfect. I reach up to my neck to find the one stray thick, coarse hair that regrows there every week. I have a reminder on my phone to tweeze it on a Wednesday morning.

This woman on the screen is who I always wanted to look like. She's who I'd be if I had some of that *Death Becomes Her* potion Isabella Rossellini was peddling. Or maybe a sprinkling of that magical Sundrop flower Mother Gothel was obsessed with in *Tangled*. She's a Disney-ified version of me.

'What do we know about her then?' Sam asks. 'This *Orla*. He's tagged her on the post. Did you look at her profile?'

I shake my head. 'I couldn't get service on the train.' I pause. 'Also, my hands were so wobbly, I was afraid I'd end up tapping the wrong thing and hearting a family Christmas photo of hers from 2016.' I shrug. 'She's probably got her account on private anyway.'

'She does not!' Sam looks up triumphantly from her phone. 'I'm on her profile now.' She looks down again, then makes a face. 'Whoa. 152,067 followers – what the fuck?' She scans the bio. 'Oh wow, she hosts a podcast. She interviews renowned, powerful women.' She glances up again, looking excited. 'Oh my god, she's interviewed Carol Vorderman, I *love* Carol Vorderman!'

'Oh my god!' I scream unhappily. 'I love Carol Vorderman, too! I met her once at a network Christmas party. This is awful!'

I yank the phone from Sam's grasp. Every photo shows Orla smiling that stunning smile, looking happy and content beside an array of fabulous women. The photos are from every angle, too, because apparently Orla doesn't even have a good side. *All* her sides are good sides. What would it be like to go through life *not* trying to trick your way onto the right-hand side whenever a picture is being taken?

'Miserable,' I mutter. Sam takes her phone back, tapping the screen.

'Hmm!' she says after a moment.

'What?'

'I googled her. She's older than us,' she comments. 'She's the same age as Justin – forty-two. She doesn't look it. I wonder what skincare she uses.'

'I knew I should've started using wrinkle cream in my twenties!' I cry, then slump back into the sofa cushions. 'You know what the worst thing is?' I enquire after a moment. 'She hasn't even shared that same photo of Justin. He's hard launched her and she doesn't even care. She's not bothered about sharing him or showing him off. Clearly, *he's* the one who wanted to do it. She obviously doesn't even care if he tells the world about her or not. Imagine being that self-possessed and unbothered about someone you're dating.'

Sam shakes her head. 'I can't. It's not normal.' She taps her phone again, then gasps.

'No way!' she says, and I rush to her side. 'I'm on her Wikipedia page. Her real name isn't Orla, though she *is* Irish . . .'

'Of course she is,' I sigh.

'But her name!' Sam says impatiently. 'Her real name is actually Olivia Rachel Leah Andrews. As in . . . ORLA.'

I look at her with pure horror. 'She's called . . . Olivia?' I swallow, feeling fury rising up my throat. 'She even has *my name*? She's got my boyfriend, my dream face, the coolest job ever and even MY NAME!' The fury bubbles over and Sam raises her eyebrows at me. I nod angrily again and again. 'Of course! Of course she does. Of *course!* Of *fucking* course. I should've known. It's a *joke* – the universe's idea of a joke. It's mocking me. The universe has teamed up with the world's daddy long-legseses to laugh at me. I'm sat here with my life in tatters, while Justin moves on with a new and improved Olivia. OF COURSE HE HAS.'

Sam regards me coolly. 'You know, you should be writing all of this down in your anger journal?' She nods at the notebook, still sitting forlornly on the table. 'You're clearly . . . er, triggered. Make a note of it.'

'I'm not triggered, I'm just truly pissed off.' I snap. 'So yeah, sure, I'll just note down how livid I am that Justin has already moved on with a better version of me. I'm sure Edward will find that really healthy and normal. And actually, you know what?' I wave my hands maniacally. 'I'm not angry actually, forget what I said, Sam. I'm *happy* for Justin. I mean, good for him, y'know? How *wonderful* for him that he's met someone so great and perfect.' I glare down at my phone, still open on his Instagram page. 'GOOD FOR YOU, JUSTIN, YOU UTTER SHITHEAD.'

Sam peers at me with a hint of disapproval. 'You know, if talking about all of this is too close to home with Edward – if that's the issue – you could always change therapists. Arshiya is brilliant! She—'

'She's a grief counsellor,' I interrupt. 'And my friend – that would be weird. It's not that Edward is the problem exactly. It's speaking to a peer at all. I'm a therapist, too! It's so patronising to be told what to do and how to deal with things by someone I consider an equal. Someone who *used* to see me as an equal! I know everything he's going to say to me anyway. I don't have anything to work on.'

'Liv, *everyone* does,' she says gently, reaching for the notebook and handing it over pointedly. 'Stop taking your rage out on me and write it all down.'

I glare at her as she stands up, ready to go. 'I love you,' I tell her sharply.

'Whatever,' she says, smiling. 'Write it down.'

CHAPTER ELEVEN

'You guys!' I stand up on my tiptoes, yelling and waving. 'Over here! This way!'

The music is pumping drum and bass all around me in the darkness, but after I scream again, Jools and Andi finally spot me.

I was going to meet my make-up pals from *Morning Tea* in a normal pub, but it turns out Friday evenings in central London are quite busy – who would've guessed? So, we've ended up in a cheesy club at 6pm, purely because it was the only place with empty seats. Yes, we have to put up with loud music and semi darkness, but at least no one else will be in here, jostling for seats, for at least another six or seven hours.

I hug Jools, then Andi, turning to wave towards Sam, who is sitting patiently in the booth.

'Andi, Jools, this is my flatmate, Sam.'

They greet her enthusiastically, taking their seats as Sam

turns to look directly at me, accusatorily. '*Flatmate*?' She blinks, mock offended. 'Is that all I get after all these years? Not "lifelong best friend since week two of nursery school"?'

I cock my head. 'To be fair, we weren't actually *friends* at nursery. Enemies would better describe it.' I turn back towards Jools and Andi. 'Every day at pick up, the nursery staff would fill my grandma in on the latest saga in our bitter feud.'

'Liv kept trying to hug me,' Sam says solemnly. 'And even at two years old, I knew my boundaries around personal space and physical affection.'

'You could've said no instead of repeatedly biting me,' I reply haughtily. 'I still have teeth marks on my shoulder.'

'Other friends have blood oaths or matching tattoos,' Sam says, shrugging. 'We have incisor branding.'

Andi and Jools look amused as I roll my eyes in their direction. 'So, okay, fine, Andi, Jools, apologies, this is my *best friend of many decades*, Samira.'

Sam reaches out a friendly hand to shake each of theirs. 'Hiya! Yeah, I'm *her* best friend, but she's not mine. She's top five on a good day.'

'You two are hilarious,' Andi says in her strong Texan accent. 'Can I get you a cocktail? I think the sign over there said it's two for twenty pounds at this hour.' She shakes her head. 'Y'know, when literally no one else is in here.'

Jools and I pick out the sweetest, most repulsive looking drink on the menu, while Sam selects a mojito inspired mocktail. She does drink on occasion, but not often. She tried binge-drinking regularly for a bit when we were teenagers, but she didn't like it. She's been on and off sober ever since – and not a bit less fun because of it.

Sam joins Andi at the bar to help her order and carry drinks, as Jools scoots closer.

'Are you doing okay, sweetheart?' she says with concern, peering at me over her sparkly Eltons. 'I've been so worried about you, going through all this rubbish. I can't believe Spencer's got rid of you, what a little arse. Next time his CEO daddy's in the studio, I'm going to tell on him. His dad always fancied me a bit, he'd listen to me.'

'Snitches get stitches, Jools,' I tell her sincerely, and she laughs.

'Never understood that one,' she replies thoughtfully. 'It seems more like you're promising the rat that he'll get medical attention should anything happen to him. Like, if you snitch, I'll make sure you're cared for by a doctor who'll stitch you back up. It's a bit kind, if anything.'

'In that case, snitches get no stitches, Jools,' I tell her. 'Snitches get left to bleed out.'

'That's better,' she says cheerfully, running a hand through her short grey hair. 'Much appreciated.'

'And Spencer hasn't actually got rid of me,' I add quickly. 'I'm just on leave while they make me have stupid bloody therapy.' I pause and smile gratefully at her. 'Thanks for all the messages, by the way. Sorry it took me so long to reply. I've been avoiding my phone a lot since . . . the videos.'

'You poor thing,' she clucks. 'It's just horrible. They're like fleas, the way they keep popping up with catchy new remixes and parody recreations.' She gives me a repentant look. 'I still feel terrible about that morning – the day it went viral – when you came into the studio beauty room. I should've said something right then and there. I'm sorry. I didn't think there was a chance in hell you'd be coming in, and then I just . . . panicked, I suppose. It doesn't happen much at my age anymore; I usually know the right thing to do.'

I cluck at this because I'm trained to protest when a woman over thirty makes any kind of negative comment about her age.

Jools sighs. 'Anyway, I assumed maybe you were trying to put it out of your head and didn't want to talk about it. I never even considered that you hadn't seen the stuff on TikTok! I would've warned you. I hate that you had to hear about it from that mean little man-child, Spencer. How awful.'

'Don't be silly, Jools,' I rush to reassure her. 'You were great – you *are* great. And it's so brilliant to see you.' I smile. 'I've missed you.'

She leans back in the booth, relief on her face, as Sam and Andi re-join us. They're carrying sugary glasses of weird-coloured drinks, and it briefly reminds me of that stupid mindless game I was playing on my phone during my Edward session.

'So, tell us how therapy's going so far,' Jools says conversationally. 'I know you love talking attachment styles on the *Morning Tea* sofa! Have you figured yours out yet?' She laughs nicely and Andi nods encouragingly.

'I don't have any attachment styles,' I say quickly as Sam makes a face.

'Liv kept postponing the start date, so she's only had one session so far. This past Monday. And she isn't giving it a fair shot.'

I shoot her an annoyed look. 'I am! I will. It's only been one hour of it so far. I've got another five to go, so we'll see what happens.'

'Have you been doing your therapy homework?' she asks judgementally, and I nod with outrage.

'I have actually!' I insist. 'I've filled in the stupid anger therapy workbook, like he told me to. But I've also spent this week trying to get my life back on track.' I nod to Jools. 'You remember I was working on a book? *Orange Flags*?' Jools nods as Andi looks intrigued. 'Well, they've paused publication on it, but I figure I might as well get it started.'

'That's a great title!' Andi says enthusiastically. 'What's it about?'

'It's a warning manual for women,' I explain excitedly. 'Everyone knows the red flags – they're easy to spot. The dickheads who like Andrew Tate or talk about body count or engage in the manosphere – yuck. Orange flags are things to watch out for in a relationship that are less obvious. They're things that need to be examined in more context.'

'Like guys who have asshole friends!' Andi shouts, immediately triggered.

'Or no friends?' Sam offers.

I nod. 'I have a chapter on that! Because there might be a

reason for those things that makes that behaviour okay, but they are still an amber warning.'

'What else?' Jools asks, looking enthralled. She's been dating again recently after her divorce a few years ago. She hasn't had much success. It turns out women on social media love her seventies Elton John look, but men? Not so much.

I start listing things from my book outline. 'Someone who texts a lot and makes you feel under pressure to reply right away, someone who never makes the date plan, someone who brags about being a gentleman, or nice guy, or mentions getting into fights. Someone who claims they have crazy exes—'

'I feel like that's a proper red flag!' Sam says hotly.

'It can be.' I nod. 'But there is probably room for one crazy ex, y'know? Because it's one thing if they've had a single troubled relationship, but if they're claiming all their exes are "crazy", there's clearly a common denominator there. Him.'

'Fair,' Andi agrees.

'Someone who doesn't like animals,' I continue. 'Someone who orders for you. Someone who makes off-colour jokes or boasts that they're not PC or woke. Someone who calls their parents mummy or daddy—'

'Isn't that just a very posh thing?' Jools offers, and I shake my head.

'It's indicative of enmeshment,' I say, pulling out the therapy terms. People *love* a therapy term. 'That's when the boundaries get blurred in a relationship. You need to be a distinct person in your own right; a grown-up, who is independent and not tangled up in another person. Especially when it comes to your own parents.' I sniff. 'It could mean co-dependent attachment styles.'

'You definitely made that one up,' Jools mutters, and I avoid her eyes.

'What about gamers?' Sam says, looking excited. 'Grown adults who play computer games all day! I dated a woman a while back who used to be talking into her headset for eight hours at a time. That has to be at least an orange flag.'

'I dated one of them!' Andi crows as we all pile on with our various dating tales and woes.

An hour whizzes by before I notice the time. We have to get going.

'Come on, Franco Manca waits,' I shout over the DJ's loud music, pumping just for us. I herd the noisy group out of the club and down the road, making our way through an increasingly busy Soho.

We turn a corner and my heart thumps violently in my chest as I spot a familiar silhouette in the distance.

It's him.

It's Justin.

He's laughing, his head thrown back, one arm slung casually over the shoulders of a beautiful, glowy woman.

Orla.

It's really them. The hot new couple, Instagram offish. Standing just a few feet away. Almost within touching distance.

Just like I planned.

YOUR ANGER JOURNAL

"Anger is never without a reason, but seldom with a good one"

– Benjamin Franklin

<u>Monday:</u>
What happened?

Justin got a new girlfriend and put it all over Instagram.

How did you feel?

Er, shit? Obviously?

What was the trigger?

Justin getting a new girlfriend, only a few weeks after dumping me. The hateful prick.

<u>Tuesday:</u>
What happened?

The WiFi stopped working. I turned it on and off about five times and it still wouldn't work. I can't get 5G in the flat so I couldn't ~~spend the whole afternoon googling Justin's new girlfriend Orla~~ get any of my work on <u>Orange Flags</u> done.

How did you feel?

Like throwing the router at the wall and screaming until the police came and took me away.

What was the trigger?

I guess ... feeling like I couldn't do anything to control or fix the situation.

<u>Wednesday:</u>
What happened?

I went to M&S and this man wouldn't get out of the way of the sandwich fridge. He stood there with the fridge door wide open for close to six minutes, even though it was so obvious I was waiting to get in there!!

How did you feel?

Furious. And confused about how people can be so selfish and oblivious.

What was the trigger?

Aside from certain men being unbelievably self-involved and unaware? Probably being really hungry for an M&S three bean Mexican wrap with tomato salsa and sweet potato.

<u>Thursday:</u>
What happened?

This is stupid.

How did you feel?

This is stupid.

What was the trigger?

This is stupid.

<u>Friday:</u>
What happened?

Sod off.

How did you feel?

Bugger off.

What was the trigger?

I've had enough.

CHAPTER TWELVE

'You never really wanted to go to Franco Manca!' Sam hisses accusatorily. She's being far too loud, so I yank her into a dark corner of the street, out of the path of drunk tourists. Andi and Jools join us, looking a bit baffled.

'What's going on?' Jools raises an eyebrow.

'Liv tricked us!' Sam declares melodramatically, with more than a hint of excitement in her voice. She jabs a finger in the direction of Justin and Orla, standing just outside a busy restaurant in a queue. They're laughing happily. I take them in as they stand there together, looking so natural and content. I wince at the feeling of needles stabbing my insides.

Justin looks so clean. He was never that clean when we were together.

'That's her ex,' Sam continues. '*And* his new girlfriend.'

'Ooooh!' Andi spins on her heel to take a better look, while Jools gives me a disapproving once over.

'The silly boy from the TikTok video?'

'That's the one,' I confirm shamefully. 'Justin.'

'You should've told me this was the plan!' Sam complains, turning to face me. 'You know I love shit like this. I would've been well up for it!' She pouts. 'I can't believe you tricked us. I would've brought binoculars and some kind of listening device if I'd known.'

'He's better looking than I thought,' Andi says, still craning to see. 'He looked a bit . . . meh on TikTok.'

'He *was* meh,' I say fiercely. 'But his new girlfriend has magically turned him into the perfect boyfriend.'

'How did you know they'd be here?' Sam says, sounding fascinated.

'Orla was talking to a pal on Instagram,' I explain, aware I'm about to sound demented, 'in the comment section of her most recent post. She said her "new fella"'—I pause to let the disgust wash over me—'wanted to take her to this fancy new restaurant tonight, and her friend said it didn't take bookings. They recommended arriving by 7pm and being ready to queue.' I shrug. 'I took a shot.'

'But why?' Jools frowns. 'Do you want to get him back?'

'Please say you don't, Liv,' Sam pleads. 'We've just spent the last hour talking about orange flags, and it's like you can't see the flaming fireball that man represents. He is a *walking* orange flag. His mum still pays his rent, for fuck's sake.'

Andi snorts at this.

'But that's the point, Sam.' I shake my head. 'You're right, he *was* a walking orange flag, but now'—I wave in Justin and Orla's direction—'now he's not! He's suddenly making all this effort and being the ideal man. For her. For *her*! He apparently chose and arranged this date! Look at how nicely he's dressed! Look how *clean* he is! Look at the shoes – he's wearing *socks*, if you can imagine it, Sam! And I bet they're not filthy Christmas ones he found at the bottom of the laundry basket.'

'But he probably made an effort for you, too, didn't he,' Jools interjects, 'at the beginning? They all start off making an effort.'

'Nope. Never like that.' I shake my head. 'This is so different – *he's* so different. This is because of Orla.' I stare at her across the way, laughing now with such ease. 'What does she have that I don't? What magical wand has this woman waved to make that useless boy-child over there suddenly become the dream man? What has she said to change him from a guy who made me pay for my own birthday present because he was broke and who then went out and spent £160 on a hat because he saw Timothée Chalamet wearing one a bit similar?' I look between the three women, waiting for an answer. I sigh. 'So, no, Sam, I don't want Justin back, but I do need to know this woman's secret. Otherwise, how will I ever meet someone decent?'

Sam grimaces and Jools gives me a pitying look. Andi nods with determination. 'I get it. I've been there. So, are we going over there to talk to them or what?'

That had been the plan. I'd wanted us to casually bump into the new couple in the middle of Soho. I wanted to make Justin awkwardly introduce me to this goddess of a new girlfriend, so I could examine her up close. So I could log whatever hypnosis she used. So I could vampire suck the transformational energy from out of her very pores.

But now I'm here and they're *right there* ... and I don't think I can. I can't face them. It would be ridiculous. They'd think I was mad, especially after my recent online notoriety. Justin would probably make a run for it.

We should just go to Franco Manca after all.

'They're leaving!' Sam hisses, as Jools pulls us all further into the shadows. Justin and Orla exit the queue, laughing again at the long wait and loudly agreeing they're not even that hungry.

I shake my head. Justin was *always* goddamned hungry. I think the only reason we ever left the house for actual dates was because he liked to be fed so much and I'm an unbeliev-ably crappy cook.

'It's now or never,' Sam says, her voice all trembly with excitement as they pass by our dark nook. 'Come on! Let's say hello, Liv?'

I take a deep breath, steeling myself, and then——

'I can't,' I whisper, and the group slumps into one another. There is relief pulsing from Jools, while Sam tuts, frustrated.

'How about we just follow them instead?' my best friend suggests happily, as Andi nods with enthusiasm. I had no idea Andi was so into drama. She and Sam should hang out more.

'I feel like this night is going to end in multiple arrests,' Jools murmurs, but the rest of us are already bundling our way down the cobbled streets. We pass over Carnaby Street, cross Kingly Street, and find ourselves emerging, blinking, onto the bright lights of one of the busiest roads in London: Regent Street.

'There they are!' Andi yells way too loudly, pointing at a huge toy store front. Justin and Orla are walking into Hamleys.

'What are they doing?' I hiss. 'Are they already planning on starting a bloody family together?'

'You created this ridiculous situation,' Jools reminds me as we creep inside, eyes peeled for the couple. 'You've made your bed, now you have to lie in it.'

'Well, that makes no sense,' I retort, 'Because a.) I never make my bed because what's the point when you're getting back in it a few hours later, and b.) I'd actually love to lie in it, thank you. Lying in beds is one of my favourite things to do.'

'You win this round.' Sam nods sombrely, as Jools points towards the up escalator. I can just make out Orla and Justin on there. They're holding hands.

How sweet, I think for just a second. Then I remember that he's ruined my life.

We stealthily make our way up to the third floor, where the lovebirds are browsing the Build-A-Bear Workshop area. They meander, chatting freely and laughing.

'Jesus, they're actually getting one,' Jools says with awe, as Orla picks out the bear she wants.

'Of course they are,' I mutter furiously. Justin mocked my childhood soft toy, Eeyore, endlessly. He said it was a hilarious thing to have held onto, and in the end, I hid Eeyore away in a cupboard at the top of my wardrobe. But for Orla? Sure, why not. Let's get her a £40 customised teddy for no reason. I'd've loved a teddy.

We settle into a corner, partly hidden by a large stand of water pistols. Two kids run around us shouting at each other to take cover.

'Ugh,' Sam says with genuine disdain, watching the kids shriek and barrel into things.

'Not a kid person?' Jools asks with amusement, eyebrow raised.

Sam shakes her head. 'I live by the advice given in every laundry detergent advert.' She pauses. '*Keep away from children*.'

As Jools and Andi laugh, sharing war stories of their own offspring, I quietly watch Justin across the store. I take in the familiar way he walks, the familiar way he smiles, the familiar way he brushes his hair back, away from his face. He is still the same Justin, only . . . better. Happier? Happier with Orla. Happier without me.

As I stare, he carefully picks out the bear's outfit, showing Orla options and swapping in a cowboy hat for a beanie. He selects adorable yellow dungarees, and I eye Orla now, as she laughs sweetly at his choices. She laughs a lot, it seems, but not in an over-the-top, fake way. She does it with her whole chest, completely un-self-consciously. She is pure confidence, even here, in this silly, crowded, touristy place meant for children. Justin reaches over and takes her hand, bringing it to his mouth and kissing it.

It hurts. A lot.

How strange, I think, that he was mine so recently. That he could've kissed me like that.

Not that he would've.

I step back, almost into the path of the playing kids, who dodge around me like I'm part of an obstacle course.

I shouldn't have come here. I shouldn't have done this. I feel suddenly very silly indeed.

'We should go,' I whisper to the group, and they nod. We file away from the Build-A-Bear area quietly.

'So, what did we learn?' Sam asks when we're far enough away.

'Only that they're clearly very happy together,' I reply quietly.

'That is a woman who is getting seriously laid,' Andi whistles, as we file down the escalator.

'Thanks for that,' I reply mildly.

'Sorry girl, but come on, have you seen a more obvious sex radiance? She is getting orgaaaaaasms.'

I snort. 'I doubt it. Justin doesn't like giving cunnilingus.'

The three of them stop simultaneously at the bottom of the escalator. Two teenaged girls behind us grunt and angrily move around the horrified group staring at me.

Sam's whole face is twitching. 'What?! Are you fucking serious? You never told me this.'

Jools regards me askance. 'Er, Liv, sweetheart, isn't one of your mottos, "Make sure he shows up *for* you and goes down *on* you"?'

I shrug. 'Well, yeah, I mean, in an ideal world, of course. But you can't have everything in a relationship can you? I'm thirty-one, the entire world is hassling me about when I'll settle down and have a baby. You don't get oral sex once you've had kids anyway, do you?'

'She's not wrong.' Andi nods from the back of the group as Jools looks gloomy. They all regard me silently.

'God, I'm so glad I fancy women too. Keeps my options open.' Sam breathes out.

'When did you say your next therapy session is?' Jools asks nicely after a moment.

'Monday,' I answer a touch defensively, and they all nod.

Sam takes my hand, and we head for the store exit. 'I think it's time you started taking it more seriously, Liv. For real now.'

I sigh, admitting defeat as we exit the busy store, zigzagging around gaggles of yet more screaming children and harried-looking parents.

'Fine,' I say into the din. 'I will. I promise.'

MorningTeaVids

22 weeks ago

RELATIONSHIP EXPERT LIV CARPENTER ON MORNING TEA SCOLDS CALLER FOR COMPARING HERSELF TO HER FRIENDS

Liv: Hiya! Have we got Zaya on the line?

Caller: Yep, I'm here. Thanks for taking my call.

Liv: Of course! I—

Caller: I'm just so sick of this.

Liv: Right and—

Caller: It's my friend, Sarah, she's such a smug cow.

Liv: Can you avoid swearing or mentioning any names? We don't want to identify any—

Caller: Fine, but how do I tell her to stop showing off about everything? It's making me feel rubbish.

Liv: Can you give me an example?

Caller: Like, she just got a new job and kept talking about how great it is and how all the people on her new team are so brilliant. I know it's way more money, too. And that's just the latest in a long line of stuff she's constantly boasting about. Everything seems to go her way, she's the luckiest person I ever met. I couldn't listen to it this time, I've had enough. I told her I wasn't interested and to stop shoving her success in my face.

Liv: [long pause] Well, god, I'm glad you're not *my* friend.

Caller: What?

Liv: We should be able to celebrate our successes with our loved ones. It doesn't sound much like she's throwing it in your face; she's just trying to share her excitement with you. Wouldn't it be sad if your friend didn't want to do that? You're so busy comparing your life to hers, you've forgotten that you're meant to love this person and should be happy for her happiness. Comparing ourselves is a dead-end road full of self-loathing and resentment.

Caller: [silence]

Liv: It's so easy to forget that we're all living here, inside our heads, feeling insecure and doubting ourselves. We assume we're the only ones feeling like that because everyone else is putting their best foot forward – by which I mean, their best photos on Instagram forward. You need to reframe your thoughts, Zaya. Instead of thinking, 'She's got everything I want and is showing off,' try telling yourself, 'She's worked so hard and is finally getting what she deserves.' She's not living her life just to spite you. So, stop comparing yourself to her and be a better friend.

Caller: [long sigh] Okay, I guess . . .

[watch again?]

Liv Carpenter says comparing yourself
never gets you anywhere

#LivCarpenter #BBCMorningTea #RelationshipTherapist #AgonyAunt #AdviceColumn
#LifeCoach #Wisdom #LivCoolAndCollectedCarpenter #KeepCalmandCarpenter
#BeABetterFriend #StopComparingYourself #LivForPresident

CHAPTER THIRTEEN

Weirdly, Edward doesn't look too impressed by my first week of anger journaling. His eyes flick across the page, his brows furrowed, and I feel a small crush of embarrassment. I shouldn't have sworn all over it, that was immature. But, in the moment, that's what I felt like writing. I was being, y'know, honest and authentic! I *wanted* to be childish and petty. I wanted to treat the assignment with the dignity I felt it deserved.

He sighs after a moment. 'I know you weren't exactly thrilled about this when your agent – he's a character, isn't he – first suggested these sessions.' He leans forward, look-ing thoughtful and intense. 'But they told me you'd had a change of heart; that you were keen to go ahead and wanted to try. Your producer, Spencer, and Fabian both said you had requested to meet with me specifically because we already had this collegial relationship. I was worried it would be unprofessional since we work together as colleagues, but they insisted. They promised me you were open to it.'

'I am open!' I snap.

'Clearly you're not!' He sounds exasperated, waving at the stupid journal. He looks up, making eye contact again. 'Look, Olivia, would you rather meet with someone else? I would understand. It's important to find the right therapist and it could be someone outside of the therapy collective. I have a list—'

'No,' I say quickly. The thought of having to start again – and with a stranger! – suddenly seems much worse, even, than being here with him. We sit in silence for another minute.

'You're sure?' he asks, eyes searching mine. 'If you're worried about *Morning Tea* finding out that you've switched therapists, I could—' I shoot him a warning look at the mention of *Morning Tea,* and he brings his hands up in a gesture of surrender. 'Sorry, I know that topic is off limits.' I scowl and he sighs. 'Okay,' he says at last. 'Well, I'm getting the feeling the journal itself needed to be noted down as something that made you angry.' He looks faintly amused.

'Sorry,' I mutter, feeling my cheeks get hot.

'It doesn't matter,' he tells me kindly, putting the journal to one side. The fact that he's being nice about it has made this worse. I thought he'd be supercilious and snotty. I thought I'd get slapped down, instead of this mildly disappointed act.

He cocks his head ever so slightly. 'Why do you think you find it so much easier to give advice than take it?'

I feel myself bristle again. 'That's not true,' I say as neutrally as I can. I fight an urge to pick my phone back up and start playing the coloured test tube game again. 'I'm absolutely fine listening to advice.' I then add quickly, 'When it's warranted or relevant.' He's looking at me, so I continue, aware I'm slightly babbling. 'I listen to Sam's advice! Even though it's mostly terrible. And I listened to Justin's advice when we were together. He had plenty of opinions on my work and my clothes and my life choices . . .' I trail off when I catch something passing across his face. It's gone before I can pin it down and he's back to being inscrutable.

He clears his throat lightly. 'Do you think your relationship with Justin was healthy?'

I blow out my cheeks, feeling like I've been slapped. You can't just go straight to a question like that! Edward should be building trust with me, not intimating that I make shit choices.

I lean in. 'Do *you* think my relationship with Justin was healthy?' For good measure I add, '*Ed?*'

He smiles tightly and I can see he's vaguely annoyed. I know I'm being a bit mean. Maybe even belittling. I'm prodding that professional façade for any exterior cracks.

He puts down his pencil. 'I wasn't in your relationship, *Olivia*'—fair enough, he's doing the same thing back to me—'so I can't answer that.'

We eyeball each other for a full thirty seconds, neither one of us wanting to back down. But he blinks at last, leaning back into his chair.

'Okay, if you don't want to talk about Justin, then let's talk instead about your week. How has it been?' he asks. I sit back in the armchair, wondering how to answer this. I definitely can't tell him the truth. I can't tell him how I wasted the whole week obsessively going through nearly ten years' worth of Instagram pictures of Justin's new girlfriend, Orla. I can't tell him how I set up a fake Facebook account just so I could request to be her friend on the off chance I could see her more embarrassing younger years. How I listened to two full series of her podcast – which by the way is hatefully smart and funny and cool. She really did have Carol Vorderman on there! Vorders!! The living legend herself! I can't tell him about Friday night, where I tricked my friends into following Justin and Orla through London, and then watched them personalise a toy at Build-A-Bear. I can't tell him how I cried all the way home wondering what name they might call the bear and what message they recorded together for it when you press its tummy. And I can't tell him how Sam had to get her daddy long-legs costume out again to cheer me up. Or the detailed plan she came up with to poison Justin's home water supply.

'My week's been ... fine,' I say simply. Edward smiles again and I think how much kinder he looks when he smiles. He is suddenly less like a Ken doll and almost like a real person.

'Would you like some cake?' he says, reaching into a bag and pulling out some Tupperware. 'It's carrot cake. My mum made it.'

'Your mum?' This completely knocks me off my feet. This man has a *family*. He is someone's son. He's probably got a dad, too! I never would've pictured it. 'Does she live nearby?' I ask, realising I don't know the first thing about this man I've been acquainted with most of my adult life and worked across a hallway from for all these years.

'Not too far.' He nods his head. 'She and my dad are in Bath. My brother and I take it in turns to visit regularly. She loves coming to London though. She says she likes to see young people having fun.'

'That's nice,' I say, meaning it. He takes off the lid and offers me a slice. I take some. It's moist and smells amazing. 'Is this your way of bribing me into engaging with the process?' I twinkle, and he laughs.

'Yes, I'm dangling a carrot . . . cake.'

I take a bite. It's *amazing*. 'It's definitely better than dangling just a carrot,' I say thoughtfully. 'What a strange thing for people to say. Carrots aren't that nice, not really. I mean, they're okay, I guess. I don't turn them away when they find their way onto my plate, but I still can't see in the dark. So why would dangling a carrot be so very enticing? Surely it's a better idea to dangle a bag of Maltesers or something.'

'True,' he acknowledges, biting into his own slice of cake. Crumbs go everywhere and he laughs at his own clumsiness. And, so I do, too.

'Please tell your mum thank you very much,' I say through a mouth full of sugar. 'She makes a mean carrot cake.'

'I will.' He smiles widely. 'What about you, do you have family close by?'

I shake my head. 'No. My mum lives in Cumbria, but we don't really talk much these days. I'm not close to my dad either. He left us when I was pretty little – three or four. I think he was in Spain last time I heard from him. He sends the odd happy birthday text.' I laugh, adding, 'Usually in the wrong month though. He mostly seems to think I was born in January.' I pause. 'My grandma was the one who really brought me up. But she and Grandpa died quite a long time ago now. When I was a teenager.'

'I'm sorry,' he says simply; sincerely.

I shrug. 'It's what grandparents do.'

'It's what we all do.' He shrugs. 'When we were training, did you ever read *Love's Executioner and Other Tales of Psychotherapy*, by Irvin D. Yalom?' I shake my head and he continues. 'I'll lend you a copy, it's fascinating. He says that the ever-present awareness of inevitable death is something that drives us from a very young age.'

I nod. 'That's a fun thing to say.'

He ignores this, continuing with something akin to endearing enthusiasm. 'We try to deny our inevitable mortality in different ways. Some people turn to religion to reassure themselves that something like immortality is waiting for us. Others have children to ensure a kind of continuance. Some try to create something else to leave behind – a legacy of some kind, so we won't be forgotten.'

I nod thoughtfully. 'You know, I've been trying to write

that book. I have a publishing deal.' I pause, wondering if I still do. 'But as you can see'—I gesture towards the anger journal at Edward's side—'writing doesn't really come naturally to me.'

He laughs again, then looks more serious. 'Look, Olivia, I do understand how hard it is for you to talk to me about all this. I know it will be strange for you to open up to a colleague. But I believe this could work and might even be genuinely helpful if you let it. We all know it's easier to give advice than to take it. We can be the wisest person in the world when it comes to other people, but it's so much harder to be objective when it comes to our own lives.'

I sigh, swallowing the last mouthful of cake and wondering if I can ask for more. 'But I know everything you're going to say to me.' I try not to let it, but I can hear the defensiveness creeping in. 'You're going to suggest we do some cognitive reframing. You'll tell me it would be a good idea to change my negative thinking. You'll give me some relaxation techniques to do when I feel the *"anger"* coming on.' I roll my eyes. 'You're going to say maybe I could practise mindfulness and try positive self-talk.' My voice is laden with sarcasm. 'Come on, Edward, am I close?' I lean in. 'But the thing is, I don't have a problem controlling my temper. I never lose my rag! What you and Spencer and Fabian – and everyone else! – don't seem to understand is that the tantrum I had in the restaurant that night with Justin was a one-off.' I consider telling him about the cinema trip with Sam and the wanking teenagers. 'If anything, it was the first time I'd

139

properly let the fury out in a long time. Maybe ever! So, I'm not going to do it again, am I? It was a one-off.'

'And how did you feel afterwards?' He's looking at me with those calm, dark eyes.

'What?' I blink at him. 'What does that matter?'

'I happen to agree with you,' he says, frowning. 'I don't think the problem is that you got angry. But I do think there is an issue here.' He repeats himself. 'How did you feel – *physically* – after you threw that, er'—he uses my word—'tantrum? How have you felt in the weeks since?'

His question takes me by surprise. I thought this session would be all breathing practice and meditation. How do I *feel*? Physically?

I think about it. 'Hmm,' I begin slowly, 'Well, since you asked, actually I feel . . . pretty good? I've felt strangely better in myself since that night.' I cock my head, considering it. 'Obviously not emotionally, since my world has been crashing down around me but physically . . . yeah. I'd been having these migraines for months, and I would wake up some days aching all over. I haven't had that since. They're gone. The pain is all . . . gone.' Shock is in my voice. 'I haven't felt this physically good in a while, if I'm being honest.'

He nods and takes a second. 'You've heard of psychogenics?'

'The body keeps the score,' I whisper, and he nods again.

'The link between mental and physical well-being. I see so many women in my office who don't know how to express anger in a healthy, productive way. They've been taught to keep it all in, socialised to be nice and polite. Women are told that they're good with emotions, but anger is the only one they're not permitted to express. Except there's so much to be angry about in this world, especially for women. It's no wonder it manifests in a physical way.'

I fight an urge to roll my eyes. He's obviously one of these 'not all men' types who claims to be an ally and then calls you a fat bitch because you don't want to give him a blowjob, even after he oh-so generously held a door open for you.

Edward meets my eye, his expression serious and earnest. Okay, maybe he's not one of them.

'You mentioned having migraines recently,' he begins. 'Did you know women are three times more likely to get migraines? That they're *four* times as likely to have an auto-immune disease? Not to mention, twice as likely to suffer from depression.' He clears his throat. 'Some experts think it's linked to the fact that women aren't able to release their anger properly. They shove it all deep down inside.'

I take this in. 'I wouldn't exactly call that scene in TGI Friday's a healthy way to deal with my emotions.' I grimace.

'That's fair,' he laughs dryly. 'But at least you were letting them out instead of forcing them back down.'

'But I feel angry all the time,' I protest weakly. 'I get *so* angry.'

'I'm sure you do.' He smiles dryly, then nods at the journal. 'But look at those examples of your anger. On Tuesday you say you wanted to throw the Wi-Fi router across the room and scream, but did you?' I shake my head as he continues, 'I'm not saying that would be the right way to vent

141

your frustration, but you could've called the provider. You could've taken a walk while it fixed itself. You could've had lunch to distract yourself.' He pauses. 'And then on Wednesday, you wrote that you were stuck behind a man at the fridge in an M&S.' He raises an eyebrow. 'Did you actually say anything or did you just stand there silently waiting and feeling furious for the whole six minutes?'

'I stood there silently waiting and feeling furious,' I confirm in a mumble, then throw my hands up. 'But what *could* I say?' I cry, feeling slightly hard done by.

Edward cocks his head. 'Well, you could've said, "Excuse me, can I get my three bean Mexican wrap with tomato salsa and sweet potato?" That might've been one option.'

'Oh,' I say, genuinely stumped by this. It honestly hadn't occurred to me. I stood there that whole time, hopping from foot to foot, silently raging at the entitlement of men and waiting for the guy to realise how inconsiderate he was being. And of course, he didn't, which only compounded my upset. But Edward's right. I could've just said 'excuse me' and got on with my life.

Why didn't I do that? What's wrong with me?

'There was one part here that felt real'—he gestures to the journal—'where you said your broken internet made you feel like you couldn't control the situation . . .'

I wait, staring at a dark hair on his shoulder. It is the only imperfection on his otherwise impeccable suit. With that much hair on his head, it's surprising he doesn't shed more.

He pauses. 'When your boyfriend—'

142

'Ex-boyfriend,' I correct quickly, then feel silly for saying it. It suddenly feels like I'm flirting with him or something.

'Ex-boyfriend.' Edward nods. 'Justin?' I gulp in acknowledgement as he continues, 'When Justin said he didn't want to be with you anymore, what were you really feeling in that moment? Sitting there at the table in that restaurant?'

I sniff, trying to take myself back to that moment. I've tried so hard *not* to think about it. I've tried to pretend it didn't happen at all.

'Angry,' I say simply.

He frowns. 'But you and I both know there would've been more to it,' he prods. 'Anger is a secondary emotion. It's a defensive emotion that's protecting you – shielding you – from some other primary emotion or feeling. I'm not saying anger isn't real or important, of course it is. Anger is natural. It's important. It's a powerful force; a good thing. Unless it's not dealt with properly and it becomes destructive. That's when we lash out or make bad decisions. You can hurt people who don't deserve it.'

'Justin *did* deserve it!' I say fiercely, and he nods.

'Of course he did!' he replies with certainty, and I feel a rush of new affection for him. 'But do you ever find yourself lashing out at people who *don't* deserve it?' I hesitate, not answering. But I think about how the only person I ever really snap at is Sam. Who never *ever* deserves it. I think about swearing all over the anger journal. That could be construed as me lashing out in the wrong direction again. At Edward. When he's actually been pretty nice.

He continues, 'You have to understand the underlying feelings, so you can manage them going forward. So you can develop healthy coping mechanisms and gain clarity.' He pauses. 'So what else were you feeling when Justin ended things?'

I take a deep breath, my head spinning as I think back to that painful evening. 'Humiliated,' I admit after a moment. 'Vulnerable. Rejected. Hurt. Sad.' I start speaking faster. 'Afraid, ashamed, guilty, weak, exposed.' I look down at my hands – they're shaking a little. 'A thousand things, I guess.'

He leans forward. 'Feeling angry is a lot easier than feeling those other emotions, isn't it? Fury can make you feel in control, at least temporarily.' I nod as he continues. 'That's why I thought the anger journal might be good for you. It's a safe space to write things down – to vent. A constructive way to make sense of how you feel. I want it to help you express, not repress. And it could help you release some of that pent-up, self-harming rage.'

'Right,' I say softly. Because it actually – horribly and embarrassingly – makes so much sense.

'But, for the record,' Edward smiles. 'I really don't think the problem was that one-off tantrum in the middle of the restaurant.' He pauses. 'I think the problem is that it was a one-off.'

I let this sink in.

CHAPTER FOURTEEN

As Edward and I finish up the session, there is a knock at the door and Sam bursts in without waiting.

'Aren't you guys done yet?' she calls out as Edward frowns.

'Please wait until I answer the door, Samira. We could've been in the middle of something.'

She raises her eyebrows. 'Oh yeah? What kind of thing would the two of you be in the middle of, eh?'

She giggles but Edward's face is thunder. 'Samira!' he sounds appalled and – I note with offence – a bit disgusted.

Sam tuts. 'All right, Mr Professional!' She holds up her hands in surrender. 'Sorry for barging in, I won't do it again.' She moves breezily past him and into the room. 'But Liv doesn't have any secrets from me anyway.' She shrugs. 'Plus, I thought you guys would be finished by now. You've overrun by fifteen minutes as it is.'

'Have we?' I check my watch. She's right, I hadn't realised.

I suddenly feel a little shy and embarrassed. It's bad enough that Fabian and the studio have forced Edward to give me these sessions against his will, and now I've taken up more of his day than I was entitled to.

Sam moves closer to Edward, openly looking him up and down with a greedy expression. To be fair, he does look even more *Edward* today than usual. The suit is immaculate, the hair glossy, that stupid jaw all square and clean shaven. Sam continues, like I'm not even here. 'How's she doing anyway? Hopefully a bit more cooperative for your second session?'

He gives this a moment, then laughs politely. 'Olivia is doing great,' he says warmly, glancing over at me with appreciative eyes. Something sloshes in my stomach at this. I feel part furious at the condescension and part warm and fuzzy.

'Two down, four to go,' I quip. 'It'll be over before you know it.'

Sam moves around the room, examining Edward's furnishings. She picks up one of his pens, then puts it back down again on the desk. 'Have you talked to her about her terrible dating choices yet?' She rolls her eyes at me, then returns her gaze to Edward. 'Honestly, her ex, Justin, was about as romantic as my last smear test.'

I squeak with horror. 'Oh my god, shut up, Sam!' I whine, sounding like a teenager, embarrassed by a prying parent.

'Sorry!' She grins. 'But you don't listen to me. I thought it might help for an outsider like Edward to remind you to stop settling for less than you're worth when it comes to men.' Edward smiles, tight-lipped and silent. Sam tuts. 'Oh, come on, Edward! Tell her she should know her own worth.'

'I do know it!' I snap. 'I know my worth. I don't need slogans and clichés thrown at me like I'm a twelve-year-old girl making a Pinterest board.'

'Sorry,' Sam says again, a little nicer this time. 'I just want you to find someone better than *Justin.*' She says his name with such disdain, my stomach prickles with defensiveness – with humiliation.

'Er . . .' I inhale deeply, pushing down my upset. 'That's all very well, but let's not forget that I wasn't actually good enough for Justin in the end. You keep telling me I can do better than him, but it turned out I wasn't even up to scratch for a guy who thinks *a lot* is one word. A man who didn't clean his ears because he said his hair protected them from dirt. Someone who hasn't been to the dentist in eleven years because he's petrified of other people's nose hair coming near his face.' I am panting a little now. 'Not only did *he* dump *me*, but he's now going out with someone ten times better than me. So, saying I can do better is actually nonsense. What you're saying doesn't even make sense. How am I supposed to have higher standards when it turns out Justin is too good for me?'

Across the room, I catch Edward frowning. He opens his mouth to say something and then closes it. 'Let's pick this up next week, shall we, Olivia?' He glances at Sam with disapproval. 'In private.'

'Babe—' Sam begins, and there is regret in her voice. She knows she's pushed me too hard.

'I'm fine!' I say brightly, smiling widely to show that I'm not upset or anything. 'Without further ado, let's get out of here, shall we?'

Sam shakes her head. 'No, wait, I have further ado. I have loads more ado. I have ado coming out of my arsehole.'

I sling an arm around her shoulders and move her towards the door.

Edward steps towards us, into our path. 'Before you go, Olivia, I was hoping to get two minutes after our session. I do need to talk to you about something. Something outside of'—he waves around his office—'this. Separate from our therapy.' He pauses and for a moment he looks deeply unsure of himself. I've never really seen him look like that before, it's weird. He continues, 'I've been trying to talk to you for a few weeks now . . .'

I frown. 'Is this about the clinical supervisory sessions I've missed?' I don't wait for an answer, feeling annoyed he'd bring this up now. 'Because look, Ed, I'm not even seeing any clients right now and it seems—'

He looks surprised. 'No, it's not that,' he replies. 'Could we . . .' He gestures towards Sam but she doesn't budge.

'Sorry, Edward,' she says with delight. 'I'm taking Liv for a break-up haircut. I want to get a fringe so I'm making her get one, too.' She nods at me. 'You know, in case it's awful. Then at least we can look terrible together.' She checks her watch. 'We're going to miss our appointment if we don't go now.'

I shrug in Edward's direction as Sam yanks me out the door. As I go, I glance back at him one more time. He looks worried.

What could Edward possibly have to talk to me about?

CHAPTER FIFTEEN

On Wednesday I get two messages in a row that have me curled up in a ball on my sofa.

The first is from Justin. He says – very politely – that he would like to drop off the rest of my stuff this week. The less nice inference rings loudly: he wants to get rid of any last, remaining evidence that we ever had a relationship. To dismiss for good the last year and three months of my life, like it was nothing.

In his message he's very keen to emphasise that I 'don't have to be there' at the flat when he drops off my things, if I'd rather not see him. Or – he adds – he would be 'more than happy' to meet in a neutral place.

It's clear he fears the wrath of Tiramisu Girl and underneath the embarrassment, it gives me a small boost to feel his terror. Until the humiliation rushes back in. I reply quickly, before I can get too sad, telling him I'm around all evening if it suits.

The second text is perhaps even more crushing and alarming. It's from Jamal, one of my colleagues at our therapy collective. He's reminding me of our group dinner this week. And that it's my turn to host.

After we set up the collective four years ago, me, Jamal, Arshiya, Fran and, of course, Edward, all decided to have a semi-regular dinner to celebrate our partnership. It gives us a chance to re-bond every four or five months; to catch up socially as normal human beings, as well as chat about work and the office. We all appreciate it, but we also all need it. It sounds strange, given so much of the job is about talking to other people, but sometimes being a therapist can be a little isolating. We go off into our own individual offices and rarely interact or overlap. Our dinners have become an important tradition that gives us that chance to properly catch up. I've always really loved them.

But so much has changed since our last one. I'm single again. I've been suspended from my TV job. I've lost a dozen clients. And I'm infamous on TikTok in the worst possible way. Even Celeste Barber recreated my tantrum video.

Not to mention how odd it will be to have my own therapist, Edward, over to my flat for a social event. At previous dinners, we've barely interacted. What will we do at this one?

I can't do it. I won't. I'll tell them I'm ill, they'll understand. I'm reaching for my phone when Sam arrives home.

'Ugh!' she yells, slamming the front door, 'I hate my job.' This is our daily routine.

'Come and tell me all about it,' I call out and she appears at the living room door.

'I don't want to,' she pouts. 'It's the same list of frustrating things it always is and I'm sick of the sound of my own complaining.' She flounces past, throwing her bag down onto the sofa, then wheeling around on me. 'Okay, since you insist. My boss is a letchy old Eton boy who thinks I'm his PA, not a highly trained and qualified legal secretary. I hate him.' She slumps down onto the sofa beside me. 'Today he asked me to fetch his dry cleaning. When I told him I was working on some urgent contracts for a client, he told me to give it to one of the "other girlies".' Her eyes bug out as she looks over at me. 'That's what he refers to the female legal secretaries as – *other girlies*. We have plenty of men working with us, but no, he'd never ask any of them to do his chores. They can have the real work and join him on his golfing trips, while us *girlies* do the household shit and fetch office birthday cake.'

'God, what a prick,' I sigh.

'He's a narcissist,' she shouts into the room, then tuts. 'Actually, no, he's not. I've decided that calling people a narcissist is over, it's lost all meaning since everyone started saying it.' Her eyes widen with emphasis. 'It's become such a cliché – everyone is a narcissist: exes, bosses, co-workers, overbearing parents. That curious cat who knocked over a vase. We're all narcissists, it's become a normal state of being.'

I nod. 'I think maybe it's just being a human. We're all narcissists.' I sit up taller. 'And maybe being one can be good! I've met a hell of a lot of women over the years who could do with walking into a room believing they're the star of the show and no one else matters.'

'I try to channel that energy.' She nods. 'I'm the star of my movie. I'm the main character. I'm no one's funny, sassy sidekick.'

'Quite right,' I say. 'I love narcissism for you.'

She grins. 'Although, I've never felt more like a side character today, what with my dick boss stealing everyone's MC vibes. It didn't help that I was hungover after my date last night.' She looks outraged. 'I only had one glass of prosecco, what's happened to me since I turned thirty?'

I grimace. 'Ugh, how embarrassing. Less prosecco, more amateur-secco, am I right?' I am delighted with this joke and Sam snorts gratifyingly. I beam, then add, 'Was the date any good though?'

'It was . . .' Sam searches for the right word. '. . . fine. She was sexy and nice, but we had nothing in common. Literally nothing.' She shrugs. 'The trouble is, all the men I meet want to hit it and quit it—'

'Are we still saying that?' I murmur but she ignores me.

'—and all the women I go out with immediately want to move in with me after one date.'

'Who can blame them?' I ask, feeling pangs of jealousy, though I know she's joking. Only one woman has ever tried to live with Sam apart from me, and to be fair, they'd been dating for six months at that point. I'm happy to report my best friend still ran a mile though, because I don't know what I'd do without her.

Sam smirks, and I add, 'You're not going to move in with anyone else though, right? You're not moving in with her or anyone else? Because you belong to me, remember?'

'God no!' she says, laughing. 'She spent a full hour discussing whether marine collagen is better than bovine collagen.'

'Ooh!' I cry, genuinely interested, 'And what did you decide?'

'What we decided was that we would not be having a second glass of prosecco,' she says solemnly.

'Amateur-secco,' I mutter my joke again, but it doesn't get a laugh this time.

Sam pulls her shoes off beside me, making animal noises with the relief. 'I think the problem with dating is that I don't really want a partner. I'm only dating in the hopes that someone will be mega rich so I can quit working. I want to be a trad wife but without doing literally any of the wife stuff.' She pauses. 'Including the actual wife bit because marriage – ew. Do you know that heterosexual marriage makes women much less happy and men much more so? There's actual research proving men suck the life out of you.'

I think of my client, Wendy, with her husband and two grown-up sons. All annoyed with her for finally finding her own life and not solely serving them. She has predictably 'postponed' her last few sessions with me after seeing my TikTok videos and it makes me sad. I felt like I could've helped her.

I reach across to squeeze Sam's shoulder. 'I hate that your job is so rubbish.'

She sighs. 'It's not really the job itself. Though that is boring as hell most of the time.' She sighs again. 'It's just the director. Team morale is so much better when he's off on another one of his little skiing or golfing jaunts.' She rolls over on the sofa, so we're almost nose to nose. 'It only seems to take one person to poison an entire office, doesn't it? And there *is* always one dick, ruining everyone's work life.'

'Do you think that one person is me at my office?' I whisper. 'At the therapy collective?'

'God no.' She sits up straight. 'Of course not, why would you say that?'

'All this shit.' I wave my hands in the air to indicate the universe and all the horribleness it contains. 'It has to be impacting my workmates, doesn't it? Do you think they've had any clients cancel on them? Ruined by association with Tiramisu Girl?' I gulp. 'It's probably why they want to have dinner on Friday, to tell me I'm out.'

'Dinner?' Sam frowns. 'Don't you have a regular dinner now and again together anyway?'

I nod. 'Yes, but surely they must know I wouldn't want to be involved in this one. Not with everything going on. But, no, they even want me to *host* it!'

'Oh, you should!' Sam's face breaks out in a huge smile. 'I missed the last time you did it here, and I'm so keen to meet Jamal and Fran.'

I regard her with horror. '*You* can't be here! It's not right. It wouldn't be professional for you to have dinner with your therapist, Arshiya! There are ethical guidelines around stuff like that!'

'Professional schmofessional! Ethical schmethical!' she says happily. 'I'm *dying* to see what she's like when she's not being a therapist. I want you to ply her with booze, get her drunk. I would love to see the human side of her.'

'Arshiya doesn't drink and that wouldn't be appropriate,' I try weakly. 'And it wouldn't be right for me to socialise with Edward either, not while we're mid sessions.'

'Don't be boring!' Sam cries. 'It'll be fun. You can put Edward and Arshiya up one end of the table. You and I can be way up at the other end, if it helps. I'll just watch Arshiya from afar and take notes.'

'We really shouldn't,' I try again and Sam pouts.

'Please let me have this,' she says. 'My job is so boring and my boss is so hateful. You are my favourite drama and I need this in my life.'

I laugh. 'Ugh, fine!' I tell her, picking up my phone and replying to Jamal, confirming the time and details. 'But you, missy, are going in the anger journal.'

Sam cocks an eyebrow. 'You're doing it again this week?'

I nod. 'I didn't exactly take it seriously last time, and I promised Edward I'd give it a proper go. So, I am.'

'I'm glad,' Sam says seriously. 'I think it'll be good for you.' She narrows her eyes then smirks. 'Sorry again for interrupting Monday's session.'

I automatically reach up to touch my new fringe. It wasn't too bad when I left the hairdresser's, but it quickly bent over into odd angles that won't be tamed. I tried to wash it this morning and it has dried into a poufy, gigantic thing that looks like a clip-in hair piece. And very much not in a good way.

Sam's new fringe, meanwhile, looks phenomenal.

She smiles nicely. 'How was the session anyway?'

'It was kind of . . .' I trail off, searching for the right word, '. . . it was surprising.' Sam waits for me to continue, so I do. 'It was actually a bit enlightening. Some of the things Edward was saying were really interesting.' I clear my throat. 'I'm not saying I *need* therapy or anything, but some of the stuff he said made a lot of sense.' I pause. 'I have to admit, Edward's pretty smart.'

'Not to mention super sexy,' Sam adds, grinning. 'Do you think he'll wear his three-piece suit to dinner on Friday?'

I try to picture Edward at any of our previous dinners. I can't. It's funny how he's come so much more into focus for me these last few weeks.

My phone vibrates with a message from Justin. Oof. The sight of his name still hits me square in the chest.

'Justin's dropping off the last of my stuff in half an hour,' I tell Sam, and she makes a face.

'Yuck,' she says loyally. 'Let's release some daddy long-legseseses on him when he knocks on the door.'

'You'll have to be in charge of that, I'd need to be locked in the bathroom,' I tell her, and she snorts, getting up and wandering out into the kitchen.

'God, did you see Orla's latest post?' she calls from the

other room. I hear the clinking of glasses and the click of our oven being turned on.

I sit up straight. 'A new post?' I call out, frantically pulling up Instagram on my phone. My heart thumps at what I might've missed in the three hours I've been offline – what was I thinking! Sam always says I should have Google alerts set up for every single person we've ever dated, but I'm not sure that would work for new Instagram posts anyway.

I find Orla's profile and there she is. I scan her gorgeous, clear-eyed face, her wide guileless smile. And there's Justin, beside her. She's done it, she's posted about him.

'I wanted you all to officially meet this guy,' she writes in the caption underneath their happy faces. 'His name is Justin and I am just the *tiniest* bit smitten. But don't tell him that, I'm totally playing it cool.'

Oh, fuck me, that's charming.

That's it then, they've both shared. They're Instagram official – both of them. It's happened. There's no going back.

Sam reappears at the door. She's drinking a pint of water. 'You see it? The smitten thing? Are you okay?'

I nod, unsure if I really am. 'What does she have that I don't, Sam?'

'Nothing,' she says firmly, coming to sit beside me.

'No, I mean it,' I say, insistent. 'There must be something. I know she's prettier than me and cooler than me, but is that all it took?'

Sam shifts uncomfortably. 'Have you considered . . . no, never mind.' I stare at her, waiting, and she sighs. 'Okay, I

just wondered if maybe she just might not . . . maybe she . . .
I don't know, perhaps Orla just . . .' She looks sheepish.
'. . . doesn't let him take the piss?'

I frown at her. 'What?'

She looks a little flustered. 'I don't want to make you feel
bad. I just mean, maybe he's had to meet her at *her* level,
instead of lowering herself to his.'

'You think I *lowered* myself?' I cringe at her words.

'That sounds worse than I meant it to,' she tuts at herself.
'But, look, babe, you did wash the guy's clothes. He's an adult
man and you did everything for him like he was a small boy.
You let him behave however he wanted without a word of
protest, and he treated you like you weren't important. And
maybe that ended up meaning you *weren't* that important to
him.' She swallows. 'I'm saying maybe this woman doesn't
take his shit and so he doesn't give her his shit.'

'Jesus,' I breathe out, unsure how to respond. Unsure how
I even feel. Is this fair? It doesn't *feel* fair. It feels really cruel
and horrible. I think I need a solid minute with my anger
journal.

'Look, I'm sorry—' Sam begins, and the doorbell goes.

'That'll be Justin,' I say robotically.

'Hey, wait, Liv—' she tries again, and I shake my head.

'Let's not,' I say lifting a hand, my head spinning. 'I have
to go take some more of Justin's shit before he leaves forever
for someone better.' I don't look at her as I head for the front
door. 'But thanks for your honesty, I guess.'

CHAPTER SIXTEEN

I can't stop thinking about how great Justin looked the other night.

Not in an I-want-him-back kind of way, but more of a ... huh? Like, what? How is it even possible that he is *this* different? In such a short amount of time? Obviously, I thought he was handsome before, but it was always more in a boyish, *potential* kind of way. Now, he's undeniably gorgeous. His hair has been cut nicely, his face is clean and shaved, his shirt is fresh and ironed. And it's not just how he looks, his whole energy is different. He's standing straighter and taller. He's walking with more purpose and direction. He's got that good narcissist energy Sam and I talked about. Like he really believes in and centres himself. It's bizarre.

'How do you cook a kale salad?' Sam asks me from across the kitchen. We regard each other blankly.

'Does a kale side salad *need* cooking?' I ask, and she shrugs.

'What do you do if not then – bake it?' She blinks at me.

'What's actually in a kale salad, other than kale, obvs?' I squint at the random groceries lined up before me on the counter. 'Like ... other vegetables, right?' Sam stares back even more blankly. 'Ughhh,' I wail, 'Is it too late to just order a takeaway? It's what I've done every other time I've hosted one of these dinners for everyone.'

'It's a fine back-up plan.' Sam nods. 'But I want to impress Arshiya. I don't think Domino's Pizza is impressive.'

'She may not be the right therapist for you if you're this concerned about impressing her,' I comment in professional mode.

'Whatever,' Sam says neutrally, reading the back of a packet of pre-chopped kale. 'Why aren't there instructions on this? Do you just, like, empty it into a saucepan and heat it up?'

'That sounds right.' I nod with certainty, trying to work out how to light the hob.

Sam and I both live on takeaways, pre-packaged sandwiches, and microwave food. It was the one area where I definitely wasn't the perfect girlfriend for Justin.

Maybe that's why he dumped me? Maybe Orla is an incredible chef who doesn't lob everything into the oven at 250 degrees because it surely cooks faster.

Our hand-off the other night was short and decidedly not sweet. He came in, politely asked how I was, handed me a Sainsbury's carrier bag of half empty TRESemmé shampoo bottles, cleared his throat and then ... left. We barely had five minutes together and yet, it has turned my thirst for answers into serious dehydration. Like, hospitalisation with an IV drip may be required.

What has Orla done to him? How is it possible?

Sam and I are still mid salad-cooking when Fran arrives a few minutes later. Since they're here first, we ply them with wine, in the hopes they might not care if any food is incoming or not.

Edward is next through the door and we exchange a slightly awkward – but warm enough – hello wave. I know this is a strange situation, but something in me – deep down, but still! – feels quite happy to see him.

'Hello,' I greet him shyly and he nods back, regarding the flat around him warily.

'You know this contravenes quite a few ethical codes . . .' he says in a low voice, his tone a little wry. 'Me being here, I mean, in your home.'

I shrug. 'I can quote the British Association for Counselling and Psychotherapy, too,' I tell him, then clear my throat. 'Any dual or multiple relationships will be avoided where the risks of harm to the client outweigh any benefit to the client.' He inhales, his nostrils flaring, so I quickly add, 'And, Ed, I thought we'd already agreed that the benefit *does* outweigh the concern about our . . .' I smile playfully. '. . . *dual* relationship.'

Edward frowns. He bites his lip, looking torn, and for a moment I try to see all of this from his perspective. His flighty, difficult and shallow colleague – a woman he's known for a decade and worked with for four years – is suddenly a client. She's suddenly someone he has to turn inside out emotionally on a weekly basis.

And tonight, he's in her home, being offered salt and vinegar crisps from a paper bowl.

'It'll be okay,' I whisper more seriously, touching his wrist lightly. He nods, swallowing, and I dance away before I can think too much more about the oddness.

Arshiya and Jamal arrive last – though not late because therapists can never be late as we see too many people with abandonment issues – and hand over their coats. Sam flutters attentively around Arshiya, chattering excitedly about a rug we recently put down in the hallway like the fake adults we are. Arshiya looks half wary, half amused by the frantic attention.

'Arshiya,' I call out across the room, deciding a host's job also includes rescuing guests, 'Can you come give me a hand with drinks?'

She follows me over to the fridge, looking relieved. 'Are you okay with Sam being here?' I ask in a low voice, and she nods, smiling.

'Yes, it's fine. We talked about it in therapy yesterday. Though'—she side-eyes my keeno flatmate, who is watching us, eagle-eyed across the room—'I'm concerned there is a little transference taking place. I think she sees me as a new parental figure.' She's only half serious, and we laugh.

'But speaking of . . .' she begins, 'I'm actually really surprised Edward came tonight. I thought he'd find it . . .' She nods awkwardly at me. '. . . uncomfortable.'

I stare at the floor, trying not to react. Some small part of me had hoped that maybe all the drama of these last few weeks might've passed my colleagues by. Like, there was surely a tiny possibility that maybe they don't speak to each other, maybe they don't go online, maybe they have literally no one in their life who might've said, 'Hey, did you see your therapist mate Liv had a meltdown over tiramisu and she's now a meme?' But no.

I swallow. 'He did message to ask me if I was okay with him coming. He offered to sit this one out – I think he kind of *wanted* to – but I told him not to be silly. Tonight, we're all just friends and colleagues, sharing a plate of . . .' I glance at the half-hearted attempts at cooking scattered across kitchen work surfaces. '. . . Domino's pizza.'

Arshiya laughs politely. 'To be honest, I was surprised he agreed to be your therapist at all.'

'I think it was very much forced upon him,' I confide, thinking of my agent Fabian and his high pain threshold when it comes to people saying no.

'It must be really weird though,' she continues, and I can see she's watching Edward across the room, chatting to Fran, 'given your . . . dynamic.'

'Our dynamic?' I shake my head. 'You mean us working together in the collective? He's already our supervisor, it's not so different.'

She glances at me, looking amused. 'No, I mean . . .' she trails off, '*you know.*'

I frown. 'No, really, what are you talking about?'

She groans. 'Oh god, you're not going to make me say it, are you?' She pauses. 'I mean . . . y'know, the *tension* between you two.'

Jeez, have I been so obvious about my dislike of Edward? I thought I'd kept a lid on the teasing about his three-piece suit and his stern demeanour – at least around the office. I mostly just complained to Sam about him. And then she would wax lyrical about his sexiness while I rolled my eyes.

'There's no tension,' I protest quickly. 'We get on fine, really.'

Arshiya squints at me. 'I don't mean *that* kind of tension. I mean . . .' She sighs. '. . . the fact that Edward has always had a thing for you.' She sips her drink. 'I mean, *obviously*. You knew that, right? Like, forever. Since, like, day one of our uni course.'

I blink at her, my stomach dropping. What on *earth* is she talking about? Edward has a . . . I shoot a look across the room at him. He's talking to Jamal, they're eating crisps. He . . . *what*? No, there's absolutely no way that can be true. Absolutely no way. She has the wrong end of the stick. It's nonsense.

'I don't think—' I begin and am immediately interrupted by a breathless Sam, unable to contain herself any longer.

'How's it going?' she yells in our faces, her eyes wild. She turns to Arshiya. 'Have I mentioned how nice you look to-night? I *love* your jumpsuit. You look *amazing*.' I suppress a laugh. I've never seen anyone so desperate for their therapist to like them.

Arshiya gives her a sad smile. 'Sam,' she begins carefully, and I can hear the professional twang to her voice. 'We talked about this. If tonight is going to work, we can't do this.' Sam looks crestfallen but nods.

The milling continues until the pizza arrives, and I carry the boxes through and into the kitchen. Sam serves the hot side salad we made, fresh from its boil, consisting entirely of steaming kale and tomatoes. We all take our seats around the table, Sam and I sat at one end, Edward and Arshiya at the other. The noise of everyone talking is loud and comfortable, but I feel all weird and itchy. I can't stop sneaking glances over at the other end of the table. Are Edward and Arshiya talking about me? Is she telling him the same thing she told me? After all, if she's so badly got the wrong end of the stick when it comes to Edward's feelings for me, might she also think I feel the same? What if she told him I was interested in him?

Because ew! Right? Ew? That *is* how I feel about the idea of Edward liking me. Isn't it? I mean, maybe not *ew* exactly. More just . . . confusion. Because he's always been so cool and distant. So professional and po-faced around me. If anything, it seemed clear he didn't like me at all.

Beside me, Fran leans closer. 'So, Liv, are you okay?' They smile. 'I'm not asking as a therapist by the way, none of us are in work mode tonight! I'm asking as your friend – I know it's been a rough time for you.'

I nudge a grateful shoulder into theirs. 'Thanks, mate,' I say quietly, then realise the whole table has quietened, awaiting my response. 'It has been rough – it *is* rough,' I concede, making eye contact with Edward and quickly looking away. 'But . . .' I trail off, not knowing what answer will placate this group of friends–cum–professionals. '. . . you know, I'll be okay.'

Sam leaps in. 'Can you *believe* that dickhead Justin already has a new girlfriend?' Her voice is outraged, but in that delighting-in-it kind of way.

Next to her, Jamal gasps. 'No way!' he says loyally. 'Already?'

I nod wanly and Fran tuts. 'What an arsehole.'

'Do you think he overlapped?' Arshiya frowns at the end of the table.

I make a face. 'That was the first thing I wondered, too, but no, I don't think so. He was a lot of things, but I'm pretty sure he wasn't a cheater.'

'I think I'd rather have a cheater than a man–child who couldn't do his own washing,' Sam mutters, and I shoot her a look.

'He sounds very immature,' Fran pronounces sourly. 'A lot of men like that need to immediately leap into another relationship. He needs to be mothered at all times.'

'That's what I said!' Sam says proudly, looking over at me with eyes that say *I am one of you*.

I put my elbows on the table, narrowly missing a slice of errant pepperoni. 'But that's the thing! This new girlfriend – her name is Orla – she seems like she would never, ever mother someone.' I eye Sam. 'She wouldn't put up with that kind of crap. She seems to have her life – her everything – so sorted. She's this evolved, level-headed queen of the world. She's cool and sexy, with a great career, great skin, great hair . . .'

'Um, it sounds like you've googled her,' Edward comments disapprovingly from the other end of the table. I look away. Yeah, as *if* I've stopped at only googling her.

'I know it's not healthy,' I say, feeling a spike of irritation at his judgemental tone. We're supposed to be here as friends tonight, not judgy therapising judges. 'But I'm just . . . I don't know, *fascinated* by this woman. She's managed to turn Justin into a fully functioning human being in the space of a few weeks, while I got nowhere close in over a year, despite all my best efforts.'

Edward frowns. 'I don't think anyone should be responsible for changing another—'

'We nearly met her!' Sam reveals excitedly, and I fight the urge to throw a cold onion ring at her. She's sharing too much; too thrilled to have everyone's attention. 'We followed Justin and Orla to a Build-A-Bear workshop.'

'Sam!' I say too loudly, and she grimaces.

'Sorry,' she says, regretful but happy. 'It just slipped out.'

I catch this group of highly experienced and qualified psychotherapists exchange looks, and I burn with shame.

'I just want to talk to her; to meet her,' I explain quietly. 'I just want to see what she has that I don't.'

'That's not how it works,' Edward says kindly. 'All you're doing is torturing yourself by obsessing over this woman.

You need to block them both on all platforms and stop looking altogether. You have to focus on your own journey.'

I hold my hands up. 'All right, Edward!' I force a laugh. 'Our next therapy session isn't until Monday. Back off!' I mean this to sound light; to defuse the situation, but instead it heightens everything. The room falls silent.

'Sorry,' I add quickly. 'I do know what you mean, and I agree with everything you're saying, of course I do. I understand it's incredibly unhealthy to be researching this woman and comparing myself to her or to their relationship.' I clear my throat. 'I will do what you've suggested – I'll block them both – and make sure I'm purely focused on myself from here on out.' I pause. 'Okay?'

Everyone around the room nods, but no one is meeting my eyes. They didn't buy what I'm selling. After a minute, the group resumes slowly eating their pizzas. Jamal is so flustered, he even helps himself to some hot kale, offering some up to Fran as well. They both peer at it with horror, their expressions confused and frightened.

Across the table, I meet Sam's eyes. She gives me a tiny smile, and I return it after a moment. We both know I'm talking horseshit and don't mean a word of it. In fact, we already have a new plan to find and speak to Orla, face-to-face. And we're implementing it tomorrow.

MorningTeaVids

39 weeks ago

RELATIONSHIP EXPERT LIV CARPENTER ON MORNING TEA SAYS SET YOUR BOUNDARIES

Liv: —And then I hid in the bathroom until Sam could get him and his thousand stupid legs out the window. I don't understand how he keeps getting in—oh we're back from the break! Er, hi everyone. Apparently we have Petra on the phone this morning. Hi, Petra?

Caller: Hi Liv, I'm such a big fan, I watch you every day. Well, when you're on! They should get you in on Mondays and Tuesdays as well!

Liv: Oh, that's really kind! So, what do you want to talk about today?

Caller: Right, yes, so it's my husband.

Host: Wuh-oh.

Caller: He hasn't done anything wrong, exactly. It's me. I can't stop obsessing over this woman from his past. His first love, from when he was a teenager.

Liv: How old are you?

Caller: I'm in my thirties, and I know how stupid this sounds! They were only together for a year, and it was a lifetime ago but I . . .

Liv: You can't stop yourself.

Caller: Exactly! It got so much worse a few months ago when I found his old teen diary and it was full of her and how he felt back then.

It all sounded so intense and dreamy. I can't stop thinking about it, and how he must still love her and compare the two of us.

Liv: Are they still in touch?

Caller: No! That's why it's extra ridiculous! They haven't spoken since they were kids, but they're friends on Facebook. I look at pictures of her every day, scrolling for ages, imagining them together and wondering whether I measure up.

Liv: Have you tried speaking to your husband about this?

Caller: God no, he'd think I was mad! I *am* mad.

Liv: You're not mad, Petra, this is incredibly common. It's very human of you, and if it makes you mad, then we're probably all a little mad.

Caller: Oh, thank y—

Liv: But it's got to stop.

Caller: Oh.

Liv: You can't keep torturing yourself this way. It isn't right or healthy. Try to reframe how you see this other woman. Think of her as someone you should be grateful for. She helped make your husband the man he is today. I'm sure you have a past, too. How would it make you feel if you knew your partner was feeling this miserable over it?

Caller: Awful.

Liv: The first – and most important – thing you need to do now, is start drawing clear boundaries for yourself. No more looking at pictures of her online.

Caller: But I—

Liv: [sternly] No! I'm serious, Petra. You have to go cold turkey here. Right now. It's a form of addiction and every time you feed it, you start another horrible cycle of shame and self-loathing that will only lead to more feelings of insecurity.

Caller: [deep breath] I know you're right.

Liv: Of course I'm right, I'm always right.

[watch again?]

Liv Carpenter says you can't let obsessions rule your life ... and that she knows everything

#LivCarpenter #BBCMorningTea #RelationshipTherapist #AgonyAunt
#AdviceColumn #LifeCoach #Wisdom #LivCoolAndCollectedCarpenter
#LivKnowsBest #KeepCalmandCarpenter #LivIsAlwaysRight
#Boundaries #ExObsession #QuitColdOrHotTurkey

CHAPTER SEVENTEEN

'Do we have any final questions from the audience, before we wrap things up?' Orla blinks into the bright lights, squinting at her audience from the small stage. She points to a woman at the back, who stands up nervously.

'What do you do to combat writers' block?' she calls out, and Orla smiles encouragingly towards her guest.

Sam and I are watching an in-person live recording of Orla's podcast at a bookshop. She's just finished interviewing a well-known author of racy romance novels, talking with frankness and joy about the revival of smut and women's pleasure in literature. There are about seventy of us here in the audience, and I have to admit it's been a really interesting and fun evening. And we got to hear about rimming, which is always a bonus.

'Everyone handles writers' block differently,' the author replies, leaning towards the captive room. 'Personally, I like to do something really removed from the writing process.

So, I'll, like, watch a horror movie or something! Take my brain as far away as possible from the latest rimming scene I'm trying to get down on the page.'

Everyone laughs, enjoying the feeling of shock.

Orla leans into her microphone. 'Personally, I don't like horror films, I have Facebook showing me "memories" from 2009 every goddamned day. That's more terror than anyone should ever have to endure.'

The audience laughs even harder, and Sam and I join in. God, she's charming.

Orla professionally wraps things up, thanking her guest and everyone who came along. 'We'll be sitting at the table over there at the back,' she tells the audience, 'so come get your book signed by those of us who've written one'—she grins pointedly at the writer—'or just to say hello and get a photo for the 'gram.'

Sam and I exchange a look. Here we go, it's happening. This is our chance to speak to her, one-on-one, face-to-face. At last.

We're really doing this.

We join the queue of adoring fans snaking their way around the bookshop. 'That was so much fun,' Sam whispers as we wait.

'I know,' I moan. 'I was hoping she'd be terrible but she's a fucking delight. No wonder Justin is so happy. And she's even prettier in real life. No fair!'

'Sorry, babe,' she murmurs sympathetically.

My heart pounds in my chest as we near the front of the queue. I feel adrenalised and scared and buzzy and ashamed.

I feel *alive*. But it's not until we're suddenly next in the line, about to stand in front of this woman I've obsessed over for weeks now, that I realise the problem.

What if she recognises me?

Holy shit, of course she will! She would've looked me up just like I looked her up. What the hell was I thinking? I glance in a panic over at Sam, but she's already excitedly edging forward. I wonder if I should make a run for it. I picture Orla watching me with bafflement as I suddenly flee from her presence and out of the building. Would that be weird? And what if someone else recognises me as Tiramisu Girl and films me being mad again?

Either way, it's too late. The queue moves me forward and I turn to face the music, waiting frozen, for Orla to look up from the table and make the connection.

'Hiya!' she says with warmth, her Irish accent coming through clearly, as we make eye contact. 'Thanks for coming along. What's your name?'

I stare at her and Sam clears her throat, throwing out a hand to shake. 'I'm Sam, this is, er . . .' She freezes, too, and I decide to go with the truth. After all, if Orla recognises me and I've used a fake name, that makes me way creepier, right?

'Liv,' I whisper, and her smile gets wider.

'As in Olivia?' She leans closer. 'Don't tell anyone, but that's my real first name.'

'It's a good name.' I swallow, still waiting for the click of recognition. It doesn't come.

'Have you had a nice evening?' She asks cheerfully,

clearly used to starstruck fans incapable of much in the way of speech.

'Yes, thanks,' I say meekly. 'You are . . . funny.'

'That's so kind,' she says warmly, and I really, really hate how nice she is.

'Do you have any, er, relationship advice?' Sam blurts, apparently doing as badly with all this as me.

'Relationship advice?' She looks a bit surprised, then composes herself. 'Well, to be honest, I've only just started dating someone new, so I'm not sure I'm in the best position to be doling out how-tos!' She looks between us. 'Are you two single?' We both nod and she smiles. 'Enjoy it. I was single for years before I met Justin – that's the new lad's name – and I loved it. I think you truly have to be happy on your own before you can be happy with someone else. Don't you reckon?'

We both nod silently. 'Do you, er . . .' Am I really going to ask her this? '. . . do you wash his underwear for him?'

She blinks with shock at my question. 'Do I . . . ?' She looks baffled, then laughs hard. 'No, we don't live together and I don't wash any of his things! He's a forty-two-year-old man, of course I don't!'

I join in, laughing robotically, though I am mortified beyond belief. Sam starts laughing, too. I can hear her laugh is genuine.

'Yeah!' she says through cackles, 'I mean, who'd date a man-child like that?' I jab my elbow into her ribs and her laugh turns into a cough.

Orla smiles. 'I'm not saying there's anything wrong with looking after one another in a relationship, but I do think it needs to feel equal, you know? Like a partnership; a team. I never want to feel like I should be responsible for or in charge of the house just because I'm a woman. I never want to feel like someone's mother'—this hits harder than it should—'and it drives me mad that so many of us have been conditioned to do that.' She makes a face before continuing. 'To look after the men in our lives as if they're small, incapable babies. We run around doing all this emotional and physical labour for them and half of them don't even notice. I never want to be a side character in my own life.'

'Exactly!' Sam says with enthusiasm. 'I was saying that very thing recently. And I've noticed so many of these dick-head men date women so much *younger* than them'—she side-eyes me—'because they know those women are not as likely to stand their ground or assert their boundaries. They don't push back in the same way.'

Orla laughs. 'You're so right! I can't tell you how nice it is to be in my forties now and not give a feck.' She pauses. 'But that's obviously a long way off for you two. Are you in your twenties?'

Holy crap, I'm in love with this woman.

Sam laughs girlishly. 'We're both thirty-one.'

'Your thirties are such good craic.' Orla nods. 'But just you wait. When you hit forty, you will realise how much you've put up with that you didn't have to. So far, my forties have been even better.'

'My friend Jools says being in her fifties is the best,' I tell her, and Orla beams.

'I can't wait.'

The organiser behind her gives us a signal to wrap things up and we nod obediently, starting our exit shuffle.

'Anyway, it was nice to meet you, Orla,' I whisper, and she stands up, reaching over for a hug. She smells incredible. Like a Lush bath bomb shaped like a human. 'Thank you,' I murmur into her shimmery hair.

'It was lovely to meet you both,' she says with genuine warmth as we move away. We catch her greeting the next person in the line with the same sort of enthused kindness.

'She didn't recognise me,' I whisper as we walk away. 'How is that possible? What new girlfriend doesn't look up the last girlfriend? Never mind my recent viral TikTok fame.'

'Maybe Justin lied about you?' Sam sounds just as confused.

'He was the worst liar ever,' I say, and then I turn to my best friend, horror dawning. 'Is it possible, Sam, that Orla just *didn't ask him about his exes?*' I shake my head in astonishment, glancing back over at this magical human-being-shaped bath bomb, chatting animatedly to a group of young women as they pose for a photo. 'Is it possible she just doesn't care? That she's *so* emotionally healthy and mature, that she isn't even threatened or bothered about her boyfriend's previous relationships?'

We stare at each other. 'Oh my god,' we say together, the idea of it blowing our collective minds. 'Oh. My. God.'

YOUR ANGER JOURNAL

"Anger is never without a reason, but seldom with a good one"

– Benjamin Franklin

<u>Wednesday:</u>
What happened?

My ex, Justin, came to drop some stuff off and didn't even seem bothered about the situation or about seeing me.

How did you feel?

Truly crappy. Inadequate. Worthless, pointless, useless. Less.

What was the trigger?

Seeing myself through his eyes and finding myself woefully lacking. Seeing how little our whole relationship – or the last year – meant to him.

<u>Thursday:</u>
What happened?

Sam left her wet washing all over the radiators in the flat and the whole place stank of damp all night. I couldn't sleep and then overslept so I almost missed my train.

How did you feel?

Irate, grossed out, and exhausted.

What was the trigger?

Someone else's thoughtlessness and my inability to point it out calmly. I want to be able to handle something like that rationally without letting it get to me. It's been sitting like a knot in my stomach ever since. And it still smells in the living room.

<u>Friday:</u>
What happened?

I tried to cook some chicken fajitas for a dinner party, and it was a disaster. Does everyone just <u>know</u> you're not meant to warm up kale for a salad?

How did you feel?

Really frustrated and stupid. And outraged at the prices Domino's charges for a bit of bread and cheese. Deal Wizard my arse.

What was the trigger?

Feeling out of my depth, I think. I've always felt like my brain is the one thing I have. I can't be the coolest or prettiest person in the room, but I like to feel like I'm one of the brightest. Feeling like I'm not good at something really bothers me. It also makes me think about my mum and whether she ever tried to teach me to cook. I don't remember.

<u>Saturday:</u>
What happened?

I went to this book podcast, Q&A event thing — just a random thing I saw advertised, totally randomly. But at this random thing, there was a woman — a random woman — who made me angry. Just randomly.

How did you feel?

Jealous. Impressed. Sexually confused.

What was the trigger?

I think it was seeing this woman being so happy with herself. She handles all these complicated things with such ease and it makes me angry. I want to be better at my life. I want to be her.

CHAPTER EIGHTEEN

I feel strangely nervous, arriving at my third therapy session with Edward on Monday.

After Friday's dinner party revelations, I know he will want to talk about Justin – about Orla – and I know I should tell him the truth about it all. The truth about what Sam and I got up to on Saturday. But I am – of course! Obviously! Duh! – very embarrassed. I know how dysfunctional my behaviour has been – is being – and I don't want to feel or hear his judgement about it.

And then there is also the other thing making me nervous.

'Good morning, Olivia,' he greets me cheerfully, as I soft knock and enter. 'Nice to see you, come and sit.'

I do, unable to look at him directly. I think again of what Arshiya said at the dinner party the other day. That thing about the tension between me and Edward. About him having a thing for me since our university days. I need to know what she meant by it. Was it just one of those silly things women are socialised to do: bonding via inane and well-intentioned baseless gossip? Or was it something else? Maybe she'd had a couple of drinks before coming over? Maybe she was tipsy.

Except of course, Arshiya doesn't drink.

Tipsy on life? It doesn't seem likely.

So where did that come from? Why did she say that?

'Friday was fun!' I leap in with the first thing I can think of as I plump cushions beside me on the sofa.

He frowns. 'I was going to keep church and state separate,' he comments dryly. 'But since you brought it up, can we talk about Justin and the new girlfriend?'

Goddammit.

He is looking at me intently. 'Or, more accurately, can we talk about how you feel and how you're *reacting* to Justin and his new girlfriend?'

'I would rather not,' I say honestly, and he nods.

'I understand that, but I do think it's something that's obviously weighing heavily on you. I think it might help you to talk about it.'

He waits, and I sneak a look at his face. He has incredibly even features. He's always so well-groomed and clean shaven. I wonder if he ever lets his stubble grow out.

Is there any chance – any chance *at all* – that what Arshiya said was true?

Let's consider it. Okay, so maybe it's possible Edward *used* to have a thing for me. Maybe back in those busy days when we were all having group sessions, working towards our qualifications. I will allow for the possibility that maybe he'd had a *tiny* crush back then. We were all in our early twenties! Everyone had a thing for everyone! We were bags of soft tissue, frail psyches with the massive horn. So, sure, *maybe* Edward would've gone there. It's possible, isn't it? And maybe from that vague old long-forgotten crush, Arshiya has extrapolated some kind of nonsensical and non-existent ongoing sexual tension.

Because even if – *even if!* – Edward liked me now, you know, like *that*, he wouldn't exactly be confiding in her, would he? Would he? He'd never casually gossip about who he fancied within the group, not with his colleagues. It's sooo not Edward. He keeps his cards close to his vest – or is it chest? – with even small inconsequential stuff, so there is no way he'd let on about an in-house crush.

So there, it's definitely nonsense. It's Arshiya being a shit-stirrer. She's been spending too much time with Sam; she's turning into a drama lover.

Edward is still waiting for me to speak, and I try to focus on the session and what he's asked me.

I can't tell him the truth, I just can't. I'll tell him … something else. I'll tell him about Sam and her wet washing.

I open my mouth to prevaricate, but something stops me. Instead of flatmate irritations, I blurt out the truth. 'We went to see her – me and Sam.' I feel the spike of shame hot on my cheeks, but his expression doesn't change. 'The new girlfriend, I mean. Orla. She hosts a podcast, and we went to watch her record one live in a bookshop.' I swallow. 'And we talked to her afterwards.' I sigh. 'She seems really nice.'

He nods sagely, like he knew this all along. Like this is not a pathetic thing to have said – or indeed, *done*.

'And how did you feel seeing her, speaking to her?' he asks in a neutral, non-judgemental tone.

I shrug. 'I don't know. Weird.'

He leans a micro-fraction closer. 'Close your eyes,' he instructs, and after a moment, I do. 'Take some long, deep breaths, and give yourself a full body scan. How do you feel and *where* do you feel it?'

I frown, then do as I'm told. Deep breath, deep breath, and then I mentally pat myself down. I can feel the beginnings of a migraine, nagging at the back of my brain. I haven't had once since before Justin dumped me. My stomach hurts a little. I try to tune into what emotions are coming up . . .

'Sad,' I say quietly, my eyes still closed because it's easier. 'Rejected, abandoned.' I swallow again. 'I feel angry that Orla is so perfect and nice and successful and pretty. I feel . . . jealous.'

'You feel like she's been chosen over you, somehow,' Edward offers, and my stomach pain gets worse.

'Yes,' I say simply. 'And not just by Justin, but by the world.'

'Is this a familiar feeling? A familiar pain?' he asks softly, and I open my eyes to look at him quizzically. His face is kind and sympathetic.

'I don't know,' I say, but the pain in my stomach has turned to nausea. 'Yes.'

'Can you remember when you've felt this way before? Where does this feeling take you?'

I shake my head, fighting it. The sickness is in my throat now. We fall silent and when he speaks again, his voice is even softer. 'It sounds like you didn't have the best relationship with your parents, when you were growing up,' he says, and I nod carefully as he continues, 'Did you feel abandoned and rejected around them, when you were a child?'

'I don't think they liked me very much,' I tell him quietly. 'I think my mum was angry with me for existing. She would constantly talk about how much she'd sacrificed for me, and the life she'd missed out on because of my existence.' I pause. 'There was a lot of guilt whenever I was living my life or being happy. Actually, the only time she seemed pleased with me was when I was doing well at school – when she could show me off. I had to be perfect or, y'know, I'd ruined her life for nothing.'

'You felt like you were responsible for your mother's emotional state,' Edward comments and I nod in agreement, though it wasn't a question. He continues, 'It felt like it was your job to make your mum happy. To be the good girl.' I shift in my chair. This is starting to feel quite hard already, but I know only too well that he's only just getting started.

'What about your dad?'

I shrug. 'Well, he wasn't really around enough for me to know how he felt about me or about being a parent.' I swallow. 'He left when I was at nursery. I'd see him occasionally, but he was mostly completely absent.' I laugh bitterly. 'Mum never left, but she might as well have done. She was absent emotionally. I would go to my grandparents' house after school every day and most weekends. It was nicer there.'

Edward pauses, breathing slowly. 'Emotionally immature parents can be very damaging.' I nod again at this, not trusting myself to speak. He clears his throat. 'Maybe anger wasn't a safe thing for you to express when you were young? Maybe your emotions were ignored or dealt with badly? Or maybe saying how you felt to people who were supposed to keep you safe didn't get you anywhere?'

'Yes,' I say with a touch of impatience. 'But I've dealt with this. I know my parents were useless, I know I didn't have the best childhood. I've been low contact with both of them for a long time. I used to have a *slightly* anxious attachment style, where I worried about abandonment and sought constant reassurance, but not anymore. I haven't done that in ages! I've dealt with this. I've *totally* dealt with this.'

He takes a moment. 'I'm not sure you can ever fully deal with feeling unloved as a child. That sits with you. It can sit with you physically and emotionally, for a lifetime, and as adults we keep having to address it. Otherwise, it's in danger of controlling us. We're often held hostage to emotions we felt as kids, but we don't have to be.'

I smile playfully. 'All right for you to say, with your perfect mum making perfect cakes for you every week.'

He smiles back. 'Nothing is ever as good as it looks from

the outside. My family has its issues too, believe me. You should see the enmeshment and parentification going on with my brother and our folks.'

I blink at this tiny bit of new insight, seeing Edward in a different light. He's a real person, I realise again. It's starting to sink in. He's more than just a two-dimensional walking suit. I don't know if I like this new development or not.

Maybe a human version of Edward *could* have a little crush.

I gather my things as we finish up, my head spinning. 'Are you doing okay?' Edward asks me nicely, and when I glance up, I can see that he has relaxed into a different mode. Edward the therapist has gone. This is just him, just Edward.

'It's a lot,' I admit quietly. 'The whole thing. There's a lot that I need to think about.'

He nods. 'I know. And I know thinking about it can be difficult. But I really do believe it will help you in the long run – painful as it probably feels right now. You're a good person, Olivia, you really are—' He stops short, like he has remembered himself. He clears his throat, turning away, then turning back. 'And I know you don't want to, but we really should talk about *Morning Tea* at some point soon—'

'Not yet,' I interrupt, shaking my head, grabbing for my coat and yanking arms into sleeves. I feel angry with myself for wearing it. The July sun is too warm for a jacket.

As I leave Edward's office I let his words wash over me. There was so *much* there; so much we talked about.

In general, I try not to think about my parents too often, but the feelings that came up in there, in Edward's office, prove that maybe I haven't processed as much of my pain as I thought. As I need to. But the stomach pain has gone, and the threatening migraine has receded a little.

I reach for my phone. I'm going to do it. I'm going to belatedly take Edward's advice. It's too late to *not* stalk poor Orla to her place of work, but I can now start as I mean to go on. I open Instagram and look up both profiles. One by one, I block first Justin's profile, then Orla's.

Then I hold my finger down on the social media app, and I hit the magic words. 'Remove App'. And then I let out the biggest sigh of relief.

CHAPTER NINETEEN

It's possible the joy I feel – the big, heavy weight that's been lifted from my shoulders – is just temporary, but I've felt like a new Liv over the last few days.

Sure, I'm still opening my phone every few minutes to automatically check Instagram, but I have – at least for now – somehow managed to not re-download it. And sure, I know deleting social media is not the whole answer to all of this. It's not even a big part of it. I also know that once I'm back on *Morning Tea*, I'll have to start interacting with viewers online again, but with everything that's happened in the last few weeks, there's no point denying it's become a bad place for me. A big fat cesspool of messy toxicity, encased inside an asbestos shed painted with extra layers of lead paint.

And I think it might be a big step that I'm taking *any* steps at all. Maybe a tiny bit of me is realising that these therapy sessions can't hurt. They might even help.

Before me, Jools picks up her large sandwich, taking a bite and speaking through crumbs. '. . . and it's obvious nobody even likes him much and the viewers keep messaging the show to say they really miss you.' Jools grins at me from across the table and I tune back into what she's saying. 'And Spencer is the same little creep as always, so you're not missing much of anything. Same old, same old.'

'Thank you,' I tell her, smiling gratefully. I pick up my own sandwich, inhaling the smell of tuna mayo.

'But never mind the show, how have *you* been?' she asks pointedly, peering over sparkly frames. I cock my head.

'Better, I reckon,' I tell her, thinking again about my last meeting with Edward.

She eyes me sternly. 'No more following your ex and his new girlfriend around, I hope?'

My face gets hot, thinking about that face-to-face confrontation with Orla. And how much the impulse is still there to find out more. Yes, I've been resisting the horrible little urge, but only just.

Jools clocks my reaction and sighs. 'It's really bad for you, sweetheart. It's like an addiction. You get that momentary boost, then the massive low afterwards. Then you have to go even further to get the same high. You have to stop, completely.'

'I know, I know!' I tell her, staring at the perfect flicks of her eyeliner behind her glasses. How much practice does that take? 'And I'm working on it, I swear. I've unfollowed them both on social media.' I say this *so* proudly, but she looks a little nonplussed.

'That's a good start, I suppose,' she says, nodding. Then she makes a face. 'God, I hate being so boring. Why am I always the voice of reason?! I used to be such a shit-stirrer when I was young.' She giggles, running a hand through her short hair. 'But there's something about being in your fifties . . . you realise how painful it all was and how sad it is that so many young people – young women – put themselves through hell. For no reason!' I try not to focus on the joy of being called young, and instead zero in on her words. She sighs. 'I don't want to see you go through more pain than you have to.'

'You're not boring, Jools, you're *so* wise!' I tell her fiercely. She's right, I need to hear this. She can be the super ego to my id. The angel to my devil. The Dec to my Ant. The Jools to my Sam.

She nods, taking the compliment. 'I think every woman should have an older female friend.' She takes a sip of her water. 'I've got one – Sophia, she's in her seventies and she's effin' brilliant. Having her around has always done me the world of good. It's important, I think, to understand where women have come from and what they've been through. To have the perspective of a different generation.'

'What *is* your perspective?' I ask curiously. 'Were things so different for you?'

'Oh god, the nineties and noughties were a rough time to be young and working.' She breathes deeply. 'You had all that ladette culture telling you the only way to be a feminist was to be like a bloke – a top bloke! You had to be front of the queue to laugh at the sexist jokes, or go, "Hoi, look at the bazookas on her!" That felt like your only option as a woman,' she snorts, 'oh, apart from being a glamour model, Jordan wannabe, who got your tits out for the ladz and shagged everyone in the name of female empowerment.' She widens her eyes at me. 'You wouldn't believe what went on in my first TV job. Everyone getting drunk together at lunchtimes, then heading back to the office to carry on drinking. Managers snogging the female interns, bosses getting blowjobs in the dressing rooms, celebrity sex tapes casually emailed around the whole team for everyone to laugh at, female staff members objectified or treated like a joke.' She shakes her head. 'Of course, they would select the odd, token woman to be promoted every now and again, but then she'd have her contributions completely ignored or stolen, while the men mocked her efforts behind her back. Meanwhile, she'd have to make sure she told everyone she was different from other girls and sabotage any other women, in the vain hope men might accept her.'

I deep breathe through this, the horror of it all travelling through my veins. It wasn't even that long ago. At last I speak. 'Did you *really* call them bazookas?'

She grins, looking amused. 'Yep. Norks, knockers, rack, jugs, melons. You got double points as a woman if you were willing to be disrespectful about your own body.' She pauses. 'Although, at least we didn't have iPhones or social media when we were kids. I thank god for that every day. Never mind the rest of it, I hate how synchronised we all are now – our watches are all linked to the bloody internet, you know? No one ever knew the real, proper time back then and everyone's mum kept the kitchen clock at least five minutes fast. It was nice.'

I laugh. 'I'm not sure I could cope with that. I'm terrified of being late for anything as it is.'

She raises an eyebrow. 'Oh, mate, you *couldn't* be late back then. If you were late, everyone would've already left Woolworths without you. You'd have missed all the shop-lifting from the sweets' section.'

I laugh again, then take a moment. 'Do you think things have gotten any better?' I ask seriously. 'For women, I mean.'

She considers this. 'No, not really.' She shakes her head. 'I think things are *different* for women now, but it seems sadly clear the likes of Trump and Tate have proved things aren't any *better* for us.'

I nod sadly.

She goes on, 'I think there was a small window of time, maybe ten years ago, where feminism got too powerful for them.' She rests her head on a hand. 'The patriarchy, I mean. We seemed like we were turning a corner. We had proper feminist icons to look up to. We were acknowledging the complicated feelings of being a woman. We had #MeToo, and we were starting to have proper conversations about intersectional feminism.' She winces. 'To me, it seems pretty obvious that men were feeling embattled and inconvenienced by having to examine something in detail that they'd never thought much about. Even the decent ones didn't like the movement because it made them feel embarrassed and ashamed to be reminded of their power and their privilege. Not to mention that the status quo had suited them all for so long. And we all know what powerful people do when they want to destroy a movement: they divide us up.' She shakes her head. 'And they've done it *so* successfully since. They convinced a whole subsection of feminists that their real enemy were trans women – how miserable is that? That the real problem lay with who was using what loo, and whether a tiny minority of already vulnerable and suffering women had the *correct* genitalia. And then the patriarchy told young women that every older woman was an awful TERF. Then young women were labelled *basic* or *pick me girls*. Then conservatives convinced another subsection of silly young women to reject feminism altogether and embrace being trad wives. As if they ever could've even made that choice without feminism! Oh, and then they piled in on women who speak up, calling them "Karens".' She shakes her head again. 'That whole Karen thing started out as a genuinely important conversation about white women misusing their power – it was a race issue – and now *Karen* has turned into something we label *any* woman who dares to be angry or moan.' She shrugs. 'I have a couple of friends who are actually called Karen, and you should *see* them bending over backwards to be nice and polite, and repress themselves, out of fear that their online namesake will hold true.' She sighs. 'It's been very effective. We've been divided and conquered. Feminism feels quite broken and confused again lately.'

I listen to her impassioned speech with awe. She's right, of course she is. The patriarchy has somehow persuaded women to turn on each other. It's the same thing the rich and powerful right wing has done – told us to blame each other instead of them. Blame immigrants, blame the even poorer than you, blame the vaccines, blame the conspiracy theorists, blame *anyone* except the billionaires.

'Women have to be in this together,' she continues with steel in her voice. 'We can talk to men about allyship and being feminists all we like, but they're not invested. They can't be trusted to really care, it's not in their interest.' She pauses. 'Did you know, after Sarah Everard was murdered in 2021, thousands – thousands! – of men signed up for a feminist course called "Exploring Masculinities and Allyship Training for Men". About ninety per cent then just . . . didn't show up. They signed up, took the credit, felt good about themselves, then went right back to pretending there is no problem. They just don't *feel it* in the same way. They see us in their workplaces, they see us in government and speaking out in public – and they think we're just being greedy asking for more. They don't know how insidious and sinister sexism still is.'

I nod vigorously, feeling furious and self-righteous and powerful. I reach over to take her hand, and I squeeze it.

No wonder we're all so fucking angry.

MorningTeaVids

41 weeks ago

RELATIONSHIP EXPERT LIV CARPENTER
ON MORNING TEA SAYS DIFFERENCES
CAN MAKE OR BREAK A FRIENDSHIP

Liv: Hi everyone! What a busy morning it's been so far on the show. And there's more to come. Next up on the line we have the lovely Julie – are you there, Julie?

Caller: Yes, hello, Julie here.

Liv: You've been having some issues with a close friend, am I right?

Caller: [sad sigh] Yes, and I don't know what to do, or if there's any coming back from this. We've known each other since we were at school, and always had the same kind of liberal views on stuff. But she's changed so much in the last few years and started saying some really horrible things. It really upsets me and I don't understand how she can see things that way. I've mostly backed down when she's brought it up, because she's so *aggressive* about her views, and it all feels so personal. But I'm so mad at her and I don't know how to get over that. Or if I even should!

Liv: The political climate right now – and in recent years – has become so fraught. It *does* feel personal a lot of the time. It's okay to feel angry.

Caller: But I keep seeing stuff online about how we should all be

able to disagree on our politics and keep a civil discourse – all of
that – without losing friends, but this shit is serious—

Liv: Whoops, sorry to the viewers about the swearing.

Caller: Oh right, yeah, sorry. [another deep sigh] I'm just so frustrated,
Liv. This was someone I used to be able to talk to about *anything*.
Now all she does is shout me down. And when I do get a word in
edgeways and try to tell her my point of view – the one she used to
share! – I just get called *woke* and sneered at for having empathy. I
don't know what to do, please help me.

Liv: I know a lot of agony aunts would tell you to put aside your
differences, agree to disagree, and avoid talking about the
upsetting stuff. Some might even tell you to do the opposite and
get into it with your friend – have the conversation and work it out!
Listen and try to understand! Run towards the fire! But I'm not going
to say that.

Caller: You're not?

Liv: No! Because I think she's behaving horribly! Let's put aside the
actual differences and how sad it is that she's gone down this
brainwashed road, because the issue at the heart of this is that
she's being pretty vile to you about it all! Is *she* in agonies right now,
worrying about upsetting you with her opinions? It really doesn't
sound like it! It sounds like she keeps insisting on shoving them in
your face and down your throat. And then insulting you because
you don't share them. How is that a good friend?

Caller: That's so true . . .

Liv: And honestly, do you actually have anything in common anymore,
beyond a shared history?

Caller: God, I guess . . . no, not really!

Liv: Sometimes we as humans think we have to cling onto things from our past, because they've been important to us once or there are good memories attached. But do you think the pain of losing her now will be worse than enduring this kind of twisted relationship for the rest of your life?

Caller: [long pause] No.

Liv: Even something that was once everything to us can become toxic and unhealthy. It's time to re-evaluate this friendship for what it really is now, Julie, not what it used to be. Because she sounds like all she is to you now is a shit friend who isn't worth you wasting your good energy on.

Host: Liv! Sorry about the swearing again, viewers.

Liv: My bad.

Caller: Okay, but Liv's right. She *is* a shit friend.

[watch again?]

Liv Carpenter says ditch the toxic friend . . .

#LivCarpenter #FriendshipAdvice #PoliticalDivides #BBCMorningTea
#RelationshipTherapist #AgonyAunt #AdviceColumn #LifeCoach
#Wisdom #LivCoolAndCollectedCarpenter #KeepCalmandCarpenter
#PlatonicBreakUps #PoliticalDifferences #ToxicRelationships #ShitFriends

CHAPTER TWENTY

Edward seems distracted when I arrive for our fourth session, and I try not to take it personally. I'm starting to really think these sessions could help me, and I want to talk about the stuff Jools said at lunch this weekend. I want to talk more about my family, too, and the correlation I've noticed with my anger.

We take a seat, and he smiles brightly. 'So, Olivia, we've talked a bit about why anger is important and where it comes from, so I think, in this session, we should focus on productive ways to express instead of repress.' He pauses. 'I think we both agree having an outright explosion in a TGI Friday's isn't the healthiest way to go about it.'

'Effective though,' I mutter, and he smiles like he can't help it. I wonder if he always used to smile this much or if it's just me having an effect on him. I've never thought of Edward as someone who smiles much, but he should. It's a really great smile. Almost as good as the hair.

'We want to practise assertiveness without aggression,' he adds and I make another joke.

'No screaming for tiramisu then?'

His mouth twitches. 'Ideally not. But feel free to have as much tiramisu in your fridge at home as you can cope with.'

'Sam's had the fridge packed with the stuff ever since I went viral.' I roll my eyes. 'She thinks it's the funniest joke ever. I tried to get my revenge by buying loads of Scotch eggs – she hates eggs – but there wasn't room in the fridge. We don't even have space for a tub of Country Life.'

He covers his mouth. 'That is funny.'

Huh. Edward finds me funny, how strange. Or maybe it's Sam he finds funny? But either way, he definitely has a sense of humour under all that calm, double breasted suit-ness.

'Tiramisu aside, I've had clients who found it cathartic to practise martial arts,' he continues, 'or – if that's too much – others try punching pillows. We could try scream therapy, or swearing at the bathroom mirror. I had one client who would go to a lake and throw pebbles as hard as she could, all the while calling the water a cunt over and over.'

It is so shocking, and so hot hearing him say that bad word. That word only women are allowed to use because we're the ones who've had it used against us for so long.

'Does any of that appeal?' he asks, and I think about how nice it would feel to scream that word over and over. And over and over and over. How freeing it would feel to make a fist and fully punch something soft and yielding.

'It's worth trying a few things, to see what might work

for—' His words are cut off by the ringing of a phone. It's not mine, I made sure I silenced it outside, before I even entered the building. In front of me, Edward pales.

'I'm sorry,' he murmurs, moving from his seat.

'It's fine!' I say, though I secretly feel very smug. It's a cardinal sin for therapists to have their devices go off during a session. What if I'd been in the midst of a big weep about my abandoning parents? I guess Edward isn't such a perfect therapist after all—

Oh. He looks super freaked out, actually. He's staring at his phone, half frozen with apparent indecision.

'Are you okay?' I ask. 'Answer it if you need to. Edward, really.'

'I'm sorry,' he mumbles the apology this time. 'My mum hasn't been very well lately, and I told my brother to only ring if something serious happened. It's him calling now.'

'Answer it,' I say earnestly, and after another second, he does.

'Jake?' he says into the receiver, and I shift anxiously in my seat. I should probably leave. I'm sure he doesn't want me listening into his calls, especially when it comes to something so personal like this. I don't move. From the phone I can just about make out a male voice on the line, speaking with urgency. Edward nods at something, then speaks in a soft tone. 'I'll come right away.'

He doesn't say goodbye, he just hangs up and looks at me with confusion. 'I'm so sorry, Olivia, I have to cut our session short, I—'

'Don't apologise.' I stand up fast, grabbing for my bag. 'I

get it.' Should I pry? I can't tell what the right thing to do is. 'Are you okay?'

He shakes his head, looking at the room around him like he doesn't know where he is. 'They've called an ambulance, they think Mum might've had a stroke. They're waiting on paramedics right now.'

I inhale a deep, shocked breath. 'That's horrendous. I'm so sorry, Edward . . .' I am lost. I want to help but don't know what to do. 'Can I help? Do anything?' He looks at me again, his expression foggy, but shakes his head after a moment. He stares down at his phone, checking something. His fingers are shaking; it's clear he's really scared. My heart hurts for him.

'Damn,' he murmurs, and I step forward minutely.

'What?'

'The trains . . .' He looks flustered. 'They're delayed, there's a shortage of crew and . . .'

I step forward again. 'I know, I drove in today because of the problems, so I have my car outside. Can I drive you?'

He stares at me a little blankly and then shakes his head. 'No, Olivia, I can't ask you to do that. It's nearly three hours, I can't . . . I don't—'

I take another step; a bigger one this time. 'I'm driving you.' I make sure it's not a question this time and he slowly nods.

'Okay, would you mind? Thank you.'

I pick up his coat for him, helping him into it. He suddenly seems so intensely vulnerable. I feel the reversal of roles keenly and fight an urge to gather him up into me for a hug.

We don't say much as I lead him to my car, and we take

off across London in the direction of the M4. Beside me in the passenger seat, I can feel he's trying to gather himself.

'I'm sure she's fine,' he says at last, finding his voice.

I nod.

'My brother Jake is a catastrophiser,' he continues. 'She's probably just got a headache or something.'

I nod again, pulling up at some traffic lights and mentally urging them to hurry up and change.

'They say the first few hours are key, don't they?' he says, and I nod yet again. 'Maybe I'll just text to see if the ambulance has turned up yet.' He adds this casually, but I catch his hands still trembling a little in his lap as he types. 'You hear all these horror stories about the NHS these days, don't you? About people waiting hours for an ambulance to show up and then they don't come at all.'

'It'll come,' I say with confidence, feeling none of it.

We sit in silence for a few minutes as he stares down at his phone, waiting for a reply.

Beside me, Edward suddenly breathes out. 'Jake says a first responder is on his way. They'll be there in the next hour to assess her.'

'That's good,' I say decisively. 'They'll know what to do.' I check the satnav, still two hours to go. *Please let his mum be okay.* I reach over to pat his arm. 'We'll be there before you know it,' I tell him, sneaking a glance across at my therapist. 'Just hold on, Edward. Hold on for a bit longer.'

He nods, as we make eye contact. And then he reaches for his seatbelt, cutting across his chest, and he literally holds on.

CHAPTER TWENTY-ONE

'*GRAND DESIGNS*,' Edward suddenly yells out beside me. It makes me jump. He's been so silent for the past hour, I almost thought he'd dozed off. But it's clear he's just been staring out of the window at the passing motorway.

'What?' I am baffled. 'Did you just yell out *Grand Designs*?'

He turns to face me. 'Sorry.' He half smiles, looking a bit embarrassed. 'It's a family tradition. We used to play yellow car — you know, where you shout yellow car if you see a yellow car—'

'I'm familiar,' I tell him dryly.

He grins sheepishly again. 'Well, that developed over time into a different car game. Every time you see some dilapidated old building that Kevin McCloud would get excited over, you shout *Grand Designs*.' He strains against the seatbelt, gesturing back the way we've just come. 'Off the motorway there, we went past a rundown, neglected old water tower that Kevin would love to see converted into a house for a couple and their three kids.'

This is the best thing I've ever heard. But almost better is how red Edward's gone while explaining it.

'I love a weird family tradition,' I tell him, and try to think of any I can share. But of course, I have none. Beyond not ever getting any real affection or praise. Is that a cute story to tell, or no?

'I'm sorry I missed such a beautiful building, so full of potential.' I shake my head. 'I'm sure Kevin would insist the new owners not change a single thing. They can't move the huge storage tanks or the neighbouring reservoir, otherwise they might endanger the *integrity* or the *poetry* of the building.' I'm using my best Kevin McCloud voice.

'Yah,' Edward pulls out his own decent impression of the presenter. 'And of course, the pressurised potable water system is vital for the *symmetry* and *winsomeness* of this domicile, even though it will add another million to the build cost. There is a *delicacy* and a *refinement* to this water tower that must be conserved and safeguarded.'

'Just look at the *exquisite dusty, ash dingy greyness*!' I signal to come off at the next junction and then point an exaggerated finger in the air. 'Regard the *pulchritude* of this unliveable new home!'

'Pulchritude!' Edwards sounds amused. 'Good word. It sounds like you're a *Grand Designs* fan, too?'

'Actually . . .' I stop at a busy roundabout, waiting my turn to pull out. 'I've had to stop watching it. There are too many episodes now where they don't finish the project, and that makes me itchy. I cannot have that kind of resentment in my life.'

'That's fair.' Edward smiles. He checks his phone for the millionth time and this time I catch a change in his expression. 'Oh, thank god,' he murmurs. 'The first responder is there.' He checks his watch. We're still about an hour away. 'She thinks Mum could've had a TIA, but my brother says she's fairly confident it's just a severe migraine.' I watch the road, listening intently. 'There's no drooping, she's able to raise her arms, and her speech isn't slurred. They've checked Mum's blood pressure and respiratory rate, and they're both raised, but the responder isn't unduly alarmed.' Beside me, I feel Edward sagging into the seat with relief.

Thank god.

He snorts. 'It's pretty obvious my brother's not that worried anymore – he's saying he wants us to grab some food en route, since there's nothing in the house.'

'That's such good news!' I say sincerely, glancing across at Edward. His whole energy has relaxed. 'There's a service station a couple of miles away, shall I turn off there?'

He nods and my stomach rumbles quietly. It's after lunch. Is it inconsiderate to suggest we get something to eat for ourselves, too? What's the etiquette when you're driving your therapist to his mum's house during a medical emergency but you're starving because you only had three spoonfuls of tiramisu for breakfast since it's the only food in the house? It's probably too niche an example for William Hanson to have covered in his etiquette books, but I'm guessing it would be frowned upon. You're not really allowed an appetite in times of crisis.

We pull off the motorway, park up, and head into an overpriced food shop. My legs ache from the drive as Edward loads items into a basket. I watch on longingly. I'm *desperate* to grab something to eat but hold myself back. I have self-control, I have willpower!

Maybe I could just shoplift a sandwich and mainline it in the loo?

As we retrace our steps down the high-ceilinged concourse, Edward pauses beside me. 'Would it be weird to suggest we grab some fast food?' Edward gives me a sheepish sideways look, gesturing towards a KFC a few feet to our left. 'I'm starving!'

Oh, thank GOD.

'I guess we could do that, if you think we have time?' I offer without much enthusiasm, and he nods, as my stomach growls again; loudly this time.

We sit down with our junk food and I tuck into my wrap joyfully, too ravenous to regret my messy choice. Across from me, Edward chews on a hot wing and we sit in companionable silence. He looks deep in thought, and I wonder if I should ask him again about his mum. It's funny that I've told him so much about my parents and I know so little about his. Beyond the fact that his mum makes a lovely carrot cake. Maybe he'd like to talk about her? Maybe he really *doesn't* want to talk about her. Maybe I should be googling reassuring things to say about a stroke – something about how clever the brain is at building new pathways. Except Google is never reassuring about these kinds of things.

He clears his throat. 'I have a question for you, Olivia.' He pauses. 'Do you say *could care less* or *couldn't care less*?' He looks at me piercingly and then picks up his napkin, wiping his fingers. 'They're now pretty widely recognised as meaning the same thing, like flammable or inflammable.' He sighs. 'And I don't want to be a snob about the way language changes, but I can't get over how wrong it sounds to say you *could* care less. Surely it undermines the point you're making if you *could* care less?'

I blink. 'That's what you were thinking about?' He nods, waiting patiently, so I answer. 'I don't think I say either, to be honest. Mostly because I do care, I always care. I couldn't care *more* if anything. It's a curse.'

He smiles softly. 'I can see that.'

'And I don't think I've ever said inflammable or flammable either,' I add. 'But that's a lot of stupidity for one English language.'

'English is endlessly stupid,' he agrees. 'Don't get me started on bi-monthly meaning both twice a week *and* every other month.'

'Oh, oh! And how is it possible that cough, rough, though, and through don't rhyme?' I ask, full of exasperation.

He laughs. 'You know, any time someone says *a lot*, I now think about what you told me and Samira after our second session. You remember when she burst in to take you for a haircut? You told us Justin would insist *a lot* was one word?'

I look down. The last person I want to think about right now is Justin, never mind the embarrassing stuff he did when we were together, that I told myself was cute.

He leans closer. 'Sorry,' he tells me quietly. 'I didn't mean to upset you. It struck a chord because I have a friend who thinks thank you is one word.'

My eyes widen. 'You haven't upset me!' I tell him quickly, my voice a little high. 'You didn't.' I sigh. 'Justin was ... he was an interesting guy in hindsight, what can I say?' I narrow my eyes at Edward. 'But wait, how does your friend think *thank you* is one word? What about when they say *you* in any other context? Is that a whole different word to *thankyou*? And do they not ever say thanks?'

He puts a hand to his chin, considering this. 'He definitely does say *thanks*, so I assume he thinks *thanks* is an abbreviation of *thankyou*. Which it is, of course. And – if I had to guess – I'd say he thinks *thankyou* and *you* are whole different words. Much like, I don't know, *making* and *king* are unconnected, separate things. Or friend and end. Or Justin and tin.' It's his turn to look down at the table. 'Sorry, I keep mentioning your ex.'

I shake my head. 'It's fine, but I'm not sure Justin and tin *are* separate things. The man clearly has a tin head, so maybe Justin is *just tin* through and through.' Edward laughs at this nicely, so I keep going, feeling a little punch-drunk on making this man laugh. 'I also think a lot – or *alot* – about how he didn't clean his ears because he said his hair protected them from dirt. It's my Roman Empire. But mostly I feel uneasy about it because I don't really know how to clean my ears myself.' Meeting Edward's eyes, I add quickly, 'I mean, of course I *do* wash them. Every day. But I've never been totally clear on what everyone else does and I think about it every time I get in the shower—' I move smoothly past this, though I can feel myself getting pink. It might be my imagination, but I think Edward's blushing, too. 'What I mean is, do you just use water to clean your ears? Or do they count as part of your head, therefore you clean them with shampoo when you're washing your hair?' He narrows his eyes at this, and I immediately need to know what shampoo he uses. His hair is *so nice*. I continue with my lengthy, multi-part question. 'In which case, what if you don't wash your hair every day? Samira does hers every four or five days, so does she only shampoo her ears every four or five days?' I pause for breath. 'Or maybe your ears count as your body, so you use bodywash? Or maybe they're part of your face, in which case you would rinse them with facewash?' I shake my head. 'But my facewash is expensive, it feels a bit offensive to waste it on my ears.' I sigh. 'It's such a conundrum.'

Edward has been listening carefully, taking all of this in. He nods now. 'Maybe Justin had the right idea in leaving them well enough alone.'

I giggle, and he joins in. 'But seriously!' I cry, genuinely keen for an answer. 'What do you do with your ears? Please tell me you wash them!'

'I do,' he confirms, smiling. Then he shrugs. 'Actually, I

just use my shampoo all over, for everything. Hair, face, legs, arms, ears, all . . . of it.'

The sentence hangs in the air as I'm bombarded with mental images I shouldn't be having. I'm realising now that talking about showering with this man was not a good idea.

But I still really want to ask him about his shampoo.

I segue quickly. 'I might give up washing my hair altogether. This damnable new fringe is a nightmare.'

'I like it,' he says, and I feel a tug in my stomach.

'You do?' He nods and I lean closer. 'Are you just saying that to be nice?'

Edward shakes his head. 'No, I don't tend to do that. My friends say I'm a little too honest at times, and with a face like mine, I shouldn't be.'

I squint one eye at him. 'A face like yours?'

He nods. 'Apparently I have a – what's the phrase? – a resting bitch face. Fran and Jamal have both independently of one another told me I have, and not just a standard resting bitch face, but a Karen-y resting bitch face.' He sits back in his plastic chair. 'My return rate for new clients is actually not too great because a lot of people think I hate them before we've even exchanged a word.'

'I thought you hated me!' I say without thinking. I'm quite taken aback to hear Edward express anything other than total confidence in his professional status.

He cocks his head, looking at me penetratingly. 'I know.' He pauses, then adds, 'I don't. I never have. I like you a lot.' He pauses again. 'And, for the record, I really respect you and your work. I've always been in awe of your job. You've demystified counselling and made mental health support more accessible. I think you're pretty incredible.'

I look down at the limp cold fries before me, feeling bad. 'Sorry.'

'It's fine,' he says neutrally. 'Let's blame my stern face.'

I laugh shortly, but the guilt weighs on me. It wasn't his face's fault. He has a nice face. It was me, all me. I made assumptions about Edward. Unfair ones.

'We should get back on the road.' I clear my throat, and he nods reluctantly.

'It's probably a good idea.' He collects our leftovers, loading up the tray, and turns to find a bin. 'I'll text my brother and tell him we're half an hour away.' I follow him back to the car, an unsettled feeling creeping through my stomach. I tell myself it's junk food-related.

CHAPTER TWENTY-TWO

We arrive at Edward's parents' house at last and I hover anxiously in the hallway, feeling like an interloper. An interloper with very stiff legs after that journey.

The first responder is still here, and she speaks in low tones with Edward, who nods, an air of authority about him.

'I'm still confident it's not serious,' she's saying. 'But of course, we're going to thoroughly check your mum over. The ambulance should be here any minute now, and we'll get her to the hospital. They'll give her a CT to double check, but I really think she's okay.' She pats him on the arm kindly as she moves away. I feel Edward sag beside me.

'I'll get out of the way,' I whisper to him, and he turns to me.

'No, please don't go,' he says with urgency, then looks horrified by his vulnerability lapse. 'I mean, god, of *course* you can go, Olivia. Sorry, yes. This must be very weird for you. Thank you enormously for bringing me here. Go and live your life.' He smiles. 'Go scream swear words at a lake.' He pauses. 'Pillow optional.'

I shake my head. 'No, no, I'll stay, it's fine! I *want* to stay. I can be here as long as you need me. I have no plans at all.' I pause, then add seriously, 'Apart from the lake screaming, of course.'

He gives me a side smile as his brother approaches. 'Oh Ed, thanks so much for coming,' he says, throwing himself into Edward's arms. 'Did you hear what she said? They're going to give Mum a CT.'

'I also heard her say it's probably just a bad migraine,' Edward reminds him, and the brother nods.

'Yeah, I'm sorry, I freaked out. Mum had this awful headache, and her vision went funny. Then she was really sick. She seemed so out of it . . . I don't know, I just panicked.'

'Don't worry,' Edward says, and his professional mask is back on. 'You did the right thing. We'll get her checked; it's going to be fine.' He turns to me. 'Jake, this is my friend and colleague, Liv, she drove me over. I've asked her to stay for a bit.'

Friend? Liv? I thought I'd get *client,* or *Olivia* for sure.

'Hi, Jake,' I say shyly.

He grins at me, then frowns. 'You two are both doctors, right? Do either of you know what a TMI is?'

'Too much information,' I supply, and Edward shifts beside me.

'The first responder said TIA,' he corrects. 'It's a mini stroke.' Seeing Jake's expression, he adds hastily, 'But it's usually not serious and resolves very quickly.'

'And we're not doctors,' I add nicely.

'You're not?' Jake looks surprised.

'Technically, I have a PhD,' Edward says awkwardly, and I regard him with shock.

'You do?' I've known him all this time and didn't know that. I guess that's what he was doing after uni, when we all went our separate ways. I started working as a therapist right away while he went off and became a doctor. Surely that's just showing off.

I glance away.

What else don't I know about him?

Edward reddens slightly. 'I'm just going to check on Dad,' he whispers, and I acknowledge this with a nod as he crosses the room.

'Sorry for intruding,' I tell the brother, who shakes his head.

'No, god, not at all!' He says this so kindly. 'Don't tell Ed, but I've sent out a bat-call to literally, like, everyone I know. Half a dozen people are about to turn up here with cupcakes so I can weep on their various shoulders. They're going to be so mad when I tell them it's just a migraine.' He grimaces. 'Two of them are abandoning their workday for me. They're probably going to get fired.' He shrugs then grins. 'It's possible I may have overreacted. Did Ed tell you I overreact to stuff?'

'No,' I reply innocently, because he said it in the car at least three times.

He pauses, then looks at me a little closer. 'I'm really glad Ed has someone he can lean on. He's usually sooo determined to carry everything alone. Older brother baggage.'

'That tracks,' I smile, enjoying this character insight.

'How did he describe you?' Jake squints at me playfully. 'Friend and colleague, eh? Is there anything more to it?'

'Oh god, no!' I bluster, feeling my cheeks get hot. 'We're just ... yeah, we're what Edward said.' I stare down at my feet, feeling Jake's eyes on me. But what else can I say? I can't exactly tell Edward's brother that we're not even really friends, he's just my colleague-cum-therapist and I've only in recent weeks started seeing him as a real human being at all. That – until this car journey and a surprisingly bonding bit of KFC – I thought his brother pretty much hated me.

'Weird energy in your response,' Jake says leaning closer to sniff the air around me. 'So, either you actually really loathe my brother, or this is ... hmm, I'm going to take a shot here.' He squints at me. 'Your ... *fourth* date?' He waves his hands as I feel sweat break out on my neck and between my shoulder blades. 'Like, you're giving that early doors intimacy vibe where you don't exactly know where you stand, but you're totally feeling it. Y'know? Am I close?' He smirks mischievously.

'You've got it all wrong.' I swallow hard.

It's not the fourth date, it's the fourth *therapy session*.

I continue quickly, 'We work together, we ...' What?

216

Because the weird truth is that the intensity of going through therapy can sometimes be like the intensity of those early days of dating someone. Getting to know one another, sharing yourself in bigger increments, revealing your most private parts. But not like *that*. I smile brightly. 'We're just mates, like he said. Really.'

'Okay, gurl,' he trills, twirling away and back over to his family. Edward re-joins me a moment later.

'Right, sorry about that.' He frowns as he takes in my expression. 'What? Was Jake talking your ear off? He can be a lot.'

'No, he's great,' I say, meaning it, despite his brother's interrogation. 'I actually really like him *a lot*. Most of the time anyway.'

He narrows his eyes at me, then lets it go. 'So.' He takes a deep breath. 'They've just declassified my mum's level of urgency – so no ambulance. Which is good because I'm betting it would've been a hell of a wait, despite what the first responder said. Dad's going to take her in, but he doesn't want me and Jake to go with them. Apparently we get in the way and make too much noise.' He smiles indulgently. 'I don't think my parents have ever seen me and Jake as any older than about fifteen.'

'Even when you're in your thirties and have a secret doctorate.' I raise my eyebrows at him, and he looks amused.

'It wasn't a secret. We didn't speak much after uni and you just never asked.'

'I hate it when people say that,' I protest. 'Why would I

go round asking people in my life if they happen to have a PhD? What else should I specifically have enquired about? Do you keep a pet zebra in your back garden? Can you speak Welsh? Did you once break the Guinness World Record for doughnut eating?'

'Actually, I *can* speak a bit of Welsh.' He shrugs as I gape at him. 'I used to anyway. We lived there for a while when I was little. *Un dau tri pedwar pump chwech saith wyth naw deg.*'

'What did you just call me?' I narrow my eyes.

'I just counted to ten.' He grins, and I shake my head in wonder. He leans in, his face suddenly quite close to mine. 'Did you know the word for red is *coch*? I found that very funny as a small child.'

'Cock?' I say too loudly, and catch Jake looking over from across the room. He's wearing an excited, knowing look on his face.

'Yes.' Edward smiles. 'But cock, spelled with an aitch.'

There is something about the way he says cock and I can suddenly feel the blood pumping around my body. My coat feels tight and I'm noticing how warm it is in here. There is a tense silence as we look at each other. The room spins a little. After a second, Edward looks away.

'Anyway . . .' He clears his throat. 'We're going to wait here until Mum and Dad get back, to make sure everything's okay.' He takes a tiny step back, pausing, and then speaking in a lower voice. 'Are you all right, Liv, being here around my family?' His eyes search mine anxiously. 'You know, just when we've started getting into conversations about your parents? I don't want this to be painful for you.'

I blink up at him as he furrows his brow, looking at me penetratingly. This is such an intensely thoughtful thing to say – to ask – and I am momentarily rendered speechless. I swallow. 'That's so . . . nice,' I answer at last, trying to recall a single other man in my life – my *whole* life – who would've thought to check in with me like this. I don't think Justin even knew my parents weren't around. He was probably just relieved I wasn't making him meet them. I nod, looking away. 'I'm totally fine, don't worry about me. I just want your mum to be okay.'

Edward steps closer again. 'Look, Liv, of course I won't ask you to stay – I'm sure you have a life to be getting back to – but if you fancied it, Jake and I are going to get the board games out and play drinking games like it's Christmas. If our parents think we're still teenagers, we might as well embrace it. You want in?'

I consider the other options waiting for me at home: an empty flat that needs a deep clean. Sam's wet washing probably still hanging up everywhere because it takes her a week to fold it up. A laptop awaiting words for a book that more than likely isn't wanted anymore. An internet full of horrible comments.

Though at least the viral sensation of Tiramisu Girl seems to finally be dimming. I might even be able to access the real world again one day.

Oh, and Justin and Orla all over Instagram, showing off

their great love to the world. My fingers itch at my side thinking about it. I'm desperate to look. I need a distraction.

'I could be persuaded to stay for a quick game of Uno,' I grin.

CHAPTER TWENTY-THREE

'Dad's texted!' Jake shouts across the din, waving his phone in the air. 'She's fine, it's all good! She's had the once over. They reckon it was definitely just a migraine, and I was being a big old worrywart as usual!'

The room cheers, clinking glasses, as Jake re-takes his seat at the table with his friends. They're playing a very competitive game of Monopoly and the shouting over Park Lane immediately resumes. A few feet away, playing our own board game at the coffee table, Edward and I make relieved eye contact.

'Phew,' he says quietly, and I smile widely, rolling the dice and moving my piece four squares. Yay, a ladder!

'Phew indeed,' I echo back, handing over the dice for his turn, 'And now we know your mum is okay, Edward, I get to ask you something I've been dying to know since before we even got here.'

His face changes in that moment and something charged zigzags between us. The rest of the room gets dark and far away. I feel my heart thump in my chest as I scramble to quickly continue. 'Er, about you and your brother, I mean.' I swallow. 'You guys are ... Edward and Jacob?' Our surroundings rush back in as he blinks at my question, then frowns.

'Yes?'

I wrinkle my nose. 'C'mon, you know what I'm saying, don't you? You're Edward and Jacob! Do you also have a sister called Bella, perchance?'

'What?' He looks baffled, and I burst out laughing. 'No, we don't have a sister.'

'You cannot tell me no one has ever pointed this out to you?' I snort. 'The characters from *Twilight*? Edward and Jacob?'

He shakes his head. 'Never heard of it. Is it a TV show? Were they brothers?'

'No,' I say with frustration. 'They were rivals or whatever ... come on, there's no way you don't know this! It was a book, then more books, then a huge movie series! Edward was the vampire and Jacob was the werewolf ...'

'Werewolf?' Edward sounds astonished. 'Was it a horror film?'

'No!' I wave my diet coke around, exasperated. 'It was romance, really, I guess. Romantasy. It kickstarted an entire generation of sexy monster fiction!'

'So, the werewolf and the vampire were in love?' Edward

rolls the dice and moves his piece up another ladder. He's winning.

'No!' I cry, grabbing the dice for my turn and shaking them furiously. 'Absolutely not. Bella Swan was the one in love – with both of them. And they were in love with her. She had to choose.'

'So, there was a vampire, a werewolf, and a swan?' His face is the picture of confusion.

'Oh my god, stop talking,' I laugh as I slide down another snake. 'Basically, they were two iconic love rivals, and the entire world – apart from you it would seem – was either Team Edward or Team Jacob.'

He's looking at me again. 'Which were you? Team Edward or Team Jacob?' He asks this in a soft voice.

'I was Team Charlie Swan actually,' I giggle again, trying to dispel the weird tension between us. 'Bella's dad.'

'That seems wrong on a few different levels,' Edward comments wryly, raising one eyebrow.

'What can I say?' I shrug. 'I have daddy issues.'

He yawns, reaching up into a deep stretch and I watch his body move. The vest of his three-piece suit rides up, along with the shirt. For just one solitary second, there is a centimetre of skin, and I feel a hotness creep into my bones.

He reaches for the dice again. 'I need a six,' he tells me, keeping eye contact, and it's exactly what he rolls.

'You get all the luck,' I complain, and he looks at me. There's something unreadable on his face.

'I win again,' he says simply, then reaches to take off his

suit jacket. He rolls up his shirt sleeves and I take in his forearms, trying to remember if I've ever seen them before. Surely I have? So why does this feel so shocking? He scratches the wrist around his watch, and I try not to notice what muscular arms he has. He's been hiding some serious buffness under all those suits. Is this a new development, or has Edward always been so . . . defined?

'How do you get your hair so shiny and thick?' I ask suddenly, trying to redirect my thought process. He raises an eyebrow.

'Is it shiny?' he asks, reaching up a hand to gingerly touch it.

'It's ridiculous,' I tell him. 'Don't pretend you don't know you have great hair. What shampoo do you use? I've wanted to ask you all day.' I pause, adding, 'For as long as I've known you, actually.'

He frowns. 'I don't know. It's one I've had forever; I don't take any notice.' He squints, trying to remember. 'Weirdly, I think it's a brand made by that American writer, Gore Vidal?'

I shake my head at how little this makes sense. 'What?'

He nods. 'I know that probably can't be right.' He shrugs. 'My dad uses the same stuff. Mum got a job lot of bottles years ago. She loves a bit of a Del Boy deal. It probably fell off the back of a lorry – as she would say.'

'Show me,' I say, standing up. He looks amused, but obeys, leading me through the hallway to a large bathroom at the back of the house. I automatically close the door behind me and then turn to face him, realising how odd it is that I did

that. How odd this whole thing is. I'm standing in a bathroom with my therapist. With my therapist's perfect hair and
his powerful arms. At his parents' house. And I just shut us in.

'There.' He points at the bath, and I pick up a bottle. I turn
to stare at him with amusement.

'Gore Vidal?' I ask, and show him the bottle.

'Oh.' He looks a little embarrassed. 'Well, I've never heard
of Vidal Sassoon. I assume there's no relation to Gore.'

'I wouldn't have thought so,' I smirk, then shake my
head in bafflement. 'So, the secret of your magical hair is a
discontinued shampoo from the noughties that you thought
was made by a dead American writer.' I'm *really* trying not
to laugh. 'You are a complicated fellow, aren't you, Edward?'

'You think my hair is magical?' he asks quietly, and something pulses between us. Something new. I no longer want
to laugh as he stares down at me, his eyes black. I suddenly
remember our earlier conversation about showering, and feel
my cheeks blister with heat.

'I think I better go,' I say, feeling very warm and strange.
'It's a long way back and Sam will be wondering where I've
got to.' I open the bathroom door, walking quickly back
through the hallway to find my coat in a jumble by the front
door. The noise from the living room would imply Jake
won the auction for Park Lane and is now building hotels to
destroy everyone.

Edward catches up with me as I go to step outside.

'You're really leaving?' he says, his hand on my arm. 'Don't
you want to wait and see my parents, Esme and Carlisle?'

I gasp as his eyes twinkle. 'You *do* know what *Twilight* is! You're such an arse! I can't believe I fell for that.'

'Are you kidding?' He shakes his head. 'Do you know how many people went on about it in 2008? It ruined my entire year. It's why we go by Ed and Jake at home – much less fantasy chic.'

'I didn't think you liked me calling you Ed,' I tease. 'I only did it to piss you off.'

'I know,' he says with intensity. 'But maybe I liked it too much.'

I swallow hard. 'And there was me thinking you were such an uptight fuddy duddy, you didn't ever concern your-self with nicknames or pop culture,' I tease, and suddenly he's standing a little bit too close. I give him a light poke in the chest. 'Always in your suits. Buttons always done all the way up.' I brush the pristine white buttons. 'Do these ever actually undo?'

'Sure they do.' He smiles, obliging with the top one. His Adam's apple bobs lightly under the loosened collar.

'Oh, come on!' I scoff. 'Is that all you can manage, Edward? Surely you can do better than that?'

He reaches up and undoes two more buttons. I can see taut skin and thick chest hair in the unleashed triangle, and suddenly feel a bit lightheaded. Edward is even closer now and I can feel the heat of his body through his shirt. I try to stop myself staring at the hint of bare chest and find I can't. It's impossible not to look. Who would've thought such a small amount of flesh would cause such a reaction in me?

I look up at last and he's watching me, his eyes dark and penetrating, nostrils flared. A heat suddenly flashes between us, and we reach for each other, right there in his parents' hallway. Next to the shoe rack. His hands are on my face as we kiss. And then they're in my hair, on my back, under my coat. Edward's tongue is in my mouth; mine in his. It's unbelievably hot. He's an amazing kisser. I want to tear his clothes off right here, right now, in front of the coats, with the front door wide open, in his mum and dad's home, with his brother's friends probably watching on from the living room. And I don't care about any of it. I want this man so much.

Edward is the one to pull away first. He looks panic-stricken.

'Shit,' he says, but I don't hear him. My gaze is too un-focused; the world spinning around me. All I want is to be kissing him again. I reach for him, but he steps back. 'I'm so sorry, Olivia,' he says, and I recognise the voice. It's Edward the therapist, talking to Olivia, his patient.

Oh my god. The realisation of what we've just done rushes in. We kissed. I kissed my therapist. My therapist kissed me. What have we done?

My horror is mirrored plainly on his face, and I feel the now-familiar crush of abject humiliation.

We stare at each other for another long moment, and then I turn on my heel, rushing out the front door and running for my car. I don't stop until I'm inside and driving away, the satnav telling me to do a U-turn as soon as safely possible.

'I'd really fucking love to do a U-turn', I mutter to myself as I try to steady my breathing.

That was the stupidest thing I've ever done. And I'm including the time I had a public meltdown over a tiramisu and went internet famous.

I kissed my fucking therapist. What the hell is wrong with me?

CHAPTER TWENTY-FOUR

'Oh my god, are you okay?' I'm barely in the front door, my stomach sloshing with acid, sick with dread, when Sam is on me.

'Yeah, sorry, I was—'

'Oh mate.' She gathers me up in an unsolicited hug for the first time in living memory. 'I've been really worried, you poor thing.'

'Whoa!' I say, feeling suddenly afraid as she squeezes me. Why is Samira hugging me? She can't know what just happened with Edward, can she? Surely she can't. Maybe I just looked *that* miserable.

'Why am I a poor thing?' I squeak from within the embrace. She pulls back, studying my expression.

'Crap, you haven't seen it,' she says quietly. I stare at her, and she stares back. After a second she continues, 'I'm really sorry, Liv, but there's another TikTok video. Another one from that night in the restaurant with Justin.'

'No!' I cry out hoarsely. 'No! They can't do that! The madness and hate has only just started to die down! They can't!'

'I think some horrible idiot was holding onto it for that very reason,' she explains softly. 'To start it all up again as soon as interest started to wane. It's filmed by the door – by the cloakroom – as you were leaving. When you . . .' She looks awkward. '. . . when you put your coat on and sat back down on the floor.'

'No!' I wail again. 'It's not fair! I've done my time; I've served my punishment. I'm on suspension, I'm having the therapy—' I stop myself there, knowing with certainty that I won't be able to have any more sessions with Edward. Not after that stupid thing we just did. We've only had four rounds – I'm not even sure that fourth session will count since it was cut short – and there's no way we'll be able to get through two more sessions together. Not after what just happened. So even if this new video wasn't enough to end my career for good on its own, Spencer will be able to use the fact that I'm not completing the six-week course as an excuse to sack me. This is all that little arsewipe needs to terminate my employment for good.

It isn't fair. My life was slowly returning to normality, and now . . . this. Why? It's not fair, it's not.

'Come and sit down.' Sam leads me into the living room and runs to fetch me a glass of water. She hands it over, then frowns. 'Or do you want something stronger? There's some leftover red wine or pink tequila in the fridge from Friday?'

I shake my head, feeling numb. What's going to happen? How much more can that one night upend my life? And how many more videos are out there, waiting to ruin everything? Every time I try to get back on my feet, will some spiteful restaurant goer be ready with yet another humiliating video? Are there more out there?

I take a big gulp of the water. I'm too numb to be able to taste much of anything but I can feel its coldness travelling down my throat.

To be honest, it doesn't really matter if there are any more videos of me anyway, because there's no way my career is going to recover from this now. I'm done with *Morning Tea*. I'm done with the book. The therapy collective will have to kick me out. I'm done, finished, finito. That's it. Everything's over.

'Do you want to watch it?' Sam asks, examining my face.

'No,' I say simply, then shrug my acceptance. 'Okay, yes.' Why not watch the horribleness? Why not lean into this sick feeling; this pit in my stomach. Why not self-flagellate and self-harm. Everything is over. 'Show me,' I add, and she pulls out her phone, taking a seat beside me.

On the small screen, I watch myself in the dim light of the restaurant, stomping over to the cloakroom in that special dress I'd chosen so carefully. I hand over a ticket with resentment. There is cheesecake on the front of my dress and some in my hair. I can just about make out the broken nail on my right hand. There I am, angrily yanking on my coat. And then I see a change come over my face. I remember that feeling of fury as what had happened hits me all over again. I remember that sense of injustice at the world. At everything. I remember how fucking *angry* I was. How unable I was to shut it down like I usually do.

And there I go. There's me, sitting down on the floor, where I start to rant. It's all coming back to me now.

'I can't watch anymore,' I say, pushing Sam's phone away. I can hear myself chuntering embarrassingly away on the device, probably insulting Justin's poor mum some more and talking about the joys of cheesecake. Sam jabs at the screen, trying to stop the video and, at last, silence descends.

'Are you okay?' she asks nicely, and I raise my eyebrows.

'What is *okay*?' I reflect back. 'My career is over. My *life* is over.'

'No, it's not!' she says fiercely, putting another arm around me. Her alien affection is making everything seem that much more terrifying. 'This will blow over. Things will get back to normal soon. Everything will be boring again in a few weeks.' She tries to smile. 'It's not even that bad. You make a really great speech in the video.'

'Sure.' I roll my eyes. 'I think they'd probably run out of cheesecake by then, so nothing could shut me up.'

'It'll be fine,' she says again. 'You've got a couple more weeks of therapy, right? By the time you're done, everyone will have forgotten about this and *Morning Tea* will be pleading with you to come back.'

I stare down at the floor. 'I don't think I'll be continuing with the therapy,' I say quietly.

'What?' She frowns. 'I thought you were feeling much more positive about it all? I thought it was helping?'

'I ...' I stutter, trying to get the words out. 'I fucked up, Sam.' My voice breaks a little. 'I ... kissed Edward.'

She audibly gasps. 'You *what*?' Her eyes are wide. 'You kissed *your therapist*?'

'I know,' I whisper. 'It's so messed up.'

She frowns, conflicted. 'It kind of is, Liv, sorry.'

I feel a spike of defensiveness. 'You've been following Arshiya around like a lost puppy,' I point out and she shrugs.

'Sure, I know that. I'm super curious about her, and maybe I wanted to impress her a bit,' she concedes. 'But *getting off* with your therapist? That's really over the line.'

'Great, thanks for your support,' I snap sarcastically, and we fall into a strange silence.

'Would it help to do some Justin stalking?' Sam offers hopefully, and I tut.

'No.'

'Oh come on!' she goads. 'It'll distract you from kissing the wrong people. And it'll be a laugh.' She smiles widely. 'Orla posted a new picture of them together earlier. I think they were at a museum, can you even imagine *Justin* at a museum? Didn't he once say he'd never actually read a whole book?'

'Sam, don't!' I snap again. 'I'm trying not to get sucked into that kind of thing anymore. Why are you pushing this?'

'What are you talking about?' she teases. 'You love this stuff. Don't be boring. C'mon, you know how tedious my life is. I need you to bring the fun.'

'I'm not here to be your live-in entertainment.' I sit up straighter, feeling a bubbling up in my stomach. 'It's un-healthy – *bad* – for me to be constantly obsessing over my ex and over Orla. You must know that. Why are you encourag-ing it? Do you just enjoy seeing me make a fool of myself?'

She makes a face. 'It's not that deep,' she says, and the throwaway comment makes my fury notch all the way up to ten. This is our generation's way of saying, 'Calm down, dear,' and I cannot *stand it*. I've had a lifetime of men telling me I should laugh things off, that I shouldn't take offence, that I shouldn't take cruelty so seriously. It's just a joke, babe! *It's not that deep.* Somehow it hurts even worse coming from my best friend.

'It *is* that deep, actually, Sam,' I say loudly. 'I think you see me as some frothy idiot who can keep you amused in your boredom. We laugh about you and your narcissistic main character energy, but I'm not the supporting character either. The sidekick in your own personal box office smash. The sweary Bridget Jones-y best friend, just there for the comic relief. Just because you're unhappy in your life, doesn't mean I'm here to amuse you. You seem to enjoy my drama, even when it hurts me! My pain is your fun.'

Sam's nostrils flare. 'That's total bollocks,' she retorts, but I don't shut down and placate. I say the things I want to say.

'It's not bollocks,' I reply hotly. 'You've been loving all this awful drama surrounding me lately. You found it hilarious that I went viral as Tiramisu Girl and you found it hilarious that I got obsessed with Justin and his new girlfriend. You encouraged me to follow them around, to stalk them, to press pause on my life so I could obsess over it. You should've stopped me going to Orla's podcast event, not joyfully joined in! You should've stopped me making a fool of myself. I was a wreck after that; it messed me up!'

'I was trying to help you!' Sam says, looking furious. 'I was trying to cheer you up and make you feel better. I wasn't going to shame you for your unhealthy impulses. If I'd said don't do it, you probably would've done it anyway, but just been on your own, feeling a lot worse about it.'

'Rubbish!' I retort as she nods frantically, her expression livid.

'It's true. Look at this ridiculous new fuck up with Edward! I was nowhere near that, was I? You made all that happen without any enabling from me.'

'Yes, thanks so much, Sam,' I yell. 'Thanks for pointing out that I fuck everything up and ruin everything all on my own. I really appreciate it.'

'You're welcome!' she yells back. We glare at each other crossly for another few seconds, then I stomp away in the direction of my room. I hear Sam doing the same, her bedroom door slamming loudly a few seconds later. As I throw myself onto my bed, trying not to cry angry tears, my phone vibrates in my pocket.

I pull it out, hardly able to see through my white-hot rage. It's from Edward, and it's the most formal message I've ever received from a person under the age of sixty.

Olivia,

I apologise wholeheartedly for my unprofessional conduct and lapse in judgement earlier today. My mother is home safe and well now, thank you for the support. I'm sure you'll agree that it's not a good idea for us to continue our sessions together going forward. Today was a clear case of transference and I will take full accountability with *Morning Tea* when I let them know we've stopped our sessions prematurely. I shouldn't have agreed to it initially, given our existing professional relationship. I can, of course, refer you to someone outside the collective, if it's of interest.

All the best,

Edward

I throw my phone across the room, hearing the screen crack as it hits the corner of the bookcase. And then I throw myself into my pillows and scream and scream and scream.

ViralVideosTranscribed

one hour ago

BRAND <u>NEW VIDEO</u> OF MORNING TEA THERAPIST LIV CARPENTER LOSING IT. WATCH HER EPICCCCCC MELTDOWN – VIDEO 3!!!

Rustle of phone moving

click-clack of heels moving quickly across the floor

Unidentified 1: [hissing] Why are you following her? Are you still filming this?

Unidentified 2: Yeah, shut up! She's going to lose it again in a sec, she's fucking nuts. Another crazy bitch. This is hilarious.

Unidentified 1: [very quietly] It's not. You're being really horrible.

LC: [in a high pitch] Can I have my coat, please? Here's my ticket. Thank you.

Cloakroom attendant: Sure.

LC: Sorry, there's cake on the ticket – can you still make out the number? There's cake everywhere to be honest. It's in my handbag, too, see? [laughs maniacally] Look at the cheesecake in my hairbrush! It's a good job there's already cheesecake in my hair, isn't it? Maybe it would make a nice hair mask? Some creamy cheesecake might finally sort out my *very* dry ends. I wish I knew a really good shampoo.

Cloakroom attendant: [sounding bored] I've seen worse. You had a scarf as well, right? [rustling noise and long pause] Here you go.

237

sound of coat being put on

LC: [half-sob] I don't even like this coat, you know? I got it because I saw Victoria Beckham wearing one like it and I think she's cool. Her and David Beckham seem really happy don't they? Apart from all the . . . rumours.

Cloakroom attendant: [still sounding a bit bored] Er, are you okay?

LC: [sitting on the floor] No, I'm not okay actually. [more half-sobs] You know, I did everything for that guy in there. And I don't even know why! I don't recognise the woman I became with him.

Cloakroom attendant: Who? Which woman?

LC: Me woman! Who was she? Who was the sad '50s housewife I became for him? Who was she who slipped into that trad wife bullshit role? I thought it was what I wanted, but do I? Why? [getting louder] It fucking sucks the way we sublimate ourselves for men. I see women do it all the time – intelligent, cool, brilliant women, dating boring, mediocre men who don't deserve them. They give up their names when they get married, they give up their careers when they have kids, they give up their lives to load the dishwasher. And all for men who will go to the pub with their mates after work and call their wives nags. We all tell ourselves we're too much, but there's barely anything left by the time we've been daughters and girlfriends and wives and mothers. We erase ourselves, and they don't even notice! And for what purpose? To become someone we don't even recognise. To become someone our younger selves would've been horrified and embarrassed by. I was there in 2017 for the Women's March, and now here I am, sobbing on the floor because a man who can't wash his own boxers just dumped me. What *is* that? [strangled noise] We're socialised to be nice, to be polite, to wear our wounds on the inside. We're told being angry is the one emotion that belongs to men. And if we do show it, we're called witches and bitches and ball-busters and aggressive and bossy and abrasive and stroppy and shrill. AND NAGS. We quietly get on with it all, even as it piles up and up on top of us – more and more, with no end in sight. We try and quieten any unease we feel over what has happened to our lives by sending ourselves off to fucking yoga retreats and reading *The Secret* or doing that detox Beyonce once tried – and why? So we don't end up risking upsetting the men in our lives by speaking up about our unhappiness? So we don't end up *inconveniencing* them with our existence? Every woman I know has Imposter Syndrome, and I know why! It's because we're made to feel like imposters everywhere we go! We're not wanted in the boardrooms or in their men's clubs or in their spaces. We make ourselves smaller and smaller and thinner and thinner so we don't bother anyone with our aliveness. We tell ourselves we're *too much*; we go to bed every night wondering if we said the wrong thing in that conversation we had earlier or looked silly in the outfit we carefully selected. [ragged breathing] You know what Frankenstein said? Mary Shelley got it right. 'I have love in me the likes of which you can scarcely imagine and rage the likes of which you would not believe. If I cannot satisfy the one, I will indulge the other.' [sound of LC standing up] I AM FRANKENSTEINNNNNNNNNNNNNNN!

Cloakroom attendant: I feel you, babe.

LC: Can you believe they don't have any tiramisu in there?

[watch again?]

239

"I am Frankenstein!"

#FrankensteinFeminist #TiramisuGirl #CheesecakeGirl #Hilarious #LivCarpenter
#BBCMorningTea #RelationshipTherapist #PublicMeltdown #PublicFreakout
#FunnyVids #lol #memes #meme #comedy #funnymemes #fun #memesdaily
#funnymeme #lmao #dankmemes #funnyshit #video #viral #funnyposts

39 comments

Ram

Oh my god another video?!!!

Janey

Tiramisu Girl!!!!! I'd forgotten all about her

> **Billy**
>
> She is maaaaaaad. What a dumb bitch. Reminds me of my ex.
> She ate too much cake, too. I tried to put her on a diet, and she
> dumped me! I was just trying to help her FFS.
>
> **Jim**
>
> No man is ever going to touch that woman again with a ten-foot
> barge pole.
>
> **Pete**
>
> I would give her a pity bang but otherwise she's totally
> unfuckable. lol

Lovesit

Have you seen they've totally sacked her off Morning Tea? They've
got a new guy already.

> **Sarah**
>
> Well, duh, they could hardly keep her on after this, could they?

ThatThing

I feel like I should read Frankenstein now

> **Soph**
>
> Me too! Checking it out of the library rn

DogLover

This is really mean! Leave her alone.

Ghit

I agree

IStandWithHer

What an amazing speech. It's giving Barbie movie America Ferrera vibes! I love her. You go, Frankenstein Feminist!

Andrew

She's a stupid hag and so are you. Get back in your box.

CHAPTER TWENTY-FIVE

I take to my bed, prepared for a night of tossing and turning furiously, but instead, I sleep like the dead.

There are no bad dreams about my latest viral meltdown. No anxious night sweats over Justin and Orla. No staring at the ceiling in a panic spiral about my kiss with Edward or my fight with Sam. I just sleep; heavy, thick and dreamless.

I wake up late, as the front door slams. Usually when Sam leaves for work, she sneaks out, moving about with care in case it disturbs me. Not today. She's clearly still furious.

Oddly, I'm not. Not anymore. In fact, I don't feel much of anything. It is tempting to try for sadness; to have a big old cry about all these things that have befallen me and my life. For a moment I consider spending the day – many days! – in bed, contemplating what my future might entail now that I've ruined everything and sabotaged all the things I cared about. But there is something like acceptance in my chest as I move about the flat, making myself breakfast.

Because a lot of this is my fault, I'm realising. Sam was partly right in what she said last night. I've been blaming all the outside factors for what's happened to me, and sure, maybe I didn't really deserve to be filmed and publicly shamed like that. But I have to take some accountability for where I am right now.

I'm the one who behaved like that in the restaurant. I'm also the one who mentioned Edward's name when Fabian said I needed to have therapy. I'm the one who resisted and behaved badly when Edward tried to help. I'm the one who went with him to his parents' house yesterday. And I'm the one who – hazy as it is, what with all the lust – made the first move and kissed him. I'm also the one who would've kept kissing him if he hadn't stopped us. And I probably would've dragged him into bed afterwards, too. I'm also the one who picked a fight with Sam last night because I needed to take my feelings out on someone.

Although, admittedly, some of it needed to be said.

Either way, I had agency in all of this. And it's time I accepted what's happened, instead of fighting it. It's time I started trying to fix things.

I remember what Edward started to say yesterday, during our interrupted therapy session. The thing about appropriate outlets for my anger.

I pick my phone up from the table and google my local gym. On a whim, I book myself into a midday kickboxing class on a guest pass.

The frustrating thing is that I felt like I *was* starting to work on fixing things. I felt like talking to Edward was working for me. It was getting through, piercing my shell. I was starting to realise how deep-rooted and messy a lot of my internal stuff was. I was starting to understand that just because I have words of wisdom for other people, doesn't mean I have internalised anything wise about my own life. I was really starting to understand that I needed to work on myself. And I was *willing to* at last.

The next thing I do is head to LinkedIn. I'm about to lose my regular work on *Morning Tea*, my clients at the therapy collective have abandoned me, and there's next to no chance my publisher will want *Orange Flags* anymore. Worse than that, I've been living off the advance money they gave me, and if they suddenly demand it all back, I'm going to have to find a new source of income. And quickly.

I search the site for roles requiring a therapist and ping off my CV to a few places, barely reading the job listings I'm applying for. At this stage, I'm aware how unlikely it is that I'd be a strong candidate for anything, but I want to at least feel proactive; like I'm taking steps to rectify my situation. I need to feel some semblance of control over my existence.

I throw on my gym clothes, my mind blank and numb, and an hour later I'm pummelling a boxing bag. I give it everything I've got, which – to start with – is not a lot. The first few punches and kicks feel awkward and futile. The bag is so big and immoveable, while I'm weak and feeble. But after a few minutes, the feelings start to rush in. I feel my rage solidifying in my fists and feet. I hit harder, I kick with more strength, I cry a little bit. I internally curse the bag and everyone I know.

Because sure, I have fucked things up and I'm happy to take some accountability. But other people haven't helped, have they?

How dare Edward toss me to one side like this? How dare Samira tell me I'm the problem, it's me (Taylor's version). How dare those strangers on the internet mock and jeer like I'm not a real person. How dare producer Spencer threaten my livelihood so casually. How dare the publishers cancel my book. How dare everyone and everything. Punch punch punch. Kick kick kick.

The trainer shouts out more instructions and I throw myself into the routine, sweat pouring down my face, my hands and arms aching with the effort. It feels so good, so cathartic. I feel strong. I feel ... powerful? This is exactly what I needed.

The fifty-minute class is over quickly, and I fight an urge to hug all the strong women around me, all just as sweaty and furious looking. I will be back, I silently tell the room, but for now, I have things to do and say.

I'm going to speak to Edward.

I rush straight over to the therapy collective building in a blaze of self-righteous anger and indignation, not even stopping to change out of my stinky exercise clothes. I run up the stairs, ignoring the lift, and burst into his office, only realising too late that he is likely to be with a client.

But he's not.

He's alone, sitting behind his desk, hunched over his laptop, studiously making notes. He looks tired, his usually perfect suit a little more crumpled than usual. And is that a hint of stubble, heaven forbid?

He looks up, starting in his chair when he sees it's me. A look of horror crosses his face, before he swiftly pulls it back to neutrality. To therapist Edward.

'Olivia?' he offers politely, like he's not sure. Of course, it's possible he's not – I must look demented, standing in his doorway wearing my old grey, gym clothes, my face sweaty and bright red.

'We're going to finish our sessions,' I tell him calmly. 'We're going to have our final two meetings, and then you're going to sign me off to go back to *Morning Tea*.'

He's already shaking his head. 'Liv, we can't. You know how transference works. It's very common and very normal for a client to develop romantic feelings for their therapist. There's no judgement at all, but we have to maintain appropriate boundaries. It wouldn't be professional to carry on after what happened.'

His words confuse me. Transference is all one-sided. Is he saying this was all me? That the kiss was all on me? And that the way I've been feeling recently is all fake? He's saying it's only my stupid psyche getting confused by his kindness?

I shake my head, trying to understand. No, he's wrong! Of course he is. This isn't transference. I'm a trained, experienced therapist for god's sake, not a personification of the silly young woman trope, easily swayed by a few words of kindness. This is more than that. Surely it's more than ... Edward's staring at a point above my head, waiting. His words echo around my head.

He's saying I don't know my own mind.

But what if I don't? What would that mean? Because if I can't even recognise the difference between real emotion and me projecting something onto the nearest nice person, what kind of terrible therapist does that make me? Maybe I really am a fraud. I feel a surge of anger at the injustice of it all, and then that same feeling of acceptance I experienced this morning.

'Okay, look,' I begin again, this time keeping my voice as calm as I can. 'It was just a mistake. Like you said, it was all just transference. It happens, it doesn't have to be a big deal, does it? And you can't just abandon the sessions now. I can't start again with someone else, and I will definitely lose my job if it gets back to *Morning Tea* that you've dumped me as a client. You can't do that to me. We've both agreed that what happened yesterday was a mistake ...' And for good measure I add, '... a *disgusting* mistake that was an all-round horrible experience ...' He has the good grace to look mildly offended. '... and it will never, ever be repeated. So why would it be a problem to continue with our last two sessions?'

He sighs, looking a little defeated.

'Edward,' I say sternly. 'We're carrying on with the therapy. Even if I have to squat in your office for the two sessions. I mean it, I'll just turn up here and sit there, saying nothing.'

He sighs again. 'Okay,' he says at last.

'Okay?' I echo back, relief flooding me. We stare at one another; resignation on his face, determination on mine. I smile tightly. 'Shall we have a session now then? Bang out number five right here.' I'm almost being sarcastic, but he checks his watch.

'Fine,' he replies tersely.

'Fine.' I flounce over to the sofa and take a seat. 'Let's do some fucking therapy then.'

CHAPTER TWENTY-SIX

It's been four days and Sam still isn't really speaking to me.

I mean, we passed each other in the kitchen yesterday and she mentioned it was bin day. And this morning she politely asked if I'd seen the council tax was going up again, but otherwise, I think we are officially in the midst of A Feud.

It's shit. I hate it. I feel wretched every time I hear her moving about the flat with none of her usual look-at-me energy. But I also don't feel like I have the emotional bandwidth to have a big conversation with her about it all.

I know I need to apologise. But there are also things I feel were true in what I said. So, I don't know how to say sorry for hurting her and sorry for being a prick, but also address those other important things. I love love *love* our friendship and I don't want to lose it, but there *are* times when she encourages my bad behaviour. I don't want her to enable my worst impulses. And I don't want her to feel like she *has* to enable them. As if that is the only way this friendship works. I don't want the Sam and Liv dynamic to be me always providing stupid drama and making bad choices, while she laughs along and screams 'yaaaas' from the sidelines, encouraging me to do something even worse. This has been an ongoing staple in our friendship over the years, and I want it to be better. I want us to make *each other* better; to bring out our best sides, not our worst. Maybe it didn't matter so much in our twenties, when making bad choices was part of the lived experience, practically a rite of passage or a requirement of youth. It was fine as long as the stakes weren't all that high. But they suddenly do feel like they *are* high. Things are too real now to keep on going the way I was. I need to make healthier, happier choices for myself. I need to empty myself of this painful, angry energy. And I need her help with that. She's my sister, my soulmate, I love her. I want us to be in this whole, complicated, difficult *life thing* together.

I roll over in bed, wondering how to fill yet another day of not looking at Instagram and not having any work to do.

I should go and do some therapy homework. Having insisted – bullied – Edward into continuing our therapy and then having strong-armed him into giving me a session right there and then, I am eager to make the most of these last couple of weeks. After some initial awkwardness, with Edward being scrupulously professional and po-faced, we ended up talking a lot more about my family again. We discussed ways of processing my repressed rage and I told him about the kickboxing – about how good it made me feel. He loved that, and made it my homework for this week. I'm to make a list of other ways I could experiment with releasing my anger in a positive and healthy way – and then I'm meant to try at least two of them out.

I pick up one of the pillows propping me up in bed. I press it to my face, and I scream and scream and scream. Like I did last week after my fight with Sam. I keep pressing and screaming until I realise I can't breathe. I pull away panting, then try to do that self-scan thing Edward told me about.

I feel better.

And I also definitely feel like that pillow needs washing and/or urgently Febrezing.

I perk up. At least that's something I can do today – some washing!

I pick up a notebook and pen, adding, '1. Screaming into a pillow – YES MATE LOVE IT', and then underline the words. Beside me, my phone beeps with a new email. I casually pick it up and my heart briefly stops when I spot it's from Fabian.

It is, as ever, short and straight to the point.

'Babe, publishers want a meeting f2f, when can you do?'

I drop my phone back on the bed and consider picking the pillow back up. I know what this means. It means they're formally cancelling the book. It's nice of them to offer to do it in person, but really, I'd much rather have an email I can weep loudly over in my own time and space.

What if they want the money back? I swallow down the bile rising in my throat. What will I do?

In my hand, my phone pings with another email. I open it, trying to comprehend its contents. It takes me a full minute before it clicks.

It's from a women's domestic violence charity. They're responding to my application to become one of their volunteer counsellors. They want to meet with me.

Volunteer? God, I *really* wasn't concentrating when I sent off my CV the other day.

I hit reply, ready to type out a speedy brush off, but then pause. What if this is the purpose I need right now? Sure, it wouldn't solve the money problems I'm about to face, but it could give me something else.

I think of Jools' female rage at our lunch. How women are turning on women, just when we need each other the most. Listening to her speak inspired something in me and I want to help. I think of kicking the shit out of that punch bag during the kickboxing class, side by side with a room full of sweaty women. It felt good.

I want to do something. And this is a really important charity with an amazing mission. This could actually be . . . great.

I gather my stuff and head out the door. I need to get out of the flat, so I'm heading to my favourite independent café to buy a ridiculously overpriced hot chocolate. I'll sit in my usual spot in the corner where I can find some peace and quiet to properly read the job advert. I'll look over the charity's website, do some research, consider it over a croissant and then respond to their email.

This might not solve my looming financial crisis, but it could help with something a lot bigger and more important.

As I enter the café, I almost barrel straight into someone as they reach for the door at the same time as me. My mutters of apology are interrupted by—

'Liv?'

I look up with surprise at the single syllable, and there I find the last face in the world I expected – or wanted – to see.

Justin.

And Orla!

They're here, together. At *my* favourite coffee shop.

I look between them in a panic. How is this possible? How are they here? Just when I'd given up on stalking them – just in my darkest hour – they're both here. Perfect. This is the *last* thing I need right now.

'Er, good to see you,' Justin says, and the look in his eyes says the opposite. He turns to Orla, who somehow looks stunningly beautiful even with a slightly sunburned nose. The freckles are out in full force. 'Um, Liv, this is Orla,' he introduces us awkwardly. 'Er, Orla, this is Liv, my . . . ex.' I watch in slow motion as she automatically smiles broadly, then falters. Her eyes narrow as she takes in my face, trying to place me. And then I watch in horror as they light up with recognition. She remembers me. She remembers me from that fucking podcast event I went to with Sam. She's going to out me. She's going to tell Justin how I turned up with a friend at her podcast recording and quizzed her about men.

This is the most humiliating experience of my life. I can't believe this is—

'Nice to meet you, Liv,' she says carefully, reaching out to offer a friendly hand to shake. We regard each other. I stare at the hand, then take it. I can see on her face that she knows me, that she knows exactly what I was doing when I came to see her that day. And – by some kind of miracle – she's not going to say it. Not out loud.

God, she's great. I think I actually fancy her more than I ever fancied Justin. Could I steal her from him? Would that be possible? And would it be even more fucked up than kissing my therapist?

'Hi,' I say, swallowing hard. 'Great to meet you . . . Orla.'

'We were just going to grab a hot chocolate.' Justin nods at the counter, acknowledging the long queue snaking around it.

'Me too,' I squeak. 'But actually, I think I'll just . . . um, I don't fancy one anymore really, so I'm going to . . .'

'Oh no, don't run off on our account,' Orla says so nicely. 'I know this is a bit weird and awkward, but it doesn't have to be. We can all queue together like grown-ups, right?' She grins cheekily and I smile back, my knees weak.

'I guess so.' We move to take our positions, the sound of coffee shop noise filling the air around us.

'I'm guessing this coffee shop was your recommendation at some point, huh, Liv?' Orla says playfully after a tense minute.

I glance at Justin, and he looks embarrassed. 'Yeah,' I

admit. 'This is my favourite place for hot chocolate. They add so much whipped cream and marshmallows, people go into diabetic comas all the time.' I sneak another look at Justin. 'But I don't think you ever came here with me, did you?'

He bites his lip. 'No, but you always brought me a hot chocolate when you went. I remembered how amazing they are.'

I feel Orla's eyes on me and wonder if she's remembering my question that day – the one about washing a partner's underwear. What must she think of me?

We move up the line at last and a harried woman takes our orders. Justin offers to buy the drinks, something he's never, ever done before, and I accept with some surprise. It's the least this douchebag owes me.

We exit the café and hover awkwardly outside with our hot cups. 'Well,' I mumble, trying to casually move off. This encounter might not have been quite as bad as it could've been, but it's still something I desperately want over. 'Thank you for the hot chocolate, Justin. Um, nice to meet you, Orla . . .'

She places a hand on my arm, stopping me. 'Can I . . .' She pauses to turn briefly to Justin. 'Actually, would you mind giving Liv and me one second on our own? I'm sorry, I know this is probably your worst nightmare'—she nods to me—'for both of you. But just one minute? Literally just one minute, okay?' Justin nods silently, terror dancing across his features, but he slowly walks away.

Orla turns back to me, but I speak first. 'God, I'm *so* sorry for being an absolute creep that day – coming to your event – I know you must think I'm a total—'

She waves her hand dismissively. 'Don't be silly. I've been there before.' She smiles indulgently. 'Maybe not that recently, but I am quite a bit older than you. It took an awful lot of learning – and *unlearning* – not to stalk the ex or new girlfriend of someone I liked.'

I think about my friend, Jools. How she says ageing has been revelatory for her. How she said everyone should have an older friend for advice.

'Thanks,' I say quietly. 'For understanding, I mean. And for not saying anything to Justin. I've humiliated myself around that guy enough for one lifetime. I'm working on moderating some of my . . . less sensible impulses.'

She shakes her head. 'It takes a lot of retraining when women are pitted against one another from day one. We get taught to compare ourselves and compete from such a young age. It's not easy and I get it.' She rolls her perfect cat eyes. 'And we rarely look at the person encouraging us to compete. I think if we looked at them instead, and stopped being mean to each other, women would be unstoppable.'

I take her in. I've mostly been able to shake my obsessive curiosity over this woman's magical powers, but now she's here, in the flesh, this close and this kind, I have to ask. I need to know. I clear my throat. 'How is . . . I mean, Justin is *so* different now. So completely transformed from the guy I dated. I barely recognise him. How did you . . . change him?'

She snorts a laugh. 'I haven't changed him. I don't think

a person can change someone else. They have to do it for themselves. I think . . .' She pauses to contemplate the question and I appreciate her so much for giving it the time of day. '. . . I think he just knew there was never any chance of me dating a little boy. I wasn't the least bit interested in him when we met at a friend's work thing. He was so rumpled and messy – a toddler! – and when my pal said he was keen, I laughed and told her there wasn't a chance in hell. Especially since he'd literally just come out of a relationship.' She pauses, looking a little embarrassed. 'With you. Anyway, I've dated boys before, and they have a way of slowly turning you into their mum. I will never, ever let that happen again. Men and women are all equally capable of looking after themselves; why should I be the one to do it for another person, just because they were born with a pokey-out bit between their legs?' She smiles wryly. 'The fact is, I'm happy on my own. Why should I ever sacrifice that happiness for someone who doesn't deserve it?'

'Fuck,' I whisper. 'So, it really is just about boundaries and knowing your worth?' I've said those things out loud so many times to other women. Whether it was sitting in my office with therapy clients, in the pub with my friends, or peering down a camera lens from that *Morning Tea* sofa, I've given this exact advice to countless women . . . how is it possible I didn't hear my own advice? Why did I never notice?

Orla wrinkles her nose adorably. 'I guess so? But it's not always that easy. It's hard to shake off a lifetime of societal training.' She raises an eyebrow. 'And I don't know what you saw about me online or whatever, but nothing is ever as perfect as it seems.' She waves in Justin's direction. 'We had a major argument last night. Today was supposed to be an apology hot chocolate, and now I find out it's his ex-girlfriend's favourite place!' She rolls her eyes but she's laughing with affection. '*And* that his ex is a beautiful, cool woman who must be ten plus years younger than me. A woman who also used to'—she makes a grossed out but teasing face—'wash his clothes for him? Yikes.'

I grimace. 'In hindsight, it is really mad that I ever thought Justin was the right guy for me.' I pause. 'I hope he'll be the right partner for you.'

She regards me warmly. 'God, that's really nice,' she says. 'And you're super chill and cool as well, how awful.' She laughs, and I wonder at her words. She thinks I'm chill? Is this irony? I'll have to check with Alanis Morissette – although I seem to recall none of the things she sang about were actually ironic. Orla continues, 'I guess time will tell if he's the one. I'm not sure if I even believe in them.' She sniffs. 'I don't love that he let you be that person for him when you were together, but now I'm aware of it, I'll just have to be vigilant about not slipping into bad habits.'

'It's not easy,' I acknowledge the truth of this with a shake of my head. 'But I'm guessing it's worth it to have a functioning, loving relationship. I hope you get to have one with him. Justin's not a bad bloke for the most part. Just a walking orange flag.'

She smiles. 'Jeez, you'd think they'd be easier to spot!' She

pulls me in for a hug and I hold onto her, feeling the tight-
ness that has sat like a stone in my stomach for weeks loosen.
Over her shoulder I spot Justin at some distance, watching
us. He still seems so very different; so unlike the man I dated
for over a year. But now that fact doesn't scare me or make
me feel horribly insecure. It's just some guy over there, and
I sort-of wish him well. I wish them both well.

Plus, that look he's wearing on his face of pure, unadul-
terated terror, at the sight of his current and ex-girlfriend
embracing, gives me a serotonin boost that should last at
least a month.

MorningTeaVids

64 weeks ago

RELATIONSHIP EXPERT LIV CARPENTER ON MORNING TEA HELPS WOMAN WHO'S LOST FAITH IN DATING

Liv: Hello, welcome back, everyone, are we ready for our next caller? Who do we have on the line?

Caller: Hi, Liv, I'm Ricki.

Liv: Hi Ricki! What do you want to talk about today?

Caller: My love life. I just don't know how to . . . how to *believe* anymore, y'know? In love, I mean? I go on all these awful, horrible dates with awful, horrible men and it never goes anywhere. On the very rare occasion I meet someone who seems halfway decent, he ghosts me, or turns out to be the kind of person who will send me pictures of his hideously ugly genitals at 2am, before we've even kissed. It's just this endless parade of disappointment and I'm really starting to feel like love will never happen for me.

Liv: [clucks sympathetically] I've been there. Tell me, Ricki, why do you date?

Caller: Er, to meet someone?!

Liv: Sure, okay, but why do you *want* to meet someone? Are you miserable on your own? No hobbies? No friends? Constant loneliness? Desperately broody?

Caller: Hmm, none of the above. I actually have an amazing life outside of the romance stuff. My friends are the best and I love my job.

Liv: What about loneliness?

Caller: Well, yeah, I do get lonely sometimes. But mostly I'm too busy to notice or just relieved to have a night to myself.

Liv: And actually, I bet the only time you feel really lonely is when you're on one of those awful dates, sitting opposite one of those terrible men with the ugly genitals?

Caller: Oh my god, yeah, that's right. I had that exact thought the other night when I was with this dude who kept talking about all the child maintenance he doesn't feel like he should have to pay for his kids.

Liv: My point is, it's clear you need a break. You need to quit dating for a while. Think of it like this: if you could get a quick peek ten years into your future and know for sure you'd met someone and were living that life you envision, would you be piling all this pressure on yourself right now to meet someone?

Caller: [long pause] No.

Liv: I've just started dating this amazing guy called Justin, so it can and does happen! It will happen for you, too, but you have to be in the right frame of mind. Instead of going on endless dates with a stream of anyones, take some time away from romance. Fall in love with yourself and your life again. Then you can come back to dating in a few months – or even a year – in a much more measured and positive way. But even then, I want you to stop with this scattergun approach. Only go out with guys who really seem worth it. You seem amazing and you shouldn't waste your precious time on anyone you're half-hearted about.

Caller: This makes a lot of sense.

Liv: Know your own worth, okay, Ricki?

Caller: I will. Thanks Liv! And good luck with Justin. I'm so glad you've met someone worthy of you!

[watch again?]

Liv Carpenter says . . . know your worth

#LivCarpenter #BBCMorningTea #RelationshipTherapist #AgonyAunt
#AdviceColumn #LifeCoach #Wisdom #LivCoolAndCollectedCarpenter
#DatingDisappointments #KnowYourWorth #LivCarpenterLovesJustin

CHAPTER TWENTY-SEVEN

As I make my way up in the lift for my next therapy session, my stomach fizzes with anticipation. I feel all bubbly and silly.

I'm excited to see Edward.

Not in a sexy way.

Okay, sure, yes, ten per cent in a sexy way. But also in a more healthy, processing way. I can acknowledge that I have feelings for my therapist, but I can also accept that it is part of a wider context – a lifetime of unhealthy patterns. I have transferred my feelings for Justin directly onto the next man who was vaguely nice to me. Edward was right. It is classic transference, and it is normal. It will go away.

More importantly, I'm excited to see him because I've realised how much our sessions are helping me. I'm seeing myself so much more clearly than before. I want to talk more. I want to tell him about my conversation with Orla, about my fight with Sam, about how okay it was bumping into Justin like that. How there was a sort of closure sense to it. I want to unpack it all with someone who gets it and doesn't judge me.

Outside his door, I check my phone. I have another email from Fabian, chasing me about this meeting with the publisher. I had hoped ignoring his last message might magically make the whole thing go away but I guess not. I shoot off a quick email.

'Hey Fabian, I'm assuming they're cancelling the contract, so any chance we can just do this over email? I'd rather not be dumped in public again, you know I don't react well to that kind of humiliation, lol.'

I feel better after I press send. I don't even want to write the stupid book anymore. It's become very clear in the last few weeks that I know nothing at all when it comes to relationships and romance. I am beyond clueless and in no position to be doling out advice to anyone. I need to work through my own stuff before I can work on anyone else's.

'Olivia, good morning,' Edward greets me from his doorway. He's wearing a grey three-piece suit today with a crisp white shirt. His tie is black and woollen. He smiles nicely – but coolly. 'You ready?'

'I am.' I nod, following him in and taking a seat. He offers me a drink of water, and I reach for the glass, taking grateful sips. It helps settle my stomach a little as I try not to look at his mouth.

These feelings are normal, I instruct myself again. Not real, but normal.

'So—' he begins, leaning forward, and I cut him off.

'Before we get started today ...' I smile. 'I wanted to say ... well, sorry.'

He blinks at me, and I sense something shift under the neutrality of his face. He thinks I'm referring to the kiss.

I quickly continue, 'I mean sorry about this whole'—I wave my hands—'therapy thing. I'm sorry I've been so resistant and so, well, *rude*.' I think of that first session, playing that stupid colourful test tubes game and ignoring everything he tried to ask me. It seems like such a long time ago and I hardly recognise myself. Edward's face relaxes a fraction. 'I didn't think any of this would help me,' I explain, knowing he knows this, but still wanting to say it. 'I feel silly about what a child I was about the whole thing. I was acting out, trying to run you off, trying to force these sessions to stop somehow. Until last week, really, when I realised how much I wanted to keep going.' This time, I *am* referencing the kiss.

I stop suddenly, considering this. Considering the timing of it and what a stupid, self-sabotaging thing it was to do.

What if I did kiss Edward to avoid closeness? Because I knew there was no way this could turn into anything real. Maybe I don't feel worthy of real love and that's why I dated Justin for so long, too. Because I didn't believe I was worthy of someone decent – of an equal.

I shake my head, the realisations coming thick and crushingly fast.

I always felt – feel – less than. Something in me is afraid that people will leave me because I'm not enough. Perhaps washing Justin's pants was my way of proving I was worth keeping around. Like, if I can make myself amenable enough and bring something real and useful to a relationship then maybe I can persuade them to stay. Maybe I've been doing the same thing with Sam, by being her entertainment.

What if I sabotage myself by avoiding anything that could be real and true, because . . . what? I don't trust love? And maybe the anger is another way to keep things and people at arm's length. When you're angry, it's hard to feel anything else, right?

'Do you think I push people away?' I say suddenly, and Edward frowns.

'What makes you say that?'

I take a deep breath. 'Sam and I had a . . . *tiff* the other day.'

'A tiff?' He is reflecting everything back; making me do the work. God, that actually really is annoying.

I take a deep breath. 'It was mostly just petty lashing out, but there was some real stuff under there.' I grimace. 'I worry she encourages my worst tendencies. It feels like she likes me best when I'm self-sabotaging and creating drama. Like, she *wants* me to be a fuck up.'

'Why would she want that?'

I consider this, feeling intensely disloyal. 'I sometimes think she needs me to be the mess in our lives, because then it makes her feel less like a mess herself. She's dissatisfied with things – she hates her job, she's still grieving her dad – and maybe if I'm even more of a hopeless case, then she can feel . . . superior. Like things aren't that bad because at least she's not Liv. And I allow myself to be that person for her because I need her to need me. I have to be useful to her so she'll keep me around.' *Because she won't let me wash her pants* – I don't say.

'Have you ever talked to her about it?'

'No.' I shake my head. 'It came up during the row, and things really blew up. We've barely spoken in a week.'

'We don't always take things said during an argument seriously,' he says. 'Especially if it was very heated. So, it might need repeating in a kinder way.'

'It was very heated,' I confirm. He regards me silently, waiting, so I start speaking again, fast. 'I don't think it's a conscious thing she does. I don't think Sam is doing it deliberately. It's just a dysfunctional pattern we've fallen into. And it was actually quite fun for a long time, but I don't think it is anymore. Another friend, Jools, said to me recently that women put themselves through so much pain for no reason, and I haven't stopped thinking about it.' I pause and he waits. 'Sam is one of the best people I've ever known,' I tell him fiercely, though he said nothing. 'She is my twin flame and I wouldn't be without her.'

'It sounds like you just need to talk to her then,' he says softly. 'Calmly – non-heatedly. If you can both see the toxic patterns and work on trying not to slip into them, you'll be fine. Sometimes we have to work just as hard on keeping our platonic relationships healthy as we do with the romantic ones. Friendships can be dysfunctional, too. Even the best ones.'

'That makes an awful lot of sense,' I say slowly. 'But being honest is sometimes really hard. Harder than it should be.'

'Why do you think that is?'

I shake my head. 'I don't know. What if telling her the truth means she doesn't want to be my friend anymore? What if she . . .'

He looks at me. 'What if she leaves you? What if you offer her love and your whole, real self, and she rejects you?'

I know what he's getting at. What if she deserts me like my parents did?

'Did you have the same struggle in your relationship with Justin?' he presses, and I stare down at my lap. 'Being honest with him about how you felt, I mean?'

'I guess so,' I say quietly after a minute. 'But I don't know if I was being honest with myself around him either.'

He leans forward slightly. 'What do you mean by that?'

'I suppose I mean'—I clear my throat—'I think I was lying to myself as much as I was to Justin. I kept telling myself I wanted this. I wanted to look after him, I wanted to be there for him, I wanted to wash and dry and iron his clothes. I told myself I wanted the relationship with him.' I shake my head. 'But I don't think I did, not really. I was lying to him and to myself. Maybe that's why I was so shaken when he dumped me. Because I was that deep in the lie. I was so entrenched in it, I couldn't fathom that our relationship was . . . well, total shit.' A wet spot lands on my hand, and I realise I'm crying. He hands me a tissue as the tears come thick and fast.

After a few minutes, I attempt a smile, trying to trick my

brain into cheering up. 'Let's talk about something else for a minute,' I say. 'I meant to ask – how's your mum doing?' His careful-therapist face slips just a little.

'She's great. She's been resting a lot and taking it easy, but she's doing much better. Thank you for asking.' He reaches around to the table behind his armchair. 'In fact, she sent you some brownies to say thanks for looking after her favourite son.' He hands me a Tupperware, and I shake my head with delight.

'Oh my god, that's so nice! Tell her that her favourite son, Jake, didn't even need my help, he had all his friends there, looking after him.'

Edward gives me a stern look that makes my stomach flip. 'Hey,' he warns.

I laugh. 'I'm joking. Team Edward all the way. You are second only to my loyalties to Team Charlie Swan.' I nod at the cakes. 'Can I have one?' He nods.

'Have them all, they're yours.' He smiles again. 'She's actually very upset she didn't get to meet you, though it wouldn't have been the best time.'

'Maybe another day,' I say thoughtlessly, and then feel myself flush. Why would I meet her another day? I take off the lid and offer him the tub. 'I will allow you one,' I say grudgingly, and he excitedly accepts. We both chew silently, regarding each other.

'Did you try out your homework?' he asks after swallowing, and I try not to notice the crumbs freckling his white shirt. He's quite the messy eater. Why do I find it cute when he shows me his flaws? Maybe because he is so close to having none. The more real and human he gets, the more I like him.

It's just transference, cut it out, Liv.

Ugh.

A chocolate chip lands in his lap, and I smile. His next patient will love seeing a dent in her therapist's perfect armour.

'I did indeed.' I reach for my handbag, pulling out the anger journal where I've made a few notes. 'I tried screaming into a pillow – a lot of fun but slightly suffocating. I also tried some painting, which ended up being a very intense black vortex of nothingness, which I assume means I'm completely fine'—I grin—'and I also went back to kickboxing.' I beam, remembering all that cathartic sweat. 'I think I'll be doing a lot more of that, it unleashes something in me. I feel amazing afterwards.'

'That's great,' he says happily, and a crumb bounces off his shirt and onto his lap to join the chocolate chip. I follow its progress then realise I'm staring at his *lap*.

'Um, so you think my parents really fucked me up, huh?' I say quickly, and he looks a little surprised.

'You asked me earlier if I think you push people away,' he says thoughtfully. 'Do *you* think you push people away?'

'I was thinking about our conversation about my mum – and my dad,' I say, trying not to get emotional. 'They were the two people who were meant to love me most. They were meant to think I was *amazing*. And they didn't.'

'Our brains love a pattern,' he says. 'When you've grown

up with love being this cauterised thing, without feeling or affection, maybe you assume that is what love should be.'

'So, I tell myself I want love, like everyone else,' I continue, 'but I'm also afraid of it, because it wasn't a good feeling when I was young. And anything real, with real passion and real care and kindness . . .'—I shake my head—'would be very alien, right? It would be very scary and even feel wrong.' I take a second. 'When I kissed you . . .' I swallow hard and he interrupts me.

'I am bound by an ethical guide . . .' he says robotically. There is panic in his eyes and I can hear the dump truck backing up – beep beep – ready to tell me to sling my hook.

'God, I *know*,' I say quickly. 'That's what I mean, it's what I was going to say. A big part of me must've known it was wrong when I came on to you. Rejection and abandonment are part of what love is for me, right? It's what that twisted inner child perceives as love. And so, I kissed someone that would have to reject me.'

We look at each other, and for a moment – just for a split-second – I think I see pity in Edward's eyes. And it stings so much.

He's not interested in me. It's oh-so clear now. Not at all. Maybe he was once, before. A while ago. Maybe he even was for half a second when we shared that kiss. But now it's obvious I'm just a client to him. A patient in need of a lot more therapy. He's seen these awful, humiliating, embarrassing parts of me, and any flicker of what could've been has been doused with water.

But there *is* someone out there who I can trust to still love me once I've shown them the worst parts of myself. Who has proven herself time and time again. I have to go see Samira right now and tell her how sorry I am. I need to be completely honest with her about all of it, and believe that she won't leave me. Because we might have that running joke between us where I say I love you, and she tells me to fuck off, but I know – bones-deep know – that she *does* love me. And I need her in my life.

Now I just have to make sure she knows it.

CHAPTER TWENTY-EIGHT

'Sam!' I fly into the flat, slamming the door behind me. 'Are you home? Samira?'

I pause to listen but there is only dead air in the rooms around me.

Dammit. I so wanted to burst in, all dramatic-like, and confess my undying love for my best friend. Her getting home after me feels so much more anti-climactic.

Maybe I'll hide outside until she gets back? I turn back for the front door, and suddenly, something flies at my face. I catch the familiar evil flicker of stupid massive wings, and I scream, knowing what's coming for me. It's the fucking daddy long-legs. It takes another run up, dive-bombing for my head and I run away full pelt, shrieking like a woman possessed. I can feel its hot breath on my neck as I throw myself down the hallway, its spindly legs grabbing at me, ready to bite my head off.

For a split second, I almost give in and let him take me. My death would be quick and painful. It'll be what I deserve. My life flashes before my eyes, and the image of my beloved Sam helps steel me. I can't die at the hands of this insect before I've told her I'm sorry and I love her – and then made her say it back.

I throw myself at the bathroom door, slipping inside and pushing it shut behind me.

I breathe hard, telling myself over and over that it's okay. I made it. I didn't lose my head to a daddy long-legs. I've lost my head to other evil males before, but not this time.

And then I hear the front door open and close. She's home.

'Sam,' I yell, and there is a moment of silence.

Maybe it isn't her, maybe it was the daddy long-legs letting himself out?

'Liv?' her familiar voice calls back at last. 'Where are you?'

'In the loo,' I yell. 'I can't come out because the daddy long-legs is back, but I need to speak to you! I talked to Edward today and it made me realise some stuff. I'm so sorry. I love you so much, you're my best friend and I'm really, really sorry—'

'Hold on,' she shouts, 'I only heard about half of that. Let me get the stupid daddy long-legs out first.'

There is a kerfuffle outside the door, along the hallway. I try to mentally follow Sam's movements, picturing her face screwed up with focus, holding the insect catcher aloft. She'll be stalking that bastard right now, rescuing me like my very own white knight. Here she is, riding in to save me—'

There is a loud shriek and then the door flies open. Sam

lunges inside, kicking the door shut behind her and landing butt first with a thud on the bathmat. She pants hard, frightened and trembly. I stare down at her. 'Oh my god, did he try to eat you?' I ask. 'I knew those daddy long-legs were bad. You see? I told you! Should we ring 999?'

She shakes her head. 'It's not the daddy long-legs.' Her lip quivers. 'It's a . . . ladybird.' Her eyes are wide with horror and now mine are wide with confusion.

'You're frightened of . . . ladybirds? Ladybugs? Those tiny little red bugs with cute little spots on their backs?'

'They're *evil*,' she hisses. 'They bite and pinch! And they have a toxic liquid they release – from their *leg joints*. Did you know that? What kind of messed up creature has toxic leg juice? And it's called *reflex bleeding*. Is that not the most horrible thing you've ever heard?'

'How did I not know that you were terrified of ladybugs?' I ask, bemused. I offer her a hand. She takes it, standing up.

'Don't you remember that was what we kept fighting over at nursery school?' she says, and I snort.

'Dude, we were, like, four.'

'We had a big fall out in Year One about it, too,' she points out. A hazy memory jogs. A tiny Sam screaming about a book – one with a giant ladybird on the front cover. Us fighting over it. Me crying at home about the fight and the mean girl who hid my book.

'God,' I say, 'our origin story was so Elphaba and Glinda.'

'I'm Elphaba!' we say at the same time. I only wanted to beat her to it.

'Either way, it hasn't really come up much as an adult. There seemed to be an awful lot more ladybirds around when we were kids. And you don't really get them inside much these days, so it doesn't come up in conversation.' She glances fearfully at the door. 'Why is it in here? How did it get in?'

'I bet the daddy long-legs brought him in with him,' I say. 'I told you they're calculating bastards. He was probably sick of you always beating him and made this plan to finally defeat you, recruiting your one natural enemy.'

'You think?' She regards me with fear plain on her face and I nod. Then a thought occurs.

'Um, did you get the daddy long-legs out before you ran away to hide in here?'

She shakes her head. 'No, they're both out there, together, in the living room. And there's no one else to save either of us.'

'Nooooo!' I cry. 'So, we're trapped?' I breathe heavily. 'We must be able to call someone!' I look about me for my phone. 'Why don't we know any of our neighbours? Why haven't we cultivated some kind of sexy ongoing flirtation with the boys across the hall?'

'Because the boys across the hall are ten and eight years old, and live with their very hostile parents who hate us,' she points out, and I nod.

'Ah yes.'

We look at each other. 'We're going to have to do this ourselves,' I say softly. 'Together. You and me.'

I see her gulp. 'Before we do, I have to say something.'

She stares into my eyes. 'I had a big chat with Arshiya—' she begins, and I interrupt.

'I had a big chat with Edward!'

We laugh with relief, then she continues, 'Look, Liv, I'm really sorry about our fight. It was all my fault. You were right, I think. There's some horrible, sadistic part of me that quite likes you making bad choices. I guess they made me feel better about my life or something. That's what Arshiya thought anyway. But I want you to know the real me – the conscious me, the non-buried-psycho part of me – only wants you to be happy and successful. I want you to make good choices and not stalk exes or date awful pricks. I want all the best things for you in the world. I think you're amazing and I'm so lucky—'

I cut her off with a sob. 'Stop it, stop it. Sam, I'm sorry, too. I was so mean, and it was totally unfair of me to blame you for me messing up my own life. I hate that I hurt you. I love you so much.'

I pull her in for a hug and in my ear I hear her reply, 'I love you, too, idiot.'

'God, you're so clingy. You have such an anxious attachment style,' I tell her hair, and she snorts.

'Shut up.'

I step back at last. 'Edward thinks I'm afraid to be honest because I worry you might reject me like my stupid parents did.'

She gasps. 'I would *never.*' She looks sheepish. 'Arshiya thinks I'm afraid to let you live your life without me because I don't want to lose you like I lost my dad.'

'You won't lose me,' I say firmly, and then we hug again. 'Not ever.'

'God, parents really fuck you up, don't they?' she murmurs into my ear. 'Even the good ones.'

'I think just existing in this world fucks you up,' I say, shaking my head. 'Our rewards are just forever chemicals and trauma.'

She draws back, looking determined. 'No. It's time to take back control of our fuck ups, Liv.' Her hands are on my shoulders. 'We need to make good choices and fight our demons.' She grins. 'By which I mean the daddy long-legs and the ladybird. They are the manifestations of our demons, and they must be defeated once and for all.' She assumes some kind of *Braveheart* energy as she adds, 'It's time to take back our land.'

I sniff. 'I assume you mean our flat. And you're right. I mean, it would be one thing if they contributed to the rent, but they don't even do that.'

Sam looks around the bathroom. 'We need weapons.'

'There's your very grimy, disgusting toothbrush?' I offer, and she considers it.

'Nah.' She shakes her head. 'I don't think insects are as germophobic as you.'

'I would argue that it's not about the germs,' I say, 'it's about the gross crud build up around the head, which you know you're supposed to change every three months—'

'All right, moneybags,' she retorts. 'We're getting off topic here.' She pauses. 'How about the toilet brush? We could, like, herd them with the brush into the plastic bit and trap them inside and—' She notices the face I'm making and laughs. 'Okay, so disgusting things are off the table.' She looks around again. 'But honestly, I'm not sure what *isn't* a bit gross in a bathroom, now I'm looking around. A hairy razor? A mouldy flannel? A cruddy soap?' She pauses. 'We really need a clear out, babe.'

'Should we just rip the showerhead out of the wall and beat them to death with it?' I suggest.

She narrows her eyes. 'No. We're not murdering them. They don't deserve to die because of our broken psyches.'

'They do,' I mutter rebelliously.

'I think if we make a run for the kitchen,' she says bravely, 'we can get the insect catcher. And then we go for it. Together. I'll get the daddy long-legs, you go after the ladybird. We'll do it for each other.'

I take a deep breath. 'Wouldn't it be healthier for us to confront our own issues? Take on our demon for ourselves?'

'Sod that!' she exclaims. 'I think it's fine to help each other. We're human beings, we all need to look after one another.' She looks me square in the eye. 'I've got your back, you've got mine.'

I take her hand, our faces serious and solemn. 'Okay, I'm ready. Let's do this.'

We turn for the door. At the last second I grab for her toothbrush. Just in case. It's got to be better than nothing, hasn't it?

And then we go.

CHAPTER TWENTY-NINE

Sweaty, broken and drained, Sam and I collapse on the sofa. It's been an intense hour of screaming and running, with a lot of IT'S ON ME IT'S ON ME IS IT ON ME GET IT OFF ME I THINK IT'S STILL ON ME OH GOD GET IT. But we've finally got the ladybird and the daddy long-legs out and any remaining open windows are now firmly shut.

Our demons finally conquered – external ones at least – I go to fetch us celebratory biscuits from the kitchen. When I return, I pick up my phone. 'I'm going to message Justin,' I say.

'What?' Sam sits up straight. For a moment she looks half excited, then remembers our new deal. 'No, you can't do that,' she instructs. 'That is not a healthy choice. You need to let him and Orla go. They will only make you sad.'

I laugh at her change in tune. 'Thank you for saying that. But actually, this isn't some humiliating "pick me" thing. I've just been afraid to be honest for so long. I want to tell him the truth.' I gasp, turning to her. 'I didn't tell you! I bumped into him and Orla.'

She echoes my gasp. 'You followed them again?'

'No!' I exclaim, outraged, as though we didn't do that very thing in Hamleys not so long ago. 'They were in my coffee shop, ordering *my* hot chocolate!'

'Not the hot chocolate with all the cream!' She looks horrified. 'That gave me a sugar headache for three days straight last time.'

'Swear to god,' I confirm. 'It was surreal.'

'Were *they* following *you*?' She looks agog. 'And wait, oh my god, didn't Orla recognise you from our podcast fan-girling? Ohhh, this is so unfair! I can't believe we weren't speaking when the maddest thing in the universe happened.'

'I know!' I giggle girlishly. 'But no, I don't think anyone was following anyone. I'm pretty sure it was just a coincidence and evidence that Justin hasn't completely changed into a different species. He's still too lazy to come up with his own ideas for coffee shops.'

'And did she remember you?' Sam is enthralled.

'Yep.' I swallow, remembering my horror. 'But she didn't tell Justin, because she is an absolute babe. She took me to one side, and we had a proper chat. She's the nicest person, it's a shame she's not single.' I grin. 'And I feel so free of it all now. I'm actually, like'—I feel my eyes widen—'*glad* for them. I genuinely thought to myself afterwards, *good for you*, and I wasn't being sarcastic!'

'Wow.' Sam is stunned into almost-silence. 'No one in

history has ever said *good for you* before, without being sarcastic. You're so evolved these days. What has therapy done to you!'

'I am evolved enough these days to realise I'm not really evolved at all,' I sigh, typing my message to Justin. 'I have a long way to go.'

I write out my message. It comes quickly and easily – a surprise even to me. There is no agonising over commas or kisses, because I am just not that invested. I want to say something straightforward, for my own sake. I'm not trying an angle or trying to force an outcome or manipulate him into saying something back. I just want to say what I want to say and then get on with my future without him. I hit send without even consulting Sam, and she looks annoyed but lets it go.

I reread the message quickly, feeling calm.

Hi Justin, nice to see you and Orla the other day. She seems great and I'm happy for you both. I wanted to say a proper sorry for the way I behaved that night when you ended things between us. You were right, we weren't good for each other, and I only regret that I wasn't more honest with us both leading up to that point. It could've saved us a lot of internet humiliation, ha. I really do wish you all the best. Maybe see you around my favourite hot chocolate place sometime. Hopefully with Orla. Take care, Liv x

Beside me, Sam makes a choking noise. 'God, you expect too much of me, Liv. You have to *at least* let me read it! I won't give you any advice, I just want to read it.'

I hand her the phone, and she scans it greedily.

True to her word, she offers nothing, except, 'Do you feel better?'

'I do actually.'

She opens her mouth to say something more, when my phone starts to ring in her hand. She gapes at it, then thrusts it at me like it's molten hot.

'It's Justin,' she whispers. 'He's *calling you.*'

'Oh my god,' I whisper back, like he can hear us. 'Should I answer?'

She shakes her head. 'I can't tell you what to do. Do you think it's a good idea? Will it make you feel better or worse?'

I stare at her, and then at the ringing phone, now lying on the sofa between us. In slow-motion, I reach for it, and hit . . . accept.

'Justin?' I ask with trepidation, half hoping it's a butt dial.

'Liv?' he answers, sounding equally horrified.

'Er, yes?'

'Hi, um, sorry for calling,' he says nervously. 'I know it's weird.' He pauses. 'Come to think of it, I don't think we ever actually spoke on the phone when we were going out, not even once.'

I shake my head though he can't hear me. He's right, I don't think we did. And I don't think it says anything good about us that we didn't.

Beside me, a wide-eyed Sam mouths, 'Shall I go?' and I shake my head again, grabbing for her hand and squeezing it.

'Thanks for your message,' he adds, and I wait, still not

knowing what to say. 'It meant a lot, and I wanted to say sorry, too. Er, properly. I don't think I have.'

'I wasn't trying to make you feel bad,' I say softly. 'With my message, I mean. I just needed to say it. For closure's sake. To end a chapter.'

'No, I know that, I get it,' he says. 'And I think I need my own closure, too.' I hear him smile. 'Hence the unsolicited phone call.' He takes a long, slow breath. 'I wanted to say that it did mean something, our time together. It wasn't nothing. But I wasn't . . . I don't know . . . fully *myself*, I guess. Or at least, I wasn't the person I want to be. I was a useless oaf, I know that, and I let myself be that guy when deep down I knew I didn't need to be. Hell, I didn't *want* to be, not really. I felt lazy and stupid a lot of the time.'

'Well,' I say lightly. 'You kind of *were* lazy and stupid a lot of the time.' He laughs good naturedly.

'That's fair,' he replies. 'But to quote the great Robbie Williams, "No one is the villain in their own story".'

I frown. 'I think George R.R. Martin said that.'

He sounds a little impatient when he replies, 'Okay, well, Robbie Williams said it more recently. Anyway, I don't think I wanted to see that there was anything wrong with the way I was behaving. The way I was treating you. I told myself that you liked doing everything for me. Y'know, it's how my mum treated my dad, and I see it happening in a lot of my friends' relationships. Not that many of them are happy.' He pauses. 'But none of that means it's okay that I acted like it. Meeting Orla made me realise that.' He laughs a little. 'Every time I act all helpless and useless about some-thing that needs doing, she does the same, but takes it even further. She's like, "Oh, you don't know how to turn the dishwasher on? Oh no, neither do I and now I've flooded the kitchen – whoops!" She's hilarious. She says she's weaponis-ing weaponised incompetence.'

I laugh, too. 'She honestly seems amazing. And I'm not just saying that. I want to be her when I grow up.'

'Me too,' he says. 'I hope I don't fuck it up.'

'Me too,' I echo.

I hear him swallow hard down the line. 'I'm sorry if it hurt you, me meeting her so quickly after we split up. I didn't intend for that to happen either. I hope you never thought I cheated or—'

'Nah,' I say simply, letting him off the hook. 'And I get it now. These things happen when they happen. You can't let someone like Orla pass you by.'

'That's . . . really . . .' he trails off. 'You're a good person, Liv.'

'Sometimes,' I acknowledge, making eye contact with Sam. 'And I'm working on being better.' I pause, thinking of the man who's been helping me with that mission. 'Thanks *alot* for calling me, *Just Tin*,' I say, knowing he won't get the joke, but also knowing it'll make Edward laugh when I tell him about it.

As we say our goodbyes, wishing each other well, I feel all glowy and light. I don't think I'll ever speak to Justin again – I don't need to – and I'm fine with that. It was what it was, and now it's time to let him go and get on with my life.

'Take care,' he says, and then — as I go to press the end call button — he says something that I barely catch. It sounds like the word internet, and then — bizarrely —*redemption*. He's gone before I can ask him to repeat himself.

I frown at the phone as Sam watches me.

'What?' she asks anxiously. 'It sounded like a really civilised, grown-up chat, until the end. What happened there?'

I shake my head. 'He said something strange as he hung up, but I didn't catch it.'

She shrugs. 'Well, he's a strange dude.'

I laugh. 'That's a fair point.'

She looks expectant. 'Are you going to call him back or message to ask what it was?'

I consider this. 'Nope,' I tell her at last. 'I need to learn to let things go.'

'Therapy has been so good for you,' she murmurs, and I nod.

'It has and I feel like I still have a lot of work to do. I'm going to stay in therapy for a while.' I swallow. 'But obvs not with Edward.'

'Oh my god,' she shrieks, picking up a cushion and throwing it at me. 'We haven't even talked properly about you snogging your fucking therapist!'

We both laugh and I stand up. 'Jesus, Sam, you and I didn't speak for less than a week and everything in the universe went down.' I head in the direction of the kitchen. 'I'll get more biscuits; this is going to be a long night.'

MorningTeaVids

78 weeks ago

RELATIONSHIP EXPERT LIV CARPENTER ON MORNING TEA SAYS CLOSURE IS OVERRATED

Liv: Aww, that advert with the puppies always makes me laugh – welcome back, viewers! We're continuing today's segment with a call from a man – for once! We don't get many of those. He wants to talk closure ...

Caller: Hello? Eloy here.

Liv: Is that a Dutch accent I'm hearing? My favourite accent of all time.

Caller: Thank you, yes! I live in Edinburgh though now.

Host: Stop flirting with the callers, Liv!

Liv: [laughing] What can I say? I'm always on the lookout for my future husband! Sorry Eloy, how can I help you today?

Caller: Right, yes, okay. So, I was with my ex for three years, we broke up six months ago, and I just can't get over it. It feels like it came so completely out of the blue and I never really got any proper answers from him. I just want to know *why*, you know? We seemed to be so happy. I thought we were going to get married. We talked about adopting kids ... And then one day he just ends things, out of nowhere.

Liv: That's so rough, I'm sorry.

Caller: I just need some proper closure. I need to have a big sit down with him, so I can ask some questions and get some real answers. I've tried to message to ask for a meeting but he just said he wants to move on, and then he's ignored my follow ups since. He's blocked me on social media so I can't DM him, and I don't think my texts are going through, so I guess he's blocked me there, too. I don't know how to get him to listen. Do you think writing a letter might—

Liv: Oh god, no, don't write him a letter.

Caller: No?

Liv: No. Because whoa, you need to back off, Eloy.

Caller: Huh?

Liv: You may not like it or understand it, but he's given you all he's going to give you. He doesn't want to see or speak to you. You can't force answers from someone who doesn't want to give them, and I'm sorry, but he doesn't owe you anything, I'm afraid.

Caller: Oh ... right.

Liv: And honestly, closure is so overrated. Even if he was willing to sit down and talk to you, I'm betting he still wouldn't be able to give you the answers you want. And you wouldn't trust them anyway. There will always be more questions in a situation like this. What could he possibly say that would heal everything? If he pointed to one particular moment, one thing you said, one look you gave him, that one thing that changed his feelings, would that help? Obsessing over it is keeping you stuck in the past. You need to realise and internalise the fact that you'll probably never get the answers you want. It's time to start focusing on you instead and your recovery from all this pain. Close the door on him and stop putting your life on hold for someone who walked away without a second glance back. Okay?

Caller: Okay.

Liv: I mean it, Eloy. Throw away that letter. I know you've already written it.

Caller: Er . . .

Liv: ELOY!

Caller: Okay, yeah I know you're right. [sigh] I'll throw it away and I'll leave him alone.

Liv: Remember what I said, closure is overrated.

[watch again?]

Liv Carpenter says closure is overrated . . .

#LivCarpenter #BBCMorningTea #RelationshipTherapist #AgonyAunt
#AdviceColumn #LifeCoach #Wisdom #LivCoolAndCollectedCarpenter
#BreakUpQuestions #Closure #ClosureIsOverrated #DutchPeopleAreTheHottest

CHAPTER THIRTY

I wake up to Sam's left big toe inches from my face. We have passed out on my bed, talking late into the night. After almost a week of not speaking, there was so much inane guff to catch up on.

She grunts awake, looking over at me blearily. 'Morning,' I say, and she looks at her watch.

'Shit, I'm supposed to be at work in twenty minutes.' She rolls over. 'Sod it, I'm calling in sick. I haven't skived in — ooh — must be at least a month. I'm long overdue.'

'Want me to call for you and pretend to be your mum?' I offer, and she shakes her head.

'No thanks, but if you could write a note to get me out of PE tomorrow, I'd appreciate it.'

'No problem,' I say.

'Can we hang out all day together doing nothing?' Sam smiles shyly. 'I've felt a bit . . . untethered without you.'

I feel the same way. We still have so much catching up to do. I want to hold her tightly and not let go.

I check my own watch. 'I would love that, but I have to go into my office to fetch some files and books. I have a meeting lined up with that domestic violence charity in a few days and I need some paperwork – my qualification certificates and that. I was also meant to be seeing Jools for a coffee at some point.'

'Oh, I love Jools!' Sam says joyfully. Her face lights up. 'She's such a style queen with those glasses – such an original.'

I won't tell her about Elton John.

She grins. 'Could we combine?' she suggests. 'Get Jools to meet us at the therapy collective office and we'll help you sort out your paperwork while we chat and drink coffee?'

'God, you're so needy.' I roll my eyes, and she tells me to fuck off.

Things are back to how they should be between us. But hopefully even better, from now on.

We get ourselves dressed and head over to my office, where we ignore the many overpriced bits of furniture I own and squat directly on the floor. It's a lot easier when you're sorting through several years' worth of ignored boxes, rammed with invoices and client notes. Jools arrives a few minutes later, bearing steaming cups of coffee that we drink greedily as we work our way through the paperwork. We're trying to locate my certificates and any old recommendation letters, but we're not having much luck. Sam has been less than helpful, instead focusing her efforts on filling Jools in on my phone call with Justin.

'God,' Jools breathes out heavily, 'I can't imagine having proper closure like that with an ex.'

'It does feel pretty good,' I admit. 'It turns out, being honest is a solid way to go. Who would've guessed.'

'And maybe Justin sort of turned out to be a halfway decent guy in the end?' Jools offers, removing her Elton John glasses and waving them about.

I shrug. 'I don't think he's an awful person or anything, but I've realised that he didn't really like me that much as a human.'

Sam pauses, hovering over a document. 'I agree, actually. I'm sorry to say it.'

'Don't be sorry.' I grin at her. 'It seems obvious now. I'm just struggling to understand why I couldn't see it at the time. He always acted like spending time with me was a chore, he never laughed at my jokes, he got annoyed when I sang to myself around the house, he thought my job was kind of stupid and boring . . .'

'Don't forget how he refused to be in any photos with you ever!' Sam adds helpfully.

'We got that one photo once!' I protest weakly. 'At Christmas.'

'You mean that one where he deliberately ruined it by scowling in every shot?' Sam asks, and I nod. Jools grimaces.

'God, yeah.' I make a face. 'He just didn't like me, did he? But why did I put up with it? Why didn't I notice?'

Jools raises an eyebrow. 'I think it's because we're taught from a really young age that boys who are nice to girls are soft. They are taught to have disdain for us and for anything considered *girly*. You can't have any girl hobbies, you can't like girl things. Pink is pathetic, romance is pathetic, crying is pathetic. Man up, where are your balls, don't be a girl. They're cruel to us, they mock our interests, they treat us with utter disdain, and we think that's normal!' She shakes her head. 'How would you know he didn't like you when we're so used to men being like that about women?'

'Oh, and plus!' Sam looks inspired. 'It doesn't help the way we tell little girls that boys being horrible and pulling our pigtails actually means they like us. We internalise that messaging too. We even make a big thing of how "nice" men are boring and give us the ick. Because we've been taught at a molecular level that boys being arseholes to us is a sexy thing.'

'Sometimes it is hot,' I mutter, thinking of every single one of my favourite smut books.

'Aaaand,' Jools' face gets thunderous. 'We've got men around us who pretend to be allies, and then vote for men who would rather let us bleed out in a car park than have any ownership over our own bodies.'

'That is depressing,' I point out after a moment of silence. 'This whole conversation is depressing.'

'Either way, Liv,' Sam says, brightening, 'you deserve someone who thinks you're brilliant. Not a person who merely tolerates your existence because you improve theirs.'

'And on that note.' Jools stands up from the floor. 'I desperately need some more coffee. Do you have options somewhere in this building? Even instant would do.'

I nod back out towards the corridor. 'There's a machine in the staff lounge at the end of the hall. She heads out and I consider her words. Why would I choose to date someone – for over a year! – who didn't like me?

I turn to Sam, who is doodling in one of my notepads. 'Do you think it's because my parents always seemed to dislike me? They barely tolerated my existence so then I thought that was normal?' I sigh as she reaches for my arm, nicely. 'I should probably stop blaming my parents for everything wrong in my life.'

'They can take it!' she says. 'And, if it's any consolation, I'm betting they didn't really like themselves either.' She turns to look me in the eye. 'Plus, they didn't even know you, so they don't get to like or dislike you. I know you inside out and I think you are excellent. I like you a lot.'

I well up a bit. 'Thanks, Sam,' I tell her sincerely, then sigh. 'There was a point back there when I really thought Edward liked me for me, too.'

'I think he did,' she says. 'Honestly! Look, I'm not saying kissing him was a sensible choice, and I'm definitely not encouraging any repeat behaviour'—she raises an eyebrow—'because that would be me falling back into bad habits and giving you bad, drama-seeking advice.' We both smile, trying not to laugh. 'But for the record, I think the chemistry between you was insane, and if not for the therapist thing, I'd have been rooting for you two.'

Jools re-joins us from the hallway.

'What are we talking about now?' she asks, and I cringe.

'Edward,' Sam says simply.

'Edward?' Jools blinks and Sam fills in the blank.

'Edward the therapist.'

'Ahaaa.' She nods. 'Of course.' She doesn't ask for more detail and I internally wince because I haven't actually told her about Edward. How awful that she obviously knows all the details. She knows I was sent for therapy with Edward, by Spencer. I imagine the whole production team probably knows. I'm sure they've been gossiping about it non-stop since I was suspended. I can't even blame them – I'd be doing the same – but the thought fills me with dread.

With my therapy time now up, it's crunch time at the studio. I haven't heard from Spencer, but surely there's still hope for my job, isn't there? There must be. They would've told me by now if I was actually sacked. And didn't Spencer say, if I completed the therapy course with Edward, then I could come back? I've done it. I've done what they asked for, they owe me a shot at returning to my slot on the sofa.

I mean, *technically,* I only did five and a half sessions. But that wasn't my fault, was it? Edward's mum got ill, so we had to stop that one.

'Your coffee machine is out of pods'—Jools shakes her head—'so I'm off to find a Costa to buy us all a nice latte.' She winks. 'You get back to Edward the therapist chat.'

'Hold on,' I say, scrambling to stand up. 'We'll come with you. We need a break, and there's a lovely coffee shop just a few minutes away.' I glance at Sam who also jumps up eagerly. 'They have the best hot chocolate ever. If your body can cope with an inhuman amount of whipped cream.'

Sam nods, then grimaces. 'Let's just hope it's not being frequented by any exes today.'

We both laugh at this, filling Jools in on my Orla and Justin encounter as we make our way down to the café. We join the long queue, chatting easily as we wait our turn. I consider how different I feel from the last time I was here. Standing in a queue just like this one, next to my ex and his beautiful new girlfriend. It feels like that happened to a different person.

We step forward at last to place our order and a large human-shaped frame fills my vision. It's a tall man with a large, expensive looking coat, and he's just shoved his stupid self in front of us, blocking our way. He's queue hopping! Who does that in this day and age?

'What the hell?' Sam mutters, as Jools and I exchange furious glances.

I open my mouth and then close it again.

I'm angry. Of course I am. And it's okay that I'm angry. It's understandable. This man just did something rude and hostile, and he should be called out.

But I'm realising in this moment that there is a certain amount of privilege that comes with getting angry. Sure, I am entitled to be angry about someone pushing ahead of me in the queue. I am entitled to tell this guy off. My sessions with Edward have convinced me of the righteousness and usefulness of anger. Women *should* be angry. It's natural and important, and we have plenty of reason to be so. In fact, I'm increasingly convinced it is actively dangerous to our health to be suppressing it. It's damaging us.

And yet. It is also dangerous for us to let it out.

As a woman in a world where men are the biggest threat to our survival, getting angry is a privilege not all of us can risk. I could tell this guy off and he could turn around and punch me in the face. He could kill me. If I'm lucky, maybe he would just call me a bitch. *Just.*

It's risky to get angry as a woman. But it's also risky not to.

So, I do it anyway.

'Hey!' I say to his back, my voice slightly louder than it should be. My instincts are screaming at me to be quiet – to hush up, to take it, to silently fume instead of saying something. He ignores me, so I do it again. 'HEY!'

This time the man turns, looking mildly surprised and irritated. He looks me up and down, his expression vaguely repulsed. 'What?' he snaps.

I open my mouth to say sorry. To ask him nicely if he made a mistake. If he somehow missed the long line of people waiting patiently for their turn. To offer him the option of pretending.

No, not this time.

'You just pushed in,' I point out. 'There's a queue and that's not okay. We've all been waiting; you can't just shove your way in like that.'

'I'm in a hurry,' he enunciates like I'm stupid and I feel the pulse of fury that wants to hurt him, fighting with my cognitive dissonance-y instinct to whimper and apologise.

'We're all in a hurry,' I explain calmly. 'Nobody is thrilled to be standing here in a queue. Nobody came here just to stand here wasting important life minutes. But it's fair. Waiting your turn is the right thing to do.' I pause as he eyeballs me with antipathy. 'So please go to the back of the queue and wait, like everyone else.'

He rolls his eyes and turns back to the counter. 'Get over yourself,' he mutters, giving none of the shits. Gnarly rage bubbles up in my belly, furious and freeing.

I clear my throat. 'Dude, I can't force you to be a good person,' I tell his back loudly. 'But I'm telling you as clearly as I can that this is really crappy behaviour and karma is coming for you.'

'Oh, give it a rest! It's not the end of the world! I'm in a hurry, I need a coffee, okay, love?' he laughs, not even bothering to turn and face me.

'DICKHEAD,' Sam yells, emboldened by my bravery.

'Stupid cow,' the man mutters back, but his tone is quieter, less sure of himself. A single, isolated woman calling him out – telling him off – is one thing, but two? That is harder to ignore; harder to bully.

Jools joins in. 'Get to the back of the line, you stupid arse,' she barks.

'Yeah!' comes a small voice from the back of the room.

A woman behind us takes a step forward.

'You're all being way more polite than I would've been,' she tells us, her face dark and thunderous. She turns to speak to the man's back. 'You are a *massive* dickhead and a total arse,' she tells his shoulders, and we watch them tighten as the woman continues. 'Why do you think you're better or more important than the rest of us here? Why is your time more valuable? I bet you do this all the time, don't you? I bet you spend your life shoving women out of the way just because you can, and because of course you matter more. I bet you just parked your car out there on double yellow lines, and I bet it's a garish metallic Range Rover with a personalised number plate that makes you feel special and important.' Her face is full of pent-up anger, as glorious insults pour forth. 'And I bet you're in a rush because you're late meeting your mistress at a seedy Travelodge where you'll bitch about your poor wife who openly hates you. I bet you buy women horrible red lingerie sets in the wrong sizes and make comments about how much they eat. I bet you text while driving and I bet you chew with your mouth open. I bet you interrupt your female co-workers and take credit for their ideas. I bet you play loud games on your phone on busy trains.' Jools, Sam and I watch the woman with awed expressions as she keeps going, a torrent unleashed. 'I bet you complain about women taking maternity leave but would be disgusted by the idea of paternity leave or joint parental leave. I bet you suddenly have to go to the loo whenever your wife asks you to do something, and then sit there having a poo for forty-five minutes. I bet you spit in public and tell women to smile. I bet you send unsolicited dick pics. I bet you—'

'Shut up!' he yells at last in a shrill voice, still facing away. He leans across the counter, his energy desperate. It's clear he wants to get away now as murmurs begin across the rest of the angry queue of mostly women. 'Hurry up with my order,' he barks at the young barista. She takes a step towards him, her face cold.

'They may not be able to stop you queue jumping,' she says quietly, 'but I can. My name's Karma and I won't be serving you. Please leave and don't come back.'

There is a moment of shocked silence and then the queue erupts into a loud cheer. Whoops and scattered applause follow as Jools, Sam and I beam at each other, feeling the release of our righteous anger.

The happy noise around the room continues as the man slinks his way, red faced and furious, towards the door. He runs out and for the hills, as a few of the queue women follow, throwing themselves at the window to catch the last of his hasty exit. 'He was parked in a *disabled space*!' one yells joyfully. 'And there's no blue badge, he's just *that* entitled.'

'Of course he is!' another yells over. 'And I can confirm he does indeed have a metallic paint job and a personalised number plate. Hold on.' She presses herself against the window, squinting hard. 'It says B1G BO1. Big boy?! How cringe!'

Everyone is laughing and shouting, full of cathartic joy and unfamiliar power. My friends and I regard each other silently, our faces sparkling with joy. *Look at what we did*, we tell one another without speaking. *Look at the power we have when we are together.*

At the counter, the barista hands us three hot

chocolates – on the house – and we tip her heavily, smiling conspiratorially at one another. As Sam and I head for the exit, we find Jools deep in conversation with the other women of the queue. She shoos us away, promising to meet us back at the office, and I catch snippets of noughties war stories. She is recruiting for the forthcoming war.

As Sam and I wander slowly back in the direction of my office, I consider how much better I feel. That was all me back there, being brave and saying my piece with dignity. And I want to give myself credit for it – but I also know I wouldn't have done it without his help. Without Edward. I look down at the overloaded hot chocolate in my hand, steam melting through the mountains of cream, and I think of his mum's cakes. How generous she was and how sweetly he spoke of her. Such a green flag. I think about his loud, warm family, who all rushed together in that moment of crisis. I think of Edward's hilarious brother, Jake, who wears all his neediness on his sleeve, in such an endearing way. I think of how he brings out that soft, big brotherly side to Edward; the one who likes to be teased and plays board games without getting competitive. I think about the family shampoo they all use that fell off the back of a lorry and must be years out of date. And how they all have such nice hair. I think about the way Edward undid those shirt buttons just before we kissed.

I think about him all the way back to the office, and collapse on my sofa, where, all at once, it hits me.

This isn't transference. The way I feel about Edward – this gooey, pathetic, marshmallowy feeling – it's *real*. I have real feelings for him. I fancy the three-piece suited pants off him, but more than that – I *like* him. He's a good person! He's kind and sweet, and curious in a non-judgemental way. And he knows *a lot* are two separate words. I'm not misdirecting my emotions, and it's not that he's my hot therapist, I just plain . . . like him.

Did I mention he's also sexy as fuck?

He's not like the men I've liked before. I've always chosen emotionally unavailable men, and yes, Edward is unavailable in other ways. But he's also open with people he cares for – *so open*! – never mind evolved and kind.

And if we've finished our sessions together, maybe it doesn't have to be unprofessional anymore to ask him out. To kiss him. To try.

God, that kiss we had was sensational. I've never felt anything like that before. I can still feel the buzzing on my lips whenever I think about it. And if the kissing was that good, what would it be like to . . .

What if I followed my own feelings for the first time? What if I see love as something for myself? What if I make a good choice – what if I *choose* someone good – instead of being flattered by being chosen? Flattered by the wrong person.

I have to tell him I like him. I *want* to tell him.

'Sam.' I sit up straight, staring at her, my chest heaving. 'I know this might not be sensible, but I think I'm going to tell Edward I have feelings for him.'

'You . . . you're *what*?' She gapes at me, and I swallow hard.

'I know he'll probably reject me, but I have to do it.' I scramble to stand up. 'You're right, I think he likes me as a person, and maybe the ethical bullshit will get in the way, but he's not my therapist anymore, is he?'

'Er . . .' Sam looks so divided. On the one hand, this is exactly the kind of crap she loves to be a part of. I can see it on her face – she wants sooo much to cheerlead me on and then watch. But she's trying to be less dysfunctional. 'Ummm . . .' she tries again, fighting herself.

'If it helps,' I say, bouncing on the spot, impatiently. 'I'm definitely doing this, whatever you say next.'

Her face breaks out into a huge, triumphant grin. 'Then GO!' she shouts. 'I want you to do this and I love this for you! Edward is the BEST! And so fit!' I grab her for a quick hug, and she doesn't resist. Then I turn to run out the door and to the lift. *I'm doing this, I'm really doing this.*

I jab frantically at the lift doors and they ding open immediately.

And standing there, as if he was waiting for me, is Edward.

CHAPTER THIRTY-ONE

Edward is standing there, in front of me, real and solid. I feel like I haven't seen him in years, and it takes all my willpower not to throw myself into his deceptively big, burly arms. I step inside the lift, trying not to stare, taking in his familiar shape.

'Liv?' he questions; surprised to see me, and I find myself unable to speak for a moment. All the excitement and energy from a moment ago has frozen in my chest and I can't think how to say any of it. I had all the words ready back in my office with Sam, and now all I have are squeaks.

'Hi,' I squeak.

He presses the ground floor button, and I stare at it in a panic as the doors shuffle closed. My first instinct is to throw myself into his arms and kiss him. To have that moment again. That kiss we shared in his parents' hallway was so genuinely glorious. I could've kissed him for hours, doing nothing more than enjoying that feeling of his rough lips against mine; his hands on my face and back. That kiss . . . it felt – I don't know – *pure*. It was kissing for the sake of kissing. Kissing for kissing's sake. I wanted more, obviously I did because I'm human and it was amazing but – in the moment – it felt like everything. It was sort of simple and beautiful. It was how kissing is meant to feel. How kissing *hasn't* ever felt for me – not properly. And I *so* want to do it again.

Instead, I clear my throat. 'How are things?' I ask, feeling the horrible hollowness of small talk ringing through my words. Our last session was just days ago. We talked in so much depth about the darkest corners of my life and now I'm treating Edward like the Amazon delivery driver dropping off my washing powder subscription. But that feels like aeons ago and everything is different now.

It's clear he hears the strangeness in my tone, too, because he laughs lightly. 'Things are, you know, pretty good. How about you?'

So formal. It's bizarre.

'Well, I . . .' I glance frantically up at the digital display. Fuck! We've nearly made it to the ground floor already. What idiot made lifts so quick?

I turn to face him because it's now or never. And I can't do never. The old Liv would've done never; she would've found another Justin.

'I . . .' I try again and he regards me quizzically.

'Is everything okay?' he asks nicely and I nod, unable to speak.

'Everything is really okay!' I tell him in a rush. 'Actually, Edward, I just stood up for myself to a bully in a queue and everyone joined in. We scared a man with a tiny penis and it was brilliant. Maybe he won't push in next time, or maybe he'll reconsider parking in a disabled bay.' I shake my head, laughing a little as I think of his number plate. 'Big Boy!' Edward looks totally confused by this, so I keep speaking. 'What I mean to say is that everything we've talked about in our sessions has really helped me. Knowing you, talking to you, has really helped me and—'

The lift dings loudly and the doors begin to open. I reach over and press the close button.

'What are you—' he asks, eyebrows drawn together, but I'm already choosing the top floor again. We start our ascent, and he looks flustered. Is this a kidnapping? Surely it wouldn't rise to that level. If the police wish to categorise it, it would be a simple lift-napping, nothing more.

'Sorry, I just need another minute with you,' I say quickly, and he frowns. It makes me giggle. 'Edward, your resting bitch face is really Karen-ing right now.'

This makes him smile and I take a deep breath, trying to re-start the speech I can't remember a word of. 'You know, spending time with you has really dampened my enjoyment of Taylor Swift,' I tell him as he looks ever more baffled. 'Say what you will for awful men who ruin your life, but they definitely make her songs more relatable.'

'Who's Taylor Swift?' he asks, eyebrows raised, and I feel a squawk of abject horror making its way up my throat – until I remember the *Twilight* prank. He's messing with me. A play-ful smile is fighting through the wide, innocent expression, and I laugh. Edward clears his throat now. 'Look, I'm really not sure I'm following a lot of this,' he says and I sigh.

Why am I talking about Taylor Swift and queue bullies when all I want to do is tell this man I like him? I'm really messing this up.

The lift dings as we arrive back at the top floor again and I groan at it with frustration. The doors open and Edward waits, looking at me expectantly.

I reach over and hit all the buttons this time, ground floor to three. The doors obligingly shut and down we go. Again.

'Look,' I begin, trying to steady my breathing. 'You told me I should start being honest about my feelings.' He turns to mirror my position, regarding me curiously. I continue in a flurry of silly words, 'And I know I'm really only at the start of my therapy journey. I'm going to carry on with my sessions and my work, but with someone else now.' An expression flickers across his face, and I quickly add, 'Not because you're not great. You've been *so* great! I will totally five star you on Google reviews or whatever, but I need to . . . I have to . . .' I take a deep breath, the lift doors dinging, shuffling open, then shuffling closed as it moves through the floors. I'm getting a bit travel sick and surely he'll start getting annoyed if I keep him lift-napped much longer. I only have seconds until we reach the ground floor again. 'Right, Edward, you know how you and your family love *Grand Designs*? And you know how I said I can't watch it because I find it too frustrating when Kevin gets you really invested in a project and then takes you around for a final look but it's miles away from being finished? It's the most frustrating thing in the world, but I am an unfinished *Grand Designs* project.'

He points at me. *'GRAND DESIGNS.'*

I smile. 'That's me. I have a long way to go yet, but I can see so many good bits glimmering in here. When I'm done, I'm going to be worth all the expense and time. I'm going to be great. And you've helped me see that. I have to do the rest without Kevin and the camera crew but being around you makes me want to be the best version of myself. You even make me like myself as an unfinished project. Do you get it? You've helped me see that I could be ... pulchritudinous.' I search his eyes, hoping he gets it.

'You're the ... water tower?' he offers in a murmur, and I shake my head.

'I hope not,' I sigh. The lift dings at the first floor. One more to go. I need to stop using in-joke metaphors, it's too confusing.

'Edward, we've finished our six sessions now, haven't we?' I ask and he nods.

'Yes, Liv, and I've emailed the *Morning Tea* producer Spencer to let him know you've completed your sessions but—'

'You have?' I feel my face light up. So, we're officially done as therapist and therapee – *and* I should be getting my job back! 'That's brilliant, and it means—'

'Look,' he tries to interrupt. 'I have to talk to you about something, Olivia. It's something I've been trying to explain for a while now.'

He looks uncomfortable and it hits me that he's going to say it, too. He likes me! He's wanted to tell me for a while!

But I want to be first to say this. I want the chance to be honest.

I grin. 'No, let me,' I say, raising a hand. 'If we've finished our sessions and you're no longer my *Grand Designs* therapist, then there's no reason we can't give *this* a go.'

His eyes widen as I gesture between us. 'I have to—'

'Please don't start with all that transference crap again, Edward,' I plead. 'Because my feelings *are* real, I know they are. And you can't deny that kiss we had at your parents' house. It was amazing and it felt so right. I'm not mad, am I? You felt it, too, didn't you? Don't tell me it was all one-sided.'

He takes a deep breath. 'Yes,' he says at last. 'It was . . . in-credible. And I have feelings for you, too, Liv – really fucking strong feelings actually – but I have to—'

'I know we have to,' I say quickly. The lift is nearly at the ground floor and I reach out, ready to again jab at the close doors button. I just need one more minute. 'And I know this is a huge thing. We've been intimate as client and therapist and it's not as easy as just deciding to move past that. I know it's a process and we'd have to work through it. It will be slow – unlike this sodding lift – and it will be difficult, and we'll have to re-learn about each other as real people again.' I swallow hard, my eyes searching his. 'But honestly? Edward?

I really don't want to bother with any of that. I just want to be kissing you right now.' I don't wait for him to reply or respond. Instead, I move in. I put my hand on his face, feeling the warmth of early stubble there. And then I reach up and kiss him.

It is easily as good as the last time. Maybe – unbelievably – even better. He kisses me back now, dropping his bag and wrapping his arms around me tightly. We pull closer, my head spinning and the whole world dropping away.

The ding of the lift pulls me back and we stop at last, staring blindly at one another for a second. I can't feel my body, everything feels far away; spinny and drunk.

In those milliseconds as we pull apart, I stare at his face in wonder. Somewhere in my brain, a kind of peace settles over me. I feel the full body relief of having said the words I wanted to say, I feel the joy of finally being honest. I feel the excitement of having kissed this man I like.

I think about the years of knowing Edward, and not really knowing him, and what these last few months have meant to me. How finding him in the chaos and ashes of my previous life has been like a miracle. I think about all those moments I've thought about him in private; in the quiet moments at night before I fell asleep. How much I thought about our conversations, about his messy eating. I think about how I can't use shampoo or wash my ears anymore, without thinking of him. How – whenever Sam asks what takeaway we should get – I think of our lunch in KFC, talking about the stupidity of English words. I think about *alot*. I think about how I've restarted watching *Grand Designs* in recent weeks – but only old episodes where all the projects have definitely long since finished.

The milliseconds pass and the doors open. Jools is standing there, waiting with her surely-cold-now hot chocolate perched haphazardly in a cardboard tray. She looks annoyed and I feel bad for hogging the lift. She blinks at the pair of us, standing stock still, too close. We probably look very sus.

'Sorry,' I try to speak, my tongue feeling swollen and unfamiliar; my lips buzzing. 'We were just—'

'Ugh, why are you talking to *him*?' she says making a face. She sticks her tongue out at Edward, then adds, 'Traitor.'

'What?' I say, completely non-plussed. Why is she ... what the hell does *that mean*? I repeat myself, 'What?'

'Just so you know, Liv.' She's glowering. 'I've not once given him a good base – not once. Viewers keep saying how sallow he looks and how orange his eyebrows are, but out of loyalty to you, I've ignored the feedback.'

I shake my head. 'What base? What are you talking about? *Who* are you talking about?'

'Edward the therapist,' she says, waving her free hand at him.

'Right ... ?' I say and glance up at him. He is frozen, staring at Jools with something like panic on his face.

'*You* know,' she continues. 'He's ... *y'know*!' I shake my head, still uncomprehending, and she continues, 'He's stolen your job, hasn't he? He's the arse that the other arse, Spencer, brought in to cover for your suspension. And now they've offered him the job. He's stolen it out from under you. And I will continue to give him orange eyebrows; my professional reputation be damned.' She frowns. 'Sweetheart, you know this, don't you? You were talking about it upstairs earlier with Sam? Why do you look so confused?'

I stare at her. I can feel Edward's eyes boring into the side of my skull. 'How would I know this?' I say, my voice trembling, my legs like jelly. 'I've not seen a single episode of *Morning Tea* since I left. I couldn't watch it, it was too real; too horrible. I didn't want to see who they had covering me on the sofa but I never thought . . .'

She shakes her head. 'But I've talked to you about the guy they brought in to cover for you. I told you the viewers don't like him.'

A vague memory of a conversation returns. I remember Jools saying something about this, something about the therapist they'd got covering my job on the sofa, but I wasn't listening, not properly. And I had no idea it was . . . Edward. No, she must've got it wrong, it can't be, he wouldn't do this to me. He would've said, he would've told them no, he wouldn't . . . I look down at my hands. They're shaking.

'But you obviously know each other.' Jools is looking between us now, confusion lighting her features. 'How then, if not from the show?' Her voice suddenly seems a million miles away.

'Look, Liv—' Edward's saying, and he sounds a long way away too.

This can't be real, can it? But there's no way Jools could

have it wrong. She's literally there, on the set of *Morning Tea* every single morning, five days a week. She's there more than almost anyone else. Even the producers swap in and out, but Jools refuses to let anyone else run the make-up room without her. Not even Andi. She says it's a Generation X thing.

So . . . it's true? Edward has been doing my job all this time and now he's stolen it from me, full-time? He's been doing it behind my back, while giving me therapy? While reassuring me and encouraging me and getting me to open up, he was spending his mornings at the studios. Was he laughing at me behind my back? Making me think he was a good guy? Telling me to start being honest and real, while the whole time he was . . . no fucking way.

'You?' I turn to face him again and I'm silently begging him to tell me she's wrong. I want him to deny it and laugh it off and gaslight me and tell me absolutely anything, just so I can pretend for five minutes that this isn't true. But the expression on his face tells me everything I need to know.

'I was trying to tell you,' he starts to say. 'I tried to tell you right away. I've been trying to tell you since the very first day, but you point blank refused to talk about the show and I—'

I involuntarily take a step back, still staring at him. Still trying to make sense of this. I told him how I felt, we kissed, and then I find out he's not who I thought. Looking at him in the hideous fluorescence of the lift lights, suddenly he's someone I don't recognise. Someone malevolent and manipulative and cruel. He's no longer my kind, sweet, benevolent Edward, he's something else entirely. He's a man who would trick me, who would lie to me. Who used me to get a gig on TV. Did he say yes to the counselling sessions, just so he could steal it out from under me? I step out of the lift, apologising to Jools in a mutter under my breath. I vaguely hear her call my name, and her look of concern is the last thing I see as I take off running down the hallway, tears blurring my vision. I make it out of the building and almost to the train station, before I really start crying.

I need to put as much distance between me and that stranger as I can.

CHAPTER THIRTY-TWO

I hear Sam come back into the apartment an hour or so later. She knocks on my bedroom door and softly calls my name, but I don't answer. I hold my breath, lying in the dark, and wait for her to take the hint.

She does, and a part of me feels disappointed. I wanted her to go away and leave me alone, but I also want her to force affection on me and hand feed me soup as I weep.

I think being human is to have a desk drawer inside you of confusing, tangled wires. You can't remember whether you need any of them anymore or what they're for – does this charge my phone, or my emotional centre? I can't ever remember so back it goes, lobbed into the drawer on top of the messy pile.

I've lost my job, I've lost Edward, I've lost the confidence I had in everything I've learned recently; the confidence I had in my future.

What was the point of any of this?

I sit up to rearrange my pillows, punching them hard into submission. It makes me feel better – marginally, but still – so I hit them even harder. Then I pick one up and scream into it.

'Liv?' I hear Sam back at the door. Clearly, screaming into a pillow is not as quiet as I'd hoped. I stand up, dropping the pillow back on the bed, and roar into the ether.

'RARGGGGHHHHHHHHH,' I yell, and Sam needs no further encouragement. She bursts in, her eyes wide and worried. When she sees me, she stares with frightened eyes as I do it again. 'RARGGGGHHHHHHHHHHHHHHHH!' She continues to look confused, regarding me for a long moment.

And then she joins in.

'GRRAAAAAAAAAAAAAAAAAA,' she tries.

'RARGGGGHHHHHHHHHHHHHHHHHHHHHH HHH!'

'GRRAAAAAAAAAAAAAAAAAAAAAAAAAAAA AAAAAAAA!' She manages to be even louder than me and I giggle. This feels good.

'RARGGGGHHHHHHHHHHHHHHHHHHHHHH HHHHH!' I shout until I run out of breath. She inhales deeply, crouching in position; ready to release her next guttural shout and—

The neighbours bang furiously on the wall. We stare at each other mortified for half a second – then burst out laughing. We laugh and we laugh and we laugh, reaching for each other to lean on, tears streaming down our faces. Sam starts choking and we both collapse on my bed, still laughing; still choking.

'That was so much fun,' she says when she is at last able to speak. 'Let's roar on a regular basis. We'll put it in our diaries for a weekly sesh, I'll send you a calendar e-vite.'

'Maybe when the neighbours are out?' I say through tears.

'Screw the neighbours!' she says loud enough for them to hear. 'They've got two kids! If they're allowed to have the volume on their stupid Playstations at a thousand, we're allowed to do a bit of roaring once a week at a regularly scheduled interval. They'll either have to learn to be out at that time – or join in.' She wiggles her eyebrows mischievously. 'We could start a building-wide scream sesh.'

'I get the feeling Mrs Finch on the ground floor could do with it,' I reply, coughing through the giggles. 'It's certainly made me feel much better. I think that might be even better than kickboxing for releasing my female rage.'

We lie there, side by side on my bed, staring at the ceiling.

'Jools told me what happened,' Sam says at last.

'Fucking Edward,' I reply calmly. 'He stole my job, and he let me think that we ... that I ... *fucking Edward.*'

'Fucking Edward,' she agrees. 'Had you already told him? Had you already found him and said what you went to say; about how you feel – felt?' She turns to look at me and, after a moment's hesitation, I nod.

'Shit,' she breathes.

'Fucking Edward.'

'What did he say though? When you said it?' she asks, and

317

I close my eyes, feeling that tangled knot of wires inside me getting more knotted and more tangled at the thought of our lift conversation. And what happened after that.

'We kissed,' I admit, remembering the feel of his mouth on mine. Feeling the shape of his fingers on my face. Reliving the way his body felt, pressed up against mine.

'Nooo!' Sam cries. 'Oh, babe.' She sighs. 'I feel terrible. The first proper test I had when it came to our newly boundaried-friendship and I failed. I immediately encouraged you to run headfirst, straight into a terrible choice. What a crappy person I am.'

'No, you didn't and no you're not!' I open my eyes and turn to her. 'This isn't your fault. Like I said, I was doing it with or without your endorsement.' I frown. 'And *you* shouldn't feel terrible, *he's* the one who screwed me over and then kissed me – twice! He's the crappy person!' I sigh. 'He *knew* how desperate I was not to lose my job at *Morning Tea*, and he casually took it from me, behind my back, not even bothering to give me a heads up that it was happening. In fact'—I sit up, pointing an angry finger—'he was pretending to help me get it back! He's the one who should feel terrible.' She nods as I sigh and then continue, 'Plus ... I'm kind of glad I said it, even after everything I found out next. It was how I felt, and – if Edward gave me nothing else – I do at least agree with what he said about me being more honest. With myself and everyone else. I need to stop pushing down my feelings. I've got to let them out. Otherwise I'm in serious danger of becoming a bitch eating crackers about the whole world. About all of mankind. About society as a whole.'

'Bitch eating crackers?' Sam frowns and sits back up. 'What the hell does that mean?'

'It's the phenomenon where, when you hate someone enough, everything they do riles you up. Even something innocuous like them eating a cracker can irritate the fuck out of you. It's actually very common, we all have something or someone we feel Bitch Eating Crackers about.'

'Yes!' Sam says loudly. 'I loathe my boss so much that even his breathing makes me crazy in meetings now.'

'He is a bitch eating crackers,' I say seriously. 'You are full BEC about him. And fair enough, actually, because he is a knob.' I pause. 'Anyway, I need to release these furious feelings, or they'll consume me.'

'Okay, so let's release them.' She turns to face me again and her expression is serious. 'How do you feel now about Edward? Right now. All of the feelings, good and bad – go.'

I consider her question and take a deep breath, sitting up straighter. 'I feel sad and angry and let down. I feel *really* disappointed. I thought he was someone I could trust and believe in. I feel stupid for not knowing he'd replaced me, and embarrassed that everyone else obviously knew.' I pause. 'I feel hurt.' My breathing gets a little ragged. 'It's uncomfortable, here in my stomach.' I move my hand to the painful centre. 'It just feels very . . . shit.'

'It is very shit,' she acknowledges. 'And is he the only one you're upset with?'

I shake my head, finding it easy to locate answers. The therapy has helped me grab onto things – internal things – more easily. 'Actually, no! I'm angry with my producer, Spencer, for doing this to me, too. Why did he say I could keep my job if he didn't mean it? Why hasn't he told me to my face that he's given someone else the role? I'm angry at Fabian, my agent, for not stopping this from happening or warning me.' I sigh. 'I guess I'm even kind of angry with Jools, even though I know it's not fair. She should've made sure I knew about Edward. And she should've quit her job in a blaze of fury and stormed out when they replaced me.' I meet Sam's eyes. 'I know, I know! That's absurdly irrational, I'm just saying it out loud.' She smiles, as I add quickly, 'And now I've said it, I'm not angry with her anymore.' I shrug. 'Also, to be fair, she did try to tell me about him and I wasn't listening. I was too much in my own head. She tried, even without knowing the history between us, and she is the best.'

'She is very cool.' Sam nods. 'But just so you know, theoretically, I would've quit my job in a blaze of fury and stormed out on your behalf.'

'That's why you're my best friend,' I say.

'In fact, would you like me to quit my job in a blaze of fury?' she offers, hope in her voice. 'I'd really love to, please tell me to do it. Give me an ultimatum if you like? If it's my job or our friendship, I'll quit right now!' She picks up her phone looking excited and I laugh, pushing it out of her hand and back down on the bed.

'Let's park that idea for now,' I tell her. 'Until we've worked out how you would, y'know, *live*.'

'Fine,' she sighs, then looks at me with a serious expression. 'C'mon, we haven't finished here. We need to dig much harder. So, tell me, why do we think Edward might've lied to you?'

'He's a little chicken shit?' I offer sweetly. She smirks but holds the silence. I tut. 'Okay, I guess . . .' I pause, then take a deep breath. 'Maybe he was worried about how I'd react.' I think about this for a second. 'We're colleagues, he was my therapist. Aaaand he'd just been witness to a very public example of how I take bad news or perceived betrayal. He might've been concerned that I would hide under a table with some kind of cake and scream at him about his mum's decor.'

'That's true.' She nods sagely.

'Okay, well, he shouldn't have taken the job in the first place!' I cry, and she raises her eyebrows.

'And why do we think he might have taken it?'

I inhale, trying not to roll my eyes at this coolheaded therapist version of Sam. Given the choice, I way prefer the drama loving bad influence. 'I guess . . . I mean, I *suppose* he probably saw it as an amazing work opportunity, that anyone would be mad to turn down. I guess Edward could see that being on TV will open him up to a whole new world of work offers and clients. Plus, well, there's very decent money involved.' I sigh again. 'But basically, if he liked me enough, he would've chosen not to hurt me.'

'To be fair, you didn't know each other so well then,' Sam points out. 'You were still ignoring him in the lift and pulling a face as you whispered about his Ken doll smooth crotch and sewn up butthole. Neither of you had figured out your feelings.'

We fall silent because I don't know that I agree with her. I can make excuses for him covering the job initially, I can just about understand him not telling me, I can even accept him taking the full-time position. But the fact is, he wouldn't have done any of it if his feelings for me were stronger than his ambition. He wants success more than he wants me.

I think about how I came on so strong both times we kissed. I made all the moves. It seems clear enough now that I was doing all the running. Maybe he liked me a little – enough for a couple of really great kisses – but not enough to overcome all of the other life stuff. Not enough to choose me.

And after a year of half-hearted crap from Justin, I know now that I deserve someone who would always pick me, over and over.

It's time to put all of this behind me. All of this question-able bullshit, all the job drama, all the Justin stuff, all my confusing feelings for Edward – all of it.

I lie back down on the bed and stare at the ceiling.

'It's been such a mad few months, Sam, such a strange summer,' I whisper into the semi-darkness. 'So much has happened; my whole world got turned upside down. I think I just need to focus on me for a while. It's time to move on with my life and forget about all of the craziness I've been through. I'm done bringing the drama and making space for men who don't deserve it – on and offline.' I give her a sad smile. 'So, I'm done. It's going to be all about me from here on out. It's the Liv Show now.'

Beside me, Sam nods. 'Good for you.'

CHAPTER THIRTY-THREE

The first week of the rest of my life flies by. I have my meeting with the domestic violence charity, and it is beyond eye opening in a horrible and soul crushing way. A nice woman named Harriet takes me around the centre and talks me through some devastating stories and statistics. I get introduced to a couple of women staying there and they tell me survival stories that put everything I've been through over the last couple of months in the kind of perspective no one ever really wants or needs, goddammit. I feel ashamed. But also invigorated. I realise immediately that I'm *desperate* to work here. I want to work here, with these women, more than anything. I want to help them. I feel excited about doing something properly important and useful for the first time in a really long time. Sure, I loved working on *Morning Tea*, but this is on another level. It feels like exactly what I should be doing.

Harriet says I can start the following Monday. There is even talk of funding in the works that could enable them to create a full-time paid position for me in the near future. Outside in the cool, summer sunshine, I skip along, my steps light. I feel myself smiling at strangers as they pass, then find a bench to sit down on. For a moment, I close my eyes, turning my face up to the sun and letting its rays perform some magic. I let it heal me.

Then I feel a little silly and re-open my eyes, hoping no one saw me trying to be spiritual.

I pull out my phone to scan through my emails, making mental notes to follow up on a couple of enquiries I've sent out. I've been researching nearby therapists and am hoping to set up some meetings with a few to see who the best fit would be. I'm determined to keep working on my mental health. Without Edward. Obviously.

I haven't heard anything from him. Not a word. Not a text, not a WhatsApp, not an email, not even a bloody video on Instagram. Nothing.

It's what I expected, to be honest, but it still hurts. More than it should.

But I'm about to email him. Along with Jamal, Fran and Arshiya – the whole therapy collective – and I know it's long overdue. I take a deep breath and type out the message. I'm giving them notice for my office space. I'll pay up for another month and then they'll have to find someone else to take over. It's the right thing to do and I probably should've done it months ago when I first got internet famous. But

I was too caught up in my own stuff at the time to worry too much about the impact my notoriety was having on my team. Either way, I'm not practising privately anymore, and I can't afford to keep renting the room – not without my TV work. So, the issue has been forced. I gulp, thinking about how much worse off I'm about to make myself as I embark on this volunteer work. But I have a feeling it'll be worth it.

The reply-alls come in quickly from Fran, Jamal and Arshiya. They're very kind and sad, telling me they will miss me, it won't be the same, and insisting I must continue attending the regular dinners.

Edward is last to respond to the group. He sends me his best wishes for the future.

I stand up, the sun not feeling so bloody healing anymore.

Best wishes for the future. Did he really just write that?

I head straight to a kickboxing class and pummel out the fury I feel, deep in my belly. The punchbag is Edward's face and those words drive my fists. *Best wishes for the future*. Has anyone ever said anything so vile to another human being? *Best wishes for the future*. Ugh, what a piece of work.

As I leave the gym, sweaty and spent, Fabian tries to call me again. My poor, beleaguered agent has been trying to get hold of me for weeks now.

Riding high on the adrenaline of kicking stuff a lot, I finally give in and answer.

'Will you – for the love of fuck – learn to fucking call me back once in a while?' Fabian rages before I can even say hello.

'Sorry Fabian,' I say, not really feeling one bit of it.

'Why are you ignoring my emails about the book, sugar lump?' he demands, and I sigh.

'Because I don't want to go into the publishers' office just to have an awkward conversation. I've had far too many of them recently. I'm spent, sorry Fabian. I'm trying not to put myself into shitty situations that make me feel rubbish anymore.'

'You owe them money,' he says sharply, and my stomach flips. 'If we have any hope of them not asking for the whole advance back, we need to meet with them face-to-face and play nice. Maybe they can be talked around about *Orange Flags*. Or maybe just persuaded not to be arseholes about it. You *owe* them.'

The fear of this stabs through my bravado. My savings are getting dangerously thin, and I've already seriously contemplated selling my car – an indulgent unnecessity bought with my *Morning Tea* money – to buy me some peace of mind. If I have to return that money, I won't be able to embark on this volunteer work for the centre. And I suddenly really, really need to do it. I can't let all those people down. We have to talk the editor around. 'Okay, fine,' I concede, adding with some sincerity, 'Sorry.' I take a deep breath. 'When do they want to meet?'

'Can you do this afternoon?'

I check my watch. 'Are you serious?'

'Yes, I just spoke to them, that's why I called again. Your editor wants a conversation ASAP. They're sick of waiting around. They need this resolved.'

I feel bad then. It's all very well putting myself first and prioritising my happiness, but it doesn't mean I can just ignore anything I don't like the sound of. I've been a child. 'Sorry,' I mumble again, and I really do mean it this time. 'Yes, I can do this afternoon. I just need to shower.'

'Good.'

We make the arrangements, and I dash home to get washed and dressed. I have just enough time to throw on some lipstick before rushing immediately back out the door to catch my train.

As I walk through the grand glass doors at the publisher's, I try not to think about how much has changed since the last time I was here. For that meeting I was arriving as a renowned TV relationship therapist with a boyfriend and my own therapy collective business, about to sign the paperwork on a halfway decent book deal. I was fussed over, I was lauded. There was fanfare and excitement in the air. There were assistants handing round glasses of champagne! There were *cupcakes*.

And today . . . well, things are certainly different, but maybe they're not so bad. My life is moving forward in a new way. I still have my Sam, and I also have this new volunteer gig.

But I can't say it feels amazing to be potentially leaving today with a cancelled contract, a massive bill to re-pay, and an indelible black mark against my name in the publishing industry.

I spot Fabian waiting in reception and he greets me coolly.

'Liv,' he says, offering only the merest hints of a double air kiss. I am massively in the bad books if he's calling me by my actual name. Which is fair enough, given what a nightmare client I've been in recent months. Or maybe this is just what you get from your agent when you're out of favour with the world and everyone on the internet hates you. Fifteen per cent of zero earnings doesn't amount to a whole lot of commission.

The editor, Jenny, comes down to greet us personally, hesitating in the lobby. For a moment I think we will have the whole meeting right here and now, in the middle of reception – with the added humiliation of the security team watching on with pitying eyes. Quick and painful. But thankfully, she turns to usher us through the turnstiles, where we take a lift up to a glass-walled meeting room. One side is lined with book posters; another features a display of recent publications. I recognise a handful and fight the urge to ask for some freebies. Now is most definitely not the time.

We sit down and there is a strange silence.

'How are things?' the editor begins, and I clear my throat. I'm fighting irritation again. Did I really have to come all the way here for this? To be dumped like this? I sneak a glance around on the off chance there is a cake stand with tiramisu.

'Fine,' I answer simply, swallowing down the resentment as best I can.

'Great, great,' she says, her eyes darting left to right. I almost feel sorry for her. This would be a horrible conversation to endure. Especially with someone who is literally infamous for throwing huge strops. 'So, look.' She leans forward across the table. 'I'll get straight to the point. This hopefully won't be too much of a problem … but we're hoping you haven't got too far with the writing of *Orange Flags* yet.' She grimaces, and I stare down at the table. I shake my head.

'No,' I admit, preparing myself for what's coming.

'Oh, that's good.' She sounds relieved. 'Phew! Because we actually think a slightly new direction might work better.'

I look up. I feel Fabian sitting up straighter beside me, too.

The editor is nodding, excitedly. 'We've been discussing it here – the team and I – and we actually think a more personal, memoir-style book might be more interesting and more exciting for readers.' She beams. 'We think you're fantastic, Liv, and we want more of *you* in this book. *Orange Flags* sounded fun and instructional, but we want more of the Liv flavour injected. After everything you've been through personally in the last few months, we love the idea of a therapist, writing about her journey, realising she still needs to work on herself.' She pauses. 'You've been in therapy recently yourself, haven't you? That's what *Morning Tea* said in their press release?' I nod, struck silent as she continues, 'Honestly, it's a better hook than yet another self-help book about toxic relationships anyway!' She laughs. 'It's more universal and more authentic. I mean, *god,* who among us hasn't felt like we know everything, only to realise we still have so much to learn?' She points to herself. 'My friends all say I'm the best at giving advice, but when it comes to my own life, I'm a hopeless case who knows nothing and makes some of the worst choices known to man.' She beams across the desk at me. 'Yours is a real and relatable story, Liv, and we'd love you to write about it.' She stops, suddenly looking a bit nervous again. 'What do you think?'

What do I think? I'm struggling to take it in. I came here to get dumped – again. I hadn't even considered any of this as a possibility.

Fabian leans in. 'I love it!' he declares, waving his hand flamboyantly. 'It's genius. I would read the shit out of that book.' He elbows me. 'Liv, honey bear, you love it, too, right, babe?'

I'm *babe* again. I frown. 'Actually, yeah, I do love it,' I say at last, meaning it. 'I think it could be really interesting.' I look her in the eyes. 'I'm about to start doing some work with a domestic abuse charity. I'd like to write about that too, once I've found my feet a little more. It would obviously involve very careful handling, and the charity's sign-off on everything, with client confidentiality, but would that be something I could include in this memoir?'

She considers this. 'Yes,' she replies slowly, the smile getting wider. 'I love that. I think that's a great angle and feels like it would give more weight to the subject matter, too. Go for it!'

My grin matches hers as Fabian claps joyfully. He reaches around my shoulder to give me a quick, happy squeeze.

'I'm so glad you're up for this,' the editor beams. 'It's always a bit awkward having these conversations, hoping a writer isn't going to be offended at the change in direction!' She laughs a relieved laugh, and I wonder at the egos she has to deal with. She continues, 'And for the record, I think *Morning Tea* were absolute idiots to get rid of you!' She laughs again casually. 'You were so wonderful with the viewers, your advice was always spot on and everyone loved you. The guy they've replaced you with is so awkward and cold. I can't believe they've given him the role full-time now!' She pauses. 'And what's up with his orange eyebrows? That make-up team clearly hates him.'

I wince painfully at the mention of Edward. I also feel something else – some other emotion – and give myself one of those full body scans. I feel . . . defensive. Poor Edward and his resting bitch face and energy. He may be awkward but he's *not* cold. Not really. Not underneath those three-piece suits and the serious expressions. He's not cold at all.

I give myself a shake. Let's not get sucked back into warm Edward thoughts.

Best wishes for the future. Remember?

The editor is still gushing. 'Honestly, I can't believe they're not begging you to come back, especially now you've had this – what would you call it? – internet redemption?' She giggles again and I regard her quizzically. Those words are familiar. I search my memory banks, and it clicks at last. There it is. Justin. That phone call we had. As we hung up, he'd said something like that. I didn't understand it then and I don't understand it now.

'I'm sorry,' I interrupt as she tries to move the conversation onto deadlines and marketing spend. 'What do you mean *internet redemption*? What are you talking about?'

She stares at me, blinking hard. 'Don't tell me you haven't seen it? You've gone viral!'

I laugh sharply. 'Er, is that a joke? I know I have! Like, three times. It pretty much decimated my life, I lost everything. It was horrendous.' I laugh harshly and she shakes her head.

'No, no, I mean in a *good* way!' She looks awkward. 'I know you didn't have a very nice time when it came to the comments on those first two TikTok videos, it must've been horrible.' She clucks sympathetically. 'But the last video that was posted? The one where you sat on the floor outside the cloakroom, ranting about men and the way women sacrifice themselves for them? Everyone loves it!' She pauses. 'I should say, *women* love it. Obviously it's deeply unpopular with a certain contingent. All the incels are ... well, not very keen. But women love you! Women like me.' She looks bashful. 'They're calling you the "Frankenstein Feminist".' I shake my head, trying to process this newly minted mantle, as Jenny continues. 'They're treating the whole thing like a battle cry. You're the new America Ferrera speech in *Barbie*. You're Saoirse Ronan on Graham Norton's sofa, reminding everyone how women have to think constantly about their personal safety. You're Julia Gillard on the front benches, decrying misogyny against women leaders. You're a feminist hero. They all *love* you. They did a whole segment on you for *Woman's Hour*!'

I shake my head at her – what's she talking about?

'I can't believe you haven't seen any of this! It's all over Instagram and TikTok. It's everywhere!' She blinks, looking incredulous.

'I've been avoiding the internet recently,' I murmur, trying to take in her words. I shake my head again. 'But that is all ridiculous. I'm not some feminist hero, I was mid-breakdown, sitting on the floor of a TGI Friday's. Women can't seriously think I have any idea what I'm talking about – I haven't a clue what I'm doing!'

'Have a look!' She throws her phone at me, the app already open. I pick it up greedily. It feels like *years* since I've let myself look at Instagram or TikTok and I've missed it so much. My hands itch with the anticipation.

Then I stop myself.

'Actually, sorry, I don't want to,' I say, handing the phone back. 'Thanks for telling me, but that all sounds quite . . . I don't know, *separate* from me. I suppose I'm glad if it's helping women and giving a voice to something important, but I really can't get sucked back into obsessing over internet comments from strangers.' I grimace. 'And by the way, I'm very aware I sound like one of those self-righteous social media puritans right now and I want to make it very clear I generally have no willpower in any other area of my life, but right now'—I nod—'I really want to focus on doing things that make me feel better, not worse.' I glance over at Fabian. He looks almost as shellshocked as I must by the news of my latest viral outbreak. I thought he was all over the internet, but maybe he's been having his own life epiphany. I turn back to Jenny, continuing, 'And this book sounds really great. It's exactly what I want to write. Thank you so much for giving me this opportunity.'

'I'm so glad you hadn't done too much on *Orange Flags!*' she says with relief, and I nod, realising how much more excited I am to write this book instead. Like, I want to run home right now and get started.

Fabian takes over. 'Actually, I know for a fact that Liv had done a *lot* of work on *Orange Flags* – despite what she just said – and since this is a whole new subject matter,' he begins in full-on agent mode, 'I think we should discuss an amendment to the payment we'd previously agreed.' He glances at me, his eyes twinkling. 'An *improvement*.'

Jenny half smiles like she knew this was coming. 'I think we might be able to come up with something,' she says, and I find myself breathing out, smiling widely.

More money? Thank god for that.

As we leave the building, Fabian grabs me for a proper hug. 'I knew it would all work out!' he shrieks happily. 'Listen, babe, schnookums, pumpkin pie, I'm sorry for being such a bitch to you lately. I know you've been going through it.'

I hug him again. 'You haven't really been a bitch. Sorry I haven't exactly been the ideal client.'

'Nonsense, you're a dream.' He waves his hands as we head off to the station. 'You should see how badly some of my other clients behave. Someone should film *them* and stick it on stupid TikTok.'

'Speaking of . . .' I side-eye him, laughing. 'I thought you were all over that app. How did you miss my latest rise to notoriety?'

He looks sheepish. 'I may have been slightly off my game lately. I was in a fuckboy situation, and it was taking up all my mental energy.'

'I hear that,' I sigh, thinking of all the messy relationships I've been in over the years. Maybe Justin wasn't quite in the fuckboy category in the end, but he was still soooo wrong for me.

I'm happy to be single, I realise suddenly. How new for me. How exciting!

Beside me, I clock Fabian's expression.

'What?' I ask with trepidation. 'Who was it? What did you do?'

'It was Spencer,' he admits, looking mortified.

I stop dead in my tracks. *'SPENCER?!'* I shout. 'The fuckboy who's had you off your game was the awful human toad, my former producer at *Morning Tea*?!'

He nods solemnly. 'Sorry.' He pauses. 'But I swear I'm done with him. For good this time. He's hateful.'

I stare at him with horror for a moment, then burst out laughing. 'Oh Fabian. You need to work on your self-esteem issues. You deserve so much better.' I raise my eyebrows at him. 'You better make an appointment.'

He laughs, long and loud, then grabs my arm, looping his through mine. 'Well, my darling pookie, sod Spencer the toad man and sod *Morning Tea*. Who needs them anyway? They'll regret losing you. And he will definitely regret losing me.'

'Honestly, I think even if they did come crawling back now, I'm genuinely not interested,' I tell him, and I suddenly, really, really mean it. My words are not coming from a place of bitterness, or anger, or rejection. I just don't want to do that job anymore. I had fun there for a while, but I'm excited to start this new challenge. To do something *real*.

Fabian sniffs. 'Well, I hear on the grapevine that it's not going well with the new guy they've got full-time on the sofa anyway, so I'm expecting a begging call from that snivelling little louse, Spencer. It would delight me no end if I could tell him you're not interested and to go fuck himself.' He sneaks a look at me. 'But perhaps we'll see how much money they're offering first.'

I laugh, then feel a stab of pain for Edward. 'Are you just saying all that to be nice, or is it really not going well for Edward?'

'Edward?' he sounds distracted. 'Who's Edward again?'

'Try and stay on topic, Fabian,' I tease. 'Edward the therapist. The guy you made me have six sessions with. And *Morning Tea*'s new relationship counsellor on the couch.'

He looks at me with surprise. 'You mean *your* therapist? Sexy Edward in the suits?' He shakes his head. 'Didn't he tell you, babe?' He sniffs. 'He did it for a few weeks and they offered him the job, but he turned them down flat. Not interested. And believe me, I know how much they were offering him. It must've hurt. No, they had to get some awful therapist called Paul for the full-time gig in the end. Really cold and unfeeling – and not even sexy to make up for it. Everyone hates him.'

I stop dead in the street. Fabian stops too, looking at me questioningly.

'What do you mean?' I ask. 'Why would Edward turn down the job?'

He shrugs. 'Well, I don't think he ever wanted it in the first place, to be honest. I'm reliably informed – because I'm informed about everything, darling, especially when shagging the head producer – that Edward was put in quite a tricky position. He was initially offered the interim role, covering for you while you were off. We were trying to persuade him to take on those six weeks of therapy sessions with you and Spencer kept pushing him to also take the temp job on the show.' Fabian wiggles an eyebrow. 'I think that little toad knew how popular Edward's ... *look* would be with viewers.' He smiles like he's picturing him. 'Anyway, apparently Edward kept saying no, but then Spencer, the awful little shit, told him the only other couch therapist he could get on short notice would be replacing you for good. So, Edward was forced to choose between taking over for a couple of months, or your job being given to someone else altogether.'

I start walking again and Fabian falls into step with me.

My head spins.

Edward didn't want the job. He only took it to keep it safe for me. He turned down the full-time role.

For me?

Why didn't he tell me!

What if . . .

No, that's ridiculous.

I can't think about this. My life is finally coming together again. I'm back on track. I've got my new role with the charity. I've got this book – this memoir! – I'm excited for. Plus the promise of some financial security. Why would I complicate things by questioning this decision I've already made?

Because what if it was a decision made on a faulty premise? Fabian and I reach the station and say our goodbyes, heading in different directions. Me for home, him back to work. I climb on board my train carriage, my head spinning, still trying to process what Fabian said. This feels like such a mess.

I have to stop this. I have a plan, a new future of my choosing. One that is healthy and uncomplicated. Edward and I would always have been dysfunctional. He was my therapist, for goodness sake! We'd never really be able to get past that. It's unethical, it's broken, it's wrong headed. And I don't want to make those kinds of choices for myself anymore.

There. Decision made and it's the same one as before. Better choices. It's the right thing to do.

No more Edward.

And that's that.

CHAPTER THIRTY-FOUR

TWO MONTHS LATER

The text comes at lunchtime on a Friday.

It's a warm, blustery day in late October and I'm in the office at the charity centre, having a break. I'm halfway through writing a chapter about being the Frankenstein Feminist. A moniker I'm still known by around the centre. Mostly, everyone thinks my brush with fame – or notoriety – is hilarious, but a few of the women look at me with wonder, like I'm some kind of celebrity. One of them said my rant inspired her to get away from her husband. I went home and cried a lot after that.

It's been a genuinely amazing experience, working here. I wake up every day ready to bounce out of bed and into work. I never felt like this with *Morning Tea*, not even on the best of days.

I'm making a difference. It's really genuinely special and I'm grateful.

The text is from Arshiya.

We have been having a raging debate about whether to invite you to the therapy collective dinner – which is tonight btw. The woman who took over your office can't make it, so there's definitely room at the table. Obviously everyone wants you there, but some felt it would be weird for you since you left, and you'd probably rather not. Either way, I'm overruling them and insisting you come. It's from seven tonight, at Edward's apartment. Please come. We really miss you. But – for the record – I'm so blown away by what you're doing at the charity. So proud xx

The text fills me with such a strange mix of emotions. For a minute, I struggle to grab onto them. Every time I think I've got a handle, they slip away. How do I feel? *How do I feel*? I don't know. Shit, I really don't. I've become so accustomed to naming my emotions in recent months, but this? I just don't know. I desperately want to call my new therapist, Dina, for advice, but I resist. I don't want to start using her as a crutch, not when I'm finally feeling quite mentally good.

Also, we haven't got to a place yet where she knows the full backstory of these last few months, and I don't think we could cram it all into the five and a half hours we have left of the day before this dinner deadline.

The therapy collective get together is tonight. At Edward's, of all places! Do I want to see them? Do I want to see *him*?

I re-read the message, wondering what to do.

'*We have been having a raging debate about whether to invite you . . .*'

I feel pretty sure which side of it Edward would've been on. After all, who the hell would want their former therapy client, slash former work colleague, slash former two-time-snoggee, to pop over to their place for a surprise catch up? I can't even blame him for arguing against this, it sounds horrific.

And yet.

Not so horrific.

There is a pull in my stomach; something magnetic. It's whispering *Go*. I've heard that voice before. It's the one Sam used to love feeding; the one who loved drama and made stupid choices.

And yet.

I haven't seen any of the group since I left. It would be really nice to see them and catch up; to find out how their lives have been.

But maybe these are just excuses. Maybe they're the lies I've always told myself when I wanted to do something wrong. Maybe I'm just looking for any old reasons, because the truth is, nice as it would be to catch up with Fran, Arshiya and Jamal, it's Edward I really want to see.

Perhaps we could put things to rest at last? Get some closure? Like I did with Justin on the phone that time? I could say sorry to Edward for judging him so harshly during our last conversation in the lift. I could thank him for the work he put into our therapy sessions together. We could part as friends. Or at least, non-awkward-and-non-weird former acquaintances?

I think about how much better I felt after I had that chat with Justin. We were able to have the most civilised conversation, admitting faults on both sides and saying sorry. What if I could have that with Edward?

And ooh, I *have* just had my hair done. I've finally fixed that bloody fringe and it looks great. It would be such a shame to waste it. I wonder how Edward's hair is looking these days. I haven't managed to get hold of any old Vidal Sassoon despite my best efforts. Apparently it was discontinued in 2002, so god knows how Edward's mum got hold of her supplies.

Before I can change my mind, I pick up my phone, my heart thumping in my chest, and quickly type out a message.

I'll be there. Can I bring Samira? X

Her reply comes immediately.

Why not? Lol. Tell her the usual rules apply x

I message Sam, knowing how excited she will be about this. Things have been a lot healthier between us since our gamechanger chat a couple of months ago, and I know her continued sessions with Arshiya are helping her massively. She's even started applying for new jobs and has a couple

343

of interviews lined up in her mission to escape her dreadful boss.

OMG YES BABE!!!

Her reply comes back within seconds. Because, sure, we're both a lot mentally healthier, but we are still human beings who like a bit of stupidity in our lives.

The rest of the day passes too quickly, and I don't feel the least bit ready when we find ourselves waiting nervously, several hours later, outside a tall front door. Sam takes my hand and squeezes it for moral support as I ring the doorbell. My heart is hammering as I wait for him to answer.

But it's not Edward who opens the door. It's Arshiya, and she leaps on me with excitement, pulling me inside.

'Liv!' She looks genuinely thrilled to see me, and I find myself grinning back, feeling the same way. Fran piles in for the hug, and then so does Sam. We all squeeze one another tightly as we bundle through the hallway and into the living room.

I hadn't realised how much I've missed this lot. We hug for ages, and I only pull away because I can feel eyes on the back of my neck.

I turn, searching for the source of the heat, and land on him. On Him. On Edward. He's standing towards the back of his large living room, watching. He's in conversation with Jamal, but he's watching me.

He looks great. His hair is glorious and thick – well done

Gore Vidal – and his face is clean shaven. For once, he's not in one of his fancy suits. Instead, he's wearing a surprisingly tight white T-shirt, tucked into blue jeans. It's all very At Home with James Dean, and boy, is it working for him.

I hold his gaze, and for a moment he doesn't smile. But then he does. Tightly. He raises the glass he's holding by way of a greeting, and I nod back. It is the real life equivalent of *Best wishes for the future.*

I turn back to Fran, Arshiya and Sam, feeling a coldness in my belly. What did I think he'd do when we saw each other? Throw himself across the room to hold me, upending coffee tables as he went?

I mean, that would've been lovely, actually. Kind of out of order that he didn't.

Arshiya is speaking and I tune back in to hear her say, '. . . I just think it sounds incredible, and I was wondering if you know, do they have any more space for volunteers?' Her eyes search mine. 'I could do a day a week at least – maybe more if they needed.' She's talking about the domestic violence centre where I work.

I nod, excited by the prospect of working with Arshiya again – and bringing in more support for the charity. 'Definitely! They always need more volunteers. I'm sure they'd be really grateful,' I tell her. 'I'll email over some info on Monday. Actually,' I say shyly, 'as of this week, I'm no longer a volunteer anymore. They've found the budget to take me on. So, I'm doing four days a week with them. Then working on the book at home on Fridays.'

'That's so great!' Fran gushes, taking a big swig of their wine. They look a little tipsy actually. And sound it when they continue, 'Mate, you look sooo happy. We really miss you around the collective. It's shit without you. Some people around here are *dicks*.' I make eye contact with Arshiya – who looks alarmed – and then Sam – who looks delighted. Fran leans closer, their breath somewhat overpowering. 'It was good that you got out when you did, really. And you're obviously really enjoying the new job, so it's all worked out well.'

I clear my throat, keen to stay on safe ground. 'I honestly am loving it,' I tell them truthfully. 'It feels so different – I feel so different.'

'You're really helping people,' Arshiya tells me solemnly. 'My mum, she had to stay in one of those places for a while when we were little, and they, well . . . they saved her, quite honestly.'

Beside me, I can practically feel Sam's eyes bugging out. Arshiya spots it and she shoots her a warning look. 'Sam,' she says carefully, 'don't go getting excited. That's all the human, personal info you'll be getting from me tonight.'

Sam nods silently. 'This is a safe space,' she tells her, and we all start laughing. She brightens. 'Speaking of workplaces, my awful boss quit today!'

I turn to her, gaping. 'What? No way!'

'I wanted to tell you in person,' she says excitedly. 'Apparently, he was the subject of a massive internal investigation – something to do with appropriation of admin funds – and was about to be sacked, so he beat them to it.

But it was proper unhinged stuff. He came storming out of the CEO's office, shouting about being betrayed. He then yelled at the whole office about traitors and started throwing staplers.'

'Do offices still need staplers?' I murmur, awed.

'It would seem so,' Sam confirms. 'And then he took off his tie, put it around his head, and tried to steal a computer.'

'Let's hope no one was filming it,' I say, sombrely, with too much wisdom.

'He would deserve to be put on TikTok,' Sam says with conviction, and we grin at each other.

'I'm more than happy to pass along my viral sensation mantle to him,' I say.

Fran leans even closer. 'I still see you pop up on my timeline a lot,' they say mistily, wobbling slightly. 'People sharing the Frankenstein Feminist, crusading all over social media, empowering women. Bloody cis men.' They shoot a dark look across the room at the two cis men here – Jamal and Edward.

Sam and I exchange a discreet glance, wondering the same thing: What the hell has been going on over at the therapy collective?

I snort, trying to keep things light. 'Yeah, well, being the Frankenstein Feminist is certainly better than being Tiramisu Girl.'

'Or Cheesecake Woman,' Sam offers helpfully.

'Either way.' I side-eye her. 'It's not a bad online legacy. The only part of the internet that still hates me is the manosphere. But I can't tell you how fine I am with a bunch of incels in their mums' basements ranting into their little boy headsets about me.'

Fran roars at this as the rest of us smile politely. They start talking about incels and snakes and politics – it's becoming clear that they're going through something.

I guess every therapist has their own issues, not just me. Every person.

I glance at Sam again, wondering if we can extract ourselves from this conversation, but it's clear my flatmate has the opposite intention, shuffling even closer to Fran and their drama. I sneak another look across the room. Edward's no longer standing in the corner with Jamal, and my eyes dart around frantically, trying to find him. I can't see him, where has he—

And suddenly he's there. Standing beside me, shoulder to shoulder, taking over my personal space. The woody smell of him fills my nostrils. I didn't even know I knew his smell so well until I am breathing it in. It sends all kinds of familiar sparks shooting through my unprepared body.

'Olivia,' he says, his head tilted sideways, looking down at me.

'Edward,' I reply, fighting the urge to laugh. It's all so formal. He places a hand on the small of my back. The warmth of it radiates through me.

'Look, can I—' he begins, speaking to me in a low voice. I turn to face him properly, feeling the heat coming off the rest of his body. 'Can we—'

We're interrupted by Jamal shouting from the kitchen about something burning.

'Dammit,' Edward mutters, heading off at speed towards the kitchen. I feel suddenly very thirsty, watching him go, and look around for the wine. Maybe I should join Fran in the bitter drunk club.

As we sit down for dinner, I find myself seated across from Edward. A part of me wants to stretch my legs out to touch his but he's got them carefully and strategically tucked underneath himself. The message is clear.

'We're so glad you came tonight, Liv!' Fran shouts loudly from down the end of the table.

'Thanks, everyone,' I reply warmly. 'And thanks loads for inviting me.'

'You're welcome,' Fran is still shouting, but there's much more in their voice. Much more *unsaid*ness. They sound even more pissed off. The table looks down at them. They raise an eyebrow. 'C'mon, let's not be fake about it.' Fran takes another long swig of their wine. Sam's mouth gapes open – she's *enthralled*.

Arshiya tries to interrupt, 'Fran, let's not—'

'Because not *everyone* wanted Liv to come, did they?' Fran yells.

I stare down at the salad on my plate. I'd decided to avoid the messier foods, given who is sitting across from me, but now I wish I had something more exciting to focus on.

'Fran!' Jamal says sharply, but they're undeterred by the table's hostility.

'We had a little argument about it actually,' they explain, nodding in my direction. I stay staring down, thinking about Arshiya's message.

We have been having a raging debate about whether to invite you ...

I hadn't taken that very seriously. I thought she was being playful. I'd taken Arshiya at her word that they were just worried about making an ex-colleague uncomfortable. But it's clear Edward didn't want me here. He *fought* to stop me coming.

I shouldn't be here.

Edward finally speaks. 'Fran, that's enough now.'

'Fine,' they say, sounding like it's very much not fine.

We eat in silence.

I daren't look up.

I really shouldn't be here. I wasn't welcome. I'm an interloper. I was the troublemaker when I worked with them, bringing my internet drama to their doors, ruining the collective's reputation and dragging Edward into things. And when I finally do the right thing and leave, here I am anyway, months later, still forcing myself into their private evenings together when I wasn't wanted.

I shouldn't have come.

'Hey, look, I'm going to ...' I push my chair back awkwardly, feeling a lump in my throat. 'I need to get home actually. I've just realised I've got a whole bunch of work I need to ...' I don't finish my sentence; I stand instead and turn on my heel. Behind me, I hear Sam exchanging sharp words with someone as I take off for the front door. I hear her footfall behind me, but I've got the front door open before Sam can catch me. I make it outside before her hand lands on my shoulder. I turn and—

Oh.

It's not Sam. It's Edward. He looks upset.

'Olivia,' he begins, '*Liv*.'

'What?' I snap, then inhale, trying to get my emotions under control. 'Look, I'm sorry,' I continue, 'I know you didn't want me to come tonight. And I'm so sorry I've caused tension with the team. But I'm going, okay? I'm leaving – you got what you wanted. You can get back in there and enjoy your evening without me causing problems. Tell Sam I'll see her at home.'

He frowns at me. 'You're wrong.' He pauses. 'I'm the one who told Arshiya to message and invite you earlier,' he says softly, looking pained. 'I want you here. I want you ...' He swallows. '. . . here.'

'You do?' I can't look at him.

He sighs. 'If you really want to know what that was all about, it was Jamal. He and Fran fell out earlier. They felt he was being two faced and unkind, but Fran doesn't know the full story. Jamal was the one who said you shouldn't come to the dinner.'

'Jamal?' I ask, feeling hurt and confused. I thought we'd always got on just fine.

'It's not—' Edward sighs again, this time with frustration. 'It's not anything to do with— Look, Liv, he was just trying to protect me, all right?'

'Protect you?' I blink.

Edward bites his lip. 'He didn't want you to come tonight because he knew it would mess with my head.' I look up now properly, searching his eyes as he continues. 'He thinks you make me crazy – and I guess you do! You have done for years! I've been so madly in . . .' He swallows again. 'I seem to have a habit of making very unprofessional choices when you're around. I said yes to being your therapist when I knew I shouldn't; I said yes to being on that TV show when I knew I shouldn't – both times because I thought I was helping you. I came to a dinner at your house. I . . . kissed you. I kissed a *client*!' He waves his hands around, looking so untethered. 'I nearly ruined my career, undermining all my own ethical guidelines. I nearly fucked everything up that I'd worked for, and Jamal was with me through all of that. He was who I was confiding in.' He sighs. 'And then you quit the group, you left the office, and I was even more of a wreck. Jamal had to pick up the messy pieces. He had to look after me when I was crying on his shoulder every night, watching old videos of you giving callers advice on *Morning Tea*. I couldn't stop talking to him about bloody tiramisu.'

I smile at this because I can't help it. But my head is spinning over his words. Edward was upset about me? He was a wreck? He cried over me . . ? God that's so hot.

So wait . . . what does this mean? What did he say? Edward . . . loves me? I can't quite fathom it. He *loves* me? Did he say . . . years?

'But why didn't you message or reach out?' I ask weakly.

He blinks. 'I thought you hated me. Our last conversation . . .' He shakes his head. 'You felt like I'd betrayed you, like I'd let you down. And I felt like I had. Plus, I still didn't know if how you said you felt was just transference or – I don't know – a rebound after Justin.' He smiles wanly. 'But then you came tonight. And the way you looked at me . . .'

'I was so desperate to see you, I couldn't stay away,' I admit, something in my chest loosening and releasing. 'And I'm so sorry for making you feel like this. I had no idea.'

'Well.' He smiles again. 'I guess it's good that I was able to maintain my professional façade for at least some of the time.'

'You were so goddamned professional,' I say, wishing he was in one of his fancy three-piece suits, so I could undo a shirt button. 'Apart from all the kissing.'

'There wasn't *that* much kissing,' he replies, biting his lip again. I can feel his eyes on my mouth. We inch a little bit closer, staring in wonder at each other. My body temperature is rising with every passing second.

'There could've been more kissing, I guess,' I concede.

He steps even closer. 'There could be so, *so* much kissing,' he murmurs, and then – at last – he reaches for me.

ViralVideosTranscribed

two weeks ago

FRANKENSTEIN FEMINIST GETS HER TIRAMISU AT LAST – AND BAGS HOT NEW BLOKE!!!

LC: . . . And just so you know, I will never, ever wash your pants and—

Waiter 1: Sorry to interrupt, Ms Carpenter, we just wanted to say we hope you've enjoyed your dinner. We're so glad to have you back here.

LC: You guys are so nice. Sorry about, er, the last time . . .

Waiter 2: There's no need to apologise. In fact, it brought in a lot of business for us.

Hot Bloke: The dinner was lovely, thank you. And Liv won't stop going on about your cheesecake, so I had to check it out for myself.

Unknown: Excuse me! Hiya! Sorry! Can I get your autograph, Liv? I'm a big fan! [clears throat] 'I have love in me the likes of which you can scarcely imagine and rage the likes of which you would not believe. If I cannot satisfy the one, I will indulge the other. I AM FRANKENSTEINNNNNNNNNNNNNNN!' That was brilliant, that was!

LC: Er, thank you very much.

scratch of pen on paper

Unknown: Thank you so much! Do you think you'll ever be back on Morning Tea? It's rubbish without you. Both the guys they got to replace you sucked, especially this latest one.

Hot Bloke: [clears throat] Awkward.

LC: [laughing a lot] No, I don't think so. But never say never. They have invited me back as a guest a few times now, but I prefer Woman's Hour these days. There are some brilliant people that work on Morning Tea though. Particularly in the make-up room.

Unknown: Can I just quickly ask you something about my partner? They're—

LC: It was really lovely talking to you, but I'm going to get back to my dinner.

Unknown: Oh right, yeah, of course!

LC: I will say that you seem like a brilliant person, and it's easy to forget that when you have a lot of hormones rushing around – not to mention all of society crushing you with their expectations and opinions – so remember who you are and make sure you like the person you are when you're with them.

Unknown: Wow, that's amazing. I will.

LC: And I think everyone could benefit from some therapy. I certainly did – and still do.

Unknown: Thank you Franken— er, Liv. Bye guys.

Hot Bloke: [murmuring] Nice boundary setting. God, you're brilliant. Shall we get some cheesecake?

Waiter 2: If I may, we actually *do* have some tiramisu on the menu this evening.

LC: No way!

sound of chair scraping

Waiter 2: Er, madam? I appreciate the hug, but there's really no need.

LC: Sorry.

Hot Bloke: Two tiramisus, please!

Waiter 2: No problem.

sound of waiter walking away followed by the sound of lots of kissing

[watch again?]

"everyone could benefit from therapy"

#FrankensteinFeminist #TiramisuGirl #CheesecakeGirl #Hilarious
#LivCarpenter #BBCMorningTea #RelationshipTherapist
#PublicMeltdown #PublicFreakout #FunnyVids #InternetRedemption
#TGIFridaysHasTiramisu #StillDontKnowWhatTiramisuIs
#HotNewBoyfriend #SexyHair #WhatShampooDoesHeUse

[shared 214,089 times]

EPILOGUE

YOUR ANGER JOURNAL

"Anger is never without a reason, but seldom with a good one"

– Benjamin Franklin

Ugh, shut up Benjamin Franklin!!!! You're such a know-it-all. You weren't even President. I don't think?!

<u>Monday:</u>
What happened?

Edward took too long getting back from work because of a train stuck in a tunnel.

How did you feel?

Frustrated and wretched because I miss him all the time and it makes me feel all needy and pathetic. But then he turned up with flowers, and I don't care that they're a cliché, they make everything better. I'm looking at them now and they're making me smile. My attachment style is flower-based these days.

<u>Tuesday:</u>
What happened?

One of the survivors I work with was upset because we couldn't get the police to take her seriously about her ex.

How did you feel?

So ragey, you wouldn't believe. Like, throwing tiramisu levels of ragey. But I took whatever steps I could to help her, and then went to a kickboxing class where I clean took a punching bag off its hook with one of my kicks. Proudest moment of my life.

<u>Wednesday:</u>
What happened?

I finally sent in the manuscript for my book — hurrah! — and Fabian immediately called to say well done. But then the conversation got a bit heated when he said my old boss, Spencer at <u>Morning Tea</u>, had called again about me coming back to the show. And then he admitted he was sleeping with Spencer again. Yeugh.

How did you feel?

Frustrated because I've told Fabian over and over that I'm not interested in going back to my old job at <u>Morning Tea</u>. I truly LOVE what I do now. And also annoyed because Fabian deserves sooo much better. Not to mention that Spencer deserves so much worse. Why don't people listen to my advice????? I'm a trained professional!!!!!!!

<u>Thursday:</u>
What happened?

Edward just arrived and he—

I gasp. 'Don't read over my shoulder!'

'I wasn't!' Edward protests, moving away and across the kitchen. He's got a black cherry yoghurt in one hand and a tiny spoon in the other. The effect is absurdly childish, and for a few seconds, I silently watch this proper adult in his three-piece suit, eating baby food while clutching a baby spoon.

He's in the navy suit today – which he knows all too well is my favourite. It does something to me. Something inappropriate.

I hug my anger journal to my chest. 'You're not my therapist anymore, *Ed*, you haven't been in a long time now.'

'Very glad to be relieved of that job,' he retorts casually, spooning more pink yoghurt into his mouth. 'I'm not qualified enough to cope with such a disastrous *Grand Designs* project. You're way over budget and we still haven't even started on the landscaping.'

I grin, narrowing my eyes at him. 'That's it, I'm putting you in my anger diary now. My therapist will have a field day with what you just said.' My eyes travel down his front, where a blob of yoghurt has landed on his tie. 'I'm also telling Dina all about your terrible eating skills.'

He picks up his tie, regarding the mess. He frowns, then laughs. 'My mum would be appalled.' He cocks his head in a way I find irresistible. I fight the urge to leap up and rugby tackle him to the ground, ripping off that tie and licking any errant yoghurt off him, wherever it may have spilled.

'As if I'm not already in there,' he says teasingly, nodding at the anger journal.

'Oh, you are. Big time,' I confirm, giving him an enig-matic smile.

'Quite right.' He nods, then pauses. 'When is your next session?'

'Monday,' I confirm.

He moves closer to join me on the sofa, his energy soften-ing. 'Are you going to tell Dina about the conversation you had with your mum?'

I make a face. 'I don't want to.' I pause. 'So yes.'

'I'm so glad I'm not your therapist anymore'—his voice is grit—'because I no longer have to be neutral and careful, and I can just call her a total arsehole.'

I smile at the anger in his voice, feeling warm and loved and supported. 'Agreed. But I'm still glad I reached out. At least I can say I tried one last time, you know? I tried to re-connect, I tried to have it out, I *tried*. And she didn't want to know.'

I think again about the brief phone conversation I had with my mum this week. I'd been surprised she even picked up the phone to me, but having done so, it was immediately clear she regretted it. She made no effort as I attempted small talk, giving me one-word, closed-off answers and sounding distracted and disinterested. When I tried to bring up my childhood, she immediately got defensive. No part of her wanted to hear what I had to say, never mind taking account-ability or working things through. Some people want to stay as the water tower, I guess.

But at least I tried.

'Anyway.' I shrug. 'Now, I can move forward with my

life, knowing I did my best and that not having her around is definitely the right thing for me. I haven't lost anything, because there was never anything to gain.'

'I like that,' Edward says thoughtfully. 'Is that one of Liv's mottos?'

'Actually, I heard it on a podcast the other day,' I reply nonchalantly. I feel Edward's eyes on me.

'Podcast?' he enquires, and I studiously stare down at my anger journal, doodling words around the inane quote at the top.

'Uh-huh,' I confirm.

'Liv,' he says in a warning tone, and I chance a glance up. He's put down his yoghurt and is regarding me semi-seriously.

'What?' I ask innocently, then sigh. 'Okay fine, yes! It was Orla's podcast! You caught me. But it's not about stalking her and Justin! I couldn't give a fig about Justin anymore.'

'I know that.' He looks amused. 'I'm not worried about him. I actually think you're half in love with Orla and I'm trying not to find it threatening.'

'I'm not!' I say weakly, knowing I don't sound all that believable. 'Or – if I do love her – it's mostly platonic.' I pause. 'And I definitely love you *more*, so it's fine. I choose you.' He laughs good naturedly as I continue. 'Either way, I only listen to her podcast because it's so good, not because I am obsessed with her anymore! She had Alison Hammond on her show the other day! Who could resist the goddess Alison? And Carol Vorderman is coming back on as a guest next week.' I sigh. 'I am just one person, Edward, you cannot expect me *not* to listen to that. Plus, it is my moral imperative to support other women in hearing about their lived female experience.'

Edward frowns. 'Is that a real thing? It sounded like it might be made up nonsense.'

'It sounded quite cool though, didn't it?' I brighten.

He comes to sit down beside me, and I eye the small wet stain of wiped off yoghurt on his tie. He pulls me into his body, and I inhale the scent of Gore Vidal shampoo. God he's sexy. I feel so lucky. And I know he does, too.

'I love you, Tiramisu Girl,' he tells me softly, into my hair.

'I love you, too,' I say, meaning it with my whole body. 'But for the record, I'm still Team Char—'

He kisses me before I can finish the thought.

ACKNOWLEDGEMENTS

Hello, you lovely lot. So, before we get into the nitty-thank-you-grittys, I want to do a quick dedication. This is my eighth romcom and I've never done one before, but things change and here we are. I want to dedicate this book to my mum. She's been through a lot and has always been there for me. I love you, Mum, this one is for you.

There are so many more thank yous needed here and I want to say, firstly, thank you to all of YOU. To all the amazing, wonderful readers out there. You're the best of humankind and your loveliness and generosity continues to blow my mind. I wouldn't be here or anywhere at all without all of you.

The next big thank you goes to Fred Attrill, my therapy guru, for all his help with this book. I love you, dude. Your wife is okay, too. I know I probably still got a bunch wrong when it comes to therapy, sorry. I am terrible for sacrificing authenticity for the sake of a cheap laugh.

Next up, let me talk to you guys for a sec about my editor, Molly Crawford. Because I love her so much. Reader, she wouldn't marry me because she's already married to some guy named Tom, but she does edit me and does the most brilliant, insightful job, I can't even tell you. She is a horrendously slow walker though. Her, Laura Wood and Rebecca Ryan should all have some kind of separate lane assigned to them for walking purposes, everywhere they go.

Sabah Khan, I think I creep you out on a regular basis with my fangirling, but you are Just. So. Good. I feel incredibly lucky to be working with you and I hope it will continue into our old age. Thank you for everything. Amy, Kate, you are queens and I am so grateful for your incredible work. The same goes for everyone else at S&S – thank you enormously. Misha, SJV, Clare, cover goddess Pip, Jess, Harriett, copy-editor Gillian, proofreader Celia, and to the extraordinary rights team, Amy, Ben and Maud.

Thank you to my agent Diana Beaumont, who is just plain awesome. Thank you to my family and to my lovely pals. Thank you to my husband, David, who I fancy SO MUCH. I also have many thank yous to dish up to my author pals who've been so kind and supportive throughout this – and always. Shout out to Diana's Dames: Daisy Buchanan, Caroline Corcoran and Harriet Johnson. Thank you Laura Wood, Kirsty Greenwood, Lindsey Kelk, Lauren Bravo, Milly Johnson (JOHNNYYYYYYY), Beth O'Leary, Cesca Major, Holly Bourne, Paige Toon, Isabelle Broom, Cathy Bramley, Rebecca Ryan, Rosie Walsh, Kate

Riordan, Caroline Hulse, Eva Verde, Sukh Ojla, Hux, Mhairi McFarlane, Salma El-Wardany, Laura Jane Williams, Lia Louis, Justin Myers, Lizzy Dent, Beth Reekles, Hannah Doyle, Poorna Bell, Sophie Cousens, Mike Gayle, Kate Weston, Elena Armas – and so many more.

And finally, I read some truly fascinating books in my research for *Good For You*, but the one I felt most inspired by and want every woman in the world to read is *Women Are Angry* by Jennifer Cox. Hard reccy, along with her podcast, *Women Are Mad*. Everything Philippa Perry does, too. Get on it!

LOVE YOU ALL

If you enjoyed *Good For You*, read on for a sneak peek of Lucy's heartwarming and funny romcom.

Available now

Narrator:

Well gosh, hello there, lovely reader, don't you look wonderful! I'm—
  'Aren't you going to open it?'
  Ahem, sorry for the interruption, I just wanted to explain that this is a novel told in three parts and—
  'Seriously!' the woman with a voice a whole octave higher than it should be shouts, her eyes bulging out of reddened sockets.
  She's not talking to me, of course. She's on a flight, where she would usually spend the whole journey clinging to the seatbelt, visualizing a burning, fiery death, surrounded by screaming families, while hanging oxygen masks violently knock into one another. But today! Ohhh, today she's been too intrigued by the haunted young woman beside her – whose name is Jemma, if you're interested. Jemma has been fingering an unopened envelope for hours. It's provided her seat partner with a tantalizing distraction from that dream she had last night – the one about the plane crashing into a mountain, where she had to eat her fellow passengers.
  The woman leans in closer, all the way over Jemma's arm rest,

giving up all pretence of watching the Sandra Bullock film on her tiny screen. She's very much in Jemma's personal space but Jemma's too polite to mention it.

'I'm sorry, I know I'm being nosy and your generation is all about' — she pauses, preparing to roll those red eyes as she does air quotes — '"boundaries".' She's practically in Jemma's lap now, puffing stale breath in every direction. 'But oh my god, I can't take it anymore. What IS it? And why aren't you opening it?' Her voice rasps, dry from excitement and recycled plane air, as she jabs a finger towards the envelope.

A subtle pinkness spreads across Jemma's cheeks.

Jemma usually resists any form of attention seeking. That's her sister Clara's area of expertise. In fact, Jemma's spent a whole lifetime trying to hide. She prides herself on being able to blend into any number of backgrounds. Physically, Jemma would describe herself as not being much of anything. In the dim light of this aeroplane cabin, her hair looks blonde, but she would pull a face and wave a dismissive hand if you told her so. It's mousey! she would insist. The kind of middling hair colour that hairdressers desperately want to highlight one way or the other. She'd also say her shape is average — too up and down to be described as curvy and too chubby to be called slim; a distinctly average height and weight that nobody would mention in the grand scheme of body positivity debate. She would, wittily, refer to herself as a beige buffet in human form.

But I would disagree. I think Jemma is shiny and brilliant.

Either way, right now — sitting in the centre aisle of this mid-flight aeroplane, fiddling with the edges of that still unopened envelope – there's no denying she's vibrating intrigue. Jemma Poyntz is the most interesting person around for miles.

Granted, she IS 10,000 feet in the air, so the pool is limited.

'Um,' Jemma hedges, clearly unsure how to answer the woman and probably wondering if her own eyes are also that red. She turns the creamy-white envelope over in her hands again, taking in the letters of her own name on the front and admiring the sloping, scrawled handwriting. She's thinking about how much she dislikes her name. Yes, she appreciates its sturdiness; its safe ordinariness. But that stupid J ruins everything. She's spent her whole life correcting the spelling and still gets 'To Gemma Poyntz' on every email and letter from British Gas.

She takes a deep breath. 'I'm sorry' – she turns slightly, feeling the woman's hot breath fully in her face now – 'I do want to open it – I have to open it – but I'm . . .' she finishes lamely, '. . . scared.'

Jemma swallows hard, staring down.

A younger woman the other side of Jemma removes her earbuds. 'Are you talking about the envelope?' she asks, leaning in as well. Jemma is now squished on either side and the social-panic is obvious on her face. 'You've been fiddling with it since we took off, it's driving me crazy.'

'Me too,' Jemma dry laughs, her pink cheeks getting redder still. 'Believe me.'

'Is it exam results or something?' the older women asks, shaking her head, already knowing that won't be it.

'No.'

The red-eyed lady sags back into her seat and an angry passenger behind her kicks it in response.

'Who's it from?' the younger woman asks as Jemma frowns.

She laughs shortly. 'It's from my book boyfriend.'

Either side, both women look puzzled. 'What on earth is a book boyfriend?'

Jemma smiles. 'Erm, well, it's meant to be the sexy hero in a romance novel. The perfect man you obsessively fall in love with.' She glances between them. 'Because, y'know, it feels like a lot of real life men are terrible. Fictional men make more sense. They're more romantic and they don't let you down.' She sighs. 'Except THIS guy is real.'

The older woman frowns at Sandra Bullock's frozen features on the chair-screen. 'I'm still confused.'

Jemma sighs. 'OK, so it started a few months ago . . .' she pauses, staring down into her lap, '. . . when my twin sister moved in with me.'

'Ohhh,' the younger woman interjects joyfully, 'that's so cute! I've always wanted a twin sister!'

Jemma shoots her a dark look. 'Everyone says that, literally everyone. But you haven't a clue.'

Red Eyes raises her eyebrows at this while Jemma breathes deeply through flared nostrils. 'The truth is, we've never got on. Clara's a selfish nightmare and the last few months have been awful. She basically ruined my life. And this' – she waves the letter – 'has been another complication I didn't want.' She sighs again. 'My life used to be so straightforward and predictable.' She looks between the women, both listening intently. 'And I LIKED it straightforward and predict-able. I don't need a rollercoaster of emotions, never knowing what's coming one day to the next. I was content in my stable little rut.' She narrows her eyes, glaring at the envelope. 'Until Clara and THIS came along.' She straightens her back and shoulders, determination lighting her eyes. 'Right, sod it, I'm opening it.'

She inserts an angry finger into the envelope edge, ripping open the top. Her hands are shaking as the two women either side watch on, agog.

At last, she's going to find out who he is, and – believe me, reader – it's going to change everything . . .

Discover more from Lucy Vine

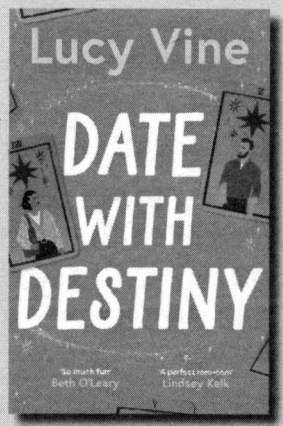

Available now

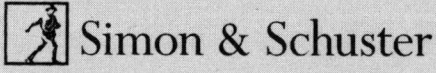